Tony Cavanaugh is a writer and producer for film and television. He has written for *The Sullivans, Carson's Law, The Flying Doctors, Fire, Adrenalin Junkies* and *Clowning Around*.

He was nominated for the Victorian Premier's Literary Awards for the screenplay *Father* and the Queensland Premier's Literary Awards for the screenplay *Through My Eyes*.

Promise is his first novel.

PROMISE

For every promise, there is a price to pay...

TONY CAVANAUGH

This is a work of fiction. All characters are fictional, and any resemblance to actual persons is entirely coincidental. In order to provide the story with a context, real names of places have been used, but there is no suggestion that the events described concerning the fictional characters ever occurred.

hachette
AUSTRALIA

Published in Australia and New Zealand in 2012
by Hachette Australia
(an imprint of Hachette Australia Pty Limited)
Level 17, 207 Kent Street, Sydney NSW 2000
www.hachette.com.au

10 9 8 7 6 5 4 3 2 1

Copyright © Tony Cavanaugh 2012

This book is copyright. Apart from any fair dealing for the purposes of private study, research, criticism or review permitted under the *Copyright Act 1968*, no part may be stored or reproduced by any process without prior written permission. Enquiries should be made to the publisher.

National Library of Australia
Cataloguing-in-Publication data:

    Cavanaugh, Tony.
    Promise / Tony Cavanaugh.

    978 0 7336 2847 4 (pbk.)

    A823.4

Cover design by Luke Causby/Blue Cork Design
Front cover photograph courtesy of Getty Images
Back cover photograph courtesy of photolibrary.com
Author photo courtesy of Jasin Boland
Text design by Kirby Jones
Typeset in Sabon by Kirby Jones
Printed and bound in Australia by Griffin Press, Adelaide, an accredited ISO AS/NZS 14001:2004 Environmental Management System printer

The paper this book is printed on is certified against the Forest Stewardship Council® Standards. Griffin Press holds FSC chain of custody certification SGS-COC-005088. FSC promotes environmentally responsible, socially beneficial and economically viable management of the world's forests.

for
Delaware, Charlie, Scarlett

PART I

'And nothing, where I now arrive, is shining.'

DANTE ALIGHIERI, 'INFERNO'

1

Make No Promises

Nine missed calls.

My gun and my phone; they were my life. Leaving my gun behind was easy. I just hurled it like a baseball into the ocean. I didn't bother to watch its dead journey from the top of the cliff. I was staring at my phone. I knew I had to destroy it too, but I shoved it into my back pocket and kept walking. Later, I told myself.

Nine missed calls, same caller ID. I'd driven for eighteen hours, until the exhaustion had finally kicked in and I'd pulled off the highway. Six coffees later, I stared at the phone, which I'd carefully placed on the other side of the table as if it were a guest.

I was the only customer in the roadhouse. Out back there was a car park stretching deep into the night, crammed full of road trains and campervans and long-haul semis but they were still, quiet; everyone was asleep. A crumpled woman wearing a name tag that said Rosie had served me from behind a counter display of deep-fried day-old food. She had also been asleep when I walked in. Now she was staring at me, which is what most people would do to a man who doesn't answer his phone when it rings and then buzzes and rings and then buzzes for twenty minutes. What's wrong with you? Answer your phone. You're hiding, you're on the run, people are chasing you.

Rosie kept a dark watch on me. I knew she'd scanned the fastest way out in case her suspicions were confirmed and I was indeed a monster slowly awakening with each bolt of the coffee she reluctantly handed me. I guess my dubious behaviour was aggravated by my ring tone: Jimi Hendrix's 'Hey Joe'.

I knew the song well. I knew similar details of real domestic murder cases even better. The ring tone was a code, plugged into all of our phones, signalling a call from Family of Victim. Even though we had a lot of victims, spread over long years and across the reach of a vast city, it didn't matter; the questions at the end of the line were always the same.

Rosie was starting to flinch on cue, as Jimi's voice rumbled on about how Joe had gun-barrelled his woman into the ground because she looked at another man.

The same number flashed up on the caller ID. I'd memorised it long ago. I gave Rosie a wide smile and asked if she'd be so kind as to give me a seventh coffee and then picked up the phone and answered, my voice stretching back over eighteen hours and a thousand kilometres.

'Hi.'

'You resigned?'

I guess that after nine missed calls the shock had worn off; all that remained was anger and betrayal. Her voice was tired. I knew she had been crying; I knew this call would cast her into a dark journey from which there was no hope. She knew it too. I just had to confirm it, that's all.

'Yes,' I said.

I heard an intake of breath: deep, slow, like the last echo from a sinking world. I burned away my shame and shut my eyes hard and kept them in a clinch while I waited for her to answer. From a place that seemed further than a thousand kilometres away I heard her say: 'So, she's dead.'

She hung up before I could reply. It would've been easier if I'd answered the first call. After nine unanswered attempts she'd distilled everything into a silent landscape of recrimination that would linger long after she hung up.

I looked out through the window. There must have been at least thirty semi-trailers and trucks in the car park. It was getting close to four in the morning; soon it would be dawn. A car sped past. I'd been following its approach since I noticed a tiny light, way off in the distance. Outside, beyond the neon spill from the roadhouse, it was black. No moon, no stars, no shape to the scrublands that stretched far and wide around me.

I put the phone down. In it were stored hundreds of contacts. I flipped off the back, removed the battery and eased out the SIM card. Before I allowed any feelings of doubt or remorse or guilt to surface, I snapped it in two.

Out in the car park, I shattered the rest of the phone with the heel of my boot. I picked up the pieces and threw them into an industrial rubbish bin. I heard the growl and rumble of a road train as its engine came to life. I heard the crunch of gravel as another truck began to ease towards the highway.

I walked towards my car. I had another six hundred kilometres to drive.

—

MY NAME IS Darian Richards. I grew up on a sheep farm, beneath a mountain called Disappointment in the soft valleys of the Western District. Every night I would lie in bed and stare out at the next mountain: it was called Misery. In the mornings I'd go outside and stare at a third mountain: it was called Despair. They were named a hundred years earlier by some fool explorer who was searching for The Great Inland Sea, which didn't exist. Every time he climbed one of the mountains he got excited. Every time he reached its peak and looked across more land, he got ... well, we know.

I couldn't wait to get out of there. I had nightmares; it was as if the feelings he'd given these places as names were conspiring against me. Aged seven, I imagined I was already doomed. I knew there would be disappointments. But misery? Despair? Was that what the future held?

I was sixteen when I caught a lift with a truckie. I didn't look back at those mountains. He dropped me off in the heart of Melbourne, two hours down the highway.

Three years later I was a Constable with the Victoria Police where I stayed, climbing the ranks until I had become Officer in Charge of the Homicide Squad. I earned a reputation as the top homicide investigator in the country. At the age of thirty I was also the youngest.

Most crews have a ninety per cent success rate. Ours was ninety-eight. People called me a legend. I wasn't. I was just doing my job. Still, investigators from other cities would ring and ask my advice. Ministers from State governments would hassle my boss and try to get me seconded to clean up a murder that was lingering too long on their front pages.

I stayed in that job for sixteen years, until I could bear it no longer, which was exactly two weeks ago, when I abruptly resigned, having decided to relocate to a hastily purchased cottage on the Noosa River, which was about as far north on the east coast of Australia as I could go unless I entered the final thousands of kilometres of rural coastland that stretched up to the Timor Sea. I'd saved enough money to live a frugal life and sit by the river for a few years.

—

'You promise?' I heard her voice echo, as I climbed into my car and closed the door. I started the engine, revved the accelerator. It was old, imported from America with left hand drive.

We'd been chasing the perp for about three years. It was always the same. A girl boards a train. Vanishes. A week later she's released into a multi-storey car park, wandering, drugged, dazed, unsure if she's alive; more likely she thinks she's dead, in an enclosed world of concrete spirals and parked cars. Always dressed in the clothes of his previous victim, ripped, shredded, now tattered, rags held together so loosely they flutter to the ground, leaving her naked by the time she's found. She's been living in a collapse of darkness and time. He said nothing to her. He raped her repeatedly, endlessly. Then she awakes, a week later, among parked cars. It's not the same world that it was a week before.

He'd stolen his ninth, Lorna, when I heard the question asked by her mother, Diane, as I was standing in the kitchen of their home, out of the way of my crew as they searched for any trail that might link the victim's stable world to his prowling one.

Diane knew how he worked. Everybody knew. Newspapers, television, radio reports were full of breathless speculation. He may as well have had his own blog. He was lord of the city and all of its homes.

'It's *him*, isn't it?' she asked in a voice only just controlling the terror. She was strong. She'd stay with us until her girl was returned. Most parents don't. They freeze and turn inwards, their lives already ruined.

'Yeah, it is,' I replied.

'Then he *will* release her, won't he? Like the others, in about a week?'

I turned to her as she asked another question: 'She'll come back to me, won't she?'

'If it's him,' I said, 'and we have every reason to believe it *is* him, then yes, Lorna will–'

I'd already said too much.

'–most likely be released.'

She stepped up to me and I felt her hand close around mine and hold it tightly in a soft embrace – something I hadn't expected or anticipated; she'd caught me off guard – and she said: 'You promise?'

I just wanted the desperation to stop. Not only hers.

'Yes,' I replied.

—

Lorna didn't come home after a week or after two; weeks became months and still she didn't come home.

After the second month I began to drop by and see Diane. Every month. She clung to me. My promise kept her going, feeding the hope that Lorna would one day return. My visits confirmed we were still investigating. I was on the case. I was active. We were closing in on the perp. In truth we were stranded. But I'd made a promise.

Once, late, after midnight, after my reassurances, she took my hand again and started to lead me towards her bed. I wanted her as much as she did me, for different reasons, all of them selfish. I pulled my hand away and left. Some cops do sleep with victims or their family members. Maybe they need it to keep going, to keep hunting or to find some joy in a world of grim trauma. I didn't. But I wanted to.

—

I DROVE AWAY from the roadhouse, back onto the highway with her voice in my head.

She was right: her daughter was dead. I knew it after the first week passed and she didn't surface. I knew it every time I visited her, assuring her, giving her hope when I knew there was only despair, made worse by my promise. It could have been worse had I not pulled my hand away, compounding deceit with the embrace of my body into hers.

Lorna wasn't coming home. Nor were the other seven girls who boarded trains after her. We never found him. He's still riding trains.

I stared ahead, driving faster, and pushed images of Diane – naked now, her bra unclasped and falling softly onto the carpet beneath us, her body pressing into mine – into darkness. All I could see was the road.

2

The Newsagent's Daughter

IT WAS A YEAR SINCE I LEFT THAT ROADHOUSE. A YEAR SINCE I tried to walk away from darkness.

A breeze swept up from the Noosa River, in through my house, a rickety wooden cottage built by a fisherman about a hundred years ago. All that lies between my living room and the water is grass, palm trees and a hammock. When it storms I get a little nervous because the house shakes.

I was staring at a photo of a young girl on the front page of the local newspaper. *Another Girl Vanishes. Killer Claims Number 6.*

Her name was Brianna.

I listened to the pounding of the surf from the beach a kilometre downstream where the Pacific Ocean sweeps through a narrow channel, over a sandbank with deep tangles of mangrove on either side.

Brianna looked as if she hadn't yet decided whether she would smile or be serious for the photo. I wondered who took it and if it had been taken inside or outside; the background was flat and grey. It wasn't intended to run on the front page of a newspaper.

I turned away from the photo and picked up the phone.

'Casey's Antique and Second-hand Emporium,' said Casey, 'a place of mystery and treasure.'

'It's Darian. I thought I'd come over–'

'Darian?' he interrupted. 'The bad man from the dangerous streets of Melbourne,' he added, chuckling.

'–maybe later today,' I finished. A small tinnie floated past me, drifting along the current, downstream in the direction of the sandbar. Standing in the boat was a local fisherman, an old guy with spidery legs firmly spread so he didn't lose balance. Without looking in my direction, he waved. He sells me mud crabs when they're in the river.

'Stay for dinner,' said Casey as I waved back. I hate waving but I like mud crabs.

'Thanks. I will.'

There was a pause. 'Cool,' he said slowly.

It wasn't cool. I never stayed for dinner; it had even become part of our friendship, a signature exchange of, 'Stay for dinner,' always met with, 'Next time.' That's how it worked. He didn't really mean it because his girlfriend doesn't like me and I didn't mean it because I don't like going out for dinner.

I like a simple life, a private life, a life without distraction. This happily leads me to the exclusion of people. Most people I've met want to talk about the patterns of the fish in the river or the clouds in the sky or, the very worst, how their baby is growing up so well. Don't get me wrong: I devoted my life to the protection of people. I just don't want to have to talk about it. I adore the writings and the songs and the poems and the thoughts of people – mostly dead people – but not a regular engagement with them. Casey was one of two exceptions.

He spoke carefully. 'Maria gets home at six.'

Maria was Casey's girlfriend, a Senior Constable in the Noosa Crime Investigation Branch. Her staggering beauty was matched by her popularity at the station; she was also very clever. The boys told her things. Trying to impress the pretty girl. Male cops, generally speaking, are dumb. Some are wooden-plank dumb, some are rodent dumb. Most are just moron dumb. Female cops, on the other hand, are not dumb at all.

Maria is wary of me. All the cops on the Sunshine Coast are wary of me. Small-town cops don't do respect. They do superiority. I didn't want to rumble the petty jealousies in the station up on the hill, so I drove into town as anonymously as I could, albeit in a bright red Studebaker convertible. I stayed low, never told anyone where I came from or what I did, and I always waved back. This was about as successful as taking out a full-page ad in the local paper.

'I thought I'd get there 'bout four,' I told Casey. 'I'll go through Tewantin. Buy some wine.'

'She likes rosé. French–'

'Chateau St Paul,' I said. 'I know.'

'Hey, stop by the newsagent, get me *Rolling Stone*, get me some other magazines too. But nothing moron.' Retired people are strange; they develop weird habits. Casey's is that he never goes into shops. Mine is that I wave at people.

There was silence. He was thinking. I didn't intrude. And then he asked: 'Should I be prepared?'

'Yeah. Will that be a problem?' I said, referring to many things, one being Maria.

'No.'

'I need a Beretta.'

'See you 'round four,' he said and hung up. I could've told him I needed a pencil.

—

CASEY LACK USED to manage a strip joint at the end of a brick lane close to the Melbourne dockyards. One night it exploded in a gigantic fireball that rose to over three hundred metres, spewing a black rain into a January night; an explosion so loud it woke old people ten kilometres away and set dogs barking until dawn, which was about the time I was shoving aside a fireman from a charcoal awning to unearth yet another victim, her body shattered into pieces like the others.

Casey and I became friends after he helped me investigate the deaths of the eleven strippers who were killed that night. He knew the Twenty-Four were responsible. I nailed them. Casey loved the strippers and was shocked anyone would harm them, let alone blow them to pieces. After giving evidence he fled the icy web of Melbourne, drove north and retired on six acres in the Noosa hinterland. Like everyone who retires up here he got bored, and he opened a junkyard, a place of mystery and treasure.

I have two cars. In one I'm alive. In the other I'm driving. I inherited the '64 Studebaker Champion Coupe from an ageing Algerian gangster whose life I'd saved back in Melbourne. It has fins. It drives like a ballistic monster. Behind its wheel I'm immortal.

I purchased the 1990-something Toyota LandCruiser soon after realising that the local terrain wasn't all smooth and flat. It's off-white. It goes. It climbs hills that are almost vertical. It knocks down small trees that get in the way. Behind its wheel I'm anonymous.

I put the LandCruiser into reverse and eased out carefully so as not to scrape the red inheritance.

Up here people are friendly. They wave at you.

This was what Jacinta-something, one of my neighbours, was doing as I crushed the gears from reverse into first and hammered the car, quickly, into Gympie Terrace. I pretended I didn't see her. That was better than making eye contact. Eye contact could lead to familiarity; she might even think she'd be able to drop by. People up here are like that. You have to be on your guard.

Gympie Terrace runs along the river, through Noosaville to Tewantin. Old wooden Queenslanders – cottages held high off the ground by thick wooden poles of forest hardwood painted white – line the broken footpaths filled with puddles of brown water. It stormed last night. The branches of frangipani and jacaranda trees twist and mingle, becoming walls of green, purple and white flowers, sometimes reaching high enough to form a canopy over parts of the road.

I drove across the bridge that spans Lake Weyba, still and calm, its surface a mirror. Maybe half a kilometre wide, on the other side of its shore was the Wooroi Forest. Rising up from inside it was a black mountain. Shaped like a dagger, it was called Tinbeerwah. The landscape wasn't enough to distract me.

Six girls had vanished over fourteen months. All blonde and pretty. The youngest was thirteen; the oldest was sixteen. The cops listed them as 'missing' or 'vanished' – that's what they have to say if they don't have a body. But I knew those girls were all dead.

Jenny Brown was the first. She vanished sometime after four in the afternoon on Saturday the fifteenth of October. Everyone – except for her parents and her friends and anybody who knew her – thought she'd run away. Especially the cops, who were the ones who said she'd run away. They would've allowed a good two or three minutes before arriving at that conclusion. By the time they'd reached the front gate of her home, before they'd even walked across the road and climbed into their cruiser, they would've forgotten Jenny Brown existed.

That's the type of police work I used to call DD: Dumb and Disdain.

After two more girls vanished, also blonde and pretty, the cops realised it was hard to say 'coincidence' any longer. There was a pattern they couldn't ignore.

Jessica Crow was the fourth. Wednesday, the twenty-third of February. She was walking along Sunshine Beach and then through the National Park, a thick forest that traverses a headland between the calm Laguna Bay and the ocean. Thousands walk through it, along a tourist path, every year. There are places to rest and signposts telling you dead facts about the koalas that live in the trees. As Jessica walked along this path I was down on the beach, walking barefoot along the sand. I'd noticed a young Asian girl. She couldn't swim and she looked like she was in trouble. In Australia we lose a few Jap tourists a year because they can't swim. There is a strong current that ebbs beneath the water's languid surface. I decided to see if she actually was in trouble.

I stripped off my T-shirt and hurled into the water, towards her. She didn't understand what I said, so I tried a bit of sign language, to which she responded by bolting like a jet ski until she reached the shoreline; there she ran on to the sand, grabbed her towel and was up the wooden steps and into the car park in record time.

As I waded back to the comfort of land, less than a kilometre away Jessica Crow was staring into the last set of eyes she would ever see. Her body, like the bodies of the other girls, has never been found.

Two months later his fifth victim, Carol Morales, was taken. I was trying real hard to ignore these vanishings. This part of the local environment wasn't expected nor was a rampaging serial killer on the loose part of the early retirement plan. I was doing a good job of pretending the killer wasn't my problem but the growing body count and the knowledge that the local cops didn't have the expertise to handle it was starting to oppress me at night, when I slept. I can erase the thoughts during the day and stare at my friends the pelicans. At night I'm as much a helpless victim as those girls.

Brianna was taken at 3.38 on Thursday afternoon on her way home from school. Three days ago. Last seen in the Noosa Civic shopping mall. Brianna played classical music. Piano. At her year nine end-of-year school concert she shocked some parents with her choice: 'Stairway to Heaven'. But when she'd finished, the applause lasted nearly five minutes and she had tears in her eyes as she stood before the parents and teachers and her school friends. She'd killed it, big time. Even the headmaster climbed out of his seat and congratulated her for her amazing talent and bravery. 'Imagine that,' he was quoted in the local newspaper. 'Who would have thought, Led Zeppelin at the end-of-year school concert? Our Brianna Nichols is going places.'

I had come up here to retire early, and that had been working, until about three o'clock this morning when I could bear the nightmares and the whispering voices no longer. So now I was going to find this guy because the cops couldn't.

Then I was going to make sure he'd never kill again. I was going to erase him from the face of the earth.

—

I PICKED OUT *Rolling Stone*. And *The New Yorker* and *Q*. Lady Gaga was on the cover of *Q*. Nude. That was the clincher, although I'd tell Casey *Q* was way cooler for a guy like him, second-hand dealer and all.

The place was packed. Cliff, the owner, was busy selling tickets to a twenty-eight million dollar Lotto prize. He used to be a coffee farmer, retired up here but soon got bored. Then, when the newsagency went up for sale – after its owner had a sudden and apparently spectacular heart attack while stacking new issues of *Playboy*, *Penthouse* and *Hustler* into his shelves – he purchased the business. This I learned, without having asked, from Silvio the Onion – 'call me Sil' – who owns the fish-and-chip joint near my house. Sil the Onion keeps me informed, even though I ask him not to.

The newsagency is in the main street of Tewantin, the next town along the river after Noosaville. Tourists don't come to Tewantin. The Sunshine Coast Council offices are in Tewantin. Tewantin is where you go to get your driver's licence.

Cliff's daughter was behind the counter. She was about fourteen. She was pretty and blonde. She wore a short skirt and a singlet cut into a v around the neck to reveal a tiny cleavage and cut short around the waist to reveal her navel. She smiled at me in a sweet and innocent way, the sort of smile some guys read as an invitation.

'You like Lady Gaga?' she asked as she zapped the magazine's barcode.

'Only the first album. In danger of selling out.'

'Yeah, maybe, but she *is* amazing.' She smiled at me again, but differently, like we shared something in common. Lady Gaga. Check the wit and stay silent, I told myself.

'Doing some bushwalking?' she asked as she zapped a local map, the only accurate chart of creeks, estuaries, forests and national parks in the Sunshine Coast.

I smiled and sort of nodded while I paid and then said: 'Bye.'

'See ya, Mr Richards,' she called out. Even the newsagent's daughter knows my name. I turned back to nod or do something. There was that smile again. Big, genuine and – I couldn't help feeling –

Dangerous. I went on my way.

'Darian!' Cliff was running towards me. What now?

'I'm sorry,' he said as he reached me. We stood on the footpath. For what? I wondered.

'But, you know ...' he said. He paused awkwardly. I stared at him. People were passing us. It was hot. The sun was hot, the footpath was hot.

'What do you want to say?' I said even though I knew where this was going; I'd already got to the end of the conversation we were about to have.

'Her. Henna.' He jerked his head in the direction of his daughter. 'Look at her,' he said, almost as an accusation.

I didn't. He went on: 'She's exactly the type of girl he targets, isn't she?'

I didn't say anything.

'Look: she's blonde, she's fifteen, she's beautiful.'

I waited.

'I'm sorry,' he said once more, in a faltering voice.

'What is it you want to ask me?'

'You were a homicide cop.'

It was that full-page advertisement I took out.

'I just want some advice. Sorry.'

'Stop saying sorry. Ask. *Now*.' I'm not big on patience.

He took a deep breath, looked around and leaned in, close, like we were brothers. He whispered: 'Should I get her a gun? A pistol, just a little one she could keep in her bag, when she's out at night, or alone, to keep her safe, from him. She's exactly the type he's taking. Look: she's a *fucking target*.' He was shaking.

I looked around the street. People were watching us. They probably knew what we were talking about. Fear permeates. When a killer is on the loose and living within your community the whole world changes. You don't walk down the street like you used to. Now everybody – even you – is wondering. Is it him? Or him? Or that guy; he's always been creepy-looking. The town was being strangled by fear and I was standing right in the middle of it.

'She'd be committing a serious criminal offence carrying a firearm.'

'Would that matter? If she was taken?' He was angry.

'You'd teach her how to use the gun?'

'Yes.'

'You'd teach her how to distinguish between a drunk who wants to try it on, a guy who scares her *and* a serial killer?'

He didn't say anything.

'Here's my advice: do not buy her a gun. If she is ever in the company of a serial killer she won't know it because he'll be just like her favourite uncle or big brother. And if, in the unlikely event that she *is* grabbed, she'll have ten seconds, maybe, if she's lucky. Ten seconds to act, and those ten seconds will be full of one thing only: terror. Okay?'

'Okay,' he said slowly.

'Okay. That's when the adrenaline kicks in. Only a person trained to operate and think clearly in those circumstances can use a gun to terminate the threat.'

He nodded.

'Do the following things. Engage a security company to monitor her movements. Buy her two GPS trackers; make sure they are on her body at all times. The first GPS *she* places. That's the one he would find. The second has to be very small and more powerful than the first. Have this one attached between two of her toes. It's about the only area of a girl's body they don't explore until later.'

He was silent.

'Are you thinking about how much this will cost?' I asked.

He looked startled and tried to cover his embarrassment.

'Don't think about how much it will cost.' Then I walked away, determined to buy all future magazines at the Cooroy newsagency, even though it was further to drive.

3

Turf

Cops don't like it when they think someone is intruding on their investigation, even dumb cops or cops out of their depth or cops desperate for help and guidance.

With that in mind I parked the LandCruiser under a massive willow tree on the side of a dead-end dirt road fringed with a forest of palm and gum trees. I looked across to the house in which Jenny Brown had lived. A cottage, made out of wood sometime in the 1930s, no later. It stood high off the ground, held up by wooden beams. It had been painted back then but not since. It was a home for poor people back then, and now. Under the house, between the wooden beams, was a scattering of junk: a TV, a couch, an assortment of rusty outboard engines and a small upturned boat. The yard was full of thick grass, unopened mail and newspapers rolled up in plastic.

This was the beginning. When the cops came to investigate Jenny's disappearance, they weren't investigating a serial killer. Their interview with the mother, days after the killer had examined the house, as I was doing now, would have been ruinously thin. Incomplete. Irrelevant. Jenny was a runaway, an inconvenience. They should have – but wouldn't have – thought to ask: Have you noticed any strangers outside lately?

I would come back here, soon. It didn't seem like there was anyone inside but even if there was, I wasn't ready. I just needed to see her home, get my first inkling of who she was and why our guy started with her. Why her? She triggered him. Why?

I drove past the other houses, as derelict and forgotten as Jenny's, until the road gave way to a forest of ghost gums and paperbark trees. It came to an end in a wide circle for a smooth turn back to the way I had come. I swung the wheel and then stopped.

There was a track leading into the bush. Maybe it led to nothing, or maybe it led to a place where kids smoked or teenagers fondled, or maybe it was just a short cut to somewhere else. Whatever it was, it looked like it led to a place of secrets.

I got out to look.

Thickets of dry scrub edged either side of the track. About eighty metres in I found a clearing, just off a turn, hidden from view by dense bush and a massive sprawling tree trunk. I pushed away the bush as I walked in and found myself in a small and secluded camping spot. Somebody had made it. Why? Did it have anything to do with Jenny or had I just stumbled into the passion palace for the local kids?

I tried to get my bearings. My sense of direction is appalling. I have no idea of proximity. Then I reached into a thicket of palm trees that formed a sort of natural wall and pushed them aside, creating a hole.

I had a clear view of Jenny Brown's house. I was standing where the killer had stood. I knew it.

4

Maria

I took the Cooroy road out of Tewantin, passing the turn-off to the North Shore, a scrubby island of forest and dirt tracks accessible only by car ferry. The four-wheel drive tourists love it over there. They get to drive like maniacs along the beach, which is technically a highway and possibly the only beach in the world that has road rules.

I drove past a cemetery, of which there are many up here, past a golf course, one of thousands, then a retirement village, one of hundreds of thousands, then out of town, following the twists of the road as it climbed a black volcanic mountain that rose through forests of eucalypt.

At the crest of the hill I turned into Sunrise Road, which runs along the top of the Eumundi Range. Very wealthy people live on one side of the road, in houses the size of Balinese resorts. On the other side, away from the ocean views, narrow roads weave into the hinterland, a land of thick bush and dirt tracks, a land where houses and farms are scattered, hidden.

Casey's Emporium is signposted. 'Magic! Antiques! Mystery! Do Not Ignore! Turn Right. Follow Signs!' I did as instructed, remembering how easy it is to be among millionaires one moment then feel lost, like the last man alive, moments later. Deep in a valley of silence, Casey's Emporium sprawls across a yard the size of a small country. It felt like driving through a safari park as I peered through my windows, but instead of animals I saw old cars and planks of wood and bathtubs and sheets of tin and washing machines. Under the cover of awnings were couches and chairs and record players and a jukebox, Singer sewing machines and piles of magazines and books, enough to keep the same small country reading for at least a year. Casey's house was as chaotic and incoherent as the emporium; it too was a Queenslander, built of wood, resting on solid poles for support, encircled by a wide verandah.

Wearing a Samoan sarong and a T-shirt that read 'Don't Blame Me: I Voted McGovern', Casey stumbled out to greet me. Casey's in his early fifties. He has long black hair tied into a ponytail that swings as he walks. He's the sort of guy who looks like he's been to a health farm, tanned and fit. He's covered in tatts, memorials to the early days when he grew up a gangster in the backstreets of Fitzroy.

'Awesome! Lady Gaga nude! Have you seen the photos of her with those conical-shaped things on her tits that shoot out jets of fire? She is dog, man! She is dog!'

We settled on the verandah and looked out over the valleys and hills to the ocean. Casey sat in his favourite spot, a passenger seat from a 1950s Dodge pick-up. I took a chair. Like wise men preparing to solve the problems of the world we stared at the view and said nothing. As he flicked through the magazines, without looking up, he said: 'I told Maria you were coming for dinner.'

'Yeah, of course,' I replied.

'She said she ain't going to tell you anything about the investigation.'

'I'm not going to ask her about the investigation.'

'I know that! You think *I* think *you're* a fuckwit?'

'I like Maria–'

'Yeah, yeah,' he said, dismissing me. 'The Beretta: next week.'

I nodded.

'The cops don't know what the fuck they're doin'. No leads: dead end. Same deal with all these serial-killer things: it's not, like, until a third or fourth vic turns up do they realise what they've got. Vics one, two and three: they were all missing persons, you know, their files are buried somewhere else; gotta get 'em out and start all over again. You know? It's fucked.'

I nodded at his wisdom. Casey had the know. Now, and back then. After the fireball incinerated his eleven strippers I instructed my crew to shake the Persians. It was obvious, I thought: gang warfare. 'Catch a fuckin' boat to Madagascar, man,' was Casey's reaction.

'Catch a boat to Madagascar? What are you talking about?'

'I'm talkin' about you goin' south when you should be goin' north.'

'Madagascar's in the west,' I said, bemused.

'You think I'm a fuckwit? I know where fuckin' Madagascar is! It's off the fuckin' map, which is where your dumb crew's headin' right now. Ain't got nothin' to do with the gangs. It's the Twenty-Four, you dumb fuck, they're the ones who did it!'

'What's the Twenty-Four?' I asked.

'Finally! Homicide investigator asks an intelligent question.' And then he answered.

The club was owned by twelve Greeks, all in their thirties and forties, slicked hair and gold chains swinging around their necks like big dicks, which is how they saw themselves. Each of these boys had a wife. Twelve wives, married with kids and staring down the barrel of a middle age that no amount of peroxide and breast implants could salvage. Each of these boys also had a mistress. Twelve mistresses, holed up in cute apartments they didn't own, staring down the barrel of inevitable replacement.

Twelve wives, twelve mistresses: the Twenty-Four. Funny thing was, each held the other in place when it came to keeping the boy locked and safe. He'd bounce his mistress in the apartment, drive home, eat ravioli with the kids then watch *The Lion King*. He didn't bounce his wife but she didn't care, too much, just as long as she knew who he *was* sleeping with. The mistress didn't care if he was with his wife or not, just as long as he didn't sleep with anyone else who was younger and prettier.

Then one of the boys, during a regular Wednesday night meeting at the strip joint, took a sidelong glance at the girl on stage: Arlene, a nineteen-year-old drop-dead-with-a-heart-attack beauty, the sort of girl men go to war over. Even though Casey warned the girls –

no cock touching or sucking or fucking any of the owners – Arlene did just that.

Word spread fast. The Twenty-Four were under threat. Arlene wasn't just one nineteen-year-old beauty; there were endless nineteen-year-old beauties. The Twenty-Four decided they would make a point. Which they sure as hell did.

A car pulled in down below.

'Gotta have a piss; back in a sec,' Casey said as he left me alone. Maria came in through the front door.

'Hey Darian,' she called out, without looking, walking into the kitchen.

'Hey Maria, how are you?'

'Casey said you were staying for dinner.'

'If that's okay.'

'Of course.'

I strolled into the kitchen to look as if I might offer to help do something, like make a cheese platter or take dips out of the fridge. Maria was in her late twenties. She had long flowing brown hair and grey eyes. High cheekbones and a wide smile. She was gorgeous, the sort of girl you'd expect to see at a *Sports Illustrated* photo shoot. As much as Casey looked like a mechanic with the brain power of a beer bottle, she looked like a goddess, good for wearing bikinis on the beach and not much else. That's how most guys treated her. They were wrong. She and Casey had met outside a local gym in Noosa Junction. Maria was leaving, walking across the road to a car park surrounded by a forest of palm trees. A couple of local heroes were hassling her. Casey happened to be riding past on a Harley-Davidson that he'd just swapped for a consignment of Balinese furniture. He turned back, aimed and ran straight through the boys. Not hard or fast enough to do severe damage but enough to make the point. She started yelling at him, going all cop on him, telling him she could've handled it herself. He got off the bike, took off his helmet, let his hair swing loose and smiled at her. He's got a winning smile and she likes a dangerous guy. Cops flirt with the outlaw. Until Casey showed up in her life she'd been used to conversations about surf and cars by guys who thought the definition of an interesting night was dinner at the local Chinese.

'Wow,' she said to me, holding up the bottle of rosé. 'That's really kind of you. Thanks.' She was trying to be friendly but doing a pretty bad job of it.

I smiled as if to say, 'Hey, that's nothing,' instead of, 'Thought I needed to bribe you with something.' She grabbed a corkscrew and began to use it with a don't-interrupt-me vibe.

Cops have this thing about loyalty. When a cop puts on a uniform, it's like they've just departed the human race and joined another clan. I used to be like that. You think you're different and, in truth, you are. You think your loyalty is to your fellow officers but it's not. It's to the victims. Sometimes it takes a little while for a cop to discover that. Sometimes a cop won't ever discover it.

I knew Maria would but she hadn't yet. I also knew, as we settled on the verandah with her rosé and my soda water, she was in possession of some information she didn't want to share with me. While we talked about Casey's eclectic range of T-shirts from the presidential campaigns of the 1970s and 80s I could see it and feel it. She was acting. There was a clue or a lead; whatever, it was important. It was secret. Everything about her was anchored to an overwhelming intention: keep the information hidden from me.

People in every home, from one end of the Sunshine Coast to the other, were talking about the serial killer's sixth victim, and here we were, ex-Officer in Charge of Homicide, a guy with more than a little experience in this area, and Maria, a member of the Crime Investigation Branch charged with finding the serial killer, talking about anything but the serial killer.

Maria knew I wanted her hidden knowledge; I knew it would be a reprehensible breach for her to reveal it. The night was an evasion of elegant steps. I knew she was smart. She knew people referred to me as the best homicide investigator in Australia. She knew my solve rate. She knew I was safe. She loved Casey, trusted him; she knew of our shared past and our bond.

We ate fish. Casey played Led Zeppelin's *IV* and sang 'Stairway to Heaven', loudly and down into the valley beneath us. Maria and I joined in. I don't think she had read the local newspaper this morning.

The hinterland at night is a place of dark forms and deep shadows, a place of dense forests and abruptly rising mountains of smooth black rock. It's eerie.

Maria whispered, 'There's something,' as we stopped where my car was parked. I stood and waited.

'He boasts,' she said.

I didn't say anything but I felt the familiar surge of a lead that, from the tone of her voice, would get me there. I gave her the silence and the space to walk away. She didn't.

'After they've been captured we find their mobiles. He leaves them for us.'

'Where?'

'Random places.'

No such thing. I kept silent.

She looked into my eyes and I could see that the nightmares and the whispering voices had begun; I could see the haunting of a righteous person captive to an evil she couldn't control or stop, an evil she didn't understand.

'He takes photos of them. On their phones. They're all the same. They've been tied to a chair and … he's taken off their clothes. It's just one photo on each phone.'

There was a long silence. I knew she was thinking about the look on each girl's face.

She took a deep breath.

'They look …'

She didn't complete the sentence. Maybe she was trying to think of words to match the image. There were none.

These moments are the obstacles on the endurance track for the cop who wants to be in Homicide. If you can absorb them – nobody really cares how – and continue the work, you can survive. I've seen good people crumble at moments like this; later, when I found them, if I cared about them, I would try to make them understand it isn't cowardice, it's survival, and if they hadn't crumbled and abandoned hopes of a career in Homicide they would have ended up dead through alcohol or suicide.

'I'm going to catch him,' I said.

She turned back towards the house. 'I know,' I heard her say before she walked through the door.

—

I TACKED SHEETS of white cardboard onto the wall of my living room. I laid out photos of the six girls. I moved furniture and pinned the map of the local area onto the next wall. The map was good, it was hand drawn; a local bushman had walked and surveyed the entire area, from Tin Can Bay in the north-east, to Maroochydore in the south-east, from the tough and grim city of Gympie – gun capital of the country – in the north-west, to the Glasshouse Mountains and rainforests in the south-west.

I then added other maps: tourist maps and road maps and bicycle-track maps. Then I added pages torn from tourist brochures: caravan-park locations, motels and bars and clubs and clothes shops, especially clothes shops. These guys love clothes shops; they hang out in the shopping centres just to watch girls going in and out. As long as it has a change room – more killers than you can imagine make the decision about a target while watching girls going in and out of change rooms.

My wall was now a vast map of cultural, tourist and shopping information. I stood back and absorbed it.

Then I began to trace the last journey of each girl.

I started with the disappearance. Where was it? A shopping centre, or a street or a park? What was she doing there? How did she get there? Who was she with? Who saw her? What did she want there? Was she meeting someone? What was she wearing? Was she carrying anything? Had she put on make-up?

With each question I added what information I had at this stage to bring her back to life. Then, making sure I'd considered everything, I slowly began to step backwards. Where did she come from? What route did she take? Did she travel alone? If it was a familiar journey, did she deviate?

Rewinding her steps as slowly as possible, so as not to miss a question to ask or an observation to note, I took each girl back to the beginning of the day, where they woke up in the morning. Home. Where was it? Was there a park nearby, or bushland, or any place that our guy could hide? How far away from the other girls' homes? Was there anything unusual at her home? Who lived at home? Had she slept alone in her bed?

And then onwards, back into the night before. Had she gone out or stayed home? Did she have a boyfriend? And on I went, until I had gone back two weeks for each of the girls.

I'd lost track of time when I stood back and looked at my wall. I let my eyes follow each of the journeys, staring at the points of connection – the schools they went to, the shopping centres they hung out in; anything that might tell me something. When I do this I have to summon an almost painful concentration so as not to let anything distract me. He was here, on the wall. My crew used to joke that it was like playing 'Where's Wally?'.

Six final journeys. Six girls. Jenny Brown, Marianne McWinter, Izzie Daniels, Jessica Crow, Carol Morales and Brianna Nichols.

Before each one is taken he'd fantasise. A world where he was king and she was the queen of his dreams, a slave in his bed. She was there to provide a mirror reflection of his power and glory. It's never about the sex. It's all about the power. Then he would go searching and find his target. Then he'd stalk her, maybe for weeks. The stalking deepens the fantasy. He watches her, in her final days, imagining what glory he and she will have together. Then he strikes, quickly. And then she's gone.

Fantasies never play out in real life, especially for the serial killer. By the time he's got her back in his lair she is going to be hopelessly unable to fulfil the role he's imagined. Maybe she's crying all the time, maybe she's aggressive. Whatever she is, she won't be his queen. She exists in only one place: his mind. That's when she'll become nothing more than a slave, a whore to fulfil his urges. Already he'll be thinking of her disposal. Now she's become little more than some rubbish to be dumped next Tuesday or Wednesday. The experience will have sated him, but only for so long. Soon the fantasy world will return, a burning need like a junkie's fix. The need to have another queen, the urge to go looking again.

He was in there, on the wall, hidden within the collage of maps and brochures, somewhere within the minutiae. Now to find him. I closed my eyes and took in a deep breath. I had to become him. I breathed out and opened my eyes and stared at the map as he was living it.

The one journey now. 'Let me shadow you,' I said.

My living room was a thorough and complete view of his world.

Until this moment I hadn't realised the Sunshine Coast was the perfect place to be a serial killer.

It's vast, awash with tourists, surf beaches, caravan parks, cheap motels, golf clubs, a big airport for hordes of holiday-makers, Japanese couples on their three-day package-special honeymoons, resorts with Italian-marble pathways with limos parked out the front, bush walks and parks – monstrous tracts of unmapped land dense with scrubby gums and mangrove swamps and stringybark trees, not a road or track anywhere; little villages with art galleries and coffee shops and lattes and psychics who'll tell your fortune, abandoned sugar-cane fields and hundreds of acres of sand dunes and low scrub pocketed with thousands of unexploded bombs from the Second World War war games when the American army lounged by the ocean as they waited for MacArthur to send them back into the jungles of Guadalcanal or Milne Bay; kids surfing, teenagers in love and escaping their parents to fondle in the camping grounds or the dark corners of the all-night bars, tourists in and out for a few days only, a population of waiters and bartenders with Canadian passports and Swedish innocence, backpackers and mums and dads listening to the waves and surf, the calming sounds of the beach, always there, always in the distant background reminding you: it's safe here, happy, it's a holiday zone.

This guy was in paradise.

Serial killers are phantoms. Invisible. They lead secret lives. Only their victims see inside these lives. Serial killers are rarely caught. If they are it's usually because they make a mistake that draws the cops to them. Either they get lazy and forgetful or their ego overwhelms them and they just have to emerge and let the world see them. Rare is it when a police investigation culminates with an arrest without that mistake.

In an investigation, bodies are like treasure: they reveal the killer's secrets. All six of this guy's victims were most likely buried, somewhere deep in the ground. That meant he was smart. It also meant he wasn't interested in the headlines.

I desperately needed to know where he left those mobile phones. Maria hadn't yet learned that there's no such thing as 'random' when tracking a killer. Everything is critical.

I looked at my watch. Almost two in the morning. Isosceles wouldn't be awake until ten. I should have called him yesterday.

At three the phone rang.

'I'm having nightmares,' said Maria.

'I know you are. It means you're a good cop who cares.'

'Do they go away?'

How would I answer that? The silence did it for me.

'So I guess not,' she said.

'No. They don't.' I stared at the river. There was no moon; it was a black flow of abrupt sounds: the splash of a fish, a waterbird, frogs from the island on the other side. It made me think I could've been in the Congo.

'Come and see me. Any time that works for you. I can't really help a lot but maybe ...' I thought back to Melbourne. 'What I *do* know is that you can't survive them alone. And I know what I did wrong and what I *should* have done.'

'Now?' she asked. I heard a little girl, scared.

'Now's good. Come down through the side gate. I'll be out front, on the river.'

—

I THOUGHT ABOUT who I was and what I had done, who I'd hoped to become and what – now that the screams and eyes had found me – I could do. I thought about the people I had killed and the times I had wept like a boy. I thought of the times I'd fled. I heard the sound of a bird landing on water. I thought about this holiday land, always warm, the blue skies and the tropical storms that lashed my home, blasts of thunder and torrential rain. I thought about the life I had created here, of ease and calm and isolation.

I thought about the life I'd left behind. An existence defined by savagery, of killers disintegrating life, closing a person shut like a door, extracting the breath of their memories, annihilating the sounds of their footsteps; a savagery of blood, of severed flesh and the mutilation of a journey, a dreaming line where day and night become anguish and despair. I spent my life walking through blood, absorbing the vision of the dead and holding the cinders of horror and disbelief inside me as each investigation became a trek, a dark tunnel that I entered, a world in which the grotesque has the appearance of the ordinary, where the demon greets you with a paper surface of emotion and feeling, beguilement a wall I must discern then penetrate with a savagery of my own.

A world to which I had to return.

5

Great Geek in the Sky

'Apologise first.'

In the background I could hear the familiar thump of Linkin Park. Stevie Ray Vaughan would be next. Then Noel Coward, Erik Satie and Neil Young.

'Sorry.'

'Level of insincerity rather high, Darian. What do I call you these days? Darian? Boss? Mr Richards perhaps? Instructions; we need new boundaries. By the way, of relevance *and* interest, the Sunshine Coast is, I posit, rivalled only by the sub-continent as a landscape suited to the behaviours of our perpetrators. Go back to that forest at the dead end of Jenny Brown's street: there was a white van parked there two days before she was taken.'

'You've been tracking me?'

'I get bored; I'm lonely; at nights I collapse with nostalgia. Prostitutes don't help. Nor does God. I've become an Existentialist; I take classes. Your departure was tremendously selfish. I appreciate that you were shot in the head; that is significant. Who's the girl on Tuesday nights? Red Celica, 2006; blonde; a hundred and sixty-two centimetres. Is she your method of sexual release? Would you like me to tell you of her movements; I have them all. Did you know the Sunshine Coast was so named by real estate developers in 1958? Until then it was called Near North Coast. He's going to be a very hard man to capture; I presume you would have chosen another location for retirement had you known he was already there.'

They used to be called analysts. Then, for a while, we called them researchers. Now we just call them geeks. Throughout my time as a homicide investigator I made it known I was the sum of many parts, the mightiest being the genius on the other end of the line; sitting in his apartment on the top floor of one of the tallest buildings in the heart of Melbourne, all curtain-less floor-to-ceiling windows, a mattress on the floor with its Raquel Welch sheet and the walls grasping for space amid two hundred framed prints of Goya's dark and horrific 'Disasters of War' – and of course his desk containing 'the Pulse', his array of computers all linked to one another and to the cloud, where all digital information was stored in cyberspace.

Isosceles.

'Tell me about the white van,' I said.

'It's white.'

'And it's a van; what else?' Isosceles had a theory that humour was an essential and much-maligned tool in murder investigations.

'Late model, possibly HiLux; imagery indistinct. That it's white is actually relevant, Darian; it's white-white; i.e. new or hired.'

'Sorry.'

'You're forgiven. You're rusty. Did you know that retirement calcifies the brain?'

'How long was it there for?' I asked. 'Where exactly was it? Have you looked at the other victims' houses to see if it was there too? Can you search the hire-car agencies up here and also recent sales, say the last two years of new and used white vans?'

'Thursday, thirteen October: it was already parked at o-six-hundred, directly across from our girl's house. It looks like a willow tree out there. Did you know the Queensland government has banned willow trees, due to their colossal water drainage? Eighteen hundred, same day: van had gone. I have not looked at the other houses due to uncertainty regarding the investigation; verification hereby noted following this communication–'

I was scribbling as he was speaking; he'd also be taking notes, one-handed, onto a keyboard, always on his left-hand side, while reading from the many screens in front of him and using his right hand on another keyboard directly in front of him.

'–which is also the case re sales and hiring of vans; I'll have that information soon.'

'You ready?'

'Commence.'

We began. It was just as if we were back on the eighth floor of St Kilda Road HQ.

'All known sexual offenders. Try Brisbane and the Sunshine Coast; it's only an hour and a half away. Stretch up to Gympie inland, Tin Can Bay, eastern edge; encompass the hinterland past the Glasshouse Mountains. The local cops would have already done this but they've missed him. He's in there and they've already interviewed him—'

'Most likely,' he corrected me.

'Most likely. In particular we need to focus on low-level obscene behaviour towards young women in a twelve-month period before Jenny was taken.' Serial killers don't just start killing. They build up to it. They leave trails, usually minor sexual crimes.

'Noted.'

'Can you hack into the Noosa police database?'

'Trying; not looking good.'

'Let me know.'

'The victims?'

'Not yet. Stay with him for now; he's boasting.'

'Is he? Good.'

'He leaves their mobile phones, afterwards.'

'I need their numbers.'

'Don't have them yet. He takes a photograph of them in captivity, alive, with their phone, then ...' I was thinking: what *did* he do then? 'This only just came to light.'

'Wait,' he commanded.

I did. At the other end of the line I could hear his fingers scattering across the keyboards. He types very quickly. I kept waiting.

'Darian?'

'Still here.'

'I'm getting them. I've just got Jenny Brown's. It will take some hours to get them all. The constabulary will have already done this.'

'Will they have your spywear?'

'Of course not. A question.'

'Yeah?'

'Who are we working for?'

'The victims.'

'Oh.' Isosceles was high profile in the investigative world. He took jobs from private and government contractors around the globe. He wasn't going to be paid on this one. I knew I didn't need to ask but I did anyway, just to make sure there weren't any misunderstandings.

'That okay?'

'Did you need to ask?'

I spent the next two hours going through each victim's profile, giving Isosceles instructions on what to look for. At the end of the conversation, as we were about to hang up, he said, 'A minor problem.'

'A problem about what?' I asked.

'Entirely everything. You don't have internet: you remember, that late-twentieth-century tool of communication? It's still in use.'

'I don't use it.'

'What happened to your mobile phone?'

'I threw it away.'

'Just an observation, a note in passing; minor flaw to the investigation.'

I hadn't even thought about it. Isosceles was right, as usual. 'I'll call somebody and get them to do whatever it is they need–'

'Done. There's a guy on the way; he'll be there in an hour. Owes me. He's bringing a computer for you as well; he's bringing everything you need. Don't complain, especially about the computer. He'll hack into the exchange and commit a few crimes under the Telecommunications Act but you'll be online by the middle of the day.'

'Do I have to wait for him and–'

'–be nice to him and make him cups of tea? No, I would not ask you to engage in unnecessary human contact; you can exit the house.'

And so I did, to visit Jenny Brown's mother.

6

Feelings

THE ZEPPELIN SAYS I HAVE TO BE GROWN-UP.

'You're not a boy anymore,' she says.

The zeppelin says I can be anything I want.

'You don't want to waste your life on those video games, Winston.'

The zeppelin is a cunt and I want to kill her but I can't because if I do my mum will get angry and say I am being irresponsible and that maybe I've gone *boomy* again and then she'll stop giving me money. I want to kill my mum and get all her money but I can't because cops always look to the next of kin as the first suspect and that'd be me and then I'd get caught. So I gotta put up with the zeppelin telling me I'm a child but I'm not, not all the time. Sometimes I am but sometimes I'm not.

Hello my brothers and sisters. Welcome to the Awesome World. I'm Big Winnie and I'm the *man*. Pleased to meet you, hope you enjoy the lessons.

The zeppelin says I should write things down. Feelings. That's what we're doing today: feelings.

'It's to help you, Winston,' she says.

She says I should start with something meaningful, like my first memory of being happy, or like the first time I felt love … or maybe like when I first saw baby girl Jenny B – not baby girl Jenny G, she's next – walking along the footpath under those big jacaranda trees that hang down on the road like icicles and that big wave of warm that came from under the ground and rose up through my body like a hot bath and gave me the tingles all over and made my cock all hard, standing still, there I was in the street, no cars, no people, just me and Jenny B with her blonde hair and tight shorts and pink T-shirt and her bare feet, and me following her along the footpath and she not knowing Big Winnie is behind her, shadowing her, making plans for her as we walk to the end of the road and cross Gympie Terrace to the bus stop in front of the Noosa River Bridge, cars going this way and that, boats on the river, kids on the sandy beach looking for prawns and baby girl sitting at the bus stop playing with her phone, texting, not ever looking up to see Big Winnie nearby under that old dead gum tree. Doesn't even notice me getting on board the bus, so close I can smell her. This is good, zeppelin, this is meaningful. Me and baby girl taking the Sun Bus ride through the streets arriving at Noosa Civic. I love Noosa Civic. It's got a Big W. It's got lots of girls' clothes shops. It's got lots of girls, they come here after school. Today it's got baby girl. *Still* she hasn't noticed me *and* I've been her shadow for over an hour *and* now I know her shape *and* I've heard her voice *and* I know she has a friend called Carol *and* she is a size 10 *and* soon I'll know even more *and* she'll know me. I'll know everything. But first we have to start with the beginning.

Step One: Retreat from target. (That's so she doesn't know I exist.) Become the ghost.

Step Two: Track the target. This may take up to three weeks before I have learned enough about her pattern of movements–

Stop.

No movement. Suck in breath. Listen. Assess. Stay absolutely calm. Concentrate all angles.

Is there a breach?

LISTEN! DO NOT LOOK AT HER. ISOLATE HER AND REMOVE HER FROM YOUR MIND.

NOW –

Concentrate.

It's a voice.

Roger that.

It's nearby.

TRY HARDER. CONCENTRATE.

Roger that.

Oh. It's the zeppelin. Wow, totally forgot about her.

'Hi,' and smile. Roger that.

'Winston?'

'Sorry, Doc,' smiling, 'I was miles away.'

'Did you come up with anything?'

Yes absolutely I did, I came up with my Tingle, all soft and pink and nude-nude-nude baby breasts with nippletops, blue baby eyes–

'Winston?'

'Sorry.' Focus. Sayonara Tingle.

Big Winnie, he be back.

What was I meant to be doing? Gotta be something. Zeppelin's like waiting for me to do something. Or say something maybe?

'Ah, maybe if you could give me a little bit of guidance?' I say.

'It doesn't have to be your first pleasurable memory but something from when you were really young. Like going to the beach or on a camping trip. As long as it is, *now*, something that you can look back on and think: that was fun.'

That's right: we're doing an exercise. I'm meant to be writing down my first experience of fun. Wow, even got a pen in my hand and a notepad on my side of her desk.

Right: that's why Tingle got involved; I'm not losing my mind. Okay: gotta think, *complete the exercise.*

She's smiling at me like I'm a dumb insect. 'Anything, Winston. Maybe a puppy you had.'

What's that word to describe that way she's looking at me? Oh yeah, condescending.

'Well,' I say, 'I reckon it was either when I was on a school camp outside Melbourne in this town called Daylesford and it snowed and so I saw snow fall, for the first time, ever, and I built a snowman ... or else it was when I–'

–snatched little Robin outside the video store as she walked under that old fig tree, into the big shadow that its branches cast across the footpath – not a fucking word or sound. WHAP. There she was, now she's gone. WHAP. So easy, so amazingly easy, fast man, amazing knowing I COULD DO IT, yay-yay-yay!

'—no, it was the snow. Cold but beautiful, you know? I love nature. That's why I moved up here to the Sunshine Coast. No snow up here, eh! Eh?'

—

'SHE, AH, SHE wants to see me again, like, the week after next.'

She stares at the computer screen.

Helen. Twenty, maybe twenty-two. Engagement ring on her finger. Thin gold chain around her neck. Slender fingers. Tapered. Size 36, maybe a D cup. Nice lips. Very good bone structure. Looks after her body. Overall, a size twelve, maybe ten.

Sensual. Can't apply eye make-up for shit. I dunno about that dark brown hair colour. I mean, I like that it's thick and the way she ties it up at the back of her head.

'How's Thursday at ten?'

Don't you really hate it when chicks talk to you as they stare at the computer screen?

'That might be a problem, Helen. Sorry.'

And now she looks up and makes eye contact with me. And just what I thought, what I thought the last time I was here: pale blue eyes. Watery. Almost whitish with a pale blue wash.

'Don't you hate guys like me? Sorry.'

'No, you're right, Winston.'

'Any time but ten actually.'

Eyes back to the screen. I sorta *like* the cleavage. I don't think she should have that top button undone though.

'Twelve?' Eyes on the screen.

'Roger that.'

'I love the way you say that, Winston,' laughing, still looking at the screen.

The cleavage *is* good, yeah, I like it. A long time ago I learned that the hidden is arousal. Mystery and wonder. That's what the cleavage is making me say: I'm an all-curious guy, Helen, all curious. I'm floating. I love it when I float. I want to see her breasts.

That's weird, huh? Because, you know, I actually haven't wanted or looked or felt *woman* breasts since –

Since when I found that drunk drugged chick, crashed out in the park that night, who was so out of it, she was like dead as I fucked her, even when I blew inside her and shouted into her ears, 'I just fucked you; I came inside you' but not too loud because we were in a park, even though there were no other people who could hear me, and then, when I grabbed her breast like hard and squeezed it and shouted, but like last time, not too loud, with my mouth right up next to her ear, 'I've still got my dick inside you' and still she kept sleeping, so then I shouted, but still soft like: 'Now I'm gunna cut your throat, ear to ear.' And still she slept. And then it hit me that it'd be real cool to do that: to cut her throat with one hand, while I had my dick inside her and the other hand on her tit; because, you know, I reckon she'd wake up then; wake up WOW: imagine that. Total sensation of being fucked and tit squeezed and blood pouring down your neck, pinned under and staring up into the eyes of the conqueror; so cool; stare down into her eyes as her blood would pour out over her and my hand would get all sticky as I squeezed harder and at the same time – all at the same time, she'd die: I'd see her eyes go all cloudy and she'd look – up – into my eyes as it'd blast through the end of my dick and deep into her and she'd die in my arms.

But none of that happened. I did find the sleeping chick in the park and I did pull off her clothes and I squeezed her tits and then I fucked her but I didn't kill her because I knew I'd get caught. Fear not, brothers and sisters, Big Winnie acts and thinks like a child but he is smart smart smart.

I'm way ahead of the cops. Which is another reason I wanna touch and feel Helen's big-woman tits: the cops will get confused after she vanishes and I leave behind her iPhone, which I can see on the desk next to her. Because Helen is raven-haired and she's old.

7

'Spit-It-Out Izzie, the Fuck Monster'

I PARKED UNDER THE WILLOW TREE. THE ROAD WAS EMPTY, just like it was yesterday. Jenny Brown's house looked the same as it did yesterday, like it would look tomorrow and for days stretching into an uncertain future. There was no gate, no fence, just a broken concrete path through overgrown grass where the unopened letters and throwaway newspapers would probably sink into the earth before someone bothered to pick them up. I climbed the wooden steps that led to a porch.

The front door was open. Nearly everyone in the area leaves their front door open and their house unlocked. People are trusting up here. Too trusting.

My place is always locked.

I knocked.

I counted to twenty and knocked again. I peered through the screen door but couldn't see anything.

'Hello,' I called. 'My name is Darian Richards.'

I waited. Maybe I'd missed her; maybe Sheryl was out. She liked the pokies. She liked bingo. She liked the pub. The list of her recent boyfriends ran for two pages.

'I'd like to talk to you about Jenny. I'm not a cop. I'm not a journalist. I'm not a psychic.' When you become a Family of Victim you start to see everybody by what they are not.

'Are ya here to give me a donation?' came a woman's voice from inside.

'Sorry, no.'

'Then fuck off.'

'I will. But first, before I fuck off, I'm going to tell you who I am. Why I'm here.'

I waited to see if there'd be another fuck off.

I broke the silence: 'I used to be a homicide investigator. In Melbourne.'

I broke the silence again: 'I'm here about Jenny.'

I heard the rustle of a chair on linoleum, footsteps, and then Sheryl appeared at the flywire door.

'I'm broke.'

'I'm not charging. I'm not a private detective.'

The door opened. I began to walk inside–

'Shoes!' she said as she walked away from me.

As well as smiling and waving at you and knowing everything that you did and will be doing in the future, the people up here have some strange habits. They say 'cheerio' instead of 'cheers' and 'hooray' when every other English-speaking person on the planet says 'goodbye'. And they have a thing about walking around inside a house wearing shoes. They don't. They leave their shoes at the front door or the back door; anywhere, just as long as they don't walk inside wearing shoes. I loathe walking in my socks; it feels disempowering, I can't explain it any other way. I have, however, learned not to ignore this customary demand and so, by the front door, I leaned down and removed my shoes then padded inside, in my socks.

Sheryl waited for me, sitting at a pale green Formica table in the kitchen at the back of the house, which opened onto a snarling and tangled garden of strangler fig and mango trees.

She was gazing at me, as if trying to figure out my real intention. Her face was sad, and showed a withered spirit. Her hair was lank, unwashed. She was pale even though her skin was parched brown from a life on the beach. She wore a man's shirt that used to be white. It was too big. Some of the buttons were undone or missing.

When she leaned across the table to grab the packet of Camel cigarettes and the bottle of cheap vodka, I glimpsed her breast. Once she would have been very pretty.

'The cops are fuckwits,' she said.

I said nothing. I knew how this would play out. I'd let her vent. That would make her feel comfortable with me. That would make her agree to what I wanted.

'Never listened when we told them she'd gone. Fuckwits. Then that fuckin' tramp down the road – number three – then she goes missing and the cops are back, all over us, asking this, asking that. Too fuckin' late, I told them. Too late.' She paused.

I made a mental note: 'fuckin' tramp down the road – number three – then she goes missing' – what on earth did that mean?

'So what makes *you* different?' Before I could answer: 'And how many times do I have to say what happened? Jenny walked out the door. That one. See!' She was pointing at the front door. 'She said nothing. I heard the door close. That's "goodbye": the sound of a door closing.'

She breathed in deeply as she fought back tears.

'You better tell me what you want to know.'

'Everything. About Jenny. About you. About this house, the street. Who comes and goes. Phone calls, visitors. Jenny's friends. Your friends; your boyfriend–'

'Get fucked.'

'What have the cops told you?'

'Not to give up hope. She's most likely still alive. Like that girl in Austria. Lots of girls get taken and they escape.'

'They're lying,' I said.

She looked at me, astonished. She opened her mouth to speak but couldn't. Tears welled in her eyes.

'She's not alive. He's taken six girls. They are not alive.'

She abruptly pushed the chair away from the table and got up. She stood by the kitchen sink and stared through the window into the garden. I saw a swing, cut out of an old tyre, hanging from the strangler fig. The truth can hurt, but it's the truth.

'Then why are you here?' she asked softly.

'To stop him from taking anyone else.'

I'd gambled hard on this, so I figured I didn't have anything to lose. I got out of my chair and stood behind her. Close. I spoke softly. 'I'll find your little girl, where he put her. I'll bring her home to you.'

She was weeping as I continued: 'She needs to come home. She needs that. You need that. It's not closure. It won't erase the pain. That never goes. But you will have tended to her spirit.'

Amid the sobs and gasping breaths, she said: 'Do you know how many people have come into this house and told me they'll find her?'

'No,' I said. 'But what I do know is, you've learned how to spot them. That's why you sit in here and listen to them at the front door. You can hear the bullshit and the promises, the liars, the journalists, the cops who pretend they've got something to say. You don't even have to look into their eyes. I bet you can even tell by the sound of their footsteps and the way they knock on the front door.'

She nodded. 'Yep.' She was still looking out into the backyard.

'I'm different.'

She nodded again.

'That's because I know how this guy thinks. I know he sat outside your house for days. He watched and he waited. He followed your girl. He probably followed you. After locking onto Jenny she became his obsession, day and night; he tracked and charted everything you, your boyfriend and Jenny did. He ensured there were no risks to his plan. When he felt safe, he swooped. There was nothing you could have done to stop him.'

—

SHERYL TOLD ME everything she could remember about the days leading up to Jenny's disappearance. She let me into Jenny's room. She opened her wardrobe, pulled out her clothes, lay them on her bed. I asked what Jenny liked to wear; I told her to be honest with me. She took out two pairs of tight shorts, said they were disgusting, like the G-strings she also showed me. I told her that none of this meant Jenny was sexually provocative. Or if it did, it didn't matter.

The tight shorts might have incited him. The clothes she wore to a club in Noosa might have incited him. Or he might have been incited simply because she happened to walk past him at the wrong moment.

I asked about her friends. I asked about her life away from home. Facebook, the beach, school, the local shopping centre. I asked about her doctor and her dentist, any place he might have spotted her. I asked about her route to school, her bus trips.

She told me everything, the minutiae of a teenage girl's life. Cheeseburgers at McDonald's; fries from KFC; chicken from Red Rooster. Hang-outs. Boys.

Sheryl hadn't noticed the white van parked out the front of the house.

I felt a buzz in my back pocket. My new mobile phone. Only one person knew the number. I quickly checked the message.

gofish

It was our old code for 'Got a lead'. I'd call him back after I finished. There was something missing here. I'd been granted complete access to Jenny's world, even her last Facebook postings, but nothing led me into his trail, not even remotely. What was I expecting? An email exchange of an innocent girl being groomed by a psychopath? Was I over-reaching? Was I pretending to be a saviour when in fact I was rusty, over the hill? Maybe I was past it. After all, I had clambered into this without even thinking to get online, get a mobile phone; all I'd thought of was the gun.

And then I remembered: 'fuckin' tramp down the road – number three – then she goes missing'.

Sheryl had almost vanished inside Jenny's bed. With the pink Doona tightly gripped around her, the G-strings and tight shorts were scattered across its fluffy surface, amid the other trinkets and memories of her daughter's life.

'Who were you talking about before? The tramp down the road?'

'Spit-it-out Izzie, the fuck monster. Why? What do you want to know about her for?' she asked narrowly.

The what?

'Are you talking about Izzie Daniels, his third victim?' I asked.

'How many Izzies you met?'

'But what do you mean by "down the road"? She lived at Mooloolaba.' At least an hour's drive away; maybe I was about to discover another local foible.

Sheryl sat up in bed. 'She lived there, yeah, but she fucked the twins and anyone else with a dick three doors down from here,' she said, jerking her thumb towards the houses in the direction of the main road. 'Carl, the ugly one, was her boyfriend, sort of – most blokes have an attitude if their sheila's a slut, but not him – and she spent all of her time up here. It was disgusting.' Sheryl sat up further in bed. 'I ain't no saint, but even I rang up the coppers to make a complaint about it.'

'About what?' I asked.

'Izzie! Most people close the curtains before they have sex. Izzie? Dead opposite; that girl was in training to be a porn star. Everyone knew about it; some of the kids along the street even made a place to spy on her, out in the bush on the other side of the road.'

'Izzie was thirteen,' I said without thinking.

'Must be a Queensland thing then, eh?' she responded sarcastically.

Which momentarily reminded me of indeed another local habit; finishing a sentence on an upward inflection of 'eh' as if a question had just been asked. 'Did Jenny know Izzie?' I asked.

'Everyone knew Izzie. Jenny hated her. All the girls hated her. And the parents and the school, 'specially after that time she was caught selling the DVD.'

The what?

—

I PUSHED THROUGH the palm fronds and scrubby bush until I was, once again, in the quiet of the makeshift camp with its view of Jenny's house across the road – only this time I was staring at the house three doors down. I had a direct view into the twins' living room where the curtains would part and the lights would blaze and Spit-it-out Izzie would dazzle the hidden spectators, dozens of eyes shrouded in the night outside, watching her as she 'fucked and sucked like a Bollywood slut', as Sheryl so vividly described.

This was it. This was the beginning; not Jenny. Izzie's fame spread like a virus in the underbelly of the local area, along the road, through the school – where she sold a DVD of blow jobs, a compilation that earned her the nickname – into the waiting rooms of the local doctors and up the footpaths and down the aisles of the nearby supermarket. If he hadn't caught up with her by then he probably did while prowling the shopping centre and eavesdropping on the conversations of the girls as they walked in and out of the clothes shops.

Izzie was number one. He would have tracked her down and watched her from where I was now standing. But her extraordinarily overt displays of sexuality might have both excited and frightened him; he liked his girls subdued. Enter Jenny, simply walking along the road, crossing his view, capturing his attention: same age, pretty, blonde. Innocent, compliant-looking. It would have been that simple, that easy, and that tragic.

I felt a vibration in my back pocket.

'Who's calling?' I said.

'Is that humour? Cease. Only your sense of direction is worse. I need you to go home and sit in front of your new computer. I have news.'

8

Fat Adam on the Jetty

THE COPS WERE WAITING FOR ME.

In a show of subtlety a white cruiser was parked on the street in front of Sil the Onion's, which I edged past as I turned into my driveway. Another cruiser was parked directly opposite, on the other side of the street. In the driveway, blocking the entrance to my garage, were two more cruisers. I counted seven uniforms; the biggest muscle on the hill. No female cops. Just the DD.

I parked carefully, blocking in both cruisers.

'Boys,' I said by way of greeting as if we'd just arrived for a Christmas party on the beach.

They didn't reply. They were stone faced and very still, arms muscle-bound across their chests. Seven statues, with eyes that trailed me as I climbed out of the Toyota and ambled my way towards the river where I knew Fat Adam was waiting for me.

Years ago Adam Cross was a Senior Sergeant stationed at Broadmeadows, a huge and sprawling suburb on the fringe of Melbourne. Somebody once told me Melbourne has the biggest land mass of a city per head of population anywhere in the world. When you're in Broadmeadows you think: maybe.

Adam never rose beyond Senior Sergeant. He was lazy and rolled with blubber, content to inhabit the other side of a desk while others caught the action of the streets. When a job opportunity for Officer in Charge at the Noosa Hill station was posted on our internal newsletter, there were eighty-two registered applications within an hour. The news that the desk had gone to Fat Adam meant his new bosses were either stupendously stupid or he had the best offer. Queensland, after all, has the most brilliant history of police corruption, easily, in my opinion, outperforming New South Wales and Victoria.

I knew Adam, not well, as the Senior Sergeant. He knew me more than I knew him. Everybody knows the Officer in Charge of Homicide; you're like a gunslinger walking into the saloon: people stare at everything you do. You don't stare back.

He was, as expected, sitting at the end of my jetty where I'd placed a solid Balinese three-seater bench, hewn from Indonesian hardwood. I didn't sit next to him. I smiled at the pelicans floating on the water, as if to reassure them he was only temporary.

'Who are you working for?' he asked.

'Nobody. I won't get in your way. You'll get the credit. Press conference will be all yours.'

I thought that about summed it all up, so I said, 'Good seeing you, Adam,' as I turned back to the house. 'Looks like you lost a little weight,' I added happily. He must've gained at least eight kilos.

'Ever listen to Bob Dylan?' he asked.

I didn't speak, but I didn't walk away either.

'Maybe you're familiar with his religious period, when he was born again.'

I stayed silent but he had my attention. I've usually already reached the end of a conversation by its first or second utterance – it's good to know where you're going so you can play it out accordingly – but exactly where *this* tangential line was taking us, I didn't know.

'One of my favourite songs is "You've Gotta Serve Somebody". Know it?'

I didn't speak but had an inkling where we were now going.

'He sings about Presidents, ordinary men and women, anyone. Says that no matter who you are, what you do, you have to be serving someone.' He turned and looked at me for the first time.

'How many's he taken now; your killer riding the trains?'

I didn't answer. Fat Adam was smarter than I thought. I wanted to push him off the jetty into the river. It would have been what the seven DDs wanted as well: seeing the fat boss trying not to drown and whacking the crap out of me at the same time.

'You think you're working for the victims. I hear that all the time. Burden of the righteous. You're working for *you*. You couldn't catch the train-rider so now you have to prove yourself up here. You won't catch this guy either. None of us will. You know that, I know that. Even the civilians know it. Everybody knows it, 'cept for him. But *you* … you gotta step in, gotta flash the badge of forgotten glories and offer hope where there is none; stand sharp in the evening sun, when your shadow is as long as your fuckin' ego.'

He started to wobble, an imitation of a walk. He was also bald and short. He was puce-red and fleshy. He looked like something you'd feed to hungry animals. No wonder the pelicans had gathered around him.

'We both know the drill. Let's see where it ends,' he said.

I looked down at the wooden bench. He'd left a newspaper, the Melbourne *Herald Sun*. It was folded to page three, an article about the train-rider. His last victim had now been missing for over two weeks.

The drill was this: they couldn't stop me as long as I didn't break any laws. I had to operate as a civilian. People could slam a door in my face; all I could do about it was walk away or knock again. They'd be watching me; maybe for fun they'd rumble me but, then again, the constabulary were wary of me – even the DD, two of whom were now walking along the jetty towards me, shouting that I'd parked them in.

My phone buzzed.

'Give Casey your number. I am not an answering service. He said to tell you the Brescian has arrived.'

9

The Doppelganger Emittance

I KEPT THEM WAITING WHILE I REVERSED, CREPT FORWARD, swung the wheel, reversed again, got out of the car and measured the narrow space between the Toyota's rear and Janice-something's wooden fence, smiled at the boys as if to say, 'Ain't life grand?' then hit the pedals with a gentle edging forward, then braked, swung the wheel again and slowly reversed. Two of them stood and watched me while the other two sat glumly behind the wheel of each cruiser.

I would have liked to have wasted the boys' time a lot longer than I did, but I had work to do. Isosceles had news and I hadn't called him back. Casey had the Brescian; my gun.

After I navigated into an eclectic position between a lemon-scented eucalypt, a little garden of Italian parsley and a wild bougainvillea tree whose heavy branches swung close to the Toyota's roof, I squeezed out and walked towards the back door. The boys hadn't moved.

Time for a message, I realised. I paused and waited.

Right on cue, number three said, 'You think you're real fuckin' smart, don't ya?' He had the blond dreamy beach look. King of the kids at the surf club on Saturday nights. If I was a champ surfer he might have asked my opinion on riding waves. Champ cops rarely get respect, they get envy rolled into put-down contempt.

I didn't say anything.

'Well, you're not,' he added, thus completing every six-year-old boy's fantasy of what it's like to be a tough cop.

Brain Surgery didn't move, nor did the genius next to him. I counted to ten. None of us moved.

The phone calls would have to wait.

By now Fat Adam and the other cops would have arrived back at the station; there was going to be a twenty-minute delay, at least, before these guys got back. Everybody at the station would be waiting for them, wanting to know what they did to me, how they intimidated me, maybe pushed me into the river, messed me up a bit, how they taught the know-it-all from the big city down south to get back into his place.

The geniuses hadn't thought that far ahead yet. But they would, after they left here. It would occur to them there would be a waiting party, including the boss.

I needed to make a point.

'Tell your friends to get out of the cars,' I said with a lethal calm that I hadn't used in a while. They looked at one another, uncertain.

'Or if it's a problem, I'll do it for you,' I said.

Both turned and stepped to the cars, one of them opening the side door and leaning in to speak to the waiting driver, the other walking to the driver's side window, knocking on it for him to roll it down.

The other two got out. They were big boys, the four of them. They stood next to one another and waited. At least they weren't dumb enough to flex their fists.

'Come here,' I said.

Cops don't like being told to go anywhere. They didn't move.

'No problem. I'll come to you,' I said and walked towards them. Cops don't like it when people approach them either. I got close but not dumb close.

I looked each of them in the eyes. They held the gaze. I could hear their shallow breathing, see their bodies tense, unflinching.

'I'm going to tell you a story, but don't worry, it's short. I was nineteen when I put on the uniform. An old guy, a Senior Sergeant who'd been at Collingwood station since the thirties and had the scars to prove it, told me the uniform never comes off. That's why they carry it at your funeral. It even follows you to the grave.'

I had their attention. I was talking about something each of them knew in their hearts but never spoke of in public.

'I've been shot at sixteen times; three times hit. I've discharged my firearm on sixty-four occasions. Never reprimanded. I've killed eighteen bad guys and feel a whole lot better for it. A number of those men looked me in the eyes before I pulled the trigger. I was glad to see those boys die before me. Three of them were cops.'

I paused again. Deep breathing now, bodies sagging just a little, muscles no longer tense. They were listening.

'When you go back to the station, say what you want. But don't you go back pretending I'm something I'm not. Brag all you need to in front of the boss but with your colleagues, tell 'em how it really is. In plain language, boys, tell 'em not to get carried away thinking I'm good for a rumble. That'd be a big mistake.' And then I turned and walked inside my house.

I heard the cars leave a few minutes later.

—

I DON'T HAVE a desk, so my new computer was sitting at one end of my dining table, which wasn't a dining table but a massive block of timber that Casey found in an abandoned warehouse on the old Brisbane docks. Beside the computer was a list of handwritten instructions: how to turn it on, which icon to press to get wired – and a very long list of what not to do.

I went to Skype.

'How were the police?' asked Isosceles.

'How did you know?'

'Casey told me. He's rung me three times. He found a ninety-two. It came in early.'

'Did he?' I was impressed; the 92 is hard to find.

'You're tanned.'

'That's because I live in the sun.'

'Loathsome.'

'You haven't changed at all.'

'I'm immortal. I'm thinking of travelling to Burkina Faso after this is all over; would you like to accompany me?'

'No.'

'Suit yourself. I'll go alone. You recall our last conversation on the matter of signals emitted from mobile phones?'

'Sort of. Not really. It was over two years ago, I'd just thrown a perp into the back of a wagon and was bleeding from a knife wound. I do recall you were incessant.'

'I am always incessant. Assumption: after neutralising the target, he destabilises her phone.'

'Correct.'

'Correct,' he repeated as if ticking off an item on a shopping list. 'A process of some ten seconds?'

'Make it twenty; some of the girls had tote bags, some had school bags.'

'In which case we now have an accurate location for each of the six disappearances. You'll see two anomalies. The first: victim five was not taken at the KFC, where she was last seen. Her final signal occurred four minutes later; it's on the map I've sent you. The second: victim three–'

'Izzie,' I added, so indelibly forged into my mind she'd become.

'–was taken twenty-three kilometres away from where the police say she was taken. The discrepancy in time is also odd. I have her being taken sixty-eight minutes after the police logged her as "last sighted".'

'Twenty-three k's and sixty-eight minutes? How did they stuff that up so badly?'

'Theirs not to reason why, comrade, theirs but to do and die.' Isosceles adored history and in particular the somewhat-obscure Crimean War. It was the source of many quotes, scattered throughout his conversations and text messages and the occasional random email.

'Recalling our last conversation on the matter,' he went on, 'I said there was no device one could use to stop the signal from a mobile phone, not even if it was turned off. To evade detection only the removal of the battery would suffice. You may remember the rather vicious debate regarding tin foil being wrapped around mobile phones as a means to evade detection?'

Geeks: they love to obsess over the obscure.

I assumed he had discovered six blinks, like stars in an incoherent sky, winking for the merest of seconds then vanishing into black; six messages from the phones of six captured girls. I was wrong.

'Once he destabilises them, they remain destabilised.'

'But how does he take the photos? He's got to turn their phones on, surely, to take the photos?'

'Add to his profile: knowledge of telecommunications, computer hardware and photography. He must be removing the SIM cards and inserting them into a homemade device that allows him to cut and paste a photo, from a hard drive, no doubt, into its little plastic world.'

'Cost? Places to purchase the hardware?'

'Irrelevant. It's the knowledge; that's your first lead.'

'The first? There's another?'

'His location.'

All geeks are like this. They can't tell you, 'Hey, guess what? I just found where the perp is.' They have to lead you there as if it were the end to a mathematical puzzle. I kept calm and refrained from yelling at him, which would have delayed me even more.

'Ah. The location,' I said, as if ordering a pizza.

'Emittances. Fragments. Apparitions. Mirages. The local constabulary won't have detected them. They are chimeras, ghosts. Maybe we could call them doppelgangers.' He giggled. 'Did you know Abraham Lincoln saw his own doppelganger? John Donne too: the poet, the rake, the man who spent half his life in luxurious intercourse and the other half in repentance.'

'Isosceles!' I barked, knowing I was close to him reciting the entire 'Batter my heart, three-person'd God'.

'Yes. Apologies. I digress. They are there. Not all of them, not all six, but enough. Doppelganger emittances, direct from the girls' mobile phones. Four, to be exact. The other two must have dithered into the unfolding universe. And they emanate from the following coordinates.'

As he listed them I wrote them down with one hand, and with the other I typed them into Google Earth.

'I've Google-Earthed it,' he said, before I'd even got halfway. 'Darian, our killer appears to be residing on the North Shore in a luxury resort.'

10

Return to the Gun

I LOCKED UP THE HOUSE AND GOT INTO THE TOYOTA, STILL wedged between a tree, a bush and a garden of herbs. I drove to the end of my driveway and paused. I looked left, and right and then left again. No cruisers. No unmarked vehicles.

I drove carefully, as if leading a funeral procession.

Cases don't break this fast. Not unless the killer is standing over a body with the gun in his hand. Cases *shouldn't* break this fast. But Isosceles was never wrong and, anyway, I knew he was right. Cops have a sixth sense; all cops, even the DD. We can spot a bad guy in a half-kilometre radius: the way he looks, the way he walks, the way he smiles, the way he stands. If I had friends they wouldn't invite me to dinner parties. I'd have all the guests summed up by the time I'd smiled and said, 'Thanks, just a glass of soda water.' There's the coke-head, there's the marital cheat, there's the wife-beater.

I drove out through Tewantin, passing the turn-off to the North Shore – my destination.

First, though, I had a gun to get.

In Queensland the standard-issue weapon for police is the Austrian-made Glock .22-calibre semi-automatic. The Glock is a very ugly weapon; it reminds me of a grey refrigerator.

The standard-issue weapon for members of the Victoria Police is the .38-calibre Smith & Wesson, an American handgun made in Springfield, Massachusetts. Every cop in Australia remembers their first time seeing Clint Eastwood play Dirty Harry. 'Go ahead, make my day.' That was a Smith & Wesson. Its barrel looked a foot long.

That particular pistol was called a Magnum. It was a .44 calibre. All cops want to be Dirty Harry. They can't, but the department can ease the frustration by giving them their own Mr Smith and Mr Wesson.

Long after I'd been assigned my Smith & Wesson and long before I decided never to carry a gun again, I fell in love with the shape, the grip and the feel of the Beretta 92. I kept the .38 as my authorised firearm but I rarely used it. The 92 I kept at home. Used it only when necessary, when I needed a gun that wouldn't leave a trace. The Beretta is my Studebaker version of a pistol: sleek, crafted with artisanship, metal with curves.

While Smith & Wesson has been making firearms since 1852, timed nicely to coincide with the American Civil War, and while the Glocks have been little grey fridges since 1963, nicely timed to coincide with the escalation of the Vietnam War, the Beretta company goes back to 1526, nicely timed to coincide with the Italian Wars which lasted from 1494 to 1559 but ramped up with the 'Battle of Pavia' in 1525. The Beretta is made in a place called Gardone val Trompia, on the northern outskirts of a town called Brescia, near Lake Como.

The 92 was designed and made in 1972. It's rare. Only 5000 were made. One of them lies at the bottom of the Pacific Ocean, due north of Melbourne, about a hundred metres offshore.

—

CASEY HANDED ME an R.M. Williams shoe box that carried the weight of more than a pair of cowboy boots. We were on the balcony, overlooking the sweep of the valley. In the far distance dark thunderheads were rising over the horizon, slowly blocking the soft metallic sky with the threat of a big storm. Casey was wearing a sarong with a pair of brand new R.M. Williams boots.

'It's a ninety-two,' he said as I opened the lid of the box.

'I know. Isosceles told me.'

'He's booking a trip to Burkina Faso. I'm going with him. You should join us.'

'Thanks. I'll stick to Queensland.'

I held the gun.

'No throwing it in the fuckin' ocean this time, all right?' he said. 'What a fuckin' waste. You know how many of these were made?'

'Five thousand,' I said as my fingers slowly clenched the soft curves of its hard metal.

'Five thousand. And because of you, now there are only four thousand, nine hundred and ninety-nine left. You hurt that one, it's down to four thousand, nine hundred and ninety-eight. And Lord knows how many other fuckwits have been sweated by madness and tossed theirs into rivers or streams or lakes or oceans far away. Look after the fuckin' thing, all right?'

I wasn't really listening. I was looking down at my right hand as my index finger took control and nudged into the trigger with familiar pressure. Like when I was a kid, leaning back on a chair, balancing on the rear legs, suspended in mid-air, the merest breath leading to a collapse backwards or an unbalancing topple forwards – this felt the same. All my senses were alert when my finger was on the trigger of the 92; I was in a zone where nothing else mattered, the feel of the trigger's pressure on my finger had taken me into another place. This was the moment where life or death was in my hands, literally.

Just like the kid leaning in mid-air on the back legs of a chair, I knew at exactly what point I would tip the balance, exactly how much pressure I needed to unleash the bullet with its abrupt, loud, deadly and thunderous force.

I looked down the barrel of the gun and saw men on their knees begging for their lives, and others fleeing, running from the hard chase of my pounding feet behind them, and another trying to scramble up his bedroom wall, some – not many – smiling as if taunting me or maybe daring me; men before me, all of them plunged into a dead end, an abyss of black, brought to them by the 92.

I don't know how long I was in that zone, but when I looked up Casey had stopped talking and, behind him, in the open doorway, stood Maria, dressed for work.

'Be careful,' she said to me, leaned towards her lover and kissed him. Then she left.

'What'd you fuckin' say to those coppers at your place, man? Maria wasn't even at work and she heard all about it; laughing her head off, said it was the biggest fuckin' rumble since Arch Raynor let off a grenade in the mayor's office.'

People up here make their point with an unequivocal ferocity. Arch lives down the river from me. He owns one of the slipways and the council try to take it off him every now and then; he gets fed up with bureaucracy sometimes and cuts to the chase to re-focus them.

'Even Fat Adam's scared of you. Maria said they think you've killed thirty-two crims and eleven crooked cops. Fuck man, even I'm scared of you.'

I flipped open the gun and loaded in the bullets.

'Whoa; hey, what? You need it *now*?' asked Casey.

'Yeah.'

'But–'

'Do you want me to bring it back?' I asked. 'Given its four-thousand-nine-hundred-and-ninety-nine status.'

He thought for a moment.

'Will there be a body?'

'No. Complete erasure.' Like the man I'm hunting, I insist on absolute evaporation. No bodies, no bullets, no trace, no forensics of any kind.

He stared at me, the kind of stare you give when taking in the measure of a person.

'You know, Darian, it's not just him. I mean, he's real bad but the others to come; what about them?'

'It's just him,' I said.

'I don't think so.'

'It's just him,' I said.

'No, it's not. It's you. You've returned to the gun. Like it or not, brother, it's yours to keep.'

11

Cereal

I FIRST HEARD THE TERM 'SERIAL KILLER' ONE NIGHT DURING an after-hours six-week course called something like 'New thinking in crime'. It was held in an old tech college opposite the sprawling nineteenth-century Melbourne University. Every twenty minutes we'd hear a tram rumble precariously along the wide boulevard outside like the clattering of a thousand guns.

Once a week we were taught a 'focus of interest'. We learned about psychology. We were taught 'victimology'. A guy with a handlebar moustache told us that computers would become essential. He said the 'mobile' phone would become our most valuable asset. One night I and an equally ambitious woman named Rhonda Blank were the only ones who turned up for a lecture on 'criminalistics'. I wrote notes. I was the only one who took notes. Most of the time I didn't know what I was writing but imagined that my scribbles would, one day, mean something.

On the very first night I wanted to sit next to Rhonda Blank. It was two to a desk. Deep eyes and dark hair and a smoky beauty; everything about her said: I dare you. As I walked into the dusty room with the frail lighting and shonky heating and desks made for ten-year-olds I saw her and felt I'd been thrust to the precipice of love. A guy from Traffic took the empty seat next to her; took it every week and spent the entire time ignoring her.

Traffic. Dumber than the Livestock branch.

I guessed Rhonda was there for the same reason I was: wanting to understand everything beyond the safe world of the 1950s and

60s where most cops still lived; a new place, a place uncertain, dark, dangerous, of unknown evil. Maybe we both sensed we'd be caught in its deep web, battling for a sense of identity as the crimes became more unspeakable and seemingly inhuman. Be prepared; that's what I'd been thinking.

I fantasised about Rhonda, and looked forward to the warm Wednesday nights in the tech college in room 118 on the second floor, when her presence suggested the possibilities of flesh, of sensuality. We never spoke. Only once did we share a look, and that was on the night a cop from Scotland Yard talked to us about a dark abyss in a person's soul that defies compassion and empathy.

Empathy. I wrote it down, not really knowing what it meant. Or what, more accurately, its absence meant. I was to find out.

Most nights I sat next to a cop named Daryl Baldock. Daryl was everything I hate in men. He was tall, blond, handsome, had strong muscles and spoke with charm and grace. He was enormously popular. On the weekends he surfed or hiked or climbed mountains. He had friends and an invisible gravitational force that would drag beautiful girls to him. He was nice and friendly and always asked what I did on the weekend. He had an uncanny knack of being sympathetic and, worse, I think he was genuine. He was also spectacularly stupid. In all his years on the force, despite being such a great guy and winning lots of surf championships he never rose beyond the rank of Constable.

The bloke from Scotland Yard spoke with a machine-gun accent that none of us could follow about the lack of empathy being a key contributing factor with what they termed the 'serial killer'.

It's a common phrase now, but back then none of us had heard it. I was trying to get a sense of it, rolling it across my mind, jabbing at it like an agitated boxer, when Daryl asked: 'Is that like a murderer who only kills at breakfast?'

The brilliant dumbness of this question, despite none of us being able to provide a suitable answer, was astonishingly radiant.

'No, ya dumb fuck!' the Yardsman spat, in the glory days before you'd be sent to anger-management classes for using that sort of language. 'Get a fucking dictionary and don't open ya mouth again.'

Daryl shut up and we all laughed and the Yardsman went on with his lecture. We'd all had our experiences with repeat offenders, guys who couldn't stop getting into trouble. Jails were full of them. It was their third home, the second being our police station where they got to know the cops, the first being the dive that might be a boarding house or a caravan in which they etched out their sordid, pointless lives.

But this was different. This was the description of a killer who thrives, as we thrive on air, on the fantasy of what they are going to do with a tied-up naked teenage girl or boy, then on the scheme of how they are going to capture that girl or boy, then finally on the enactment of their fantasy in all its appalling reality. In the mind of the serial killer the finale to this grotesque three-act play is the disposal of the body. And as much as we need air to continue living, the serial killer needs to do it all over again. Another boy or girl. And again. And again.

The room went quiet. The Yardsman took out a smoke – a Kent – and lit up, surveying us, like it was a game to see if he'd horrified us yet. I heard the scrape of a chair from behind me and the clumsy exit of one of my colleagues. I didn't turn to see who it was. No-one did.

I raised my hand.

'Yeah?' he barked.

'Do they ever stop?' I asked.

'Killing?'

'Yeah.'

'The marriage between psychology and traditional police work has really only just begun, laddie,' he said, 'so we cannot give you an answer that'd be scientific-like or definitive, you know what I mean?'

I nodded.

He looked at us for a moment, this lanky Glaswegian with a twitchy, hard-to-understand accent, two-quid haircut and etched face; a bloke whom, up to now, I'd dismissed as a twit. I saw in his eyes what I would come to recognise in mine, every morning, in a fleeting glance in the bathroom mirror: the pressing weight of futility like a tomb pushing against the slender barrier to your soul.

'But no,' he said. 'They cannot. As much as you–' he pointed at me, 'and you–' he pointed at someone behind me, 'all of you, as much as you all need water and air and food and shelter, maybe sex or maybe laughter or alcohol to survive, to keep you alive–'

He took a deep breath.

'–they need to kill. The abduction and enslavement, the degradation and mutilation, the torture of their victims, the pleas of help, their agony, these are as necessary to the serial killer as breathing, eating and sleeping are to you. They cannot stop.'

Another silence filled the room, as the incoherent sounds of a city echoed outside the windows, faraway; distant voices, shouts, maybe laughter.

What I love about really stupid people is their staggering lack of perception. Utterly oblivious, Daryl broke the silence and asked another question.

'Is this–' he searched, rifling through some place in his brain that could match his thoughts, 'is this serial-killer thing, you know–' again, searching, '–is this, like, new? I mean, have these people always been around, or are they, like, new, a modern thing?'

I heard a couple of people say, 'Yeah,' as if affirming the question with their own thoughts. I turned around to see who they were. That was when I caught Rhonda's look. Like me, she knew the answer, and a bond formed.

'Lad,' he said to Daryl, 'I'm sixty-five years old and have worn a policeman's uniform since I was seventeen. Let me tell you something and don't you ever forget it.'

He walked up to Daryl at his desk, stood right over him and looked into his eyes. 'There are "us" and there are "them",' he said to Daryl, who stared into the older man's eyes as if he understood.

The Yardsman may as well have told him he had lemon chicken for lunch. He stepped back and looked at us all, scoping us, an old traveller in a horrible world. The look, the click, the recognition, the connection, calmly looking at each of his young students for their brief tutorial on this clammy Melbourne night. Feet shuffled, people moved in their seats. Silence is awkward. I guess most of us felt the old guy was eccentric and maybe he'd forgotten what to say next. He looked at me and I held the gaze. He looked away and in Rhonda's direction. I knew she held his gaze too.

After an awkward pause he smiled, stepped back and laughed.

'Look at the time. Thank you for coming.'

Everyone packed up quickly. We'd all arranged to meet at a pub across the road afterwards. The publican gave free beers to cops.

I moved slowly, putting my lined notepad into my pocket, screwing the cap of my pen on tightly. I heard the others leave, a rushed scuffle of uninterested bodies pushing down the corridor and the staircase onto the street below.

Left in the room were Rhonda and me, two young cops, and the Yardsman, an old cop from a faraway city who understood that this world of ours had an undertow of depravity we were about to embrace, like he had. I'm not religious and this wasn't a religious moment, just an awareness we shared: a common bond.

'What's your name?' he asked me.

'Constable Darian Richards.'

He looked to Rhonda.

'Constable Rhonda Blank.'

'Fergus McDowell. Chief Inspector.' He didn't offer his hand to shake. 'You understand what I meant, back then, about them and us?'

'Yeah, I do,' I said and went on: 'But – I'm new at this. Is it really that black and white? Because, surely, Chief Inspector, "them" – they – surely they can't be totally bad? Evil, I mean.'

I thought he hadn't heard the question. He stared at us without speaking for what seemed like ages. Maybe he was recalling the past or maybe he was sizing us up, wondering if we were worthy of his stories. He leant forward, his gaze penetrating.

'I sat as far as I'm sitting from you, and you, girlie, from a man who'd abducted an eight-year-old girl. Her name was Gladys. He stripped her naked, he tied her to the concrete floor of his basement, he raped her every three hours for two days, doping himself to stay awake. He cut this little girl, long slices down each leg then along her arms; he masturbated as she cried in agony – that made him climax, he told me with pride. He told her he was going to kill her in the most painful way possible, he told her he'd then go on to kill her little sister in the same way. He cut off her ears and her toes and after he'd exhausted his imagination and her body, sliced open her throat, cut off her head and slowly began to clean up after himself. He told me this in detail, like it was a holiday or a great meal at a gourmet restaurant, savouring the memories, and afterwards there was, in his eyes and his mind, only one regret: that he'd be unable to do it again. He was married and every Saturday he took his eight-year-old son to a river where they'd fish for trout. At night he'd sit on the edge of that boy's bed and read him a Roald Dahl story. He dreamed his son would study law at university in London. His wife slept by his side every night, waking up to him every morning. Gladys wasn't the only one. Just the one we caught him on. There were lots of others. All little girls. All vanished from the streets, long forgotten. All taken by this person who'd come home every night to read to his son and climb into bed with his wife. Does evil exist, Darian? Yes it does. But will you, and you–' turning to Rhonda, 'will you understand it? I still don't. But what I do understand is the effect "they" have on "us". You be careful of that, you two. Their darkness is insidious. The nightmares will be the first signal. Not the normal nightmares you have as a cop, we all get those; no, the nightmares where you are no longer you but one of them.'

He snapped into another place. 'Enough. I'm gonna get pissed. G'night to you both,' he said, and left.

'What about you, Rhonda? Feel like a drink? I know I do,' I said.

I turned to face her. She'd already left.

I was on my own.

12

Vampire Slayer

I turned off the Tewantin road and drove down Moorindal Street for about two kilometres until the road stopped at a gathering of trees and grass and sand; the river's edge. I pulled up behind a line of about twenty four-wheel drives, all patiently waiting for the car ferry to return to our side of the river and carry us over to the North Shore.

Accessible only by water, the North Shore is shaped like a long flat island, the ocean on one side, the Noosa River and three massive shallow lakes on the other. About one hundred kilometres long and three kilometres across, it isn't an island – at its very northern tip it joins up with the mainland, just below the southern end of Fraser Island – but it may as well be. Up there, after the river has shrunk into a meandering narrow creek, snaking its way through mangroves and everglades and flat deserts of sandy shrublands, the North Shore finally connects with the rest of civilisation at a town called Tin Can Bay.

The North Shore is home to the world's only beach highway. Road rules, as much as there are road rules, do apply; you stick to the left. That's about it. As the highway is one or two hundred metres wide – instead of its boundary being a wall or a fence, it's an ocean that swells – you can pretty much swerve all over the place, just stay left of the oncoming, and drive as maniacally as you wish. No traffic lights, no stop signs, no intersections, no cops. It's great if you're into driving off-road up and down sandy hills and getting bogged. In fact the getting-bogged bit is the best, I'm told; everybody stops and helps drag you out of the sand. The worse the bog the bigger the party. Sometimes people bring out canvas awnings and chairs and light up barbeques and crack open tinnies.

Just down from where the asphalt road runs into dirt, a luxury five-star resort began construction a few years ago. The resort has over a hundred apartments, set back a little from the beach, surrounded by forests of black wattle and wild grass. There are street signs and street lights, roundabouts too. Palm trees have been carefully planted along narrow avenues and manicured swathes of lawn. It's a community of wealthy people. They don't deliberately bog their cars in the sand here, they don't scrunch their tinnies and chuck them into the sea; they drink wine and eat shaved ham and d'Affinois in this part of the North Shore – or, they would if they could. After that big financial crime – when a bunch of perps in New York cooked up a scam to drain people of their money, their jobs, their homes, their lives – spread over here, the consortium building the resort sank under the weight of derivative-driven debt they probably didn't even know they had. The place just stopped being built. Some of the local builders ripped out fittings from kitchens as a desperate means to be paid, knowing they weren't ever going to see money in the bank.

But, sections of the resort had been completed; apartments were for sale, which was why a high-smiling woman in her late thirties was waiting for me outside the gate to the Noosa North Shore Dreaming Resort. She was rake-thin with platinum hair and red lips. She wore a black suit.

'Hi!' she exclaimed with a smile that looked so wide and forced it had to be real. 'I'm Paula and you must be *Darian*. That is *the* most fantastic name I think I've ever heard!' she exclaimed. I'm not a big fan of real estate agents but I liked her as soon as I'd glanced at her car – a black Mercedes – and saw the back seat appallingly full of clutter, ranging from clothes and old newspapers to empty Coke cans and chocolate-bar wrappers.

'Agh!' she exclaimed when she saw me looking at her portable rubbish bin. 'Don't look at that; I'm as messy as a drunk tit on a Tuesday night! You'll hate me and never listen to a word I say, let alone spend half a million dollars on the best apartment this place has to offer.'

'Come on Paula,' I said, smiling, 'come and show me the place of my dreams.'

'You betcha!' she exclaimed. 'Jump in the Merc,' she said as she walked around to the driver's side of her car. 'We'll go and meet up with Eddie. He's going to help show you around.'

'Who's Eddie?'

'He's like the caretaker. He lives on-site. Sweet guy. You'll love him,' she said breezily, then paused and took a sidelong glance at me. 'What line of business are you in, Darian?'

'I'm retired. Used to run a security firm.'

'You know, as soon as I saw you get out of that car, I thought you were in that line of business. You reminded me of my first husband; he was a homicide cop in Perth.'

As we drove down Sea Breeze Avenue and approached the resort – a cluster of mud-brown buildings in that fake Tuscan look – I asked Paula how many of the apartments were occupied.

'Darian, I don't actually know,' she replied. 'Eddie will. There's always somebody here. Even though it's not totally finished, two of the four wings are completely liveable. I think they're great. Only place on the North Shore that's like it.'

We turned onto a roundabout and stopped out the front of a building named Ocean Breeze. No taller than the tallest palm tree, it was three storeys high. There were eight apartments on each level, and each had a balcony. It looked like a nice place to retire if you loved golf, except there are no golf courses on the North Shore. There's nothing on the North Shore except a highway beach for bog parties. It didn't look like those sorts of fun-lovers would be living here in Ocean Breeze. It didn't look like anyone was living here in Ocean Breeze. It had the atmosphere of a cemetery.

'He's meant to be here,' said Paula, reaching into her handbag. 'Sorry about this,' she said as she pulled out her phone and hit the speed dial.

After a moment: 'Eddie? It's Paula. We're out the front.' And then: 'Good.' And then to me: 'He's on his way.'

I nodded, looking around. 'It's pretty quiet. I guess there aren't too many occupants at the moment.'

'It *is* quiet, Darian.' Real estate agents will never disagree with you, no matter what. Same with car dealers. Experts at accentuating the positive. 'But,' she added, 'it's different during the school holidays.'

'Ah,' I nodded wisely, 'school holidays.' If I were a kid I'd take one look at this joint and hightail it out of here faster than Batman.

'Here he is!' exclaimed Paula.

Eddie lumbered around the side of Ocean Breeze towards us. I try to distinguish my impressions of people, especially on a case when many of the people you meet could in fact be the killer you're searching for. It's important not to be distracted by extraneous issues like ugliness or slothfulness or sheer creepiness.

Eddie had all the above. He was stout, flabby; the sort of guy who's always smiling as if he knows the secrets of the universe. As he got closer I noticed his lips were fleshy. As he got even closer I saw that his lips were glistening, wet. He was like a toad. Wearing an idiotic uniform of khaki shorts and safari jacket made especially for the resort, Eddie was about twenty-eight years old but could easily pass for seventy-eight given his glacial pace and grotesque ugliness.

'Hi Eddie!' exclaimed Paula. 'This is Darian.'

Eddie held out his fat hand and I shook it. He licked his lips, fat pink tongue rolling across the top and then the bottom lip. I tried not to flinch.

'Hello Darian. That is a very interesting name,' he said in a rodent voice.

I nodded and quickly withdrew my hand.

'Darian is interested in looking at some of the apartments that are for sale. I thought we'd show him the three in this building here and then those over in Sunset Breeze.'

'No dramas,' said Eddie and pulled out a key that hung on a chain around his neck from beneath his shirt and waved it. 'Gets us in anywhere.' He smiled at Paula and licked his lips again. I fought off an urge to go back to my car, grab the shoe box from its hiding place, take out the gun and shoot this monster for the crime of being ugly and creepy.

'Lead the way, Eddie,' I said. 'We're in your hands.'

He slothed forward, Paula and I following. 'Darian was asking how many of the apartments are actually occupied,' she said.

'I like to have people around me,' I added.

'You mean occupied as in sold or occupied as in people here now?'

Good, Eddie: excellent clarification.

'People here now.'

'Gee,' he said.

We'd walked up the steps and through the main doors to Ocean Breeze and were now crossing through the foyer. It was large and ornate with brown marble floors, Tuscan-brown walls, all-purpose forgettable prints of frangipanis and girls in bikinis and palm trees in large pots. As we stopped by the lift, Eddie repeated: 'Gee.'

'Well, there's the Goldmans and, are the Robinsons still here?' Paula added by way of a prod.

'Gone.' The lift doors opened and we stepped inside, Paula first, then me then Toad Eddie.

'Their three months was up.'

'Their what?' I asked.

'Oh!' exclaimed Paula: 'Silly me. I just assumed you knew.'

'Can't live here longer than three months,' said Eddie, who had taken over half the space in the lift as we rode to the third floor.

'I'm sorry,' she said and touched me on the arm with a reassuring grip. 'One of the provisions made by the council was that occupancy is limited to three months a year.'

The Sunshine Coast: it gets weirder by the day.

'You can't live in a place that you own for longer than three months a year: is that what you just said?'

'I know!' she said with arms outstretched as if to show me she agreed it was crazy. Finally we'd reached the third floor. 'The council is–'

'They're Greenies,' Eddie said, completing her sentence. 'Fuckwits.'

Paula shot him an admonishing look, short, sharp, professional.

''Scuse the language.'

Paula jumped in: 'The council never let anyone build over here, not for decades. There were forty or so housing approvals dating back to the 1920s and that was it. They want the North Shore to be world-heritage listed ... and it *is* beautiful over here,' she added in real-estate mode, 'so when the developers finally got this resort approved it was with this three-month condition.'

'Why?' I asked.

'They're concerned about population levels. It's actually really good–' here came the real-estate speak again, '–because it means the Noosa area doesn't become overrun and crowded like it is down on the Gold Coast. You know: Noosa is special. There's nothing like it in the entire country, and this resort – being over here on this amazing island – is special too.'

'But what if you want to live here?' I asked. 'As in *live* here.'

She reached out and held my arm and whispered: 'No-one would ever know.'

'That's right,' added Eddie. 'I've been living here for two years now.'

'And the people who are living here now; what about them?'

'Well,' said Eddie. 'There's the Goldmans, and Naomi who used to be an investment banker in Sydney, and Ian who was a lawyer in Sydney and his wife Wendy, and then there's John and Anna – he was an accountant then went into garden supplies just before the drought – and ... oh yeah, Ron. And me. I'm over there,' he nodded towards another identical three-storey Tuscan brown building called Sunset Breeze. 'That's it. Gets pretty busy during school holidays, though.'

Goldman, Ian the ex-lawyer, John the accountant-turned-garden-supplier and Ron, whoever Ron was.

And Eddie.

And anyone who had regular access to an empty apartment.

Eddie was unlocking a door to one of Paula's properties. She'd been chatting about the advantages of living on a remote island where there are no shops or pubs or clubs or ... anything, really, just a nearby beach that was like something out of *Mad Max*.

The apartment was unremarkable. The view from the balcony was of trees. I knew the ocean was close. I could hear the surf. I turned to my guides.

'It's great,' I said.

'You like it?' She looked surprised.

'Yep. Just the sort of thing I'm looking for.' A view of trees.

'One thing,' I said, as if I had just had a flash. She leaned forward and Eddie turned towards me.

'Internet. I'm on the computer most of the day; I need to be wired to check my stocks, keep tabs on the portfolio.' I looked at Eddie. 'Have you got wireless here?'

'Yep. Free wireless throughout the resort.'

'I've just bought this new computer–'

'What sort?' he asked.

'Apple. That's the thing: I don't know jack shit about it or how to connect to wireless; I can hardly turn it on, I'm so useless. Is there like a person around here who's good with that sort of stuff? A brilliant in-house geek?'

'Sure is,' said Eddie. 'You're looking at him.'

—

TED BUNDY, WHO killed a string of young women, was a handsome guy. Harold Shipman, who killed over two hundred of his elderly patients, looked like a mild and sweet family doctor. Dennis Rader – of BTK (Bind, Torture, Kill) renown – looked like a bus driver. Rapist, torturer and murderer John Wayne Gacy looked cute and funny. Before he carved a swastika into his forehead Charles Manson looked a little weird but could easily pass as an intense guy with a story to tell. Only Ivan Milat looked like the personification of evil that he – and each of his colleagues – was.

Eddie looked creepy and smug, and licked his lips. He had an air of self-importance about him. But he didn't look right. He didn't feel right.

I've been wrong before, and the first rule of investigation: eliminate.

I SAT, WAITING. From where I was hidden within the scrub, I had a perfect view into Eddie's apartment. I was about twenty metres away, framed by stunted tea-trees and tall grass.

I'd said goodbye to Paula, taken her business card, promised to touch base once I'd made up my mind and watched her drive away, down the asphalt towards the river ferry. I drove my Toyota in the opposite direction, as if heading towards the beach highway, passing the entrance to the resort.

Just before the dirt road gives way to sand, a little distance from the entrance to the beach where the 'road' passes between two large dunes, is a car park. People leave their vehicles there to sleep off the grog before they drive home; or else they rest there before embarking on the highway race; or they stop and set up camp if the tide might be coming in and night is approaching, when the highway becomes deeply hazardous. People have been caught as their cars were swept into the ocean.

My white Toyota looked right at home. It was as anonymous as it could ever be. Nobody noticed me slipping away into the bush, or if they did they wouldn't have cared, just assuming I was off to have a pee.

Easy for me to be anonymous, easy too, for the killer.

I only got lost for an hour and finally pushed through a wedge of trees to see the Tuscan-brown buildings in the distance, the orange glow of sunset reflecting in dazzling bursts from each of the windows.

I edged along the building, trying to make out which apartments were occupied. Eddie made it easy: he walked onto his balcony and started doing calisthenics; a revolting sight.

Normally at this juncture of an investigation, I'd be working through the arguments to put to a magistrate for a search warrant. I'd have the crew trolling through the suspect's life: applying to Telstra for the release of his incoming and outgoing phone records – a frustrating process that can take days – interviewing friends and colleagues, checking out priors, building up a profile before the hammer strikes. The silent investigation that can last for weeks before you finally arrive at a residence and he hears a knock on his front door.

I felt my mobile phone buzzing; a text message.

nada

No priors. Eddie was clean.

Homicide cops go insane while waiting for a magistrate to decide whether they can search a suspect's house. They scream at the phone, yank it from the wall and hurl it across the office while the bureaucrat at the other end of the line calmly explains it'll take five working days to get the incoming and outgoing phone records of their suspect, regardless of whether the suspect might have a child or a woman or anyone locked inside his house, that a person's life might be at stake–

I'm sorry, I really am, but I'm bound to adhere to the Privacy law. My hands are tied. And I do understand your frustration, Inspector, I really do.

I lay in wait outside my suspect's residence, gun tucked neatly into my belt. I was dressed in my usual clothes: black jeans, black T-shirt, black Converse. The darkness of the night embraced me. I felt an exhilaration knowing it was just Eddie and me, and that whatever I was going to do, nobody would ask me to answer to it.

13

Cling Wrap

Eddie's apartment was on the second floor. I was on his balcony within thirty seconds of leaving my hiding spot. It was just past midnight. I'd been waiting seven hours. It wasn't entirely boring; Isosceles had sent me sixty-five text messages, all of them quotes from his collection.

He was trying to alleviate my boredom. And he did.

Alas! It was but too true –

their desperate valour knew no bounds and far indeed was it removed from its so-called better part –

discretion.

William Howard Russell on the idiotic Charge of the Light Brigade during the Crimean War.

If any question why we died,
Tell them, because our fathers lied.

Rudyard Kipling, in consideration of the above, during World War I.

Eddie had spent the evening on his computer; the blue wash of its screen was the only light in his apartment until half an hour ago when he ambled off to bed, leaving it on. The computer went to sleep, plunging the apartment into darkness a few moments later and I figured: like computer, like man.

Up here people don't bother to lock their homes. I might've mentioned that. I do; I've got this thing about leaving all my possessions open for a stranger to walk in off the street and take.

Eddie had not only left the place unlocked, he left the balcony doors wide open. I stepped inside. I didn't take off my shoes.

I could hear the sound of sleep from the next room; deep and sustained breathing, a clean noise, uninterrupted by an anxious movement or the giveaway sounds made when somebody tries to be still and silent. I let the dark take me over, standing still, waiting for my eyes to adjust. After two minutes the room was clear and I could see everything. I stood there, carefully examining it as a whole.

Was this the space of a man who tracks, abducts and then kills teenage girls?

It was a one-bedroom apartment. It had a large living and kitchen area – which was where I stood – and a bathroom and bedroom. Eddie obviously wasn't big on entertaining. There was a two-seater couch and a table with a chair. That was it. No TV. No coffee table. Everything was on the dining table, which wasn't being used for dining: it had two flat screens connected to a large hard drive that sat beneath the table and quietly hummed with a couple of tiny lights that indicated it was still on. There was a large keyboard in front of the screens. I recognised the hand-held devices that gamers use. Then I recognised an Xbox.

The wall was covered with posters of *Star Wars* and *Buffy the Vampire Slayer* and photos of the actress who played Buffy, Sarah Michelle Gellar. I know all about her because of my friend on the top floor of the glass tower down in Melbourne. He once forced me to watch an episode of *Buffy* called 'The Body' under threat of industrial action.

Aside from the lip business, Eddie was, so far, as unusual as eighty-five per cent of men under the age of twenty-five.

I hit the keyboard to wake up the computer. It asked for a password. I typed in 'eddie'. Wrong. I typed in 'buffy'. Wrong again. I looked up at the poster of Buffy, with her stern look and tough stance carrying her vampire-killing stake. I typed in 'angel' and the screen opened up for me.

Buffy loves Angel, and even though she had sex with Spike, quite a lot, she'd dump him at any time for Angel. He's the dude. Eddie's alter ego; the guy Buffy wants. I went to his bookmarks to see what my potential suspect was up to in the abyss of cyberspace.

Eddie liked order: he had helpfully created a file called 'porn'. I clicked on it – and eliminated him immediately.

Eddie liked porn – what man doesn't – but not the porn of the guy I was looking for. Eddie was a purveyor of large-breasted women. In particular a 1980s porn star called Crystal Canyon who no doubt chose the stage name after her body shape. Back in those days women in porn had pubic hair. No shaving then. I'm sure Isosceles had the encyclopaedic knowledge on when and why pubic hair went out of fashion but all I knew or cared about was that my killer didn't like to look at it.

'Robyn, is that you?'

And there was I thinking I'd been so quiet on the keyboard.

'Robyn?'

Robyn? There was a girl in King Toad's life? I had about five seconds and four choices: run, leap off the balcony and vanish into the night; introduce myself and my real purpose; pretend I was Robyn with a sore throat; or–

I grabbed Eddie from behind in a jaw-lock, one arm held tight against his throat, the other at the back of his neck, as he stepped out of his bedroom. Thank God he wore pyjamas.

'The master key. Where?' I said in a deep, unrecognisable whisper.

Between gurgling and trying to point with his hand, he managed to show me it was on the kitchen bench, next to a flashlight.

I dug in with both arms and sent him back to sleep. His body sank in my arms and I lowered him to the floor. I took the roll of duct tape that hung from my belt and bound his ankles, his wrists and his mouth, keeping his nostrils free.

I dragged him back into the bedroom, locked the window and closed the door.

I had the keys to the kingdom; time now to find the apartment I was looking for.

—

If you are interested in purchasing an apartment at the North Shore Dreaming Resort my basic advice is: don't. If, however, you are determined to spend half a million dollars for the privilege of being allowed to spend three months a year in an apartment looking at either dirty scrub or ugly trees, then I would recommend 24a in Sunset Breeze and 20 or 22 or, at a pinch, 26 in Ocean Breeze. That's it.

I'd trespassed into the Goldmans' apartment where they have a very fetching collection of stuffed birds, then into Ian and Wendy's who have a magnificent collection of books, then into John and Anna's who sleep in separate beds like out of a scene from a 1950s sitcom and had boxes of cereal already laid out for morning, then into Ron's whose walls were adorned with maps and photos and masks and paintings from Africa. I closed the door on each of the sleeping inhabitants and moved across the courtyard to the last building.

None of the apartments in Sunrise Breeze had been finished. As soon as I walked into the first one I knew this was where the builders and contractors, realising they weren't going to be recompensed, ripped out anything of value in lieu of payment never coming. Because of the vandalism, each of the apartments had its own individuality. No calm Tuscan walls, no framed prints of frangipani flowers or girls in bikinis, just dust and debris, the detritus of righteous anger; even though these men were stealing they thought they had every right to.

On the second floor at 3.16 a.m. I opened the door to apartment 28 and stepped into the empty lair of the man I was looking for.

The dust and the clutter of broken plaster and chipboard edges and the short ends of wooden planks had been neatly swept into a corner next to the kitchen benchtop that in architect parlance is called an island. There was nothing in the main room. It was completely empty of furniture. No chair – on which the six girls sat. No table – on which he placed his equipment: the computer that took in the image of the girl in the chair from his camera; her mobile phone without back flap and battery; and the hardware into which he inserted her SIM card, then opened for the download of her last image alive.

I ran my fingers along the tiled floor to see how much dust had gathered since he'd last swept it. Not much; but of course Brianna had only been here days ago, when she was abducted.

Or had she?

I still hadn't asked Maria for any more information about the mobile phones: where exactly were they left and how long after the abductions were they found? And – had Brianna's been found?

A sudden urge swept through me. Had I made it here before his appointed hour? I took out my phone as I quickly scanned the bedroom – empty – and the bathroom – empty – and dialled.

'Yeah?'

Casey answered on the second ring; it was 3.30 a.m.

'I need to ask Maria something.'

After a moment I heard her mumble, 'Who is it?' and without any response to her question, I heard: 'Hello?'

'Brianna's phone: has he left it yet?'

There was a pause. This was collusion. This was much more than a whisper in the night. I waited. I didn't need to say anything. She knew I wouldn't be asking unless it was urgent. It was up to her.

After what felt like a voyage to Madagascar and back: 'Yes. We got it this afternoon.'

'Fuck!' I shouted, throwing my arm full stretch so she wouldn't be deafened.

'Sorry,' I said, calm now. 'Can you tell me where?'

'Noosa Civic, where she was last seen. They're always in brown envelopes addressed to the parents. No prints. Where are you, Darian?'

Now it was my turn to pause.

She waited, without saying anything.

'I'm at home,' I said.

'No, you're not. You're lying to me.' And she hung up.

I re-dialled. She didn't speak, just waited.

'Old habits. I'm in the room – I think I'm in the room – where he takes the photos of the girls.'

There was a sharp, sudden intake of breath.

'How? Where? Where are you? How did you do that?' While she was asking questions I was completing a thorough search of the apartment to ensure that, before I left, I hadn't missed anything. There wasn't much to search. I was in the shell of the kitchen, checking the cupboards and drawers.

'Are you sure it's his?'

'Yep.'

'How?'

'Doppelganger emittances.'

'*What*? Where *are* you, Darian, *where*?' I could see her either sitting up in bed or out of bed, pacing; whatever, she was fast becoming the cop with the customary impatience of not being answered immediately. Calling her back was necessary, I needed her to continue, but it carried a bunch of problems and they were gathering apace, now, right now, as I pulled open a drawer in the kitchen and found that my man was not as thorough as he imagined.

Evidence.

I spoke slowly: 'It might be better you don't know any more.'

Like telling a kid to choose water over Coke.

'Tell me everything.'

'Come to the house, I'll be there in ninety minutes.'

I hung up, put the phone in my back pocket and stared down at an oblong-shaped cardboard container – 'quality assured, microwave safe, caution: sharp cutting edge underneath; Black & Gold, value you can trust' – of cling wrap. One hundred and eighty metres of plastic cling wrap – a lot. The box was open, some of the wrap was spilling out.

It could have been left by one of the contractors before they abandoned the building site, but I didn't think so. More likely I was looking down at one of the tools of his craft.

I took off my T-shirt, placed my right hand inside it and gently lifted out the box by one of its ends, careful not to place too much pressure on it, lest I smudge any possible print.

A hint of silver, the beginning of day, was pushing into the night. It was past four. I thought about Eddie, tied and bound on the floor of his bedroom; freaking out at the mysterious, sudden and random attack. I knew I should go back and release him. After all he was innocent.

I didn't. I was in a hurry. I had the strong likelihood of evidence and I needed to follow its trail; fingerprints to start. Isosceles was already on standby. He had the software to do the latent check. Apparently I had software on my computer that would enable him to do it. Black & Gold was a cheap brand sold through one supermarket chain, either Coles or IGA or Woolworths, I thought, and that too needed following up.

I left the master key in the foyer of Ocean Breeze, imagining it would lead to questions about why it was there and hoping those questions would take whoever asked them up to Eddie's apartment and that the lack of response to banging on the door would lead to it being knocked down and that Eddie would be found ...

Fuck it: I'd come back tonight, in about sixteen hours' time, and release him.

I leaped off the balcony into the scrub and ran quickly, careful not to taint the possible evidence. Within moments I'd almost fallen into a creek, one of the estuaries that snake from the river. It looked deep. It was about two metres to the other side, its black trail of still water stretching off into the bush. I changed direction. I soon found an open trail that didn't look familiar. As usual I was lost.

I took a deep breath, and concentrated. The rumble of the surf was to my left: east. I headed in that direction.

—

IF I HAD been running an investigation and a civilian had done what I just did, I would have engaged in the following. I would have charged them with obstructing an investigation; trespass; hindering police officers in the course of their business; larceny; aiding and abetting; accessory to murder; manslaughter; affray causing damage to property; urinating in public – and that's just off the top of my head without even seeking some help from the rest of the crew.

And that's if the civilian had immediately divulged their activities. If they chose to withhold the information I would do all the above, and then I would hurt them.

I'd briefed Isosceles. He was checking to see if there was anything leading from apartment 28 to anyone – there wouldn't be – and what vehicles he could see with his satellite imaging over the last seventy-two hours – there might be something, but it would most likely be a nondescript white van, the favoured vehicle of serial killers – and putting together a list of all builders and building contractors in the area, cross-referencing them with sexual offenders and, in fact, all offenders.

I needed to know who came and went out of the resort; on that basis I'd made a bad mistake by leaving Eddie hogtied in his bedroom.

I realised this soon after discovering which way was east. Following the sounds of the ocean and then walking onto the beach highway, I realised I was about a kilometre from where my car was parked. As I trudged up the centre of the highway, I knew I'd committed an error, an error I wouldn't have forgiven if it had been made by one of my crew.

Finding the possibility of the perp's prints excited me so much I went blind, deaf and dumb to the equally important trail of the comings and goings into the empty resort.

What *was* wrong with me? Was it the gun? Again? I knew I'd rumbled into action because the nightmares had returned and I knew they wouldn't go away until I'd ground the killer into dust, but was Casey right? Was I now the gun, in a detective's clothing?

I decided not to think about it; there'd be other times for introspection. All that mattered were the six girls and making sure there wouldn't be a seventh.

14

Helen 36D (i)

'Hi!'
  'Winston? Hi. What are you–'
  Last words, Helen. Last words.

—

WELCOME BACK, MY brothers and sisters. God is great: he makes it easy to abduct a person. Guess he didn't mean to, but he surely did. It is so fucking easy. Listen up, my friends. Listen and learn from the greatest. Over the course of our lessons you'll learn many secrets of the craft as it has been perfected by me, the Awesome One. There have been many kills and many lessons learnt. It is with great pleasure that I am here with you now, brothers and sisters.

  'But Winston,' I hear you asking, *'how many kills? Tell us now.'*

  Patience, my brothers and sisters. Let it be said though, my friends, the answer is: a lot.

  Snatching the target: like everything, the key to success is in the preparation. You must have not only zoomed in on your target but you must follow her and watch her closely. You have to know her movements. A perfect snatch is done through speed and the minimum of noise. But you have to be prepared. For instance, Helen arrives at work at least an hour before the others in the medical complex because she likes to get a coffee from the dirty Greeks across the road. She parks in the underground car park that is empty for an hour after she arrives. Perfect. See? That's preparation.

Be aware, friends, that sometimes you might need to improvise. Always be alert and ready for the random. What if, for instance, the cleaner who comes in on Fridays was going away and had to come in on the day you intend to snatch?

Also it's very important to do it quickly. I like to use tasers. That really works on the girls. It's fast and very effective. I used to try other methods but none have been as reliable as the taser so I'd suggest you try that out.

The best thing to remember about the snatch is that the girl is unsuspecting and most people are nice. They never think, *oh, here comes a serial killer,* they always think in the positive. Remember that: nice people think everyone else is also nice.

Now, once the immobilisation is complete and the package (that's my name for the girl once she's in the van) is secured, you must must must find her phone. You have to remove the battery immediately. If you don't then the little GPS tracker will track you down. And then you'll be caught. I've warned you.

Stop giggling. Focus.

Where is her fucking phone? In here? The bag ... oops, there it goes, all of woman-breast Helen's stuff onto the floor. Scattered like lollies. No phone. Roll her over, pat her down. No phone. There's got to be a phone. Fuck! I have to take off her clothes. I don't want to do that now – you bitch, you'll pay for this but I have got to find your phone! Do it fast. Nice-tits-nice-tits-nice-tits–

Focus. The phone. Focus!

Roger, roger, roger ... that. Slow. Calm. Okay: not in her bag. Searched it, patted it down, searched it again. Not in her clothes. That means–

She left it in her car. Great. What's the time? Ten past six. She's always here at least an hour before any of the others, but, but what if? What if the random? What if the unexpected? I'm safe now. Woman-breast Helen and me, just us and no-one knows or ever will. I love underground car parks, 'specially the little baby ones, 'specially when there are no cameras, 'specially when they're empty. Remember that Show Day in the car park, watching through the one-way rear window? Ooh: all those baby girls. Almost as good as Sportsgirl and Supré in the shopping centre.

Okay. Take the risk, gotta take the risk. Gotta get the phone. Where did I put her car keys? There – Jesus! Is that a tampon? Is she in the blood? I'll fuckin' kill her if she is.

Slow down. Anyone out there? No. Nobody's coming down the ramp to this car park for at least another fifty minutes, Helen.

Sliding door open, sliding door shut.

Whup! Car open. Pull down the sleeves, carefully my boy, don't let flesh touch metal, my man, and–

Hey presto. What's that I see, Helen? Silly girl. You forgot your iPhone. But that's okay because we have it now. Ooh, you've got a message. It's from loverboy.

Hey loverboy, I'm going to send you a photo of lovergirl, looking *real* pretty, *real* soon. You ain't *never* going to forget it, either, loverboy.

Whup! Car locked.

Sayonara car.

Hey Helen. Got the phone. Gee, the battery's gone. That means you're off the radar, sweetie; that means you can't be found; that means there's no GPS of you. Modern technology; you could be dead.

Check: parcel is secure? Yep, tied nice and tight to the side in the back of the van. Arms stretched out, bound together and secured to the mesh wall? Yep. Her legs? Ditto. You'll be safe, Helen; no rolling across the floor in the back of the van for you.

Roger that.

Check: parcel is unable to speak or – ho-ho-ho – scream, shout, yell.

Duct tape from Bunnings; on special at $3.99.

Roger that and avert eyes forward: any sign of alien activity?

Nothing. Forty-five minutes before anyone drives down the ramp into the little car park; forty-five minutes before they see Helen's blue Mazda parked where it always is; fifty, maybe sixty minutes before that someone – the zeppelin? – bothers to ring the dead iPhone and leave a message: *Helen, are you all right? Just checking.*

Loverboy will get to hear that and all the other messages, including all of his, when he gets it.

The gift.

Focus. Coast is clear, captain! Roger that.

Let's go, Helen, let's go have some fun, just me and you and those big-woman breasts, lots and lots of fun, lots of steps, all the way to the chain.

A pleasant journey we shall have. But be patient, brothers. Stay calm, sisters. Ride with us a while.

—

Jesus H, look at that sun; look at that blue sky. Goddamn, I love it up here. Okay Winston, no faster than 50 k's and concentrate, be a polite driver and wave at the old folk as they drive past you.

—

Helen had stopped screaming into the duct tape. She knew no-one could hear her but that hadn't stopped her from screaming. Exhaustion stopped her. And the knowledge.

She was going to die. Maybe, maybe she could pretend to like him and say things like he was handsome and she wanted him.

But she knew.

It was all futile.

She was going to die and before she did he was going to hurt her.

She closed her eyes and remembered her sixth birthday when her mum and dad took her to Luna Park and she rode the Ferris wheel eleven times.

15

The Deal (i)

I'D CALLED MARIA BACK AND TOLD HER TO MEET ME AT THE house in two hours instead of ninety minutes, then asked her to hand the phone to Casey. 'Please,' I'd added.

She was angry and frustrated. She was a cop answerable not to a rogue but an established investigative team and a job with clearly defined boundaries. I was pushing it; she was pushing it. I guess neither of us knew where this would lead, but what we did know was we were moving forwards in the hunt.

I watched the car ferry as it pulled away from the shore on the other side of the river. It is dragged across the water by pulleys in which two thick cables are wound; stretching tight as the journey commences, tighter when the wind whips at the vessel, as if trying to push it off course into chaos.

It was 6.20 now; dawn had come and gone. It was baking hot, the sun was in full bloom.

Casey's car swept off the ferry as soon as it hit land, not waiting for the fishtailing to stop, which is what most drivers do, nervous of driving forward while the rear end erratically swishes in the wake of the journey.

Maria ground his car to an abrupt stop by mine.

Another error in judgement; of course she was going to commandeer his task. She's a smart woman. Why hadn't I put myself in her shoes? One year off the game and I was worse than rusty; at this rate the killer would die of old age.

'You're not Casey.'

'Just pretend,' she said and indicated the 1964 Lyndon Johnson T-shirt she was wearing with its delightful commentary on rival Barry Goldwater: 'In Your Guts You Know He's Nuts'.

'What's going on? Why did you need Casey over here? Tell me. Everything.' She wasn't looking at me, but into her rear-view mirror.

'There's a dirt track a hundred metres up the road, to the left; meet me about two hundred metres in. It's secluded, no-one will see us.'

I pressed down the accelerator and burned away.

As I turned left, into a barely noticeable and ill-defined track, I saw she had begun to follow.

As I waited for her, stuck in a dusty copse among gums and golden canes, I worked through the angles and they mostly came to one end: this was it, I'd just made myself redundant.

I needed to stay in the game. The very worst thing that could happen was the cops taking over, arresting this guy and watching, after a few years of legal dancing, him walk free because of hot lawyers and the usual reliance on circumstantial evidence. Call it justice, call it revenge, call it murder; I just needed to ensure I was the end-giver.

She pulled up, climbed out and swatted a mosquito from her face. 'Talk,' she said.

I told her everything that had happened since yesterday afternoon, especially about Eddie, because I needed someone to release him and ask him about people coming and going in the resort. This task would have been easier for Casey, a civilian who just happened to drive into the resort, happened to wander into the main foyer, happened to see a key with a note that said something like 'Help the fat toad in apartment 20 on the second floor' – but now Maria was going to have to do it.

I left out a few things, like the name of my cyberspace warrior and exactly how Eddie came to be trussed up in his apartment.

And the cling wrap. I forgot to mention that as well.

As I began my recitation, Maria pulled out a small notepad – the little flip-over ones that cops use – from the back pocket of her jeans. I didn't like the look of that. She took notes as I spoke, just like cops do when they're at the scene of a crime and you're a witness, or maybe a suspect. It wasn't something I was used to.

'That's it?' she asked when I'd finished, flipping her notebook closed.

'Yep,' I answered untruthfully.

'I've got to call this in, Darian. Sorry. It's the end of the road. But what you've done, it's amazing.'

That's me: amazing.

'I'll keep you out of it as much as I can. I promise.'

She was talking about the litany of my crimes: Break and Enter; Assault; Grievous Bodily Harm; Kidnap; there was some sort of Denial of a Person's Liberty crime, which I'd never bothered to study up on – I was guilty of that too – and then, of course, the numerous crimes that both I and Person Unknown had committed in relation to hacking into a murder victim's phone records and generally abominable behaviour regarding the use of spywear, satellite imagery and the internet for the dissemination of information likely to impede a criminal investigation.

I was like this once: eager and impatient, hot to prove my skills as the investigator who broke the case; kid on the curve of the big time. Blindness; that's what ambition does to you. It can be a rough learning curve downwards. No need for condemnation; indeed the opposite: ambition is admirable, especially when you're smart and you care.

'Here are some questions,' I said, indicating her notebook, which she was putting back into her pocket.

She stared at me with a 'We're done' look and continued to put the notebook away.

'Let's start with Izzie. There's a twenty-three kilometre, sixty-eight minute gap between when she was recorded as being taken and when she was actually taken.'

The 'We're done' look began to erode.

'That might have something to do with the complaints made to the police about Izzie's public sex antics. Izzie was a big-time nympho and put it on display for all to watch. A very public display. There were six complaints made by the parents in the street where this was happening. That's the same street Jenny Brown lived in.'

Maria was now staring at me in growing shock.

'First up: which of the boys went out to answer the complaints? Next up: why is there a sixty-eight minute gap between Izzie's official time of disappearance and the actual abduction? New question, same query: who logged Izzie's disappearance at the station? I'm not one to draw conclusions or make assumptions. But I think they're good questions. What do you think?'

She didn't answer. I could almost see her mind racing, trying to catch up and get ahead, but I wasn't going to let that happen: 'Now, what are you going to tell the boys back at the station? Really? Let's bury the bullshit about you being all nice and covering for me. That ain't gunna happen, you know it and I know it. That's because you're fucked.'

By the look on her face I judged she hadn't been spoken to like that for a while, maybe never. Gorgeous girls get it easy; it's not fair but it's true.

'I'm the enemy. You've colluded. You're out. Think they'll forgive you because you've broken the case? No way: they're going to hate you even more. And those pretty looks that've helped get you into CIB – all of a sudden they've become the looks of a slut. When you're gorgeous, you can only play it one way: quiet, under the radar, you don't take credit for anything. Those boys are just waiting to turn on you. As much as they want to fuck you now but know they can't because you're smart and quiet and straight, they'll fuck your head space instead because at least they get to fuck you – one way or the other.'

Eyes flashed with rage; she swung her fist at me. It was a good, hard shot and could have connected but I've had years of practice; I knew it was coming. I leaned backwards and watched her punch arc through the air.

'You prick!' she shouted as she lunged for another. This time I grabbed her fist with my open hand and held it. Locked, mid-air, frozen.

'Would you have preferred if I'd lied? Some people enjoy the thrill of the unexpected. Me, I like to know what's on the road ahead.' I let go of her fist.

She was breathing heavily, furious at me and maybe, somewhere inside, at herself.

We stared at one another for a few moments. I was bargaining on her ambition. She was loyal but, more than anything, she wanted to 'touch the flag', rise up the ranks. Riding rogue with me was disloyal but it would help her achieve what she wanted. At least that's how I hoped she saw it.

'I could arrest you now. Take you in. Did that possibility occur to you? Because, from where I'm standing it seems like a good idea. And those boys you're talking about? I'd be their hero, dragging you into the station. What about that? What about that as an alternative to your brilliant summary?'

'Then do it. Maria: do it, and do it now.'

16

Helen 36D (ii)

Here we are my friends, almost home.

Take notes, my brothers and sisters. Note: it is important that you choose a place in which you will not stand out. It is important you blend in and make yourself appear to be normal.

What the fuck is normal? I hear you asking me. Ah, good question. Here's the answer: there isn't an answer. Normal doesn't exist. But here's something to remember, friends: everybody thinks it does and nearly everyone tries to live it out.

So I live in a nice street in a nice suburb with nice lawns and nice cars and nice people who watch the TV every night and go to jobs in the morning and come home after a trip to the supermarket. I do that sort of stuff too. Well I don't really. I pretend I do. Take notes: pretend to be like the others around you.

See, it isn't normal to be driving a van down a nice street with a package tied up in the back. So you gotta make it look normal. You gotta look like the other creeps in the street, you gotta look like the ice-cream man or a delivery man or a dude who might be a plumber or an electrician. And it's so fucking easy. Helen, you listening? You're part of this too. Normal people think you might be a roll of carpet or crates of wires. That's why I call the girls, after I get them, *the package.*

Slow down, soldier, don't alarm the neighbours with excitable driving.

Sometimes I feel like I'm a real community member. Sometimes I feel like I could be a member of Rotary or I could be a Boy Scout.

Slower now. Watch the kid on the bike riding like fuckin' Spiderman in the middle of the street. Wave to the little turd. Smile at the little creep.

Here we are. In front of the Gates to the Castle. Rollerdoors are good. Best to not only get a house that looks like all the other houses in the street but try and get one with a rollerdoor. Very secure. I love love love it when I'm finally inside the garage with the package and the rollerdoors go bang onto the concrete floor, closing us in.

—

Helen was tied extremely tightly to the mesh so it was almost impossible to move. But she managed to turn her head and stare up at him as they drove. She heard the sound of the electronic doors closing. With it came a dark gloom. She knew she was in a garage.

Winston smiled at her.

'Hi Helen. I've been doing this for a little while. So: the more you struggle the worse it'll be. For you.'

She watched as he unscrewed the mesh wall and rolled it across; he climbed from the front seat into the back of the van, and kneeled next to her.

Why her? What had she done to him? Was it something she said? At one of the times when he'd come in for his sessions? She tried to remember his file. Anything she could recall might help her. She knew, from watching movies and TV, that you had to create empathy with these sorts of people.

But that thought came from a place called hope and that place was fast losing light. Helen knew there was no hope. All she bothered to recall was that he had a long name, was twenty-four years old and had a rare pigmentation eye condition that gave his irises an orange colour.

He touched her breast. He squeezed it. He stared at it, squeezing harder. She tried not to show pain but it was hopeless. Everything was hopeless. 'Remember what I said,' she heard him say.

She went still. She didn't take her eyes off him.

'There's a list of rules inside the house. We'll go through them soon. Before we do that I'm going to fuck you.'

He spoke without emotion.

'This will be fuck one. When we get to fuck thirty-two – can you remember that? fuck thirty-two? – I'll tell you if you're going to live or if you're going to die. But you have to remember fuck thirty-two because if you don't, if I ask you how many times have we fucked and you get the answer wrong, then–'

He shrugged as if to say, 'It can't be helped.'

'Oh, and just to be fair about it: a fuck doesn't include the mouth. There's a big difference. Don't count them. Okay?'

Helen had long stopped moving and stared at a horror she didn't imagine possible.

'Let's start. You just lie there, it'll be fine.'

—

HELEN REGAINED CONSCIOUSNESS and looked around her. A bedroom, dark. But not dark enough. On the walls were photos. Hundreds of photos.

Of teenage girls. Naked, bound, helpless, abused, cut, bleeding, crying, begging, on their knees, pleading. So many girls.

Helen screamed again, screamed louder than she would once have imagined possible, a scream that welled up from deep within her soul, a scream silenced by the duct tape around her mouth.

17

The Deal (ii)

If I were Eddie I'd be pretty happy: Buffy the Vampire Slayer is sexy but being freed by a meltdown gorgeous cop would be in the realm of a fantasy he wouldn't even have imagined. About now that fantasy would be coming true.

I stayed in the copse, having watched her drive away like a banshee of anger. I don't think it was the warning about his lip-licking habit.

This was the deal: she'd rescue him, making up some bullshit story about seeing a shadowy figure fleeing mysteriously from the walls of the resort. (Me.) Then she'd flash her badge and ask poor Eddie about everybody who has access to the resort, all the people who might have so appallingly and for no reason perpetrated the attack on him. I'd noticed that the four buildings each had an underground car park with electronic gates. Who's got access to them, Eddie? Especially over in Sunrise Breeze. Doesn't matter you weren't assaulted over there; got to be thorough, Eddie. Get that? Thorough.

Then she would return and report back to me. That was the plan. She still hadn't thought further ahead; she was running on adrenaline. She hadn't grasped, not properly, that I had tainted her. The deal was more profound than she realised. I'd let her discover that later, after we had squeezed Eddie for all he had. I made circles in the dirt with the tip of my boot. I was happy to wait.

—

BEING A COP meant a lot to me. I'd wake, shower, put on the uniform. In it I was someone. I believed in what I did. I worked hard. Maybe too hard. But I got where I wanted to go: I rode the lift up to the floor of Homicide. All cops want to be in Homicide, no matter what they tell you. There are two reasons for this. One: all other police work is bullshit. Drink drivers, car accidents, arson, fraud, fisheries, livestock, even rape. All bullshit. Sure, they're important, but there is an order to the world, a hierarchy. In Homicide you deal with murder. Someone has taken the life of another person. A life. If among all the chaos that wanders the world in which we live we have anything in common, it's the simplicity of life.

You don't kill innocent people. If you do, you go down. Homicide lures all cops because all cops, even the bad cops, want to get the killers who sweep among us with smiles and lies.

The second reason is more basic: if you're not in Homicide you're a loser. Walk through the foyer of the downtown station and ride the lift. First floor: pen pushers, don't even wear uniforms. Second floor: payroll. Third floor: Arson and Fisheries. Fourth floor: CIB. Fifth: Fraud, maybe the internet guys. Sixth: Child-abuse teams. Seventh: Rape and Missing Persons.

Now we're hot: two floors left, one of bureaucrats, the other the Sons of God. Homicide. We'd step out onto the eighth floor, with its clusters of four desks pushed together as one, boxes of evidence, whiteboards, filing cabinets and a lot of empty coffee cups. We kept the beer hidden in the meeting room, behind the screen where we'd watch VHS tapes of interviews or of crime scenes. The floor above us housed the Commissioner, in a very large office that had a commanding view over a city of millions. The Commissioner, whoever it happened to be, always positioned their desk away from the city so they could look at Port Phillip Bay, a panoramic vista of grey ocean peppered with sailing boats and windsurfers. I guess the view's better but it always struck me as an avoidance of responsibility to the safety of those millions.

Once, I spent an afternoon with the Commissioner in his office. We drank Johnny Walker Blue: $260 of taxpayers' money. He stared through a gigantic telescope the entire time, as we drank and as I talked about my arrest of a serial rapist in the deadbeat suburb of Frankston.

'Are you looking for possible crimes being committed, Chief?' I asked.

'No, you fuckwit. Come here,' he answered, leaning back to let me in and downing a $40 swig.

I peered through the telescope and saw a topless woman, sunbaking on the beach.

'And here.' He tilted the telescope delicately, as if we were on a space station. 'Check that out.'

Another unsuspecting – topless – member of the public, quietly passing her Friday afternoon on the beach, oblivious to the fact that the most powerful policeman in her city was perving on her while supposedly undertaking a serious discussion about the man I had just arrested – Davo, who had beaten and raped sixteen girls over his 'spree of sperm' as he laughingly called the time between being released from jail the previous year to his arrest a few hours earlier.

Davo's dead now. He went back to jail. The Office of Public Prosecutions was understaffed and sent a pimply kid, a year out of law school, to argue the case. Six months later Davo walked free. I watched him walk out the front gates, and followed him to his new home, a scummy boarding house. I waited until he stumbled down the steps and along the footpath to the nearby girls' school. I made sure he didn't make it.

The Commissioner didn't make it either. They never do. Up there on the padded floor of the executive wing, the Commissioner and his or her Deputy Commissioners are harangued daily, endlessly by politicians who fret about the crime rates that haven't gone down, then spend long hours in group meetings with consultants trying to figure out how to bend the crime rates down, re-defining 'violent crime'.

Can we take out manslaughter? Do we have to include rape?

After a while that gets to you, no matter how much Johnny Walker you drink. Then, if you haven't been sacked, you take yourself down.

On the eighth floor our reason for living was what we called the kill board: the list of dead victims, in chronological order. We listed each name, in blue felt pen, down the left-hand side of the board and drew a long line from the left side of the kill board to the right. After any basic information about when and where came the important bit: name of killer and a tick if they had been tried and convicted. By Christmas we were usually at a hundred – that's about the kill level you should expect for Melbourne in an average year.

It was past eight o'clock when I climbed back into the Toyota and turned on the engine to get a blast of airconditioning. No wind; it must have been an easy thirty-five degrees. I closed my eyes and let the cold air consume me. And I went back, to the eighth floor, to the kill board.

Long after I'd shed the uniform for a suit, I rode the lift every morning watching the losers climb out on the second floor in their Big W suits and ten-dollar shoes into Fisheries, Arson. Leaning smugly against the back wall as the lift doors closed, I would erase the losers as they went about arresting guys who'd caught too many mullet or tiptoed through the dead embers of a house fire.

The lift would rise, floor by floor, losers exiting, until I reached my floor, the floor that I ran.

After I joined Homicide I was assigned to a crew along with another detective, also new to the eighth floor. Carita. There aren't many female Homicide detectives. We were on the same crew for over four years.

Once Carita and I tracked a killer, chasing him down a South Yarra backstreet on a Saturday night. He tripped and fell and so did we, right on top of him, all elbows and knees. He had killed an eighty-seven-year-old woman named Doris. She'd never married, which had something to do with the Second World War. She collected stamps from Tahiti – they were strewn across the floor near to where the killer had stabbed her in the throat with a corkscrew.

Carita and I pummelled the shit out of the rat-faced killer as he whined and squirmed on the wet cobbled bluestones. I broke his nose. Carita kneed him in the genital area so hard I think she sent them up into his windpipe. He was crying and he was broken. Nobody cared. Two constables in their mid-twenties turned up and dragged him to the back of the paddy wagon. He couldn't stand. He couldn't talk either, which was good because no-one wanted to hear what he had to say. It was still raining. We were soaked, but that didn't matter. We'd caught a bad guy and beaten the shit out of him. No-one would know. There was no danger of an internal inquiry. Nobody cared about him. We were high. We had to go back to the eighth floor and write out sixteen thousand pages of reports about what happened but we just stood and stared at each other as the paddy wagon, sirens and lights, grew distant. I started to laugh, like you do when you win something. It must have been infectious. Carita and I laughed like morons in a dead-end street in South Yarra, big sombre oak trees above us, fat drops of rain on our heads. I made the first move. I said: 'Carita, what I'm about to say could get me into some hardcore trouble, but you know what? I just don't care. After what we've been through all I wanna do is take you back to my place, which happens to be a few streets away, neck a bottle of vodka and–'

She just smiled and nodded, and so we did: drank vodka and fucked each other like it was the last night on earth.

The next day she whispered across to me at our desk: 'I'm transferring. Just came through. Going to Fraud.'

'*Fraud?*' It was an abdication.

She looked at me with an edge of sympathy as if I hadn't understood something.

'The bad guys are charming in Fraud,' she said. But that's not what she meant. The next day her desk was empty.

I saw her once, years later, maybe I'd been seven years in Homicide. I was riding down the elevator, from eighth to the lobby. It had been three years since we rumbled the rat face in the wet alley and spent the night with vodka and sex. She stepped into the lift and smiled. I said hello and she said hi. She was wearing a dark blue suit. She smelled like a sea of flowers. She watched me as I took in her scent and she followed my eyes. She looked happy.

She must have read my mind, because she said: 'I love it.'

'Charming bad guys, huh?'

'Sweet-talkers all.'

'I hear it's a growing field,' I said. The Nigerian fraud scam was top of the pops. Everyone was talking about internet crime being the hot new thing. Fraud were down on the fifth and there was always a buzz when the elevator stopped there. We were still the Sons of God up on the eighth but the high had faded with the emergence of the new thing. We were always stuck with a hundred kills. We were a constant.

After seven years in Homicide I no longer fraternised with cops from the other departments and they all responded accordingly. When I rode the elevator it was silent; when I stepped into it, conversations stopped. But not on this day, not with Carita on this journey. We talked and I even said something like, 'I hear it's going to rain on the weekend.' As the elevator came to its slow-motion stop she said, 'The nightmares have gone,' like she was whispering to me, like she was sharing a secret; because I'd never told her about the nightmares.

She looked away, or maybe she didn't, maybe I looked away, but we'd reached the lobby and the doors opened and fresh faces ready to step inside were waiting for us to step out. Kevin, one of my colleagues who'd tallied over eight hundred murders in his career, stared at me with dead eyes as he pushed in first and stood at the back, waiting for the less important to follow him in.

I could still smell the sea of flowers, which seemed utterly wrong in the lobby of the Police Department HQ, and I had a sudden, almost desperate urge to be with Carita. But I couldn't take my eyes off Kevin. He wasn't looking at me but his staring eyes were.

'Darian?' he asked. 'Problem?'

I shook my head and the lift doors closed. He was gone. Dead-eyed veteran Homicide cop taking the slow road up to the eighth.

I turned around. Carita was walking away from me, towards the front doors. For some reason, that angered me. I wanted her there, waiting for me. I wanted the smell of her perfume and her expensively clothed body. I wanted to ask her about the nightmares but I never would. I never talked to anyone about the nightmares even though I figured that all of us in Homicide had them. She was the only one who ever spoke of them; she and the Yardsman.

'Two of the builders didn't return their access keys. Also the electrician who was contracted to do all the wiring. Eddie thinks he was attacked by Tonto.'

We were at the end of the dirt track, by the ferry road. It was quiet; the highway drivers hadn't assembled yet.

'Who?'

'Tonto. He's the Lone Ranger's sidekick. He's really ugly.'

'I'm a *sidekick*? And Eddie thinks *I'm* ugly?'

'No, you moron: *Eddie* is ugly; uglier than you said. But you got the sidekick right. Follow me,' she said and drove off.

She'd smiled. It was just like we were partners.

18

The Curse: A Shadow

THERE'S A PERFECT STILLNESS BEFORE DAWN. I LIKE THAT TIME, more than any other. It's quiet but for the gentle murk of the river as it swells past, and the faraway monotonous sounds of the ocean. I heard the car, the sound of the door closing and her approach.

'Here,' I said. It was still dark. Voices carry far on the river. After she found me on the jetty, she knew to whisper.

'I always wanted to be a cop. But I don't know if I can handle it.'

'How many years are you in? Five?'

She nodded.

'What you're seeing, what you're being forced into is the province of seasoned homicide detectives. You're not meant to be dealing with this stuff so early.'

'But I am.'

Yeah. She was.

'It's not just a job,' I said, 'and you have no friends there; there is only you.'

'But the nightmares. The faces of the girls ... it's like they're haunting me.'

'They are. That's exactly what they're doing.'

The river glimmered up a reflection from its surface of the shocked expression on her face. 'That's because they know you care. They *don't* go away. They'll always be there. It's part of the curse–'

'Curse?' she interrupted me, fear showing in her eyes.

'–of being a cop who not only cares but won't stop. This is your first killer. When he's caught and dealt with there'll be more and you'll be stronger, ready for them, ready to seek them out, no matter what, and eradicate them. Embrace the girls, they want you to. Don't be afraid of them. I was. I fought them. You can't. You lose.'

'Eradicate?' she asked.

'Whatever it takes,' I answered.

'I don't believe in that.'

'I just said whatever it takes. I didn't say you have to shoot them dead.'

'But you do,' she whispered in a voice I could barely hear.

'*I* do.'

—

IT SEEMED LIKE a conversation from another era, but it was yesterday morning. After Maria left I realised I hadn't slept in almost forty-eight hours. I'd need to or else I'd make a truly dumb mistake. Just a few hours, that was all I'd need. But not yet. There was still work to do; I needed to show Maria exactly what the deal was.

It was her day off but she parked her car down the road in a side street and took a narrow path to the river then sloshed along the water for about a hundred metres, past my neighbours' front lawns and beaches until she reached my front yard with its thickets of palm trees lining either side for complete privacy.

By now I'd told her about the cling wrap. We Skyped Isosceles, who asked if she would have intercourse with him. He spoke at length about Barry Goldwater and asked to see her T-shirt a number of times, to which she obliged, all of us aware that it was really her bust he was studying. We dusted the cling-wrap box and searched for any signs of prints – there were some possibles – then did as he instructed with my computer and another humming metal box so he could run any prints to a match at his end. We went through the list of building contractors at the North Shore resort and paid close attention to the electrical contractors. There were about sixty-five on the Sunshine Coast but we narrowed down an A list of companies in a reasonable proximity to the North

Shore. Each of them subcontracted; there were over a hundred electricians. Still, it was a good lead and connected to one of the few things we knew about our guy: his knowledge of computers and telecommunications.

As it seemed we were done, Maria looked surprised when I told Isosceles to stay with us. I wanted her to know there was an audience, albeit of one and an eccentric one at that.

We had already agreed to a shadow dance of twin investigations. That was easy. Sort of. She was bottom-rung Crime Investigation Branch, not even officially assigned to Operation Blonde, the task force chasing the killer. But she was in the room. No eighth floor in Noosa. Crime worked out of the one big room. When the annoying missing girls' case became a murder investigation they made extra space by pushing the Fisheries desks closer towards the back door; when the murder investigation became a hunt for a serial killer they pushed the Drink Driving and Marijuana teams up against the Fisheries guys. Maria was in on it, but not in it. Fat Adam was the driver; he had his own office. I assured her I knew how to stage-manage the information and remain in control. I assured her it would work. Once we had the killer locked in our sights she would be the one to bring him to the attention of the task force. She knew she wouldn't get the limelight – no-one would stop Fat Adam from that – but her ideas that led to the capture of the killer would be noted, applauded and, of course, rewarded.

There was a bit of an issue about exactly what would happen once we found the killer. She was young and believed in the justice system. It would take her some years to discover it was a game riddled with a distinct lack of justice. She knew I had a gun and she knew how I liked to end these matters. I told her I wouldn't do anything before discussing it with her first. She didn't believe me, and I didn't expect her to. I told her we were being presumptuous; maybe we wouldn't catch the guy and maybe it was bad karma to talk about it as if we would. She bought that; she had a hyperactive sense of the superstitious. I also told her that all that mattered was the incontrovertible discovery of his identity. Once we had his name we'd soon find evidence. These guys love their trophies, I reminded her. They might bury their bodies but they hang on to trinkets, spoils of victory. She felt better after I said that: he could be gone but the investigation would still be resolved.

That wasn't going to work for me of course; he and I had some talking to do. I needed to find where he had buried the girls. They needed to come home, to their parents. They needed the respect of a funeral, a proper goodbye.

'Have you thought any more about those sixty-eight minutes?' I asked her.

'No,' she answered, surprised.

'I have,' I said.

'It's just random,' she said.

Random; that word again. By now she had told us where each of the mobile phones had been found, which I'd added to my wall board.

'There's no such thing. Random doesn't exist, not in the hunt for a serial killer,' I said. I could see Isosceles nodding in agreement.

'Someone altered the times. Why would they do that?' I asked.

'It'll be a mistake,' she said. 'They happen all the time.'

'What if it's not?'

She didn't answer.

'What if it's deliberate? It most likely is. Somebody is papering over a sixty-eight minute time frame. Why? Because they have something to hide. They're not papering over Izzie's sixty-eight minutes, they're papering over theirs. Most likely time spent with her.'

She didn't speak, just kept her eyes on mine.

'What if the killer is a cop?' I said, as if the thought just occurred to me.

'*What?*' she shot out.

'You think that's absurd? Do they psych-test cops? No. They do in the Fire Services; ten per cent of applicants are pyromaniacs.'

'Eight,' said Isosceles, correcting me.

'Of all the men on the Sunshine Coast, all the men you've looked at and wondered: is it him, or him, or maybe him? Have you ever looked and wondered about *them*? Those guys in the station. How many of them are there? Fifteen? Sixteen? Has anyone eliminated them? Ever thought to wonder: how do they get their kicks? Do they dream about fourteen-year-old blonde girls? Ask yourself: have you ever heard one of those boys mention how pretty or sexy or hot one of the victims was? Has anyone said: she deserved it? Walking around with a T-shirt stretched tight over her chest, school dress altered to sit high up above her knees, maybe so high that when she leaned down they could imagine seeing her underwear?'

I was creating a dark tunnel from which there was no escape. I could see, from the look in her eyes – glassy, faraway, in the squad room – that she was deep inside it.

'How many times did they get a complaint about Izzie having public sex? Who went out? What did they do when they got there? They watched. Izzie didn't stop fucking in the full view of the street, for anyone to see – the complaints to the police did nothing. Except create a bigger audience. How many of the boys do you think went out to watch? But who among them decided to do a little more than just watch? To do something; we don't know what, but it led somehow to the erasure of sixty-eight minutes.'

She blinked and stared at me as if I'd hit a chord.

'At the other end of those sixty-eight minutes was the killer. Waiting for her? Or simply changing identity at the sixty-ninth minute?'

'It can't be.'

'Because you say so? Get real. You want Isosceles to recite some data? Cops who kill? Look,' I said, leaning in to her, 'only you can do this. You have to be me.'

I startled her.

'When you go back to the station, you have to be my eyes and ears. You wear the uniform and you play Maria … but I'm your shadow in there. You look at them with my eyes and ears as you laugh and make jokes and talk about the surf and the dumb tourists and the river poachers with their boatloads of fish. My eyes, my ears: Is it him? Him? Is it him? No-one is immune.'

She got up and left without speaking.

'Whoa, man, that was really freaking intense,' said Isosceles. 'Do you seriously believe that shit?'

I shrugged. 'Is the killer one of the cops? Unlikely. Did one of them fuck Izzie? Yep. More than one? Probably; probably they all took turns to go watch her, and one of them went a step too far. Does it matter? Only in that the killer was watching, following. He most likely swooped down on Izzie as soon as the cop dropped her off. That information will help.'

'So why the mind-fuck, if you'll pardon the expression?'

'She's smart, she's resourceful, she's independent, she's ambitious; she'll go rogue. She has to be captive to my lead.'

'Oh. Right. That makes rather good sense. Tremendous breasts.'

On that note we signed off, he to follow up on all leads emanating from the North Shore Dreaming Resort and I to bed for three hours, no longer.

I woke up to the sound of someone unlocking my front door.

19

Angie

I HEARD FOOTSTEPS ON THE WOODEN FLOOR AND THEN A SOFT voice. Angelique. Tuesdays at eight, every week. Angie, the woman I quietly loved.

It was dark. I had slept seven hours, way too long. I was angry at myself, for oversleeping and for forgetting.

I don't get lonely. Indeed solitude is a friend. He and I sit by the river, content. But I do need the touch and embrace of a woman's body. I've never been married and I was a catastrophic boyfriend many times over. Being on time or, actually, just 'being', was impossible. In Homicide, even on my days off – which I never took off – I was always on the job. Women in the force, like Carita and Rhonda, either disliked my intensity or maybe just me. Most likely they sensed a complete absence of the possibility of commitment.

The first time I hired a girl to sleep with me I was more nervous than I had ever been in my life. The business of bartering: How long did I want her for? Was it an in-call or an out-call? Did I expect GFE or PSE? Phrases I hadn't heard of. But after I'd emerged unscathed through this world of negotiation, I lay and closed my eyes as she swept across me and I felt an absorbing completeness.

From then on, and that was many years ago, I found solace and refuge in the company of prostitutes. About a month after I arrived in Noosaville, I sought out that solace and refuge again. It wasn't a cop thing. It was a me thing.

You find prostitutes a number of ways. You can go to a brothel, which I've never done – the idea of bumping into a gangster or fellow cop seemed best avoided, and as a general rule I hate people; this deal, the deal of sex, was only going to be done in the dark of my home. Or, you find prostitutes by going online or reading the ads in the classifieds where it says 'escort' or 'private services'.

There's a sense of desperation in these classifieds: 'eager to please', 'new to town', 'porn-star body', 'unforgettable', 'open-minded', 'all natural'. It's a ruthless game and words are disguises. I stared at the page in the newspaper for two hours, re-reading each one but always coming back to the simplicity of: 'Angie. Nineteen. Sweet.'

'Darian, you here?' she asked.

'Yeah, sorry, I was asleep. Hang on,' I said as I climbed off the bed like a drunk, still half asleep and dragged out of it by the sounds – innocent though they were – of an intrusion.

I walked into the lounge room. She'd poured herself a glass of Sancerre. I don't drink anymore but keep a cold reserve in the fridge for when she stays the Tuesday through to the Wednesday, eight to eight. We sit at the end of the jetty, we talk, we have sex, we lie in each other's arms naked, hour after hour, pressed tight; more talking. She studies at university and tells me about which philosopher she's reading or, my favourite subject, what beat from African colonial history she's learning. Often she asks me questions about my past life, but not dark questions that might lead to images of horror. I censor my stories and tell them as if they were fables.

Her real name is Rose but she hasn't told me that. She lives with two other girls near the campus, the University of the Sunshine Coast, but she hasn't told me that either. Nor has she told me her real age, which is twenty-seven. She doesn't have a boyfriend. I think she's lying when she tells me that.

'Hi,' I said. She was staring at my wall, now a massive crime hunt. This was not something she should be looking at. I'd forgotten it was Tuesday. Had I remembered I would have cancelled.

'Jesus, you've come out of retirement.' She put her glass down and held me tight. 'Are you all right?' she asked. Angie knew more about me than anyone.

'I'm fine. I had to …' I let the sentence linger without finishing.

'Wow,' she whispered to herself. I followed her gaze. Wow indeed. She was staring at the Beretta.

'It's a ninety-two. Very rare. They only made–'

'–five thousand, I know. One of them lies at the bottom of the ocean.' She was still holding me. She kissed me, a kiss that was really an embrace; support, affirmation. But I could see she was shaky. Her eyes were darting across the room, from the gun to the wall to the new computer and the metal boxes next to it.

But always coming back to the gun. It's one thing to know a person by what they once did; entirely another to know that person as what they might do.

'Should I go?' she asked. By now, normally, we'd be walking down the jetty and she'd be regaling me with stories of Cicero or questions like: 'Can you believe how many times Kurt Vonnegut wrote "so it goes" in *Slaughterhouse Five*?'

'No,' I thought. 'Yes,' I replied. I wanted her, I wanted her company and I wanted the feel of her soft warm body pressed against mine, I wanted to hold her in my arms and tell her stories and listen to hers. In the year of Tuesdays we'd been together I had utterly fallen in love with her. She was beautiful and she was funny and she told me, time after time, how dumb I was; teasing, prodding, joking, laughing, holding me. The challenge of her brilliant mind and gorgeous body kept pushing me forwards into a life of brightness.

Each week I paid for the twelve hours and she took my money. I paid her random amounts, whatever was in my wallet; it was always double, maybe triple the rate that had long ago been abandoned. A couple of times she left while I slept, slicing out of my bed; exams to study for, an assignment overdue.

She kept looking at the wall, at the faces of the six girls.

'It's terrible,' she said.

I sat at my computer and opened my email. She picked up her glass of wine. There were seventy-five unread messages, all from Isosceles.

I got up and hugged her from behind, kissed her gently on the back of the neck. 'I have to work.'

'I'll come back next Tuesday? You can tell me to go but I'll just check in. Okay?'

'Yeah, that'd be good.'

She finished the glass of wine, rinsed it out and then left.

20

What's the Frequency, Kenneth?

Helen doesn't like *Pocahontas*. She should. It's a really good movie. My favourites are:

Pocahontas.
Toy Story 2.
The Incredibles.
Jungle Book. When I watch *Jungle Book* I get up and dance and sing along with the animals.
Snow White.

I sort of like *Beauty and the Beast* but it's at the bottom of my list.

I hate *Fantasia*. I-hate-it-I-hate-it-I-hate-it.

When it comes to real movies (I'm making my own film) I like *Henry, Portrait of a Serial Killer*. I wrote to the director once but he didn't write back. Hannibal Lecter is awesome but only in the first one. The rest are shit. I wrote to Anthony Hopkins but he didn't write back. The first real-life movie I ever saw was *Clockwork Orange*. Alex is a droog and I was too. That was when I was eight. Alex is so cool. The way he gets that huge sculpture cock and kills the chick with it, bang, on the head. Awesome. I wrote to Stanley Kubrick, the director, and he didn't write back. I wrote to Anthony Burgess, the man who wrote the book. I told him his book was stupid but the movie was awesome. He didn't write back. I wrote to Alex. He didn't write back. I wrote to Carol Drinkwater who was fucked by Alex in that fast-motion scene that did my head in. I recognised her in a TV series about a vet called *All Creatures*

Great and Small that my mum and my aunt used to watch and say, 'It's just like home.' But Carol Drinkwater didn't write back. I loved the bit where Alex kicks the old guy and he's singing a song at the same time.

That's what me and Helen are doing now. We are singing. I am singing. Helen can't. I'm singing the songs from *Pocahontas*. That's because we are in a canoe. Me and Helen-big-tits and a canoe too.

Helen is all wrapped up, all shiny and silver. Woo-hoo. In the canoe too. Helen couldn't keep count. None of them can keep count. I don't think they teach maths anymore. I should write to the minister for education but I'm not going to because I don't care.

I don't know about *The Lion King*. *Taxi Driver* is really cool too. The way he shoots off the bad guy's finger. That's awesome. But the big problem with *Taxi Driver* is that Jodie Foster didn't go nude. What's the point of her if she's not nude? She gets down on her knees to suck off Robert de Niro but she's not nude. That's just stupid. I wrote to her and told her she was stupid and she didn't write back. Brooke Shields is all nude, all gorgeous and nude and beautiful like a gleaming wet Pocahontas in *Pretty Baby* which is the best movie ever made. Best real movie ever made. Not a cartoon movie. When she stands up out of the bath all nude, that bit is the best bit of a real movie ever. I wrote to Brooke Shields and told her she was beautiful. I write to her every week. I know she is all old now and wrinkly and she had a kid and she and Tom Cruise had a fight about anti-depressants but she is immortal. Standing up in the bath with the wet water running down her baby body, she is immortal. That's what I tell her in all my letters. When I find out the name of her kid I'm going to write to her kid and tell them that their mum is immortal. I wrote to Tom Cruise and told him if he ever said another bad thing about Brooke Shields I would kill him. He stopped soon after. He even apologised to Brooke Shields. I told her in one of my letters but she never writes back to me. But she knows who I am, that I am her saviour and the man who stopped Tom Cruise from saying terrible things about her.

I haven't really enjoyed fucking Helen-big-tits. I did. On the first day I did. I guess on the second and third days too. Now I just want to get rid of her. Go back to the original plan and get Jenny G, not Jenny B who was the first, Jenny G. She's going to be my youngest yet, which is really awesome and when you think about it, pretty cool because Helen-big-tits is my oldest and then the next one is the youngest. I think that's really cool. Sometimes amazing things just happen. Like, I didn't plan it that way. It just happened. I think sometimes that God is guiding me. I think he wants me to understand things. I don't know what they are. I think I'll know when I know, like, I think it'll be the moment. I'll just realise it. Like I just realised Jenny G is the youngest and Helen-big-tits is the oldest.

Maybe–

Hang on.

Wow. Yes. That's awesome, what an awesome idea. Why didn't I think of that? I did. Or did I? That was God. Was that God?

That is so cool.

Roger that, captain. Better turn the vessel around, captain.

'Helen,' I whisper. 'Helen, I've just had the best idea. It's awesome. You're the oldest and Jenny G, she's the youngest. I'm gunna put you two together. You can share the room together. She'll fit on the bed, won't she? Course she will.'

Helen is so boring. She doesn't say anything. She just stares at me with this stupid blank look. I'm gunna fix that.

—

HELEN WAS TRYING to stare at the stars. Lying on the bottom of a canoe. She watched as Winston leaned across to his rucksack, unzipped it and reached inside. She couldn't see what he was doing but thought she saw a glint, like the flash of a torch popping in the moonlight, and then she felt an incredible, deep pain in her leg. Something sharp and long was tearing into her flesh and she could feel the rush of warm blood erupt into the tight wrapping of plastic in which she was bound. He turned and looked at her like a child dissecting a frog in a science experiment.

Again she was screaming into silence. Winston smiled.

—

Sometimes, my brothers and sisters, torture or just simply some random pain of the strong strong strong kind is most necessary.

21

The Boy Who Bragged (i)

MUSIC, SUDDENLY. A RING TONE.

Hilary Duff? Lady Gaga? Amy Winehouse? Which was which? I asked myself as I ran into the living room to the four mobile phones laid out on the dining table: each was a different colour, each with an assigned ring tone. The yellow one was vibrating: Henna.

'Go,' I barked.

No words. Sobs. Deep, heaving sobs.

'What happened?' I asked urgently as I shoved the other three phones into my pocket and grabbed my keys and ran. Seconds matter.

'I shot him.'

'What!?'

'It was dark.'

'What happened?'

I swung open the door of the Toyota and turned on the ignition while I clambered inside. I hadn't set up the hands-free yet, which was extremely annoying as I steered with my knees, using my free hand to turn on the GPS.

'I've killed someone.'

'Where are you? Exact location.' The arc of my headlights cut across the empty street as I turned right, in the direction of where she lived, hoping it was the right way.

'Bus stop.' Barely a whisper.

'Street?' The headlights flooded a jacaranda tree and for the merest of seconds all I could see was a world of purple flowers and then it was gone.

'The highway. Near home.'
'Is it the closest bus stop to your home?'
'Yes.'
Good. Close. Four minutes away. 'Are you alone?'
'Yes, I–'
'Where is the person you shot?'
'On the ground. By his car.'
'Any sign of life?'
Between sobs: 'No.'
'Did you use the gun?'
'Yes, it was–'
'Where is the gun?'
I checked the rear-view mirror; no-one behind me.
'It's in my hand. I was–'
'Are you alone?'

A roundabout loomed ahead; they love roundabouts up here. I swerved to avoid driving straight across it. She hadn't answered.

'Listen! Do what I say! Okay?'
'Yes.'
'Are you alone?'
'Yes.'
'Look in every direction. Can you see anyone? Any cars?'
'No. Nothing.'
'Behind you is a park. See it?'
'Yes.'
'It's dark.'
'Yes.'
'Walk towards it. Stand by the low wooden fence.'
I heard the crunching of her shoes on gravel. And sobs.
'Are you by the fence?'
'Yes.'
'Throw the gun, as far as you can, into the park.'
'But ...'
'Do it.'
I heard a noise. The shops and main street of Tewantin were

behind me as I passed the little police station that's open between the hours of nine and five and looks like a kindergarten.

'Okay,' she said.

'How far did it go in? Roughly.'

'Thirty metres?'

'Good. Turn back to face the road. Can you see anyone?'

'No. It's, like, totally empty.'

Amazing. 'Good,' I said. 'Now listen very, very carefully.' I paused. I knew she was listening. 'I am less than two minutes away. Other people may get there first. Police.' I paused again. She was still listening. Focused. Good.

'You must only say the following: "I can't remember anything. I'm in shock."' I paused then said, 'Repeat it.'

'I can't remember anything. I'm in shock.'

'No matter *who* asks you. No matter *what* you are asked. You say one thing …'

'I can't remember anything. I'm in shock.'

'But you fuckin' killed a guy!' I shouted. *'What have you got to say 'bout that!'*

There was a pause then, wobbly and uncertain, she replied: 'I can't remember anything. I'm in shock.'

'Good. Say nothing else.'

There was a pause and I heard an intake of breath.

'They're here.'

'You know what to say?'

'Yes.'

'Say nothing else. Nothing else. Okay?'

'Okay. How long till you'll be here?' she asked. Through the phone, from behind her voice I heard the sound of a car pulling up on the gravel, a deeper crunching noise this time. The cops.

'That's me to your left, two hundred metres away. I'm here too.'

—

I'D ASKED SHERYL Brown if I could borrow Jenny's school end-of-year book. Jenny went to Tewantin High School. So did Izzie and Brianna. Three girls out of six. There is no such thing as a coincidence in a murder investigation.

Days had passed. I hadn't heard from Maria but wasn't expecting to; I'd be the one making contact, not the other way around. In the meantime we were exhausting the list of electricians. It was slow and frustrating but we were moving forward; just as long as we were moving and not treading water. In less than a week we'd gone a long way.

I had asked Isosceles to get me as many names and addresses as he could of the teenage girls the killer liked: pretty, blonde, young. It was a flawed request. It required subjectivity on behalf of the man in the glass tower whose adoration of females was confined to Raquel Welch and Sarah Michelle Gellar. It was flawed also because many parents these days refuse to let their children's images be published on school websites.

End-of-year school books are different. They carry photos of all the classes, of the chess club, the sports teams, the debating teams, the choir; a kid would have to be invisible not to make it into the end-of-year book.

Searching through it I came across Henna and three other girls about the same age who looked like everything the killer sought. I knew Henna's father had already bought her a gun; he hadn't been asking my advice, he was seeking affirmation. That he didn't get it from me was irrelevant. He would have found it elsewhere, and from whom, didn't matter. Any voice was enough. All Cliff needed was *someone*'s voice: *Yeah, mate, it's fine, go ahead and get her the gun, that's what I'd do.*

22

Henna and Me, Lady Gaga Too

'What make of pistol did he get you?' I asked. I wasn't in the mood for subtlety.

She spun around. It was her lunch break and, like every lunch time, Henna left the newsagent and strolled down the main street of Tewantin, crossed the road past the rambling old Royal Hotel and ventured into the park that sloped down to the river. She sat on one of the wooden benches that the council had placed along the river bank. A row of pandanus trees clung to the edge and provided thick cover from the sun.

She was feeding a flock of pelicans.

'What are you talking about?' she lied badly.

I sat next to her on the bench.

'Your dad has given you a gun, to use in case you're abducted by the serial killer.'

She said nothing, just stared at me with sad eyes.

'It won't help. It won't save you. *This* will.'

I handed her a mobile phone. 'Take it,' I said.

She did but clearly didn't know why.

'There's two hundred dollars' credit on it.' She looked startled. 'And only one number: mine.'

'What's going on?' she asked.

'Do you know who I am?'

'Mr Richards,' she said, seemingly relieved to have locked onto something that finally made sense.

'Darian,' I corrected her.

She smiled softly. Even though she had no clue what was going on, she knew to trust me. She was a trusting kind of girl. All the more reason I was giving her the phone and the low-down.

'Do you know *what* I was?'

'Yes,' she said quietly. 'Everyone knows.' There was that advertising campaign again.

'There's a killer in our midst.'

She nodded.

'You're his type.'

I could see as she fought back tears that she knew, she really, really knew. 'I was thinking of dying my hair black but I'd look so gross.'

Teenagers.

She reached into her bag and started to pull something out: the gun. I quickly grabbed her wrist and held it firm.

'No,' I said. 'Just tell me what it is.'

'A Glocken,' she said. I didn't bother correcting her. 'Dad took me into one of the national parks and showed me how to use it. What's this for?' she asked, holding up the phone I'd given her.

'That's your life-line, if you ever get into trouble. That. Not the gun. You get into trouble: call me. Only me. No-one else. Immediately. I won't make false promises: I may not be able to save you, but nobody else can help as much as I can.'

Once again she looked as if she was about to cry. Then: 'Did you really kill fifteen people? Fifteen murderers?'

'No.' She looked deflated.

'More than that,' I said. She looked delighted.

Teenagers.

'Call me – find me on the contact list – and call. Now.'

Her fingers scrambled across the keypad, efficiently, with confidence.

I'd bought a lot of phones. The one I'd just given her was matched to one that came in a yellow case. I watched the number from her phone come up on the tiny screen.

'Now,' I said, handing her my phone, 'save that number to your name so I know it's you.'

She typed in 'Henna' and saved it.

'Now we do a ring tone. I'm going to need a specific song so I know it's you.' And, as I was about to offer her a choice of 'The Wind Cries Mary' or 'Purple Haze' by Jimi Hendrix, or 'Cortez the Killer' by Neil Young, she took my phone and downloaded a song, the name of which I cannot recall but one that was instantly recognisable and, given our previously established Gaga bond, entirely appropriate.

I stood up. 'Phone first, remember?'

She nodded. 'Phone first.'

And then, as I was about to leave, she jumped up from the seat, frightening the pelicans, scattering them across the river's glassy surface, and leaned across and kissed me on the cheek.

'Thank you,' she said. 'Thank you so much.'

I was taken aback, didn't know what to say, so I smiled, nodded and walked off wishing she hadn't done that, sweet though it was, wishing she hadn't touched my emotions with the thanks of that kiss.

23

The Boy Who Bragged (ii)

She looked small but not vulnerable. She stood straight, her gaze focused in my direction. One cop was talking at her, notebook in hand. I was closing in fast, less than sixty metres. He began to look familiar. One of the DD statues that Adam brought around to my house. Maybe. The other cop was a woman. Not Maria. She was talking on a mobile phone while examining the body of the boy who was slumped on the ground near his car. Henna hadn't yet told me exactly what'd happened but it was easy to guess the basics: a random guy making a move on a terrified kid who resorts to using a gun to stop the problem as the first, not last, option.

I too was on the phone. 'I need you,' I said.

I could hear sirens on approach; it sounded like two police cars and one ambulance. Henna wasn't speaking and I could see that, fifty metres away, the cop was getting aggressive. I could see, also, the look on Henna's face: *Quick*, it said.

And so I ran.

'Hey!' I shouted to the cop.

Both of the cops looked at me at the same time; she was still on her phone by the dead guy.

'What are you doing?' I shouted to the cop with medium-level aggression. I'd need room to amp up.

'Move away please, sir: this is a crime scene,' he said. He wasn't one of the statues. He didn't know who I was. His partner did, I could tell from the way she was now talking on the phone with her eyes on me. She was doing a running commentary on my arrival.

'No,' I answered. 'I am this girl's legal representative. She is underage. She is clearly in shock. You cannot ask her any further questions. Have you called an ambulance?'

While he was thinking: *who the fuck is this?* and before he had made up his mind to whack me or wait for reinforcements he blurted: 'Of course we have. There's a man over there who's dead.'

'Not for *him*!' I shouted, amping up a notch. 'For *her*: she is a minor. You have a child, in shock, who has witnessed a terrible crime. Have you alerted the paramedics and the local hospital? If you have not, you are in breach and you must do so immediately. This girl needs medical attention. If indeed that gentleman over there *is* dead – as you've declared him prior to the coroner even seeing the body, let alone checking it – your duty of care as an officer of the crown is to this young lady. Again, I ask you: Have you alerted the medical authorities that a minor has witnessed a violent crime and is in need of immediate medical attention?'

Henna had shut down now I'd taken over. That was good. The cop, however, was freaking out. I'd spoken with a force and authority and a threat that he wouldn't have heard before and, clearly, I'd hit a nerve. DD.

'Just a minute,' I heard. It was the female cop. She'd approached and overheard my rant. She hung up on whomever she had been speaking to, and turned to me. 'You're Darian Richards,' she said in an accusatory tone.

Remember what I said about female cops? They are not dumb.

'I am,' I replied.

'I don't think you have any business here, Mr Richards,' she said. 'We'll look after the girl. Don't worry about that, please.' She was smart. 'We know she's a minor and we know she's most likely in some degree of shock but it's also true she was the only person at the scene of this crime. It is, I'm sure you understand, imperative that we speak to her.'

'Of course it is ...' I replied with the soft diplomacy of a UN official, 'imperative.' I spoke without irony but her eyes narrowed and her lips grew tight. Be careful, I warned myself. I was in the right, the law was on my side, one hundred per cent, but that didn't matter. Talking to cops is dangerous. Never talk to cops.

'I'm representing the interests of this young lady–'

'How did you know to come?' she asked, interrupting me with a good question.

'–and, as such,' I went on, ignoring the good question, 'all I'm asking is that we observe the appropriate guidelines and regulations when a minor is involved in a major crime, particularly given this young lady is clearly in shock.'

The female cop was about to interrupt again. I didn't let her.

'And any form of interrogation might well exacerbate her condition. Not to mention the regulatory stipulation that a minor must be accompanied by an adult, preferably a psychologist, during any such interview. You agree with all that, don't you?' I said with a smile that made it look like we were partners.

'No, I'm afraid I don't,' she said. The sirens were deafening; over one hill came the ambulance and a cop car, their lights whirling dazzling blue-and-red 360s through the trees of the park and splashing over the facades of the houses, from which people were starting to emerge. Soon we'd have a circus.

'I'm going to have to ask you to move along, sir,' she said. The ambulance pulled up, the cop car almost screeching into its rear end.

'No,' I said casually.

The DD was looking at us, lost. We'd left him behind when we started using three-syllable words.

'Excuse me?' she asked, clearly shocked by the blatancy and the casualness.

And then two things happened at the same time: the paramedics leaped out of the ambulance and I shouted: 'We have a child over here, in need of immediate medical attention!' which drew them away from the dead guy, and the DD grabbed me by the arm and said: 'Did you hear what she said, mate? Get the fuck out of here before you regret it.'

Even before I had begun to respond, the female cop knew he'd made a big mistake.

'Dennis–' she said, in a warning voice that didn't go any further because the moment he touched me I stepped backwards, took his arm and slammed it violently down onto my femur bone. Snapped it like a piece of kindling.

He fell to the ground howling.

'I'm charging that man with assault,' I said. Always best to take the offensive.

The paramedics had begun to guide a dazed Henna towards the ambulance. I heard one of them say, 'Better call another ambulance,' as they kept walking, leaving me, the female cop and the howling DD on the ground between us. The cops from the other car had emerged to stare at the dead guy. The howling grabbed their attention.

The female cop was staring with slack-jawed astonishment. I'd made my point and she was folding. There'd be no more fight from her, even as the other two cops were walking our way.

'I'm charging that man with assault,' I said again. 'Get out your book and record the details of the incident.'

'You broke my fucking arm. I'm gunna fucking kill you,' we heard from below.

'What's his name?' I asked her. Another cop car pulled up. Henna was safely in the back of the ambulance. One of the paramedics had put a blanket around her.

'Dennis.'

I looked down.

'Dennis, shut the fuck up. You physically assaulted me: that's a crime called assault. You just verbally threatened me: that's also called assault. They're serious crimes, Dennis; you obviously didn't study them before you took the oath to uphold the laws of the state.' I turned to his partner. She hadn't moved. The other two cops were standing next to her, all three of them staring at me unsure what to do. If I was just a civilian it'd be easy: whack me, arrest me, haul my sorry arse down to the station and whack me again.

'I'm not joking. Get out your book, record the crimes, get this idiot to hospital. I'm going over there now,' I said, pointing at the ambulance, 'to be with my client. Tomorrow I will advise you as to whether I wish to proceed with these charges. Give me your card.'

She fumbled in her top pocket and pulled out a card with the Queensland Police Service badge embossed in red and blue, with her name, Sergeant Jackson Toyne, under it. I took it, put it in my back pocket and walked away.

'Richards,' she called out to me.

I stopped and turned back to face her. More cops had arrived. Two of them joined her. I recognised them. They were part of the statue contingent from my house last week. That was a total of four boys and her and the DD, who had passed out by her feet.

'I'm not sure you know who you're dealing with, mate,' she said.

Only one of the four boys standing behind her nodded; the other three had received the message.

The cops would come back for me. You don't whack a cop and get away with it. But I'd confused them enough to buy time and thankfully they didn't have the clarity of purpose to arrest me then and there. They were intimidated by me. They wouldn't do anything until they had direction from Fat Adam and he wouldn't do anything until he ate a few burgers and contemplated all the angles. Can't go round arresting an ex-cop like me without being sure the publicity will be all shiny.

'I do, Sergeant Toyne. I do. And so should you.'

She looked askance and instinctively made a move towards me. I don't think she was aware of it. One of the statues reached out and grabbed her by the shoulder.

'Come on, Jack,' he said and turned her away.

—

As I stepped into the back of the ambulance I noticed another two police cars arrive, I heard the sound of a second ambulance and saw the neighbourhood crossing the street. Photos were taken with mobile phones, fingers were pointed at Henna. Had it been warm and the sun out, people would have brought chairs and barbeques.

'How is she?' I asked the paramedics.

'In shock but fine,' one of them answered warily, clearly not sure who I was or if I'd break his arm too.

I looked at Henna. She met my gaze. I raised an eyebrow: *Are you okay?* She nodded, imperceptibly: *Yes.* I nodded back: *Good.* I flicked my eyes in the direction of the cops beyond us: *It's not over yet; be careful and stay silent.* She nodded: *I understand.*

'I'll be riding with her to the hospital,' I said to the paramedic.

'Sorry, mate, that's not allowed.'

Hearing me being turned down, his partner looked as if he was about to faint.

'You can follow us in your car,' he added helpfully.

'I'll be travelling in the ambulance, with her.'

He was about to argue.

'Don't argue with me,' I said. And he didn't.

'We're leaving now,' said the other one. 'I just have to inform the police that she's being taken to Noosa Emergency. They'll want to send somebody to ask her questions when she's ready.'

'Of course,' I said with a smile. He looked relieved I didn't crack open his head; he jumped out and scampered off towards Jackson Toyne. Another police car arrived. Someone was wandering around taking photos with a Nikon D3000; had to be a journalist. I tried to turn away but was snapped, sitting in the back of the ambulance next to the huddled teenage girl. He worked with his zoom and took more photos; they'd be of her. They'd be the ones the newspaper would print.

I quickly scoped the area past the bus stop, the dark gloom of the park. I thought I could see someone walking through it.

I turned to look at the vehicles lining the road, parked every which way, like they'd come to a jumble sale at a football oval. In the distance I could see a 1950s Dodge pick-up. Casey had arrived. That meant he'd neutralised the threat of Henna's dad staggering his way into the crime scene with wails of guilt. Now Casey was lurking in the dark, unseen by the cops, looking for the murder weapon, which would also be neutralised.

—

Before we departed I told the medics to leave us alone. They did. Henna then told me, through gobs of breath and rolls of tears, what had happened. She'd been waiting for a bus, going to see her boyfriend. It was running late. A car drove past, stopped and a boy stepped out to offer her a lift. She refused. He started walking towards her. She freaked, thought he was the serial killer. Then he bragged. About what a great lover he was, how he'd send a pretty young thing like her all the way to heaven with his wonderful cock. He grabbed his crotch to emphasise the point and she shot him.

She reached out from under the blanket and took my hand. I returned the squeeze, a show of support. She was only a kid. What she had done would forever be the most appalling and terrible thing in her life. She started to cry again.

It was a bumpy ride; there are no seatbelts in the back of ambulances and the medical equipment is more important than passengers.

'I'm so sorry,' she said.

Riding in the ambulance, the crime scene growing more and more distant only made the horrors grow with every passing moment. The full impact of taking another person's life was beginning to overwhelm her. She was about to be plunged into a world of guilt and remorse from which there is no escape.

I didn't blame her. She was fifteen years old. A frightened child given a gun like it was a reassurance button; just switch it on when scared. Only there wasn't a switch, there was a trigger and a bullet.

At least my intervention had saved her from the damnation of a murder charge, a trial, probable incarceration and a life destroyed. I couldn't stop the demons in her mind but I could stop the law from getting hold of her. The cops could blow all the smoke they wanted but it was over. Casey had texted me.

got it

I erased the text and kept holding her hand. She was sobbing now, deep, wracking sobs that would carry through for years to come.

24

Oh Sweet Saviour, Bless You, Bless You a Thousand Times

I STOOD OUT THE FRONT OF THE HOSPITAL. HENNA WAS under the care of doctors. She had stopped crying. I reminded her of the mantra. She didn't need reminding. Despite the demons, survival had taken its place at the head of the rank. Two angry-looking cops had arrived to take down her record of interview when the doctors would allow it. They'd get nothing. They walked around me, careful not to get too close.

A car pulled up and parked in the handicapped zone. Cliff jumped out and ran towards me.

'Bless you, thank you, bless you,' he said.

I wanted to hit him and hurt him but I controlled myself. 'You almost destroyed your daughter's life, you idiot.'

I grabbed him and thrust him against the wall of the building. 'There is a young man dead, lying on the side of the road, shot dead. That's your fault. *You* killed him. *You* are responsible for having taken a life. *You* put the gun in her hands. *You* shot the bullet. She's fifteen, for God's sake.' I let go of him and pushed him away in disgust.

'I'm sorry,' he blubbered.

'Make amends,' I said. 'Find out who he was; his girlfriend, his parents, his drinking buddies. Find them all. Each one of them. You, you alone. Go see them. Apologise. Atone. And not just the once. Take note of the time and day he died and put it in your diary so you remember, every year.'

He was nodding.

'And if you don't I will come after you,' I said and walked away. I was shaking. I needed a drink. I don't drink, not anymore. I called Angie.

'Darian?'

I didn't reply. I couldn't. She heard me suck in a mountain of air.

'I'll be straight over,' she said and I flipped my phone shut and kept walking.

—

EVERY MORNING AT about four o'clock a boy named Harold rode down Park Street and delivered newspapers. Harold was saving for an iPhone and his mum, who couldn't afford it, living on her own and barely paying the rent, told him he better get a job, even if he was only thirteen. At age thirteen there's pretty much only one job available and that's what Harold was doing now. He had, after three months, perfected a backward swing whereby he'd cycle past the house and, just as he was reaching the house next to it, hurl the rolled up copy of the *Sunshine Coast Daily* across his left shoulder with his right arm. Occasionally he'd hear a 'thud' which meant his throw was too strong, that the rolled up newspaper had hit the house and not the lawn but nobody ever complained. It was four in the morning and everyone was asleep.

Harold liked Park Street; it was the easiest street on his run. That's because every house got the paper, not like Duck Street, which was the worst, where he kept on forgetting if it was number eight or twenty-eight or eighteen that got the paper and Cliff, his boss, would yell at him; by the time he got back to the newsagent they had rung up to complain.

Harold's newspaper run lasted three hours.

—

I SO WANT to kill that fucking newspaper boy. But occasionally, my friends, you may have to put up with extremely annoying wasps, like the newspaper boy who rides past my house every day. Wasps are people who get in the way of your fun. They really should all be killed and disposed of but you can't because if you did you would draw attention to yourself. I have two wasps. Harold and my next door neighbour. They interrupt me. But I deal with it.

I used to love love love creeping into the girls' room at about four in the morning (note: don't be worried if your sleep patterns go weird on you when you have a package at home; run with the fun, that's what I say) and wake up the girl with a big fright and do lots of fun things but in the middle of it, every now and then, not always but enough times to make me really very fucking angry, I'd hear this thudding sound at the side of my house.

Let me tell you: the first time this happened I thought the world was going to explode with an earthquake like in that old movie *Krakatoa, East of Java* but when I ran out to the front room and looked through the window I see this kid on a bike delivering newspapers like he was the fucking Green Hornet or something. And then the next day the kid did it again. That's when, friends, I realised the lesson. Put up with wasps. If I complained I'd be noticed. First rule of the craft? Be normal. That means: don't be noticed. *Hi*, I would have said, *your newspaperboy is really annoying. Oh*, they would have said, *what's your name and where do you live?* Get it?

The absolute most worst thing about a wasp is that you have to live to *their* routine. I have to endure that little shit riding his fucking bicycle every morning. I had to change my ways.

One day that will change. One day I *will* kill him.

For those of you who might ask *why didn't you just cancel the newspaper delivery, Winston?* the answer is this: it's not an option, friends.

That's because the local newspapers write about your triumphs. That's where the legend grows. Without the local newspapers writing about the packages mounting up the people don't get scared. They have to be scared and have to start thinking that you are God God God because when you die and release to the world all the details of your Awesome Life you will become immortal.

—

I'M NOT GOING into the girls' room this morning. I'm getting sick of Helen. Sometimes this happens early, my brothers and sisters. It will always happen. Eventually. Sometimes, though, the package just isn't up to scratch, as my mum would say. It's like when you get a new game and play it a few times and get bored. That's me with Helen now. After we came home the other night I just tied her to the bed again. I didn't really want to do anything with her but then I thought I'd fuck her, which I did. Then I went back to bed and slept like a soldier.

Routine is very important, friends. I have lots of routines. I have morning and afternoon routines and night routines with the packages. But it's also important that you are flexible, like when you have to deal with wasps. This morning's newspaper front-page story was all about me.

I love it when the newspaper is about me.

Today was special.

Bless you, I said to God and then I said it again. Bless you.

—

ANGIE NUDGED ME. 'Wake up,' she said. I could smell her soft body.

'What time is it because it's too early,' I said, reaching across to bring her to me.

'Darian.'

I sat up. She was holding up the newspaper. On the front page was a story about last night's 'Near-Miss With Killer' and, next to the side-story titled 'Serial Killer Expert: Is He Involved?' was a close-up photo of me, in the back of the ambulance. No photos of Henna, no photos of the dead kid, just a wide-angle shot of the crime scene and close-up of Darian Richards, 'well known as Australia's leading expert at solving serial-killer crimes'.

I stopped staring at Angie's naked body as she sat on my chest and read from the paper. My mind was racing: where would this lead?

'A source from the Victoria Police said that Richards, who abruptly resigned a year ago and relocated to Noosaville, was, among all homicide investigators, the absolute best there is.'

—

I AM THE best. I am. The absolute best. Only the best can try to catch the best. Welcome and bless you a thousand times, bless you. You cannot catch me but I can show you how awesome I really am. You'll understand. You'll appreciate. Friends, we now have an audience.

PART II

PART II

'In violence, too, we turn
against ourselves...'

DANTE ALIGHIERI - 'INFERNO'

25

Families of Victims

AFTER ANGIE FINISHED READING THE NEWS REPORT A SECOND time, I heard the sounds of crunching gravel: a car pulling up outside, in my yard. It was not yet five in the morning.

Angie looked panicked.

'Don't worry,' I said, climbing out of bed and dragging on a pair of jeans, 'it's not the cops and it's not the press; too early.'

I told her to stay in bed and closed the door behind me as I walked out of the room. I could live with the glare of the press but not her; that would be catastrophic. She knew I'd protect her anonymity with lethal conviction, if required.

As I opened the front door and walked outside I knew who it was out there. I'd recognised the desperation in the sounds of the car's brakes as it ground to a hard stop. It would be one of the missing girls' parents.

It was all of them, except Sheryl Brown. The rest had parked out on the street. They stood in my yard like something from *The Magnificent Seven*. In an angry line. Wanting answers.

'Who the fuck do you think you are?' was their opening comment, made by a little guy in tight shorts and a T-shirt that advertised Foster's beer. Izzie's dad. He was their representative, their spokesperson, and by the looks on the faces of the others, self-chosen. In other words, he was the loudest. They were all grieving, all confused, all living in a terrible world of limbo, so I made an effort to keep my attitude in check.

'I'm Darian Richards. You've no doubt come because of the story in today's paper–'

'Why weren't we told?' interrupted Izzie's dad. I seemed to recall his name was Alf. He looked like an Alf. I wondered if he knew about his daughter's antics.

Even though I could see there was dissent in the ranks about Alf's role as spokesman, there were nods of agreement to his question. Why *hadn't* they been told what I was up to?

'I'm not doing this officially. I'm sure you're all well aware that newspapers get things wrong; the story in today's paper is a good example of that–'

'Was it him?' asked one of the mothers. I wasn't quite sure whose mother she was but I was beginning to feel sure I wasn't going to be able to finish a sentence.

'The man who was shot,' she went on, 'was it *him*?'

Before I answered that, I needed to clarify a few things. 'I'm not officially involved. You'll have to direct those questions to the police–'

She was about to interrupt me again, but I didn't let her: 'But,' I added forcefully, which silenced her, 'I very much doubt that the young man killed last night is the person the police are looking for.'

'So we're not important, eh? That the fuckin' deal? You don't need to come and talk to us? Talk to fuckin' Sheryl Brown–'

'Alf,' a woman admonished him; Izzie's mother, probably. She was short and stubby, just like him. I could see the aggravation in him causing ripples of anxiety among the others. They were taking steps backwards as if to remove themselves from his anger. Some of them were looking at me with pleading faces, as if to say, *Sorry*.

'*What?*' asked Alf of his wife, spinning around in self-righteous admonishment. 'This bloke here starts to investigate our daughters' disappearances and doesn't ask, doesn't have the fuckin' courtesy to *ask*?'

Point made and without argument, Alf turned back to me and spat out the question, yet again: 'So what gives you the right? What makes you think you can just walk in and investigate our loss without asking, without telling us? Who do you think we are? Eh? Who? Who are *we*?' he asked, thumping his chest.

—

THE SAD TRUTH is they were irrelevant. I didn't need them, I didn't want them. I wasn't going to tell them that, but it was true.

In victimology you learn that through studying the victim you discover information about the killer. A mirror reflection of who they are tells you at least something about who he is. It's important and so basic and obvious some investigators tend to ignore it. Access to the victims is, of course, granted by the ones they've left behind: in this case, the parents in my backyard. But I already had all I needed; all I needed about the girls and his shadow trail with them was on my living-room wall. Of that I was certain.

The Families of Victims, especially when the victims are kids, develop an inevitable clan-like brotherhood, bonded together by the shocking commonality of their loss. Their grief and stupefying incapacity to actually do anything usually morphs into self-importance, self-righteousness and, sadly, eventually destroys the people they once were. When a kid is taken, when a life is taken, everything changes. What you once were is as dead as your child or lover. You're a remnant.

Back on the eighth, when I came up with the idea of assigning different ring tones to different categories of people we'd be dealing with, there was no debate that it was Jimi Hendrix or Neil Young only. I don't do democracy. My word rules. But there was debate when, after we'd assigned 'Purple Haze' to the Commissioner's office and 'Spanish Castle Magic' to informants, we needed to decide on a suitable ring tone for the Families of Victims. Most of the crews argued for 'The Wind Cries Mary' because they quite rightly thought the elegiac lyrics matched the sadness of these people. They were pretty fired up when I overruled them and said no; said it would be 'Hey Joe' with its angry and confronting lyrics about Joe's irrational decision to kill his girlfriend because she'd been with another guy.

They asked me how I could be so heartless.

'The families grieve,' I said. 'Beware emotion, beware sorrow; sorrow is not in our domain. Of course we feel sorry for them but sorrow, regret, sadness – these are not the emotions for the hard warriors of justice.'

Nobody agreed with me, and every time 'Hey Joe' rang out in the office I saw them flinch, which was exactly what I wanted.

—

'Who are we?' he'd asked.

'I don't know,' I said by way of reply, an answer that caused a visible response of shock, consternation, bafflement until I stepped forward to Izzie's dad and said, 'Except for you. Alf. Right?' I held out my hand to shake his.

He blinked away tears. In his eyes flashed fury, and sorrow, deep, prolonged, dreadful sorrow. He took my hand. We shook.

'Darian.'

He just nodded, then released my hand and took a step backwards. I turned to his wife.

'Darian,' I said again, my hand outstretched.

'Angie,' she said. Sometimes, I corrected myself, there *are* coincidences in murder investigations. Angie and Alf: Izzie's mum and dad.

We shook. I moved to the next parent. And the next and the next.

Rob; Curly. Curly and Rob: Marianne – victim number two: aged fourteen, short blonde hair and a gap between her two front teeth that an orthodontist was scheduled to fix, came from and went to school at Maroochydore, a beach town half an hour south from Noosa.

Donna; Neil. Donna and Neil: Jessica – victim number four: aged fourteen, who was taken while I swam nearby, came from Nambour, an old town that was once the hub of the sugar-cane industry; railway tracks from the days when the cane was carried by train through the main street of town are still there.

Johnno; Tera. Tera and Johnno: Carol – victim number five: aged sixteen, long dyed blonde hair, last seen walking to the hairdresser where she was going to have it coloured again because she had a birthday party that Saturday and was embarrassed about the dark regrowth, also came from Nambour.

Juanita; Jim. Jim and Juanita: Brianna – victim number six: aged fourteen, the girl who sang 'Stairway to Heaven' at the school end-of-year concert, lived in Noosaville, eight streets from where we now all stood.

I think they expected me to invite them in, maybe offer them tea. But I was done. I'd paid my respects.

'Thanks for coming,' I said.

'But ...' said Juanita, her words petering out before they found form and content.

I knew she didn't know what it was she wanted to say. I said it for them: 'You're all living in a world of hope and despair, I know that, I understand, but the cops are doing a great job, they're on this twenty-four seven. Me, I'm just a retired homicide detective. If I can provide help or advice to the official investigation, I will. I wish I had more to say, I wish I had answers. But I don't.'

'You told Sheryl Brown that the girls are all dead.' Juanita again. Their real spokesperson was emerging.

'I lied,' I lied. 'Don't give up hope.' They were so relieved nobody thought to ask me why I lied to Sheryl, which was good because I hadn't quite arrived at an answer.

'Can we come and see you?' Juanita again. The question all of them wanted to ask.

No way. Families of Victims just get in the way. There's a reason cops tell people to stay home, wait by the phone, so we know where you are. It means, 'Leave me alone because unfortunately, you're a distraction.'

'Best not. I wish I could say yes but, you know, this is not my investigation, not by a long shot. I'm working to the lead of the cops. They're running this. Twenty-four seven. They'll always know more than I do.'

They believed me – except for Juanita, whose stare told me she knew bullshit a year away – and thanked me. Some even blessed me before they silently left. Even the sound of Alf's car reversing from the yard was soft and respectful. It was like a sweet Sunday morning.

When I went back inside Angie was sitting cross-legged on the bed, still tremendously naked, reading her stars from the newspaper. Capricorn.

'You're really good,' she said in genuine approval, having heard everything that was said outside.

'I am,' I said, removing my jeans.

She held up my mobile phone. 'What's "gofish" mean?'

26

Step 1: Retreat From Target

Jenny G does not know I exist. I, on the other hand, know a lot about Jenny G. I know where she lives, I know her mum's a teacher at the primary school and her dad is a concreter. His name's Rocky. Jenny G is twelve and her little boobies are like little buds – I know because I saw them.

Supré in Noosa Civic is totally the best because you can sit on the wooden bench out near the front of Big W and you get a straight view through the front doors of the shop, past all the racks of clothes into the change rooms. You can see the girls' legs up past their ankles, not much but a bit. I measured it with my fingers. I reckon you get about five inches. That's halfway between ankle and knee. The doors in the change room at Supré in Noosa Civic are also totally awesome because they are saloon doors and they never totally shut, like, all closed, so there's always a bit of space where you can see flashes of pink and things. If I had a telescope I could sit on that bench and I would see cunt. But I can't take a telescope in and use it nor can I take in binoculars or even a telephoto lens on my Nikon camera because people would see me and know that I was perving and that would be me gone.

Cotton On in the Sunshine Plaza which is a ginormous mall is totally cool because you can also sit on a bench and get a clean view through the shop to the change room. Once I saw a girl totally nude. Just for, like, a millisecond but that was enough. That was Brianna, wasn't it? Or Jessica? Fuck. Can't remember their stupid names. Doesn't matter. After they come and stay with me we don't really use names. I think names are stupid. I hate my name.

Anyway, this horrible fat girl who I reckon was a Greek moved the bargain rack and I couldn't see in through the shop anymore. I went and pretended I was looking in at the shop next to it and accidentally on purpose bumped the rack which was on wheels and then I had a clean clear view again and after I went back and sat down I looked and watched Jenny G who I followed here from her school because it was after school when all this happened as she tried on two red singlets. I didn't like them. I thought they were common. I thought they would make her look like a slut. I followed her as she went into the change room and just as she was taking off her T-shirt, up over her shoulders and head, the doors to the change room opened, for a little second, longer than a millisecond – a real second, maybe two or even three – as if God had blown them open like a gust of wind and that's when I saw her boobies and her tiny little red nipple buds and knew then that she and me would be together forever.

That's when you have to engage in the exciting but very hard bit: step back. Soldiers call it 'disengage'. Retreat is another word to describe it. What it means is that I go into hiding so there's no way she knows I'm shadowing her. Retreat from target actually means the opposite: engage with target but only via disengagement. It's really clever and it always works.

I retreated from target Jenny G two weeks ago. Then, after I decided to be real clever and take Helen-big-tits, I put Jenny G on the backburner and told myself that I would come take her soon, not now. But now I am going to take her.

Step 2: Track the Target. Done that.

Step 3: Establish Target's Schedule. Done that too.

Step 4: Determine when to Steal Target. Done that also.

Step 5: Determine Likely Danger and Potential Problems. Did that. But now that is under review. That's because of my new friend with the silly name of Darian.

That article about him got me so excited I went in and told Helen and as I told her I got even more excited which made me pull out the Tingle and fuck her but she went unconscious on me. I guess she fainted. I dunno. I was gunna stab her in the ankle but I didn't feel like it. I wonder if Jenny G would like being fucked like this. I bet she will and I bet she'll like *Pocahontas* too.

27

Sparkie

'I THINK WE HAVE A CONNECTION,' SAID ISOSCELES, HIS VOICE resonating with urgency. 'Likelihood: strong.'

gofish. Angie kissed me on the top of my head and slid out of the house. I needed her last night, I needed the rational calm of a person with sense and grace. If it had not been for her, I might have gone next door and hurled Janice-something's dog into the river.

It felt good to be alone now but it wouldn't last; not with my newfound front-page fame. I wondered if Sil the Onion would give me a discount on his fish and chips or if the spider-legged crab man would reduce the cost of the muddies.

'Tell me,' I replied.

'Oh! Look at that,' I heard from the other end, wondering what distraction we'd be going to now.

'You're on the front page of the local newspaper up there. I would have seen that a lot earlier were it not for my current habit of reading *L'Hebdo Madaire du Burkina* – that's one of the local newspapers in Burkina Faso, did you know that? – an excellent broadsheet, I might add. Dear me: you *did* get into a little trouble last night. How are our friends at the constabulary? Out surfing?'

He giggled.

'Can we go back to the connection?' I asked.

'Indeed, Darian, indeed. A gentleman by the name of Winston Daniel James Promise – I'm sending you his details now – was questioned by the North Brisbane CIB after being observed spending an unseemly period of time outside a private girls' school in the suburb of Ascot.'

'Charges?'

'Nothing. Just the record of interview.'

'Date?'

'Six years ago.'

This was so far under the radar of a normal police list, so much a breach of a person's privacy that I had to comment: 'Impressive work.'

'You are speaking to a very clever person,' he affirmed without irony.

In policing terms there is a phrase known as Pre-P. It refers to the time before 1988 when you could make a phone call and request information on somebody who you thought might have abducted a child and be holding them in their home – and you would get the information you'd asked for. You could find out whom they'd been calling, seeing, what they'd been up to – you could, in other words, get a picture of their life. It helped tell you whether your guy was the one or you'd got it wrong. In 1988 the federal government enacted the Privacy Law. That was a black day for law enforcement. Don't get me wrong: I'm the first one to argue the rights of a person to their privacy and I'll be in the front ranks fighting for a person's right to stay silent and hidden – just as long as my murder investigation is not impeded. When I'm on the hunt for a killer, all bets are off and that includes anyone's right to privacy. The days of Pre-P were glory days. Now, to get information about a person you have to put in a request, justify the request, and then you have to wait. Patiently. Maybe you'll have to ask the person's permission to get the information. Queensland, God bless its backward ways, enshrined its Privacy Act in 2009, twenty-one years later. When I lived in Melbourne people used to laugh and mock the barbarians of the north; not us in the police department. Give us back the old days any time.

Guys like me – in fact all good cops – found ways to circumvent this law. Break it. Until the geeks tumbled into our work spaces with their laptops and the cloud to connect to, we had to rely on bribery, mateship and basic threats to get the sort of information I had asked Isosceles to come up with. Anyone with a sex offence against their name. I needed a complete list. Isosceles had it. I had it too.

It was long. Longer than you can possibly imagine.

It was also meaningless. Just a list of names, last known addresses and a catalogue of evil. To breathe life into it we needed to find the connection – in this particular hunt – to a guy who might have worked as an electrician at the Noosa North Shore Dreaming Resort. And Isosceles had found that connection. It was thin, but it was strong. And it was, I suspected, light years ahead of where the official investigation would be.

'Mr Winston Daniel James Promise is currently registered as an employee to a company called Zap Electrics, which was a major contractor at the resort.'

'But nothing more than the complaint at the girls' school?'

'Not for Winston Daniel James. But …'

I felt the surge.

'… Danny Jim Winston was a very naughty boy up until the ripe old age of seventeen. As you know, Darian, the Queensland Juvenile Justice Act of 1992 allowed him to partake in all sorts of inappropriate acts involving his penis and young girls without being registered. Here comes that email now …'

I clicked on it and a list of sex offences perpetrated by our Danny Jim, starting at the age of eight, unfolded before me. Little Danny Jim's identity was protected by the courts, but when he turned eighteen and could no longer hide, he varied his name and went off the radar.

The list was what I expected: indecent exposure, lewd behaviour, inappropriate sexual advances, that sort of thing. Then a gradual escalation to sexual assault and rape. He had been on a trajectory and now, it seemed, he'd developed into a full blown sexual predator of the worst kind.

He was a smart kid, as well. Self-disciplined. Dangerous. I wanted to meet Danny Jim.

I signed off from Isosceles and reached for my phone to text Maria. I'd promised to keep her in the loop. Only if it suited me.

It suited me. Most interviews go down a whole lot better if there's a girl asking the questions. Maria would be perfect for Danny Jim: mature, confident, busty, sexy, a cop. She'd bring out all his anxieties like an allergic reaction to peanuts.

28

LA Woman

'That cocksucker's gunna pay. I'm gunna fuckin' fuck him over till he wishes he never set foot in this town.'

Ha-ha-ha-ha-ha.

Maria laughed along with the rest of them. 'Pinning on a smile' as her mum would say. Beneath the smile was contempt. Jackson Toyne, or Jack as she preferred to be called, was perched on one of the desks in 'the room', the large, scrambled space that was Crime Investigation. Once ordered, it was now a jumble of desks and a free-for-all with cops coming and going. Over by the door to the toilet were the Fisheries guys. The room was, of course, dominated by the 'special squad' running Operation Blonde, the huge weight of the search for the serial killer.

Maria sat at her desk on the outer edge of Operation Blonde and pretended to be part of the gang as they were held enraptured by Jack's cataloguing of vengeance. It was her day off but she had been called in for a briefing.

'Fuckin' foot touches the street: bang, I'm gunna get him for jaywalking. If I hear him cough: bang, I'm gunna do him for urinating in public.'

Ha-ha-ha-ha-ha.

'And you know what? I got a mate in the tax office and I'm gunna make sure Mr I'm The Big Expert From Melbourne is gunna get his arse audited from now to eternity.'

Ha-ha-ha-ha-ha.

'I'm gunna run that cocksucker outta town. He's gunna wish

he never set foot up here, he's gunna wish he never fucked with us. Right?'

Right!

From around the time she was fifteen, guys had tried to crack onto Maria by telling her she was pretty or, mostly, sexy. Despite the conviction she was plain, in need of Botox, a boob job, a chin job and a severe diet, Maria knew that Jack was not in her league – or at least she knew that's what Jack thought, and that Jack hated her for it. Jack was cute but had the desperation of a person needing to fit in. Jack put out; she'd even slept with a couple of the guys to try to become part of the group. Dumb, Maria knew.

However, sometimes, like now, Maria would look at Toyne and find it impossible to deny the twinge of jealousy as she sat on the desk with eight of the guys surrounding her, lapping up her raucous but pathetic aftermath of last night's humiliation.

Everyone wanted to get Darian. He'd assaulted their manliness, of which there was an abundance in the station, most of it radiating from Jack the girl.

Her phone buzzed with an incoming text.

gofish

It had come from Agnew. To preserve anonymity and to give him a name that reflected how she felt about the Big Expert From Melbourne, she'd asked Casey who was the worst, most appalling person he could think of. While her lover's mind was vast and eclectic, it usually defaulted to American politics.

'Easy, babe: Spiro Agnew, Nixon's vice-president who resigned for evading income tax, and supposedly took bribes as well. Big-nosed, fat, bald arsehole.'

Perfect. As she plugged the letters into her phone Casey had continued for quite some time about the balance between Nixon's criminality and Agnew's but, love him though she did, she hadn't listened. Her mind was contemplating the position Agnew had put her in.

She looked at her colleagues one by one. Was it him? Or him? Indeed, could it be Jack, the girl? Female serial killers are rare but they exist.

Billy was the likeliest choice. He'd been the one who constantly talked about how sexy the chickies were, how he'd love to fuck a 'little blonde girlie'. Fat Adam had overheard the talk and suspended Billy for a week, almost threw him out with an official lodgement of conduct unbecoming. But, like everything in here, it was a boys' club and the loyalty to a mate was stronger than the perversity of expressions of paedophilia by one of the cops searching for a paedophile.

'Hey Maria: hello!'

She snapped out of her reverie and realised she'd been staring at Billy.

She quickly smiled and covered: 'You left out Creating a Public Nuisance. That's a real easy one,' she said and they all laughed, even Jack, although her laugh seemed forced.

She deleted the text message and sat, waiting. They were to have an eleven o'clock briefing from the boss. He was, as usual, late. Probably eating breakfast at McDonald's.

Even though Agnew had poisoned her in the most repulsive – but clever – way imaginable, even though her loyalties lay with the badge she proudly wore and with the people in this room, she felt a surge of adrenaline with the message from her secret-sharer. She was so far ahead of the others it made her dizzy to think about it. Darian was a prick in the way he used her but he was brilliant, he and the extraordinarily odd Isosceles. Maria wallowed in the eccentricity of her lover but Isosceles had introduced her to a new level: a world of investigative genius that none of her colleagues would ever experience, let alone appreciate.

For that – and for the secret buzz – she had Darian to grudgingly thank.

'Learn from the best,' her mum always said. 'If they cross your path and if they can teach you things and if they'll allow you to shadow them, follow,' her mum had said.

It had taken Maria two years to tell her mum she wanted to be a cop. She was scared. Her mum had been one of the first female detectives in Queensland. That was in the 1980s, when Queensland was still a backward, narrow-minded, nasty, corrupt, bible-bashing place ruled by fat criminals dressed as God-fearing, people-loving politicians and their tribes of equally fat, corrupt male followers. Old men. All men.

In their minds women in Queensland were good for two things: cooking and fucking. The first female cops in Queensland were Ellen O'Donnell and Zara Dane, who both joined at the same time in 1931. Throughout their lifetime careers on the force, they were never sworn in. In 1984 Lorelle Saunders was the first woman to become a detective in Queensland. Her male brethren congratulated her on this milestone by charging her with conspiracy to murder her lover, a cop, a charge of which she was innocent. Suspended without pay, thrown into jail on another trumped-up charge, she begged to be put into solitary confinement where she languished until the justice system finally exonerated her. Welcome to the club, sister. Maria's mum became a detective around the same time and watched with horror at the way the boys in the Queensland Police Force, from the very top to the very bottom, dealt with the chicks.

'If only we lived in LA,' her mum would say. More than a town, it was a symbol: Los Angeles, where the first woman to become a cop, Alice Stebbins Wells, was granted the power of arrest in 1910.

More than a hundred years later, Maria sat looking around the room, at Jack sitting on the desk with her hurls of masculine threats amid the boys, and wondered what had changed, really, and if by the time she retired in another thirty or forty years' time, what, if anything, might *have* changed. Nothing, she figured. Nothing at all.

—

MARIA HADN'T GONE to the records yet. She'd deliberately stayed away from finding out who filled in the logbook and disguised a sixty-eight minute gap. She thought about it every day. Every day she told herself today but never did anything about it, shirked the call, put it off until the next day. She knew she'd eventually succumb. Just not yet.

For the time being and for the foreseeable future, not knowing, she told herself, was better than the inevitable change to her world that the knowledge would bring.

Adam came in and told them about the incident the night before in which a twenty-two-year-old man was shot dead; told them the girl at the scene when the police arrived, whose name was Henna, had been eliminated as a suspect; told them to keep their eyes and ears to the ground in trying to solve the killing. No mention of the ex-cop they were all thinking about. Adam then asked for the latest on Blonde. Billy told the group one of the psychics had rung and wanted to go back into the forest near Fig Tree Point because he thought the bodies were still there – about a hundred metres from where they'd looked with him last month.

Nobody laughed. This is where the investigation had led: psychics in the forest.

29

The Woman in the Park

PATIENCE, MY BROTHERS AND SISTERS, IS VERY IMPORTANT. You must never be impatient. I learnt this early on, I learnt this from sitting in the bamboo. You must be very patient and not at all impatient when you are waiting to secure the package. You will have followed her and you will know what her routine is and you will have planned, in great detail friends, when and where is best. You will have bought your van and you might have even put some sort of sign on it to say that you are a plumber or an electrician so that you can blend in. You'll be parked and waiting for the girl to appear, as you've planned. Now hear this friends: you will be agitated. You will be really very excited because of all the fun fun fun things you have planned to be doing with her. It's like when you were six and you wake up on Christmas morning or on your birthday. Same thing. But with the package you have the fun of Christmas or the birthday for days and days, until you get sick of her and then you get rid of her. So it's better.

Because you're all excited you could get impatient and that, friends, is where you might make a mistake, that's when you might do something silly and bring attention to yourself.

Your guide, the Awesome One, taught himself how to be patient when he was very young. This he did by walking across the road from where he lived into the park and he would sit in the big forest of bamboo. Like a warrior. And not move. Like a sniper. And watch and wait. Like a soldier.

—

AT THE MOMENT I am sitting in my van. Watching, waiting. In nine minutes' time Jenny G is going to turn the corner and walk towards me. I must be still and I must blend in. I must be patient and wait as if I was having an afternoon tea break or if I was checking a map to figure out a direction because I might be lost.

—

FRIENDS, LISTEN CLOSELY.

Many times people think I am a child and it is true that, even in our journey together you too may have said, *Winston acts like a six-year-old kid with his love of Disney cartoon movies; how could he also be such a commander and a leader and a visionary?* And it is true: I am a child at times and at times I am wise. But it is also true and most important for survival that you know, as I do, when not to be a child, when you must be like the others around you. I am very good at being like others around me, when I need to and take a note on that, brothers and sisters. To survive you must be like a chameleon. I am also very well educated. When my mum thought I was mad she put me into good schools and hired tutors. I am particularly good at history. Surprised? Don't be. I am going to surprise you on a journey many times.

I was boomy from the beginning. Weird kid, dumb kid, fucked kid, mental kid, ugly kid, *'fuck off kid.'* Everywhere I went, everyone I looked at, who looked at me, that's what they thought: fuck off kid, weird kid, dumb kid, ugly kid, fuck off. Gave me the heebie-fucking-wheelies. Didn't know what was going on. I thought I was okay, just plain okay but every time someone looks at you and thinks you're a fucking idiot weirdo dummie creep, you dunno what's going on. Who am I? that's what I'm thinking.

Weird stuff, brothers and sisters, weird stuff going on in my head. And then I found her. Everything clicked and went *hello, you're home now.*

Washington chopped down a tree. That's how it began for him. Charlie Manson listened to a Beatles song. That's how it began for him. I found a woman in a park and that's how it began for me.

AT NIGHT THE park got all quiet and there was all this bamboo which was wide and deep and really high and that's where I sat. In it I felt I was in a forest. Nobody could see me but I could see everything. Sometimes I felt like I was waiting for the enemy to appear out of the dark. I'd sit in the bamboo and wouldn't move for hours. I'd hold my breath and stay real, real still. This is what warriors do.

Most nights it was just me because the park was pretty small and was in a little suburb where the nice people drove home and watched TV. But one night there was a person there. A body, lying on the grass under this big huge pine tree. The body was there when I moved into position. At first I didn't see it but after a while of sitting in the bamboo and holding my breath and staring to see if there was an enemy advancing I saw it.

It was a woman. She didn't move. It took me about five minutes to figure it out. It was just me and her. It was real dark this night. That's because some kids had broken the lights in the park over Christmas. I watched them, from my place in the bamboo, as they yahooed around the park, drunk, pricks, throwing rocks at the lights. Smash smash smash. They thought they were clever. I wanted to shoot them with an M16 to show them who was clever.

At first I thought she was dead but after watching her for a while I figured out that she was alive. Maybe she was drugged or maybe she was sleeping but I could tell that she had bombed out. The way she was lying and where she was, on the grass. If she was like a homeless person she wouldn't be in the open like she was. She'd be curled up under shelter. She'd be lying near the toilet block or she'd have a blanket or something. And homeless people move around because they're uncomfortable which is what you'd expect if you had to sleep in a park. But she looked like she was real comfortable, like she was in a bed of clouds, friends, a bed of clouds.

I crept out of the bamboo forest. I was wearing my camo's. I looked around me like a hunter or one of those Viet Cong dudes when they came out of the tunnels. The park was ringed by four little streets. We lived across the road from it in one of the nice houses, next to all the other nice houses and because it was real late, like about two in the morning there were no cars on the streets and no sounds or lights from the houses. It was just me and her.

She was lying on her back. She was pretty and had long dark brown hair. She had a little red dress on, like the sort that chicks wear when they go out to parties or get drunk on the town. She had a sparkly purse and high heel shoes. She was older than me. About twenty-five I thought. My mum would have called her a slut.

So I walked around her a bit and checked to make sure that no-one was around and could see me do what I was going to do and then when the coast was all clear I knelt down in front of her and lifted up her dress and pulled down her blue undies and undid my belt and my zipper and pulled out my dick and fucked her while she lay there and didn't move.

She wasn't the first chick I fucked but she was the first and only, my friends, who slept through it. I'm not sure if I recommend it, brothers. It's weird. But I was fourteen and it did give me some terrific insight into the World of the Awesome. She just lay there under me and, to be truthful, I was a bit freaked out. Not so much by fucking her in the park because it was quiet and dead all around me but because she didn't move around a lot and she didn't look at me. Now, when I'm fucking the packages, I get to feel them trying to break free of the binding around their wrists and ankles and they look up at me with big fear in their eyes which I love love love.

So I just fucked her like I guess you would cut open a frog and then I got up and did up my pants and left her. I was sure it was that date rape drug thing that makes chicks go all dead but not really dead. She also smelt of alcohol. And she had some sort of sticky sweet stuff in her hair like rum and coke had splashed up in her face. She was real pretty.

—

If you went into a park and found a PlayStation hooked up and ready to go, would you leave it there? If you found an Xbox?

What's the point? You wouldn't, would you? You'd play on it and have fun. Same with the nude woman, I thought, as I was about to walk across the street into mum's home. Why just leave her there when I could be having more fun?

—

THE SECOND TIME was better and it was in the second time that the Awesome World came to me. This, friends, was the start of the journey.

She hadn't moved. Still the park was empty except for the two of us. I could hear this big storm coming in, from up Noosa way. Up north. There was wind in the park now and I could hear the forest of bamboo trees banging against each other. Time to get you nude I said.

Friends, I would also advise that you carry a Swiss army knife at all times. You never know when you'll need it. They are very useful tools. Sometimes I use them to cut ropes or stab the packages in that little fleshy bit next to the ankle but on this night I used it to cut open her red dress. They are really sharp and the blade just slithered right through the material, from the neck to the bottom and then I just folded it open. Her blue undies were still on the ground, from where I'd tossed them before. Her bra was red too. Have you tried taking a bra off? Forget it. Use the knife. Hold up the bra at that middle point between the breasts and cut. Pop. Easy. Folded each half over on each side of her.

Now she was all nude and Big Winnie standing above her, like a tower.

You know, it was like four in the morning and I had her and the park all to myself. I didn't rush and there's a lesson in that: enjoy what you do. Take your time. Different from being patient. That's when you are excited. That's control. This is enjoying the moment. Making the most of something good. Remember that. I don't want any of you to miss out on some of the pleasures that await you. The craft is fun. Enjoy it.

So I started and then I stopped, still with my dick inside her. I looked into her eyes which were sort of half sleepy now, half dead.

'Hey,' I shouted at her.
Didn't move.
'Hey, you,' I shouted at her.
Nothing.
'Hey, I'm fucking you,' I said.
Nothing.

I could do anything with the chick and get away with it. Power, brothers and sisters. This was the biggest rush I'd ever had, better than all the other times when I'd raped those other chicks.

I kissed her. She had red lipstick on and it was smeared on one side of her face. Drunken, drugged out bitch. Bet she'd been putting it out to guys in a bar somewhere in the city. Well, now she was getting what she deserved. I grabbed her hair and pulled it.

'Hey,' I shouted.
She moved like a little bit and I pulled it even tighter.
Nothing. So I bit her on the cheek.
'Hey, I am fucking you, bitch. Maybe I'll kill you too.'
Nothing. Awesome, just awesome.

—

I ROLLED HER over and started fucking from behind. But, friends, there was a problem and it was this: where did I have my orgasm? In what part of her would she receive my blast, my force, my power? She was all mine and I had a choice. Because, my brothers and sisters, I was feeling it. The nude woman, she didn't feel it. She just breathed in and out and occasionally she groaned. Sometimes I leant down and put my head against hers to see if she was waking up. But she didn't.

I rolled her onto her back again.

I moved on my hands and knees so that I was kneeling at the top of her. I took her head with both hands and moved it so that she faced me. She had this red lipstick smeared across her cheek like a gash, like as if I'd sliced her with a knife. There was black make-up around her eyes, and dribble on the edge of her mouth. I lent down and licked it off. Swallowed it but couldn't taste anything.

Her head was real heavy. I laid her out like a doll. She was lying exactly as I wanted. I opened her mouth with my fingers.

The mouth my brothers, this is where I was going to have my orgasm.

—

AND I DID. Then I laid her head back down on the grass. She was beautiful, she was my princess. I told her I loved her.

Then I left.

I sat in the bamboo. I watched her. Soon, I knew, it would be dawn. We'd had fun, the sleeping woman and me but now I wanted to see her wake up. She'd either wake up herself or someone would see her and call the cops. Whatever, but I'd be there, watching. I really wanted to see the look on her face when she woke up and realised she was nude, that her clothes had been cut off. Would she know that she'd been fucked? Would she know that someone had had an orgasm in her mouth?

It was really funny but I had to be real strong my brothers and sisters, as I sat there, still and silent. Like a Samurai.

But then, after about ten minutes, I had this new feeling come over me.

I had to fuck her again. I had to, had to, had to.

—

I WENT BACK to her. There was probably another hour before people came out of their houses, those early-morning people who go power walking or dog walking.

I had a name for her now. Tingle.

Brothers and sisters, this was a terrible moment. I unzipped my pants again and pulled out my dick. I fell to my knees, so desperate was I to fuck her. I was overrun with the urge. It was beyond anything else I'd ever felt.

But as I started to rub it up against her, ready to force myself inside her, can you imagine what happened?

I went limp. This was shocking. What had happened? More important, friends: how could I fix it? I sat down on the grass and looked up into the sky. I thought about nude women. Different types of nude women.

I heard a moan and turned around.

She had changed. She was blonde, almost golden and her body was different. Her legs were thin and her breasts were small. Petite. In fact they looked as if they had just begun to grow. They were little mounds and her nipples were buds. I felt my dick grow hard, brothers, and I felt the urge return, sisters, even stronger than before, the need to fuck her and come inside her, to take her body and hold it tight in a grip she could not escape from.

Her face was different because, like the rest of her, it was the face of a girl and not of a woman. A beautiful little girl with blue eyes that looked into mine with longing.

And her name was Jenny G.

Look at her: all pretty and perky, all ready for the taking.

Ready?

Roger that, captain.

Darian? Ready?

Roger that, captain; silence on the deck. No incoming from Mr Darian.

Not for long.

—

'Hey, excuse me?'

'Yeah?' asked Jenny. *Ow!* she thought, what was–

30

The Stones of Kurtz

I STEPPED OUTSIDE AND INTO THE WAITING GLARE OF THE PRESS.

When I try to find a word that best encapsulates my feelings towards the press – television news crews, reporters, print journalists, basically anyone who is responsible for the dissemination of news – I can't. Words elude me. All I'm left with are images of gunning down people with an AK-47.

While Noosaville is far from the centre of news-gatherers, the story of six missing girls, pretty and blonde, plus a serial offender, psychics in the forest, a stalled investigation and now the meddling of an abruptly-retired-best-there-was ex-detective made a string of news editors send out their herds – coiffed and cool morons all popping inane, impossible-to-answer questions at me. Worse than this ambush was their response to my, 'No comment,' which was to repeat all the same questions, just louder than before.

In my head I heard the burst of the AK-47 and saw a mass slaughter of Texan proportions as I walked towards my Toyota. I climbed in, started the engine and saw more bodies, now mown down by my bullbar.

I tried not to hit any of the press; they're a thin-skinned fraternity, protective of their own. I drove out quickly, knowing they'd all be running to their cars to follow me, turned left, then right, drove too fast, turned left again, parked by the side of a road and waited until I was sure I'd lost them. They're a lazy bunch too; I knew they'd give up looking for me and retire to the nearest pub or just set up boot camp outside my house. If that was the case I'd worry about it later. I needed to focus on the investigation and ignore the flow-on effect of a photo on the front page of the local paper. I should have realised that the killer wouldn't be ignoring it. I should have considered what the article would do to him.

———

'You're the fella searching for the serial killer. What are you doing here?'

That's the flow-on effect.

Zap Electrics was a business run from a tin shed in what's called 'the industrial area' of Noosaville, which is a street that runs for a few kilometres on which, on either side, stand many tin sheds. Inside the Zap Electrics shed was a tiny front office divided in half by a bench. Maria and I stood on one side, a woman in her sixties with a dog on her lap sat on the other. She had today's newspaper folded on the bench, among a scattered pile of phone books and Yellow Pages – it was clear they didn't throw out the old ones at Zap, they just put the new ones on top. I squinted to look at the bottom of the pile to see when this process began: 1997. Languishing in disarray around the surrounds of the office were invoice books, old filing-card systems and, being an electrical shop, an astounding array of wires and old engine parts. Junk. Behind the woman and her dog was the 'shop' where a couple of guys in grime-covered blue overalls toiled over wooden benches upon which were more engines and piles of electrical things.

'We need information about one of your employees,' I said, ignoring her remark about my new-found fame.

Her eyes narrowed. This wasn't going to be easy.

'Why?' she said.

'It's a routine check. We just want to talk to one of your guys,' said Maria.

She'd told me about everyone being called in for a briefing after last night's shooting; Fat Adam keeping the troops focused. It was a good move. Fat Adam wasn't as dumb as I originally thought. I needed to remember that. He'd be anticipating me.

We were both very aware of the dangerous nature of our 'private investigation'. Ex-detective and Senior Constable. We looked official, we sounded official and nobody would be the wiser, but we needed to stay discreet. Fat Adam couldn't stop me, but he'd annihilate her. I can't say she was overwhelmed with love when we met up, but she was jazzed by the news of the sparkie and insisted, without me even asking, that she come along. She'd done her best to dress down; gorgeous girls don't go unnoticed: plain white T-shirt, blue jeans. Her hair was out instead of the official tied-back look. Sunglasses and a baseball cap when we were outside. Very different to the woman in uniform. She could easily pass as a plain-clothes detective.

'What do you want to talk to him about?' asked the woman. Even the dog on her lap was developing an attitude towards us.

'It's just a simple police matter,' answered Maria.

'All the boys are out in the field,' the woman said.

'The surname's Promise,' I said. 'Winston. Dan or Danny. Also possibly Jim. Promise,' I added for good measure. A shower of red sparks shot out from one of the electrical things in the shop behind her like fireworks. The guys pressed on, ignoring the sparks.

She looked at me. She didn't move. The dog stared at me. It didn't move either.

'Can you tell us where we might find him?' asked Maria.

The lack of positive response meant Promise was close to her in some way or she had something to hide. I'm happily ignorant about what it is that an electrician does but I know a little about the time-honoured habit of cooking the books and lying to the tax man. I took a punt: 'We're not interested in anything to do with your books or your accounting records. We just want to know where we can find him.'

Snap. That was it. She looked relieved. The dog looked relieved.

'We ain't done nothing wrong,' she said, confirming they had.

'What's wrong with you then?' joked Maria. 'It's your civil duty to avoid taxes.' She turned to me and laughed. 'You should see my husband's books. Unbelievable what he claims on,' like we were all in it together, a big happy family of tax cheats.

She bought it; she laughed along with Maria but said nothing that would implicate herself.

'So, Promise: is he around?' I asked to get us back on track.

'We don't use him no more,' she said. 'Creepy guy. Lazy, that was his problem. Turn up late, if he ever turned up at all. You get a job, right? You gotta do it, right? You tell the client, "I'll be there at seven," right? You gotta be there at seven, or at least by eight. Right?'

'Can you give us his details? Have you still got his address? And a phone number; that'd be great,' said Maria with a fine sense of focus and control.

She and the dog, whose name was Tweet, leaned across to a metal filing box that sat amid the junk on the bench, and flicked through the cards. Clearly, and no doubt to help confuse the tax man should he ever turn up to Zap, personal records and files had not been computerised.

'Did any of the guys talk to him? Did he have any friends here?'

'Not him. Real loner. Creepy too, like I said. Here you go,' she said as she lifted out a card with biro scribblings across it.

'Creepy how?' I asked before we left.

'Hard to explain,' she said. 'He was always staring at you like he knew all the answers, 'cept no-one had asked a question. And then …' she paused. 'He had, like, eyes that …' Again she paused for a moment and then looked up at us. 'Eyes that looked sort of orange.'

—

WE DROVE DOWN the coast road, with its wide sweeping views of the Coral Sea, through the beach towns of Sunrise, Castaways, Marcus, Peregian and Coolum, passing hordes of backpackers and kids with surf boards and families with suncream and umbrellas until we reached the flatlands of Marcoola, a town recently built around the edges of the local airport and resembling a kilometre-long strip out of New Jersey: sex shops, chemists and Chinese takeaways. This, and our destination – the next town, called

Mudjimba – were the junk yards of the Sunshine Coast. At sea level there were no views of the ocean and, with a firm Green policy of not cutting down the mangroves or the scrubby tea-trees, they were mosquito-infested and swampy. As we drove, mansions and recently built apartment blocks gave way to 1970s council homes built from brick and blocks of flats built from fibro and asbestos sheeting.

Mudjimba is a dump; utterly grim but for the spectacular Mount Coolum, a lonely massive volcanic mountain that dominates the horizon. Like everything on this coast it has a mystique and meaning that we can't possibly understand.

We turned off Suncoast Boulevard and drove through the awful, poverty-stricken streets, the Maroochy River Conservation Park – another dump – looming ahead. We slid up quietly out the front of a three-storey block of flats named Passion. It was rubbish-collection day and one of the bins had toppled over, its contents spilling onto the footpath. We circled it and the millions of flies and walked towards flat number 3.

The place looked like a cheap motel. We knocked on the door. No answer. We knocked again.

'Stick 'em up!'

What? We turned around to find a young woman, about twenty years old, pointing a Second World War .22 rifle at us. She'd come out of the flat next door. Clouds of marijuana smoke wafted out through the door behind her.

We did as instructed. Always best to let the person with the gun assume they have the upper hand.

'You tell the Pirate to go fuck himself,' she said.

'We're not here about the Pirate,' I said. 'We don't know anything about the Pirate. We're looking for the guy who lives in here,' I said, jerking my head in the direction of number 3.

'You're not from the Pirate?'

'Not from the Pirate,' I confirmed.

'Number three,' said Maria. 'The guy from number three.'

'He's weird,' was all she said and kept staring at us suspiciously.

I can only keep my arms in the air for so long and that time had arrived.

'Hey!' I shouted, distracting her long enough to reach out, grab the rifle, take it out of her hands and kick her to the ground. Not hard but hard enough for her to get the point.

'Ow!' she complained as I slid back the bolt on the gun and removed a long, slender bullet especially made for this antique but still deadly weapon. It was hardly a sophisticated set of moves on my part but, even though she had a weapon, she was about as dangerous as Tweet the dog.

'Tell us about the guy from number three,' said Maria.

'Give me my fucking gun back,' she replied.

I kneeled down and said: 'We're cops. We want information. You give it to us, now, or we bust your sorry arse for about twenty violations, starting with attempted murder of a police officer ranging down to possession of marijuana. Now I'm going to count to ten. By the time I get there you're going to nod yes, which means you'll answer all our questions or else you'll be eating lunch from one of the holding cells in Maroochydore. One. Two–'

'Okay, okay!' She got up off the ground, mumbling, 'Prick,' for good measure and then said, 'What do you wanna know? He's weird. I reckon he plays with little kids.'

She told us about a man in his early twenties, tall and thin with blond hair cut 'not short, not long' and 'everyday, ordinary-looking, know what I mean?' who wore jeans and white T-shirts and workman's boots, 'sandy brown, not black, know what I mean?' who had moved into the flat late one night about a year ago. All he carried was a suitcase, 'black, normal-looking, know what I mean?' She didn't know his name. He didn't actually live there, she said, because he came and went at odd hours, 'like, at three in the morning and be gone by five, know what I mean?' She and the Pirate reckoned he was a serial killer who used the flat to chop up his victims, 'although if he did that, the place would smell, wouldn't it, know what I mean?'

'Why do you reckon he plays with little kids?' asked Maria.

She just shrugged and stared into space for a moment. 'Dunno,' she finally said. 'He just looks like he does.'

Keeping the bullet, we returned the rifle and let her go back to the sanctuary of number 4. As she shut herself inside we heard the sound of a six-dollar safety bolt slide across the ten-dollar chipwood door.

We looked at the door handle to number 3. Possible prints. We went back to the Toyota and took out a roll of clear tape, which we applied to the cheap aluminium door handle and then lifted off, carefully placing it face-up on the back seat of the vehicle.

Then we broke in.

Low ceilings, grey walls, small windows with white metal blinds, grey linoleum floors – it had all the charm and character of an empty packet of cigarettes. That was important; the absence of decoration – in any form – told me something about this guy. He was myopic. The space in which he physically lived was unimportant; the colours of his imagination were buried within his head. And elsewhere. Not here. It was as clean and empty and devoid of life as the apartment he used for taking photos in the North Shore resort.

The box of cling wrap at the resort had been devoid of prints; it was most likely this place that he used – for *what?* – would be too. Isosceles rang and told us Promise paid in six-monthly packets of cash that he dropped off at the receptionist's desk twice a year, telling her to send the receipt in the mail. He'd tenanted the flat for eighteen months and had given a fake Brisbane address and used an 18+ ID card as proof of identity.

'I've now got his old Brisbane address too, where he grew up. The house was sold three years ago. A family named Ngo are the current owners. Still tracking for a relative; there is a mother and a stepsister or aunt, I'm not quite sure yet. I haven't found either of them.'

Even if we did find them I wasn't sure our Mr Promise was the sort of kid who wrote home on a regular basis. Danny Jim Promise was the killer, of that I was sure. He was emerging before us but he was clever and he'd anticipated us. Queensland Transport had no record of him, so while presumably he drove a van, to stalk and snatch, he didn't have a licence with a photographic record on it. The 18+ proof-of-age card was useless. It had a photo and a name only. It was what kids used to get into nightclubs and bars. No passport. He had a tax file number so he could ensure his earnings were maximised. He had a Medicare number. But that was the sum total of his official identification: two numbers, leading back to this empty address. He was as well-prepared and as professional as the best of them.

And all this done before I'd made front-page news. Now he'd be acutely alert.

Maria and I searched the flat. It was empty but for a roll of toilet paper in the bathroom and, in the kitchen, two large aluminium pots pushed up against the back of a shelf near a stove that looked like it hadn't been turned on since the 1980s. The only sign of anything out of the ordinary was a plastic container filled with small, round stones and another plastic container, larger, filled with sand.

'So what does he use this place for?' asked Maria.

'Good question.'

We stared at each other, wondering what to do next. I didn't want to go, nor did she, despite the emptiness in which we stood. It was, we both knew, *his* emptiness.

We sat on the floor, soaking it in.

My phone buzzed: Isosceles. Her phone buzzed: Casey.

'Yo,' she said.

Yo? I said: 'Yep?'

'Casey has the hardware, I have the software, the cloud has the spywear. The sparkie's abode in which you sit will soon be under constant surveillance. In colour, I might add. I'm in discussions with a strange woman from the small town of Hamilton in New Zealand about surveying in 3-D imagery–'

I had to cut him off. 'Casey's talking to Maria now,' I said.

Overhearing my conversation, Maria nodded at me and said: 'He's on his way down. Do you want to wait for him?'

'Ask her if he's downloaded the Ouagadougou forest information,' said Isosceles.

Ignoring him and answering her, I said, 'Do we have to?'

'No,' she said to me. 'He can do it on his own–' She stopped and listened to Casey at the other end. Then smiled and said, 'And he'd prefer it if you weren't here because you always tell him what to do and when it comes to anything technical you're a shitbox fuckhead, quote unquote.'

'Has he downloaded the Ouagadougou forest information?' I asked.

'Did you hear that?' she said into her phone, listened for a moment then said to me, 'Gonse looks better than Nakambe.'

'Gonse is better than Nakambe,' I said to Isosceles.

'It is not!' was the response.

'Isosceles,' I said, 'I am going to hang up now.' Which I did.

'Are you doing this crazy African land-locked-country thing with those two?' I asked Maria.

'Not in a million years,' she said. 'Once this is all over I'll just sit at the end of your jetty and catch fish. That's if I'm allowed,' she said.

'Only if you cook them as well,' I answered.

'Deal.'

We smiled. For a moment it was like we were partners. Would it last? I wondered. I looked around the creepy place. Even Fat Adam and the boys from Operation Blonde would have trouble justifying the expense of twenty-four-hour surveillance – three eight-hour shifts; precious people-hours slumped behind the wheel of a car staring into space – on a flat that a possible suspect comes to once in a blue moon.

Cops still do it, though. Surveillance is critical, but it's expensive and the time spent rarely yields a worthy result. In an investigation, of all the actions I would sanction, surveillance was the one that always nagged. Next to 'outcome' invariably I'd write, 'nil'.

But, brilliant if unconventional partners that we were, Maria and I had solved this one and called in the twin eccentrics – the Ouagadougouns – and arranged for unpronounceable machines with cameras and movement sensors and internet connections to filter twenty-four seven into a screen on Isosceles' monitor and, he said, mine as well. I didn't ask how and I didn't care.

Then Maria did something that cops hardly ever do: she spoke openly and honestly about how she felt. 'It's weird. One part of me just wants to get out of this creepy place but another part of me wants to stay, it's like I'm drawn to it, like I can't leave. I know he does bad things in here but it's not that; well, maybe it is, I don't know. I've never felt like this before.'

I stood up. 'Let's get out of here.'

She looked at me as if I'd just reprimanded her. I hadn't but I was being protective.

'These guys, they fuck with your mind. Everyone thinks the worst comes when they're on the other side of the interview table regaling you with their glories of depravation. It's not. Sure, the stories are disgusting, as are their smiles, but they're chained to a chair and going down. Worse are the times like now, when it's just you and him – and he's a ghost – and your imagination.'

She followed me out and I glanced back at the shabby motel-like block of flats. Sand and stones. What did it all mean? I wondered.

I knew I'd find out, eventually. I knew it'd be ugly. But as we left the place he came to, sometimes in the middle of the night, I had no idea just how ugly it would be.

31

Thor's Hammer

I DECIDE I'LL BE REALLY NICE. WHEN WE ARRIVE IN THE GARAGE and it's just me and her in the back of the van, I say, 'Hi, I'm Winston,' and I say, 'You're really special, you're number eight – that doesn't make you special, being number eight, what makes you special is you being twelve because that means you're my youngest, which is going to be really interesting. The other thing that's going to be really interesting is all the fucking, especially the – hey, do you like *Pocahontas*?'

—

HE'S ASKING ME about that old Disney movie? What's going on? thought Jenny. She knew what had befallen her and she knew she was in desperate trouble. But what did it mean when he asked if she liked the old Disney movie?

The man waited for an answer but Jenny couldn't move her head and even if she could she was so frozen with terror that she hadn't heard anything he was saying. It seemed like he was asking her a question but she didn't hear what it was. All she knew was she had woken up in the back of a van, tied up really tight to one of its sides. This guy with creepy orange eyes was kneeling down next to her in the back of the van and talking at her as if everything was normal. She tried to slow down her breathing and listen. Maybe, if she listened, she might figure out a way to escape.

'So I guess that's a no,' he said. 'That's a real shame. But we're going to watch it anyway and maybe you'll change your mind. Now here's where you have to listen carefully. In a little while we're going to go inside and there's a list of rules. They're on the fridge and I'm going to make you read them and you have to remember them. Then, and this is one of the exciting bits, I'm going to introduce you to Helen-big-tits. She's a lot older than you and she's got real tits but you don't have any.'

The man took out a knife. Jenny freaked. Was he going to stab her? She tried to move and escape but he clamped his hand over her head.

'Don't fucking move. You can't anyway but I hate it when you girls try to escape when you can't. It's just really annoying, so don't do it, all right?' he said as he pierced her shirt with the sharp tip of his knife and sliced it open, cutting it in half. 'This is going to be really cool,' he said as he lifted up her bra with his fingers and sliced that in two and tossed each half across her chest. 'Very little boobies. Very cute little boobies. I can't wait to put you and Helen-big-tits together. We are going to do the most amazing things. It's going to be so awesome. Here. Look. This is Thor.'

What is he saying? she thought, panicked.

'I used to call him Tingle but that's a silly name really. Now he's called Thor. That means God's hammer of thunder. That's olden-day stuff. Thor's hammer would crush anything. It was really powerful, like my Thor.'

What is he saying? she thought.

'Say, "Hello Thor."'

She didn't speak, she couldn't speak. She had duct tape around her mouth. He seemed to ignore that. He kept on talking.

'You and Thor are going to be best friends. Now you have to do something, because this isn't just about me, you know. You have to participate. You have to count every time you get the Thor. I guess you're just a little kid so you might not understand what I mean. I'll talk real basic, okay. Don't want any misunderstandings. Misunderstandings lead to mistakes and mistakes lead to immediate death. You don't want that to happen. No point in you getting killed ahead of time because of a silly mistake. Listen carefully. You have to count every time Thor goes inside you and shoots out his bolts of lightning. You have to count each time so that when we get to thirty-two – remember that, thirty-two – you say to me, "Winston, Thor has fucked me thirty-two times now," and then you win a prize. Did you understand what I meant by bolt of lightning? I can't remember being twelve, if I was dumb or not. What I meant was cum, or, let's pretend it's school and we're doing a sex education class, sperm.'

What is he saying? she screamed to herself.

'I've been doing this for a while. I like my routine, even though putting you and Helen-big-tits together is real new and I haven't even taken the photo of Helen-big-tits yet which is way off the grid, but we're going to do that tonight, all three of us, so anyway back to the ritual.'

He reached down and held her.

'This is, like, you know, the beginning,' he said with a smile.

What does he mean? What's happening to me? she cried to herself.

—

GET IT, FRIENDS? Rituals. They're important. Discipline is required to perfect the craft, as is routine or, because the craft is divine, rituals. The package is told what the rules of the house are and she obeys. It's simple and the packages always obey. It makes the fun fun fun all the more fun.

Afterwards I untie the package from her bindings and frog-march her into the house. Jenny G had gone all unconscious on me so I carried her. That was a shame because I didn't get to show her the list of rules that I'd pinned onto the fridge in the kitchen. Doesn't matter. Another time. We have lots of time and remember: be prepared to improvise.

I dumped her on the floor outside the girls' room and opened it. Big surprise Helen!

I dragged Jenny G in and tossed her onto the bed with Helen-big-tits.

'Here,' I said to Helen. I was getting bored now, wanted to go play on my new PlayStation.

Make sure the bindings are tight and secure. I like to have the packages nude. Remember to make sure their mouths are gagged. Basic rule of capture, friends. If you forget that and a girl cries out and is heard and you are caught, well, you're welcome to it, you deserve it.

It was pretty cool seeing both Jenny G and Helen-big-tits lying naked on the bed together. In actual fact I got real excited and wanted to cut off their heads then and there. Put their heads right up in between their open legs. Ha ha.

But I didn't. Because that's for later.

That's a much later step. Stick to the plans. It's okay to improvise, sure, but it's important, I think, to stay focused and stick to what you've got organised. Who knows what might happen if you didn't.

I thought about getting a Nintendo as well as my PlayStation but I really love my PlayStation. Each model gets better and better. Their games are awesome. Soon they'll be 3-D and virtual. I've got all the games but sometimes I get bored after a month or maybe two of playing them. You know what really sucks? Waiting so long for the new releases. I dunno why they aren't faster. Movies come out, new, every week and TV has new things on every night so why can't the games industry get its act together? That's what I want to know. I like to go online and play Warhammer.

Normally I would fuck a new package and I was all tingly about Jenny G but I had to focus. Gotta get the Ida chick.

The Ida chick is only in town for a few days. She's staying at the backpackers on the hill and every day she goes down to the dark and foresty car-park end of Hastings Street, which I like but not a lot because there are lots of people coming and going and snatching girls isn't as simple there as it is in other places. But I know it. Done a snatch there before. Know what the dangers are. (Other people, friends, they're the dangers.)

Ida is real pretty and oh holy God above, it is going to be so amazing watching the most famous and very best homicide investigator unwrap his present and watch his face as she gives him the message. Holy fuck, this is so much more fun now. Now I've got someone who can really appreciate the craft as it's practised by the

Awesome One. I never imagined I'd have someone out there who understands me, someone who can marvel at my work. It's like being a chef and knowing there's a reviewer in the restaurant, or if you made a movie like *Pocahontas* and watched it all dark and silent, like, next to the film reviewer for a newspaper. Awesome. Everything is so much cooler now that Darian and I are in it together.

32

The Gift

I WOKE, AS ALWAYS, AT THREE. I CLIMBED OUT OF BED, MADE A cup of black coffee and ambled towards my front glass sliding doors. I unlocked them to let in the river sounds and breeze and saw, at the bottom of my lawn, a large, shining, silver, cocoon-like thing.

The river's flow occasionally leaves driftwood or palm fronds; even boats, unsecured from their moorings, can turn up at the bottom of my yard on the Noosa River. I stared at the object a moment, drinking my coffee and trying to make out exactly what it was, when it moved. I suddenly knew.

Cling wrap.

He wraps the girls up in cling wrap and there was one at the end of my yard. I bolted. It was the most bizarre sight I'd ever seen: a naked girl, rolled in swathes of plastic film, two clean circular puncture marks from which she could breathe through her nostrils. Beneath the wrapping I could see eyes wide open in terror.

'It's okay,' I quickly said as I lifted her from underneath with both arms and gently, carefully, carried her back up to my house. 'It's all right, you're safe, you're okay,' I kept repeating. 'I'm an ex-cop, you're safe, I'll get you out of this, you're safe.'

I carried her inside and laid her on my couch. The plastic wrapping was thick. Promise must have bought cling wrap by the ton. I grabbed a knife to start cutting it away from her, but before I started I said: 'I'm an ex-cop. My name is Darian. I'm going to cut you free now, okay.'

Every part of her body was wrapped tightly; she couldn't nod or even blink. Her arms were wrapped across her stomach but I managed to ease a space between her thumb and her index finger. I began to cut, ever so gently into that space, all the while talking inanely but reassuringly about being an ex-cop, about her being safe now. She must have been rolled up in about forty layers of cling wrap. I hate the stuff. I always cut my fingers on the metal claw line and can never release the paper tab at the beginning of each roll. I concentrated hard as I edged the knife, gently teasing the film away, cutting through the layers, careful not to cut her, all the while thinking, What's he doing? Why has he done this? Is it some sort of challenge? Will she know? Will he have given her instructions? Did she see him? Where he lives?

I knew our killer would have been careful. He'd taken a huge risk in delivering her body to my house like a gift in the night, but he would have ensured that it was done on his terms. He would not have allowed her to know anything that might lead me to him.

But I'd learned something: he knew the river, and he used the river. It was the only way he could have left her where he did. And he was strong enough to carry her.

I cut through and released her index finger. I grabbed it: human contact. 'This is going to take a while,' I said, 'but I'm going to be as fast as I can. I'm going to cut upwards. I want to get that plastic off your face as quickly as possible.' I cut and unrolled and sliced. After about ten minutes I had arrived at her neck and told her I'd be really careful and she had to be as still as possible. The upper half of her body was now exposed. She'd managed to wrest her arms free and cross them over her breasts. She looked older than his usual takings but I kept my eyes averted, as much as possible, from her nakedness. The last thing she needed was to think she'd been dumped by one pervert into the hands of another; with a knife.

I edged the knife under her chin and gently began to peel away the layers of cling wrap. Every few minutes I'd put the knife down and unfold the wrap, like opening a present. This part took a long time. I was as delicate as possible. Finally I began to remove the film from around her mouth. As soon as her airways were free she began to hyperventilate. 'Slow,' I cautioned her. 'Sit up.' I leaned behind her to unwrap and slice at the rest of the plastic wrapped around her head. I threw it off, discarding it like the rest of the shards, onto the couch and floor around us.

I leaned back and let go of her. She was sucking in air like she'd been trapped under water.

'Just take it slow. Okay? I'm going to go and get you some clothes.' I gave her the knife. 'Use this – carefully – to get that stuff off your legs. Okay?'

She nodded. She was staring at me with a haunted, sunken look in her eyes.

'What's your name?' I asked.

'Ida,' she said. She had an accent, maybe German or Scandinavian.

'I don't know if you heard what I said before. My name is Darian Richards. I'm an ex-cop. You're in safe hands. Okay?'

She nodded. She wasn't looking at me anymore. She was looking at the wall board, at the photos and trails of each of his other victims.

'Ida?' I said. She turned back to face me. She looked like she was about to weep.

'You are alive.'

After a moment she nodded as if just realising that yes, she *was* alive.

—

As I grabbed a T-shirt, boxer shorts, pair of jeans and a belt – my clothes were going to be large on her – I started to run through the angles. He'd most likely assaulted her – raped her – so she might be carrying his DNA. The procedure was to call it in. The team at Operation Blonde needed to be informed, and Ida needed to be whisked off to the local hospital and put through the rape-kit drill, invasive but necessary, then asked a million questions in a formal record of interview. I'd already broken the law by not having called it in straightaway, and I didn't see any immediate need to change tactics.

'Here,' I said as I passed her the clothes, walking back into the living room. She'd fully freed herself of the plastic wrapping and was sitting, huddled, in the corner of the lounge. I turned away and said from over my shoulder, 'I'm going to make you tea and get you some water. You're dehydrated.'

'Thank you,' I heard. She wasn't thanking me for the tea and water. I stared out through the window. It was still dark but I could see the river flowing past at the end of my yard. How did he know where I lived? Had he been tracking me for longer than I imagined? Had he been anticipating me? If others knew I was an ex-homicide cop then why not him? Maybe he even bought his fish and chips from Sil the Onion. It bothered me.

'Are you dressed?' I asked after a moment.

'Yes.' I turned around and crossed the room and pulled up a chair next to her. I gave her a glass of water; she inhaled it.

'Thanks,' she said.

'I'm going to ask you some questions. Let's start with the basics. How old are you?'

'Eighteen.' She was older than his usual victim. Other than that Ida was the right profile: blonde, pretty. Age eighteen, she was an adult. Still, I asked: 'Where are your parents?'

'I'm from Vienna. I am backpacking around Australia. I just arrive in Noosa on Saturday. What day is it?'

'Tuesday.'

She nodded. 'I worry that he drug me and I've been unconscious for longer, but no, he take me last night. Who are these girls?' She was looking at the six victims.

'They're missing,' I said.

She looked away, back to me.

'Because of him?' she asked.

'I want you to tell me what happened but first I have to ask if you were sexually assaulted and, if so, if you would like me to take you to the local hospital?'

She shook her head. I read that to mean 'no hospital'.

'Did he sexually assault you?'

'No.' She was staring intently at me. 'You are a policeman?' she asked.

I nodded. 'I was. Not anymore.'

She looked away from me to the wall, at the faces of the girls. What seemed like quivers of horror swept through her. 'Why did he let me go?' she asked.

'I can't answer that,' I said. 'Let's go back to the beginning. I want to ask you what happened but first, do you want me to call the police?' I had to ask. She was, after all, a victim of a heinous crime. I hoped she'd say no and allow me to question her but I couldn't deny her the right to be taken in by the real authorities.

'No. No police. You promise?' she asked.

You promise? Not my favourite words.

'No police,' I answered. I was about to interrogate a material witness then let her go. If Maria was here she'd freak. Ida's testimony in a trial would be essential, maybe the clincher in convicting Danny Jim. Lucky for me Maria was back at home, curled up in Casey's arms, oblivious to the massive break in our investigation.

'He was so fast. So quick. One minute I am walking through the car park and I hear footsteps behind me and that's it. Black. Next I wake and I am in a van, in the rear of a van, tied up by the wrists and the feet, bound to the side. I cannot move. I turn my head, a little, and I see the back of his head. But not his face. He never shows me his face.'

I kept check of the questions I needed to ask as she rolled through the story, one by one, starting back at: 'Car park: which one? Where were you?'

'At the end of Hastings Street.'

This is the five-star-resort and three-dollar-latte strip, the 5th Avenue of Australia. At the end of Hastings Street is a large car park set amid a forest of pandanus and palms and jacarandas and frangipanis. Kids on the dole, surfers and backpackers park their panel vans or Kombis there. The parking's free, so it has become a makeshift camping ground, with the occasional rousting by cops who try to enforce the don't-sleep-here rule, to little effect. It's a large and sprawling area where the tropical forest is so deep that people and cars are often lost within it.

'I cannot speak because he has wrapped bandage – tape – around my mouth. I think I am going to die.' She looked up at the wall again, at the six girls. 'I didn't know of this.'

Of course not. In a land where tourism is the major industry, why muddy the sunshine with a warning about a serial killer on the loose? Or so the council said. Fat Adam asked for permission to put up warning signs in areas where young girls frequent – the council said no. Fat Adam told them it might save lives – the council said it would scare away tourists. 'Might' versus 'would'. The definite wins.

'What happened next?'

'We drive for maybe twenty minutes or half an hour. I cannot see anything. He does not speak. Then he slows down and the van turns, slowly. We drive very slowly now. We have been driving along roads. I can tell. Stopping at traffic lights, turning corners, but now it is different. I think he is driving me into a driveway.'

'Stop for a second,' I said. 'Are you going up? An incline? Down? Is it steep? Or flat, this driveway?'

'We are driving up. A little. Not steep.'

Good; we're in the suburbs or one of the towns in a half-hour radius from Hastings Street. It's a big area dense with many thousands of houses, but it eliminates the hinterland and the ranges.

'I hear a garage door. Electronic, you know?'

I nodded.

'He waits then he drives in. I hear the garage doors close behind us. It is darker in this place now. Now I think he is going to hurt me.' She paused. I didn't speak, I let her take her time and work through the memory.

She wiped away a tear. I'd put a box of tissues on the table with her tea, discreetly, as if one came with the other. She hadn't noticed, not till now.

'He climbs out of the van. I hear the door close.' She looks at me as if suddenly remembering something. 'It closes softly,' she said. 'I hear another door close. Further away. Not a car door.'

I held up my hand like a traffic cop. 'Have you seen anything at all while being in the back of the van, aside from the back of the van?' I asked.

'No,' she said. 'There are no windows, it is all covered in. And I am on the floor, even if I could turn my head to look out the front it is too high. I see nothing. Only hear.'

Most witnesses are too freaked to recount anything and just desperate to get the hell out of Dodge. Ida was none of that. Danny Jim nicked her because she was blonde and pretty; inadvertently he'd targeted a thorough and intelligent girl.

'Then, after I don't know how long, I hear the door of the van being opened, the front door and I crane my head to get a look to see what is happening but he has opened the other door, the side door, passenger door so I am confused for a minute and then nothing. It is black. I don't remember.'

She stared as if trying to colour in the black space. Without success.

'I hear before I wake. Stretching sounds. It is the plastic. The plastic being stretched out of its box. I don't know what is happening to me. I am face down. I am naked. I am rolled up in plastic. Tight in this plastic. I cannot move. It is stretched tight around my head. I try to breathe but I cannot, I think I am going to die. I start to freak out, I don't know, I can't move. I'm wrapped up but I start to freak out and then he says, "Your nose," and keeps wrapping me up, lifting my body and wrapping the plastic around me, round and round, you know? "Your nose." That is all he says. I can't see him–'

My question answered.

'–because he is at my feet and my head is face down. But I can breathe now.'

As I listen I make mental notes. If she was unconscious and during that time he removed her clothes, did he sexually assault her? More often than not a woman knows after she's come out of a drug-induced coma that something's happened. But what was he using to induce an unconscious state? And, waking up in a tight cocoon of cling wrap would warp your perceptions to the point where the possibility of rape or assault was less important than survival. I wasn't going to spook her about that now, but a morning-after pill and HIV test were necessary.

'Then we are driving again. It is night. We drive for I don't know how long. We stop. When he opens the back of the van I can hear water. Like little waves. It is the river. I know that now, but then … he lifts up my head and puts something on it. I can't see any more.'

'What do you mean?' I asked.

She shrugged. 'Maybe it is a hood. It's loose. I can still breathe but I cannot see anything. He drags me out of the van and kicks me. Here.' She pointed to her back. 'I fall onto the ground. But it's like sand. He picks me up and carries me and then I am in some sort of boat because I can feel that I am floating on water. He is paddling. It is very quiet but I can hear the river. I think he is going to throw me over into the water.'

Again she stopped and stared away for what seemed like a very long time. I waited.

'Then we stop. I hear the sound of the boat on sand. A beach maybe. I can feel it under me.'

Again I held up my hand. 'Is it a wooden boat or metal? Tin?'

She looked at me, trying to remember. 'I don't know. How do you tell?'

I guess you don't, not if you're wrapped up in layers of cling wrap.

'Forget it,' I said.

'He picks me up and carries me. Not far. He places me on the ground. Soft. I can smell grass.' My lawn. 'Still I am face down and have not seen him ever. But now he speaks to me.'

Here it is. Here's the message, the challenge, the boast: his voice.

'He says, "Upriver Darian go to Neebs," and then I hear him walk away and the boat I can hear as he climbs into it and then there is just the sounds of the river. And then later, I don't know how long, you save me.'

Upriver Darian go to Neebs.

—

AND WHEN YOU get there, Darian, you'll find a gift.

Mr-Best-Ever-Homicide-Investigator, I can see you sitting like a good soldier in your living room with my first gift, blonde Ida from Vienna who has rented a motel room for fourteen days of fun-fun-fun, one of those little rooms up on the Noosa hill. Room 1a

Ida. Look at that. Ida is leaning across and giving the-best-ever-homicide-investigator a hug and a kiss for being her hero and saving her life. Hey Ida, 1a Ida, it's Big Winnie here. I can see you with my binoculars. I am comin' back. You're in what's now called Step 5a.

New step. Contingency plan. Remember what I said about improvisation?

5a: distract and disarm the likely danger and potential hazard.

5b is next. That's also new.

5b: return to captured party and kill. I'm not going to take her, because I've already got Helen-big-tits and Jenny G tied up on the bed together and frankly three's a crowd, so that's why I've invented Step 5b.

Disarm, secure and bind, enforce silence then commence rapture. This will be in Room 1a between the hours of four and six because that's when even the loudest of the louts succumb to slumber. All is good and quiet between four and six. And Ida's screams will be all inwards, her mouth taped up real good, which is a bit of a shame because it means I can't mouth-fuck her but that's okay because I've got some super-duper alternatives, new ones for Ida 1a from Vienna. That's where Hitler came from.

Focus.

Roger that.

Look at the time.

Fuck: holy fucking jumping tornadoes. It's going to be dawn in an hour. Get out of here, boyo.

4.30 a.m. Good. The river will be empty for another half-hour, before the rowers and the fishing guys scramble into it. Normal people. Doesn't matter anyway. They all knew me by sight. I'm one of the normal people in a little tinnie going up and down the river as if I was a fisherman or out looking for mud crabs. They wave to me and I wave back.

We're all buddies on the Noosa River.

33

Twelve Into Sixty-Eight Goes ...

IT WAS DEAD. SHE HAD THE WHOLE PLACE TO HERSELF; JUST her and a couple of constables out the front to answer questions from blow-ins off the street. First reports had it being a teenage girl at the wheel, car spiralling out of control on the Bruce Highway near the Eerwah roundabout turn-off, clocking three others including a mini-van. That sounded bad enough to start draining the manpower from the station, then the next report came in. The teenage girl wasn't the driver; she'd been hurtled through the front window and died on impact with a tree. The driver was a boy. Dead on impact. Driving without a licence. There were four others in the car. All under eighteen. No seatbelts. Six empty bottles of vodka on the floor. It got worse. The car had hit another car head on, instantly wiping out a young family – mum, dad and baby – and then side-swiped a ute driven by a plumber who was still alive but, while trying to avoid the collision, rammed a Tarago eight-seater carrying an over-full load from the Under 16 Noosa Girls' Cricket Club.

Maria had volunteered to stay behind and man the fort as the entire clutch of uniforms and detectives ran to their vehicles to help with the catastrophe. Fat Adam had gone. Even the Fisheries guys had offered to help.

Maria had done her time with road carnage. After she tried to calculate how many dead people one drunken kid had created with an 'accident' she allowed her mind to wander to the real reason she stayed behind.

The police filing on Operation Blonde was pretty basic. There was a filing cabinet and three cardboard boxes holding the most recent files. Every now and then someone went through the boxes and filed some papers in the filing cabinet. On their computer system an Excel spreadsheet held an official record of investigation, updated every week by CIB and emailed to Fat Adam as the summary of the previous seven days. Rarely would it be anything more than yet another summary of the last week's summary and the one before that. It wasn't hard to access. All you needed was to be on the secure Noosa Police Station server and know the password. Everyone knew the password. As far as she knew Adam wouldn't even be able to notice who'd logged on. They all did. It had become a distraction, like going on a picnic.

Isosceles had begged her for this information but she'd told him no. She felt enough of a traitor now, just by staring at the computer screen, her fingers poised above the keyboard.

She was just going in to check on one thing. No more. She would find out who logged Izzie Daniels' time of disappearance and then she would log off.

She had to admit she was learning a lot from Darian. It was like an apprenticeship with an expert but she also knew he was using her. He'd tried to poison her mind by making her think that one of her colleagues could be the killer, and he was using the doubt he had created to manipulate her. She knew that when the time came he wanted to shoot the killer dead, not let her take him into custody through the proper channels. He wanted her to be so under his spell that she'd let him do it. No way, Jose; not on her watch. And it *was* her watch. He was the expert, he led the investigation, he'd find the killer, but she would take over. He had the Beretta, sure, but he wouldn't use it on her, of that she was certain. As certain as she was that she *would* use the Glock on him. Not fatally; somewhere soft, in the flesh. She'd already worked it through, she'd already sized him up and practised, in her mind, various angles in which she'd disarm him.

But all that was for later. Now, she had a name to unearth. She pushed aside the minor reports on her desk: a couple of break-ins, a tip-off about marijuana plants next to a pineapple plantation in Yandina, a guy ringing up for the sixth time about his fiancée named Helen who'd gone missing days earlier – twenties, dark-haired, busty – no doubt having second thoughts and holed up in a motel thinking about her future, and countless complaints about hoons on the river and on the beach and on the streets with too much grog and spare time. Nothing important.

Maria hit a few keys and brought up the Operation Blonde spreadsheet. When she opened the online folder of the victim, the page defaulted to an image: Izzie. She wasn't sure if this default was to remind the cops who was who because all the girls looked alike: young, blonde and pretty. Or maybe it was for a deeper and more personal reason: to remind them of the young and innocent life taken. To keep the victim alive. She'd heard Darian talk about keeping the dead victims alive, their spirits within, until you'd caught and dealt the blow to their killer. It was, he told her that time when night turned to day at the end of his jetty, to do with the nightmares and the whispering voices that wouldn't go away. Then he told her of his relentless nightmare of being trapped in the tunnel, running, running, chasing without ever catching, running without ever reaching an end.

She stared at Izzie Daniels. All that stuff about being a fuck-monster vanished as the innocent face of a thirteen-year-old girl stared back at her.

Thirteen.

She stared at her too long. She hit 'return' and went to the file, to get the information she'd been putting off finding.

There was the name.

But worse was the link to 'other', which took Maria to a list of all the names and times of people who rang about Izzie's improper behaviour; next to the record of complaints were the names of the police officers sent out to investigate, and next to that list was a series of blithe dismissals in the parlance of official police bureaucratic language. A total of twelve cops, twelve of her colleagues, went out to answer the call of Izzie's antics and none of them came back and recorded anything more than 'complaint withdrawn' or 'unsubstantiated'. Even Jackson Toyne – good old Jack – was in on it.

Twelve cops, almost the entire team that made up Operation Blonde, sharing the secret that one of their victims had performed sex in front of them while they watched from the darkness of their cars, lined up under the willow tree on the other side of the road, late at night.

How could they search for her killer? How could they be serious about it? That's what *he* did. *He* hid and *he* watched – they in their cars, he in the bushes. What was the difference? She wanted to throw up. She wanted to yell and scream and pull out her gun and shoot somebody. But she didn't. She did, instead, what Darian used to do.

Logging off and shutting down, she left the station, telling the constables on the front desk that she had to race out for an emergency.

34

'And This Stillness of Life Did Not in the Least Resemble a Peace'

ASIDE FROM DRINKING AND TAKING SHOWERS, I'M NOT MUCH into water. I like to look at it, but when it comes to actually being in it – especially a brown river or even a blue surf beach – I keep a wary distance. I don't like walking into houses unless I know who's inside, and I don't go jumping into brown rivers for the same reason. Only tourists and drunken teenagers swim in rivers.

I extend this approach to boats. I hate boats. They can tip over or be swamped with a big wave and you can sink and suddenly find yourself wet and in the brown land of sharks.

Upriver Darian go to Neebs.

It didn't take me long to figure it out. Neebs Waterhole is a tiny speck of water, way up the Noosa River, past the last mooring, way past the last outpost of civilisation. It is kilometres away from a narrow sandy track that has no name but connects between a dirt track called Cooloola Way, accessible only by four-wheel drive, and a road that's actually a road, almost, during the dry season, called Rainbow Beach Road. This is in the middle of the Great Sandy National Park. This is what we call remote. For about a hundred square kilometres there's pretty much nothing, just a couple of tracks and the spidery narrow end to the Noosa River, which winds its way through dense forest for about forty kilometres. It's not mapped. Nobody goes there. On Google Earth, if you go searching you'll actually find a location called 'this is where we got lost'.

This place is so far off the map I couldn't help but grimace. Worse was that Promise was running the show. Sending me Ida and a message; watching and having a grand old time as I did what he wished. It also meant a change in his pattern. Was he showing off? Probably. Was it because of my front-page newspaper article? Most likely. Which meant my intervention had changed the way he thought and now, with Ida, how he operated. Maybe that was to my advantage; it was hard to tell.

All I could be certain of was he wasn't going to meet me at Neebs and give himself up. He'd have something up there to taunt me. By now he would have done his research and checked out my past. I keep a low profile but there's nothing you can do about news reports and there were dozens about me, especially about me and the train-rider.

'Oh yes! There!' said Ida.

We were in the Toyota and I was driving her back to her motel. Her sense of direction was worse than mine and we'd been driving around for close to an hour.

'That's the hill. It's on top of the hill,' she said excitedly. I'd driven through Noosa Junction, a strip of shops and cafes and cinemas surrounded by the hills of a national park – there are lots of national parks up here – situated halfway between the rugged surf of Sunshine Beach and the calm Laguna Bay. Ida was pointing to Noosa Hill as I was circumnavigating the roundabout by Ho's Chinese and an Irish pub for the fourth time when she finally recognised where she was.

'It's a motel, a little motel next to the pub,' she said. I turned off the roundabout and drove up the hill. She was talking about the Noosa Hotel, a colossus of indoor drinking taverns and restaurants and terraces with views across the Bay and the ocean beyond, stepped into the hill over three levels. It's also a bottle shop and a nightclub for teenagers and, up on the top level, near the cleaner's shed, are five or six motel rooms banged together like something out of a 1950s American highway stopover. The one in *Psycho* comes to mind.

After she'd told me everything she could remember she went and had a shower. I had never been in the situation where a victim had been released into my personal care, so I was travelling by instinct and learning as I went. Ida was in the shower for ninety minutes before, I guess, she felt she'd washed off the smell and feel of plastic, the touch of his hands and the whispers of his voice. I fed her toast with honey, and forced her to drink another few gallons of tea.

I drove into the car park and pulled over by the motel rooms.

'I'll wait,' I said.

'Truly, I'll be fine. I will, I promise.' She wasn't very good at lying.

We'd been arguing even before we got lost. She wanted to return to the motel and continue on with the holiday in Noosa for the next ten days.

'You won't be fine. You've been targeted. You're in danger.'

'He let me go. I lock the door at night, I won't go into the forests anymore, I stay only where there are lots of people.'

She'd been through a horrible ordeal and I didn't want to add to it by spooking her or getting homicide-inspector-tough on her but I needed to win the argument.

I took the honest approach. 'Up until recently I've been working with guys like the one who took you. They are ruthless, they are relentless, they enjoy killing. If you stay he will come back for you. He didn't let you go just to send me a message. He let you go so he can recapture you. Like how a cat plays with a dying mouse. Same deal. You think you got away? You didn't. You got lucky. You've got a temporary pass. You want to go back in there and stay? You'll be dead, like his other victims, within forty-eight hours.'

Maybe I was too blunt because she burst into tears and asked me to protect her. It wasn't quite the response I was looking for.

I went into her room with her, helped her pack up her belongings and within five minutes we were on the road, heading towards the Nambour railway station. Ida was going down to the Gold Coast, about three hours south of where we were.

My phone buzzed as I was driving into Nambour.

'There is nothing there,' said Isosceles. 'Simply a pool of fresh water, a circle of cumulation in the Noosa River – which should, at this juncture, be referred to as a creek not a river, given its narrow width. The only access is via aforesaid river – or creek – or a track that leads between Rainbow Beach Road and Cooloola Way, both of which are allegedly viable options for transporting vehicles, although I might say neither of which appears to be up to the task.' He giggled. 'I could call you Marlow.'

'You could. That would be very helpful,' I said, wondering who the hell Marlow was.

'"The tranquil waterway leading to the uttermost ends of the earth flowed sombre under an overcast sky – seemed to lead into the heart of an immense darkness."'

As we were discussing the potential lair of a serial killer, I wondered what possible response I could muster to that. I decided on none.

'Are there any signs of camps, huts, anything he might have built or stayed in? Unless he's just fucking with me and sending me on a trip to nowhere just for the fun of it, he has to use it or find some sort of purpose from it.'

'That was a quote. From a rather famous novella. Did you not appreciate my literary allusion to your circumstances?'

'Sorry, I was distracted.'

'Apology noted. Nothing. Nada. Zero. Absence only. It would seem to be, within the vast and diverse range of forests and tourist attractions on your Sunshine Coast, a forgotten and remote speck. A mere circle of water in the middle of a very large nowhere. It was *Heart of Darkness*, in case you were wondering, which I know you were not, but what is the point of quoting something without an attribution to its source? How will you get there? By vessel or vehicle?'

Brilliant question: I hadn't even considered the possibility of driving and then walking. It would be longer and harder but there'd be no water involved.

'You're a genius,' I said.

'Oh, but you make me blush. Where's Maria? I miss her bosoms. Tell her to Skype me. Ask her to wear a singlet.'

'Gotta go,' I said and hung up. The phone rang again.

'I need you,' said Casey.

I was pulling up at the Nambour railway station, forty-five minutes' drive from him. Under normal circumstances I would have dumped Ida at the Noosa bus stop, but I was concerned: she had been targeted by our boy and he'd almost certainly want to complete the taunt by killing her, thus proving I was incapable of keeping her safe. She was in danger: hard-core, grade-A danger. I didn't regret my decision to drive her but I was concerned. Casey was not a man to call in need of help.

'What's up?'

'Maria. She's stared down the barrel.'

'I'll be there in forty minutes.'

I didn't exactly push Ida out of the Toyota but I didn't linger, and to her credit she realised from listening to the brief phone conversation that there was urgency. She grabbed her backpack and waved a kiss goodbye; I did the same as I dropped a U-turn and began to hurtle back in the direction of the Eumundi Range Road, making sure I stuck to the main roads and highways so that I wouldn't get lost.

35

The Tunnel (i)

EVERY HOMICIDE COP HAS NIGHTMARES. AFTER I BEGAN hunting the train-rider mine were always the same.

Distant, rumbling vibrations. Thunder? A storm?

I can't see anything. But it's getting closer, the faraway drawing towards me. Maybe there's a horizon. Maybe, over its edge, that's where the sounds are coming from.

Not thunder. Cannons? Whatever: it's coming towards me.

I don't know where I am. What's happening? Have I killed somebody? Have I found another victim?

I can feel the weight of my body, pressing down onto the bed, being pressed down into the bed. My bed is a prison; no escape. I can't move … but I'm running. Fast. The darkness is becoming visible now.

A tunnel emerges. Its ceiling is arched and its walls are made of stone. There is no end.

I'm chasing him. I can hear the sounds of his panting, the exertion pulsing through his chest, his footsteps as they pound along the cobbled surface of the tunnel floor.

This time I'm going to catch him. This time I'll make the distance. I can feel my muscles bursting and my head pounding, my chest colliding as I push and push and gather speed. I can see him now: a little man, wiry, a taut body. This guy works out; he can run fast.

—

THERE'S A BUNDLE. On the ground, clothes or rags on the tunnel floor.

As I get closer the clothes take shape and I can see a broken body, a little girl, limbs and arms askew, hair smashed into her face – I know her – blood seeping out of her mouth and a hole in her temple where he pressed the gun. Her little body is wrecked, crushed.

I turn away, try not to look as I run over her body, leap *over* her. But I do look down and her eyes, open, follow me, watch me, as I continue running, chasing her killer.

Leonie.

I'm yelling but there's no sound in this tunnel, only the pounding echoes of his feet and of mine.

Turn around, let me see your face. He never does, he keeps running, I keep chasing. Up ahead where he's just passed, another crumpled, tangled, twisted body appears out of nowhere, lying on the ground, while he gets further away down the tunnel. Rachel? Diana: she was eight. I went to her grave and I made a promise to her.

'I'll find him,' I'd said.

And I have. In the tunnel, but I can't catch him.

—

SOMETIMES I GET close, so close I can reach out to him, almost touch him, my feet pounding the ground as I try to push myself harder, faster but I never touch him and I never see his face and I never catch him and we never stop running, the tunnel never ends, it has no end, it only has him and me and the girls, scattered at whim, bundles of dirt and twigs and clothes and broken body parts, wet with blood and the seepage of the earth into which they have been folded.

What good am I?

36

Down The Barrel (i)

Casey ran down to meet me. Today's T-shirt was 'Bozo and the Pineapple', a slogan mocking Gerald Ford and Bob Dole from the 1976 campaign.

'What happened?' I asked.

'Came home early, about twenty minutes ago. Carrying a bottle of Grey Goose. Two-thirds gone. Another one in the car, empty.'

'Where is she now?'

'Up on the balcony, in the hammock. I knew she could hold her grog but, holy fuck, she's telling me to go get a third, doesn't have to be Grey Goose, Smirnoff will do. I told her to fuck off and poured a jug of water on her.'

'That's very helpful,' I said.

'Yeah, she wasn't too happy about that but, you know, I've seen this sort of shit before, man, you too. But it's your score, brother. I was just on the other side of the fuckin' bar. Whatever the fuck happened to her is something that you're gunna understand. Right?'

He stared at me, expecting me to solve the problem. All I knew was a young Senior Constable was shit-faced at eleven-thirty in the morning when she should've been at the station. I guessed what had happened, but two-thirds of the Goose down I'd have some trouble making much sense of it.

'She told me all about the nightmares and what you said to her, and she told me even though you're a prick you understand. I reckoned that that talk you two had on the jetty that dawn last week was, like, real fuckin' helpful. So ...' he stood back as if to let me pass on the journey up to the drunk-in-the-hammock on the balcony.

Most cops who work in the destruction of human life survive through some form of substance abuse. Coke or dope or alcohol, Xanax, Cymbalta, Valium – I've tried them all, and they all work to keep the demons at bay. Alcohol is the most popular because it's part of the culture anyway: you go to the pub at the end of the day, on Fridays and whenever you've closed a case, and you get yourself good and smashed and it's considered part of the ritual. Knocking back the vodkas in front of your workmates is more normal than asking them how their weekend was.

Vodka's good because it leaves no trace on your breath, so most of the crew in Homicide knock down a swig or two first-up in the morning, especially if they have to go down to the morgue or visit a Family of Victim or, the worst, go and tell loved ones that their father or mother or son or daughter or husband or wife isn't coming home, ever.

I never let it become an issue. I didn't care if the crews were on the piss as long as they weren't drunk on the job or driving under the influence, and as long as it wasn't going to overtake them.

It almost overtook me. I started drinking vodka at six in the morning before my first coffee, and then I stopped bothering with the coffee. I was like that for a month before a bullet lodged in the side of my head and I spent a week in the black void of a coma.

'Hoy!' I shouted at the form swinging in the hammock.

'I wanna drink. Get me a drink,' she said. She leaned up to force the point and almost rolled out of the hammock. I held it straight and looked down at her.

'Get fucked,' she said in response. 'I'm pissed, all right?'

'Yep.'

'But I wannanother drink. All right?'

'Nup.'

'You're a jerk, you know that?'

'You found the name. Who is it?' I asked.

She stared at me for a long time. Eventually she slurred the word that I sort of already knew was the answer: 'Adam.'

37

The Tunnel (ii)

I'D BEEN SHOT IN THE HEAD AFTER CHASING A PERP WHO figured I was faster than him and knew he was going to get caught. He just stopped running and turned to face me. Oh shit, I thought, knowing exactly what was next: a bullet. That was the only reason he'd stop. I ducked; got hit in the side of the head. I fell face down, heavy and hard. I couldn't move, couldn't see. This is it, I thought. Dead, courtesy of a random burglar I'd stumbled on while walking home from the supermarket. Lying in a wet alley like a sack of wet cardboard, me, who'd left his gun in the office, bleeding out, shooter's footsteps getting fainter and fainter. In that half-conscious moment I decided that if I lived, which I didn't think was on the cards, I'd stop doing this job; the pay was shit, the clients were shit, the hours were shit and people shot at you. It didn't matter if I was good at my job, the job wasn't good for me.

'I'm leaving,' I told the Commissioner.

'I know,' he said. 'No cop gets shot in the head and keeps being a cop, unless the smart bit of brain got lost.'

I packed up and left Melbourne for good. I quit being a cop, quit Homicide, quit the eighth, rode the elevator down and walked across the foyer and out the door. When you're a Homicide cop, you've got three choices: retire with a farewell party and old stories, burn out in shame and bitterness, or vanish. I took the last option. I didn't need the nightmares and the crushing self-disgust that enveloped me every morning, the righteousness within me ebbing away slowly.

I'd suffered the affliction of these nightmares before, a cacophony of my victims' screams in a dank and endless tunnel of broken bodies and eyes, so many eyes staring at me, following me as I ran helplessly along the tunnel that had no end. Back then I almost went mad, maybe I did go mad; the blast of a gunshot and a bullet lodged in my head put me down, collapsed my world into a safe and quiet void that was black in every direction.

When I emerged from the void, in a hospital ward with vases of dead flowers and faded cards, the nightmares had gone.

I left Melbourne in my Studebaker Champion Coupe, with some clothes, my CDs and a cardboard box of books. I left my dreams and ambitions, my bright career, my reputation as a good Homicide investigator, and as the man who ensured that the guilty perps who managed to get off in court didn't get off in life. They vanished, from outside the pizza joint or the rail siding brothel or the dockyard cafe at dawn's first light, as if an avenging angel had swooped down on them spreading his righteousness and tilting the axis of the world back into harmony.

I left it all, the Hume Highway leading me through the desolation of northern Victoria, eucalypts and red dust, a highway baking without remorse or care as the journey stretched into dead hours, a blanket of numb time, a solitary land, followed by the western suburbs of Sydney, abandoned factories and playgrounds and houses that all looked the same and dead-eyed boys in their shiny cars. Then came the smokestacks of Newcastle where the main street was silent and the cinemas were long shut and the shops boarded up and the mining families broken, gone, dead. Then into the endless stretch of highway listening to crackling radio waves from distant Tasmania, brief and incoherent like strangers from another planet, inky black nights and a landscape without any form of life.

I left behind, as my doctor said, the anxiety attacks, the teeth-grinding, the sense that I was being watched, the black shawl that spread through me as I woke, knowing that no matter what I did, for how long I lived or how hard I worked, they would never go away. There would always be those last terrifying moments as your victim, for hours, days, maybe even weeks before you found her, always her, looked into the killer's eyes and saw the confirmation of evil, the flee of hope, the desperate sadness of loved ones far away. It would never stop, but that dreadful burden that often had taken me to the brink of sanity, pulled back by alcohol or the plunder of sex or the sounds of music, had begun to evaporate.

Country and kilometres passing, my new life drawing near as I drove further and further north, the burdens and nightmares leaving me, not ever imagining I'd have to impart my lessons to a young girl, my 'partner', who seemed to be heading on the same journey I had taken.

38

Down The Barrel (ii)

THERE'S A LOT TO BE SAID FOR PSYCHOLOGY AND THE general process of therapy, but in my experience there's only so much conversation you can have about a problem and then it really comes down to making some hard decisions and taking action.

Maria drifted into a slumber after calling me a jerk and a prick a few more times. Casey and I let her sleep it off for a couple of hours while we talked about the best way to get to Neebs by land; Casey is one of those guys who likes to give directions.

We eventually heard her groan, which we figured was a sign of awakening. Casey left me to it.

When she did wake she looked startled. She was staring down the barrel of a gun. My Beretta. I had it pointed directly between her eyes, about four inches away from her so she had a clear view of the dark hole at its end.

'What the–'

'Shut up,' I said. I had the gun gripped firmly. My hand did not waver.

'This is the second choice. The gun. The first is the grog. The two bottles of vodka you've already had won't get you past tonight. You'll need another in the morning. And every morning after that. The third is: you resign because you can't hack it and don't want to become an alcoholic or a suicide. Look down the barrel. That's you, in there, you're in the barrel of the gun. You've discovered they're as bad if not worse than the crooks you've sworn to catch. Final choice,' I said and lowered the gun so that she was now staring into my eyes. 'You get on with it.'

'But–'

'No buts. You get on with it. Embrace it for what it is and keep moving. You just deal with it because, Maria, if you don't and you can't you will end up dead. The grog will do it or you'll pull the trigger or you'll resign and hate yourself for being a loser. Deal with it. Just fucking deal with it.'

I stood up and put the Beretta back into my belt. She was staring past me, out to the valley and the ocean. It was a blue sky but a squall was coming in from the north. They usually blow past, out to sea. God's parade, the forces of nature, Casey calls them. I call them squalls.

I needed to get on with it, keep moving, but not with a maudlin half-drunk. I wondered if I should tell her about Ida and Neebs. She answered my unspoken question by getting on with it herself. Point four had won the day.

'Adam was the officer who logged the time of Izzie's disappearance. He was also one of the twelve officers who'd gone out to investigate the complaint about her having sex in public.'

'Did you–'

'Yes,' she pre-empted me. 'He recorded in the logbook that he was meeting with the mayor. He was gone for two hours.'

As I took out my phone I said, 'We have two, maybe three possible scenarios. First: he tracks her down, makes her fuck him then leaves her. Later he discovers she's become one of the victims so he realises he has to cover his tracks because all eyes are now going to be on her movements. So he changes the time and place of her last known sighting – he'd have to be careful so he wouldn't be contradicted by witnesses, unless he picked her up and left her in the middle of nowhere. Second: he's the killer. Third: he's covering for the killer.'

'Covering for the killer: you mean he knows who the killer is?'

'Yeah, that's a possibility. One thing we can say with certainty: the killer knows what Adam did. So the killer, if it's not Adam, has got something over him. He's got leverage, good leverage. Adam's career is totally fucked if it comes out that he manipulated the time of her disappearance. And if it's revealed that he had sex with the thirteen-year-old victim of a serial killer before she was taken then he's spending the rest of his days behind bars. Be good for his diet.'

She didn't laugh; the repercussions of her boss's sexual urges were starting to spread out before her. 'Guys and their dicks,' she said. 'Eighty-five per cent of violent crime comes from guys and their dicks.'

—

'Are you at Neebs already?' asked Isosceles.

'No,' I said. 'I need you to ransack Adam Cross.'

'Fat Adam, the dustbin? Certainly. Why, pray tell?'

'He's the missing sixty-eight minutes.'

'Oh dear Lord, imagine having sex with someone that vile. He's so fat he probably hasn't seen his penis since The Beatles released "Hey Jude". Are we then to posit that he may be our killer instead of the sparkie?'

'Maybe. Unlikely. But we need him 3-D'd. Go right back, as far as you can.' Thirty years ago nobody bothered much on profile checks. If you had a conviction then you'd be marked, but stuff like flashing or having a wank out the front of a girls' school didn't get much official attention. No computers and nobody cared back then. Victoria didn't even have a Rape Squad until the mid-1980s when a number of guys including my colleague Claude Minisini got sick and tired of seeing too many girls being questioned by dumb-arse constables who didn't have a clue about how to deal with trauma and thought rape was just another word for either regret or revenge. Back then getting a history on Adam would have been as sophisticated as asking what pub he drank at.

'I'm sorry,' said Maria after I signed off from Isosceles.

'You don't need to apologise.'

'I know. But it makes me feel better.' There was a pause as she stared at me. 'I always wondered why you only drank water.'

I just nodded, not wanting to reflect on my dark past. 'We've got a lead,' I said. 'Our guy's made contact and he's got something for us.'

39

Smasher of Rocks

Helen's first thought was that she was now going to die. Why else would Winston bring in another victim? The new girl, her mouth duct-taped tight like hers and tied to the bed by her ankles and wrists, like her, was young and blonde. His type. The same look and age as the other missing girls.

Why me? Helen wondered. She was older, dark-haired and busty. Why did he have to take me? What did I do wrong? *Is it temporary?* she wondered. *Will he let her go?* she wondered.

No, she knew was the answer.

She hated the other girl. Although she was only about thirteen years old and desperately scared, Helen could only look at her and think of her own mortality. A new victim surely meant her use, and time on earth, was over.

A bond had developed between them. They had little choice but to look into each other's eyes. The other girl had been crying. A lot. Despite hating her, Helen wanted to reach out and hug her. But, of course, she couldn't.

Helen was all cried out. She was capable of consoling the other girl. At times she tried to send her messages through her eyes, messages that would have been clear if her mouth hadn't been duct-taped, messages passed through a smile, that would have offered hope and reassurance when, of course, there actually was none, but messages of consolation nonetheless.

The other girl stared at Helen with a look of abject terror, her eyes bugging out of her as if begging Helen to explain what was going on.

Helen tried not to look at the other girl's body. She was so young. Sometimes Helen thought about Winston killing the other girl and what a tragedy it was going to be that such a young girl was soon to die. Most times however Helen only thought about her own imminent death. And then the feelings of hatred returned because the other girl's arrival meant that her death was now going to happen very soon and the other girl would survive her.

The other girl and Winston: they were going to be the last faces she saw before she died. Not her boyfriend, not her parents, not the kids she imagined she was going to have. A crazed serial killer named Winston and a naked young teenage blonde girl with no name.

Even though Winston came in to the room and raped her at any given time, there was, Helen realised, a routine. In his weird half man, half child voice and manner, he had explained the process of 'ablution' to her. It was disgusting. He made her crawl, naked as always, on her hands and feet, tied up like a dog, along the hallway to the bathroom where she then crawled into the shower and sat, huddled, as he turned it on. He'd watch as the water doused her. She hated it when he watched her. It made her feel like she was a science experiment. He'd told her about a girl called Izzie who had tried to fight back and had to be punished with scalding hot water.

In Helen's mind Izzie was a hero. She fought back. Helen didn't. She lived in hope. Hope that he would see she'd done nothing wrong, hope that he'd release her, hope that was, she knew, futile. Hope also made her angry.

Helen would lie on the bed and stare at the photos of all the other girls on the wall and wonder which one was Izzie. There were so many.

The sound of the door opening to the bedroom freaked her more than anything. She never knew what it would bring. Another rape, a lecture, a series of questions about old cartoon movies, the ablution. It would, now soon, bring her end.

She heard the door opening.

He leapt onto the end of the bed and stood above her and the other girl. He smiled. She hated his smile. It was like he knew everything. He pulled off his T-shirt and sucked in his chest and flexed his muscles. He undid the top button of his pants and then the zipper. He let his pants fall to his feet and stepped out of them. He did this every time. He thought it was funny.

'Here's Thor,' he said. 'Thor's hammer.'

She knew what was next: he would stand right above her, and the other girl, and wave it around, laughing. Then he'd rape her. Or maybe he'd rape the other girl. She wasn't sure. The routine had changed.

'Eenie, meenie, minie, mo; catch a nigger by–'

He smiled at Helen and sang:

'his–'

He grinned down at the other girl.

'–toe!'

—

I'M NOT CALLING her Jenny little-tits anymore. It's rude and demeaning and it's sexist and not very nice. We're going to change her name. After we had sex I realised that Jenny loves me. She had an orgasm at the same time I did and that's never happened before and I know that means we are special together. I love her. Helen-big-tits turned away while Jenny and I made love which was good because I didn't want her to watch. Jenny is special. I was going to make us all sit in bed and watch *Pocahontas* on the TV but after Jenny and I had our orgasms together and she fell in love with me and I fell in love with her I decided to make some changes to all the plans.

Good changes. I undid her and carried her into the lounge room which was a first because no-one has ever been in there before and I told her that we could play the PlayStation together but because we are in love now I have to be better about things so I went and got her a blanket and covered her so she wasn't nudey-nude anymore and I told her that I was going to take off her mouth bandage but she really-really-really had to promise me that she wouldn't yell or scream or do anything like that and she nodded and I told her that she looked really nice under the blanket and that I was sorry if I upset her in the back of the van the way that I did but I didn't realise then that we were made for each other and then I told her she was the most beautiful girl I had ever seen.

She is, it's true. I love her.

I took off her mouth bandage and said,

hello,

and she said,

hi,

although she said it very quietly and I think she was still a bit shocked that we had just fallen in love which was understandable and I said,

I want to change your name because I think you are too pretty for Jenny,

and she said nothing and so I said,

how about Boadicea,

and she said,

that's a weird name,

and I said,

it was the name of a very famous queen who was not only beautiful but very powerful and rode a white horse,

and she said,

okay then,

and then she said,

are you going to hurt me,

and I said,

no,

and she said,

really because you already have and I think you are going to kill me,

and I said,

no,

and then I said,

sorry,

and she didn't say anything so I said,

sorry,

again and then I said,

we should get married,
and she didn't say anything so I said,
it's okay you can think about it because we have to figure out where we'd go on our honeymoon,
then she said,
but I'm only twelve,
and I said,
maybe then we just do it in secret, like, you know, we write it up and sign our names on a bit of paper,
okay, she said,
and I went over to her and kissed her on the lips and said to her,
now you're my wife,
and she nodded and sort of smiled and I said,
call me husband,
and she said,
husband,
and then she said,
you have to be really careful,
and I asked her why,
but I knew what she was going to say because we were soulmates, she was worried that very famous and the-best-in-the-country-detective was looking for me so I had to watch my guard. It was most important that I didn't get caught being a bragger or a boaster like BTK who totally screwed up by sending letters to the newspapers, and because I was now her husband she had to protect me and make sure that I didn't step over the line, that this thing about Neebs Waterhole was a case in point and that if I spent too much time thinking about the-very-famous-detective then it would undoubtedly lead to a mistake because up until then I had been clever and I was still really clever calling her Boadicea which was such a cool name and that Thor and Boadicea should have three orgasms every night and I said,
you're really smart, come with me,
and I led her into my bedroom which was also a special new thing because nobody except me has ever been in my bedroom and I lay her down on the bed and said,

do you want to have an orgasm now,

and she said yes with her eyes

and we made love again and this time it was really cool-cool-cool because she held-held-held me and when I came inside her she went oh-oh-oh and whispered into my ear that I was the most amazing man she had ever met and she wanted me to hold her tight to protect her from any enemies,

so I did,

and she lay in my arms and it was really nice to have my wife holding me too.

—

WHAT'S THAT YOU'RE saying, my friends?

Winston, how could you take such a risk? Letting a package into your bed and then falling asleep? Isn't such behaviour wrong? Won't she escape? Aren't you confusing the fantasy with the real-life dangers of the craft? Of getting caught?

It's true, my brothers and sisters, that I've gone out on a limb with my Boadicea, but it's also true that I haven't forgotten one of the very important rules: be alert. So, while I am lying with my new baby wife I am also awake. Waiting.

It's a test, friends.

If my baby wife stays in my bed tonight then I'll know she truly loves Big Winnie.

If she tries to leave while thinking I'm asleep, then I'll know she lied to me and was pretending while we spoke.

What do you think, my friends? What do you think will happen? Let me tell you, because I know: she will try and escape.

What will you do then, Winnie? I hear you asking.

I'll punish her, friends, that's what I'll do.

While we're waiting, my brothers and sisters, let me tell you a little about feelings. I don't really have any. Like a good soldier learning all about the craft I've read much on the world of serial killers and psychopaths. You must do this as well. You have to do your research, my brothers and sisters. I can guide you and reveal many of the rules and approaches to this world but you must also read the books that are widely available. I understand that I, along with my fellow craftsmen, and you, my friends, do not have what's called empathy. We don't care about other people or their feelings and we don't have that thing called guilt. I know that normal people, if they did what we do, if they had to practise the craft, would get all teary and go boo hoo and feel that thing called remorse and they might go to the church and say I'm really sorry for having killed little Jenny G or, if they had a zeppelin doctor, would say, please forgive me, doc, ain't going to do it again. We're different. We don't care, don't give a fuck. In fact, some of us, really really really like it. I've studied up on all this.

Are we weird? Is there something wrong with us? I hear you asking. Is that doubt, my friends? Is that concern? No is the answer. We're not weird and there is nothing wrong with us. Read the books. We're born like this. It's called an illness, like if you were born with a hole in your head or with three eyes and, as far as I'm concerned, friends, the illness is as bad as if you were born with a big long dick or, my sisters, with big titties.

But, and don't be alarmed, I really liked lying in the bed with my baby wife, my Boadicea. I've never been in bed with a girl before, as a package or as a normal girl. She is warm and her body smells nice.

Sometimes we can work as partners. There have been times, in the past, both in America and Australia and probably elsewhere, my friends, when a man and a woman, who love each other, work the craft together. That's real love. I can imagine that Boadicea and I could do that. I could see her helping me snatch other packages and we would have fun fun fun together and we'd be partners on the PlayStation and have orgasms together and because she is only twelve I wouldn't have to even think about her getting old-old-old.

But I know, my friends, and I can hear you telling me: *Thor and Boadicea and Pocahontas are all destined to live alone. That's just how it is.*

Stay alert, I am; stay cautious, I am. Because she will try to escape.

FRIENDS, YOU DON'T have to have lessons on how to guess that someone is trying to leave your bed without you knowing. They move really slow and don't breathe. They get out in real slow stages. Not like you and I, when we just heave ourselves out. No, they do it like a sniper moving into position. Slow and all stealthy like.

'Are you trying to escape?'

'No.'

'What are you doing then?'

'Nothing.'

Nothing. The biggest lie-answer of all time. Nothing always means the something the other person doesn't want you to hear.

I held her firmly down on the bed and turned on the bedside light. She looked scared. Scared-looking people are people who have something to hide.

'Sorry, I–' she tried to get out some feeble excuse but, sorry honey, it's too late.

Punishment, friends. It comes in many ways. Betrayal is bad bad bad and needs severe punishment. Choking little girls is easy. I've done it many times. I just moved my hand beneath her chin and closed my grip around her neck and tightened it, choking her. Simple. She fought back but she wasn't very strong and I am. I had her dead and killed in three fast minutes, my brothers and sisters.

Really, this was annoying. My fault, I can hear you telling me, but now everything with the photos and final steps will have to change. But remember what I said? Being able to improvise is important.

Knowing she wasn't going to escape anymore, I turned the light off and lay quietly, knowing it'd be all good and safe to sleep now. Which I did, my friends, for about two hours, missing the four o'clock creepy newspaper kid riding by.

She was still soft when I woke up. Cold but soft, like there wasn't any of that dead-stiff-person thing. Not ice-cream cold just medium cold. Being under the blanket and next to my body while I slept made a bit of a difference I reckon. Her eyes were wide open and she looked really pretty. But I knew I couldn't stay there. It had all changed and I had to make plans.

—

THE DOOR'S OPENING again, Helen thought. She was cold. Winston liked to see her naked all the time and so never put a blanket or a Doona on her.

Is this it? she wondered. Is this the time that he's going to kill me? She'd been alone for hours now and had slept fitfully. Ever since she'd been captured she'd slept with nightmares and terrible dreams of her past, happy life. It felt like she'd been sleeping for half hours at a time, waking up, remembering the dreams and nightmares, remembering where she actually was and lying and waiting, in terror then falling back to sleep again.

'Wake up, Helen, look what happened to little Jenny overnight.'

Straight away Helen could see that the other girl was dead. He was holding her in his arms and her body was limp and her mouth was open in a horrific way that made Helen think the little girl died in great pain. Winston threw the other girl on top of her.

He laughed.

'Helen-big-tits was asleep but now she has dead Jenny-little-tits lying on top of her,' he said.

Helen watched as Winston rearranged the other girl's body so she was lying face-to-face with her. Like they were in an embrace.

'It's been a topsy-turvy night and we've got things to do. We are behind schedule on some big stuff, Helen,' he said. 'We've got to get your picture to your loverboy.'

Back in the real world Helen would have hated herself for what she thought as he left the room. Relief. If he's killed the other girl, then maybe he'll spare me. At least I'll live longer, she thought.

—

FRIENDS, I COULD have used the girls' mobile phones there and then and taken the photo of dead Jenny lying on top of Helen, two nudies, one dead, the other alive. That would be the coolest and most awesome picture and would so freak out the cops and the-best-ever-homicide-cop-in-Australia. Bet he'd never seen that.

But I had to remember what Jenny said when she was Boadicea, my wife: be careful and don't let the boasting get in the way. It could be your very downfall, Winston, she told me. And frankly, she was right. What is more important? Showing off how clever I am or getting the girls and doing my things with them? *No contest, captain.*

—

ONCE I RAPED a year-ten girl in the toilet block at lunchtime but most of the time I just tuned out at school. Except for History. I love History. All famous people who are remembered through time have studied History my friends and I'm one of them. My favourite subject was Cecil Rhodes, who wasn't really taught very much. My teacher just mentioned him like he was a loser while we were studying about that Nelson Mandela and South Africa, a dumb-arse boring class about reconciliation. Blow their fucking heads off, that's what I think about reconciliation. What was real cool about old Cecil was what they called him at the time: 'the smasher of rocks'. Mrs Tonkins said he was called that because he forced thousands of natives into making roads through hills and mountains in the country named after him: Rhodesia.

Friends, I see myself as a smasher of rocks too and I'd like you, brothers and sisters, to remember that when talking about me. Not like in building roads through mountains or like in ordering millions and millions of natives around even though that'd be cool, like having your own concentration camp, but when I kill off the girls. It came to me when I snuffed out little Jenny tiny-tits, my Boadicea. When I crushed down on her windpipe and watched her die die die I was thinking I was like old Cecil, the Smasher of Rocks. When I pull out Thor and use it on the girls I also think: I am the Smasher of Rocks.

See, like old Cecil, I can't be stopped. Nothing stops Big Winnie, the Awesome One. Nothing gets in my way, not even that number-one-best-detective-from-homicide-in-the-world, not even him, no-one.

Yes, yes, I hear you calling: *one day you'll be caught or you'll die and then it'll be over.* True, my friends, but when that day comes, I will be remembered. I have made plans, be sure of that. The chain and the answer to your question – how many kills – will be revealed to the world. And then I'll be immortal.

I always asked Mrs Tonkins to talk more about Cecil Rhodes in her classes but she never did and sometimes she shouted at me. It took me way too much fucking time that really would have been better spent elsewhere but eventually I discovered where the old bitch lived. She lived alone which made it real easy so one night, after three in the morning, I just walked into her house. Dumb people never lock their houses in Queensland. I was dressed in black like a ninja. I tied her to her bed and raped her. She was about thirty years old or something. If she was real old I wouldn't have fucked her because that'd be gross. I didn't say a word, just fucked her and slapped her across the face a lot and punched her in the guts and then stabbed her dog dead dead dead. It was an old thing that dribbled in a basket in the living room. I wanted to cut its head off and throw it onto Mrs Tonkins who I left tied up and nude and punched up real fucking good but it was too much hassle so I didn't bother. She never came back to school but the worst thing was that the new teacher who replaced her, this real sexy bitch whose name was Annie something, had never even heard of Cecil Rhodes.

I love the Smasher of Rocks because mountains were blasted out of his way but also because he had plans, my friends. Roads. He knew where he was going. That's another reason I'm just like him. The steps, the plans, the routines, just like Cecil and his native army. Really, when you think about it, taking a girl is like building a road. You plan ahead, my brothers and sisters, you make certain all the possible things that could go wrong are thought about, you look this way and that and then you go in and just fucking do it.

Maybe the Smasher of Rocks wouldn't have let Boadicea into his bed but on the other hand with a country full of natives that he owned, maybe he would've. Maybe the Smasher of Rocks stole little black native girls and gave them Thor's bolt too. Who knows? Sexy Mrs Annie the new school teacher didn't.

The Smasher of Rocks was a man of focus. Just like me. Focus: stay on track. Wait till night, then upriver we go, in the canoe too, to take some pretty photos and tomorrow, yoo-hoo, when the cops see the photos on the girls' phones, rock and roll, my friends, rock and roll. Two for one. Why would he do that, they'll ask and then they'll say: it's because of the-best-and-most-famous-homicide-cop-in-the-land, that's why. Now that the best is on the case the *perp* has changed his game. Ramped up. Another level, just like when you play the PlayStation.

It'd be real cool to be at Neebs when the-best-and-most-famous-homicide-cop finds his next gift but that would be way dangerous and stupid. Like Boadicea, bless her little soul, told me last night, watch out and don't get ahead of yourself. Stay on course, just like the Smasher of Rocks carving his awesome roads through mountains.

Smash!

40

Breach

ADAM HAD TRIED REALLY HARD NOT TO CRY WHEN HE WAS interviewed for the evening news. It was so sad. All those bodies, all that carnage. And for what? A kid without a licence, drunk on vodka, speeding through a roundabout. All those lives. Kids. A baby.

'Please,' he said, after confirming the death toll, 'please be careful. Don't drink and drive. It's not just a matter of breaking the law. It's a matter of destroying lives. These were kids ...' That was when he started to break up and he turned away and the news crew, who knew him, were kind enough to stop rolling the cameras, just after they got the moment of the Officer in Charge of Noosa Police about to break down in tears. That'd be a great lead-in for the news tonight.

After the last of the bodies was taken away from the accident scene and the tow trucks, like vultures on the side of the highway, were allowed to move in, Adam told his men he was going back to the station and if they needed him, just call. He'd been out there longer than necessary but he couldn't leave, not with such a terrible human toll. They'd got most of the names and he'd assigned the best he had to go and tell – in person where possible – the next of kin. Adam would make the call to the parents of the girl who was flung through the front window into the tree at a force of about a hundred and sixty kilometres an hour. They lived in Hobart.

On his way back to the station he paused at McDonald's and ordered two Big Macs, partly because he hadn't eaten for six hours and partly because any delay in the grim task of informing parents that their child was dead was welcome.

He ate the first Big Mac as he drove, always a mistake because the lettuce spills out onto the seat and he had to be careful not to have a collision. The next Big Mac he unwrapped in his office as he fired up his computer and logged on.

Anyone could log on to the Operation Blonde folder as long as they had the access and the passwords, but Adam kept a close watch on this file because he had things to hide. Secrets. They were well hidden. He'd done a good job and he was pretty sure he'd never be caught but, best to be vigilant and make sure no-one ever decided to snoop around.

He immediately saw that this was exactly what had been happening while he and the rest of the boys were out at the accident site. Someone had been snooping.

He had never liked Maria, not from the very first time he laid eyes on her. She'd been hired by his predecessor a few months before he arrived. She wasn't really part of the gang. Even though she pretended to be one of them, she was a loner. She kept watch, as if storing information. She was smart. At first he thought she'd been hired because she was so incredibly beautiful but he soon realised that, even if that were a reason, the fact was she was highly intelligent and ambitious. She kept a low profile. She was the sort of person he remembered from his Melbourne days. 'They're gunna touch the flag,' was how people would refer to them. Touch the flag: reach the top. She would quietly earn her way up through the ranks. She'd already done all the courses on offer. Any time a course came up, no matter what it was, she did it. She'd even done a course on Fisheries and Wildlife.

People like her were dangerous.

He scrolled through the spreadsheets and tried to figure out where she'd been and what she'd been searching for.

There. Bitch. She'd gone to Izzie's time of disappearance. The computer had that page logged into at 10.28 that morning.

She knew.

How?

It was no secret her boyfriend was Casey Lack, a small-time low-life who used to run strip clubs in Melbourne. That was the connection. Melbourne: Casey Lack and Darian Richards. There's no such thing as a coincidence in an investigation.

Richards had got to her and made her his spy.

He leaned back in his chair and began to relax. His appetite returned, now that he knew he was okay. He reached out and swallowed the Big Mac in three mouthfuls. He loved Big Macs.

Adam hadn't been sure what to make of Noosa when he first arrived. Of course he was excited, not by the challenge of the police work – because there was hardly anything serious in the region – but by being in control of one of the most famous tourist regions in the country. Most tourist destinations were in third-world countries where the cops were blatantly corrupt, like Bali or Cancun, or they were in dangerous places where the cops were just downright dangerous, like Miami or New Orleans. But Noosa was none of that. It was a first-world destination in a first-world country with a first-class reputation.

He knew it would be relaxed. No stress. He quickly discovered that he wasn't the only one who'd moved up here. Almost every one of the cops under his care had moved from down south for lifestyle reasons. They were all at Noosa, like him, to chill out.

He loved the laidback life. It suited him perfectly.

Maria was one of the few who weren't like that. She came to work as if she were in downtown LA or Rio or Kings Cross. Ready for action. Alert. Holy hell, he'd think, get a life. The others came in relaxed. Get up, go for a surf, walk along the beach, chill out. You want to walk through the doors of work with your fist clenched on a weapon? Go find a battleground where you can pull the trigger. It made the others tense. It made him tense. If she wasn't so pretty he'd have been able to mount a campaign to get rid of her, but the boys liked to perve on her and she was smart enough to laugh along with them and flirt – just enough – to make her one of the most popular on his team. There wasn't a single guy in the station who didn't want to fuck her. That made her popular. Hard to get rid of popular people.

But now she was in the way and was going to become more of a threat. Indeed, exactly how much of a threat had she actually become? What if she'd revealed his secret?

This was *his* country. After two weeks he felt pride in the knowledge that the Sunshine Coast was his. Even though there were cop stations scattered in the various towns and a large base down at Maroochydore, the focus of the entire Coast was Noosa, and the centre of its law enforcement was his station up on the hill.

He was king of the hill and she was an ant that needed to be squashed. In quick time.

'Where's Maria?' he shouted out through the open door of his office.

'She went home. Sick,' was the reply.

'Call her. Tell her I want to see her. Pronto.'

'She went home *sick*,' as in, *Didn't you hear me the first time, moron?*

'Unless she's fuckin' dead, tell her I want to see her. Pronto,' as in, *Didn't you hear me the first time, moron?*

41

'We Are on the Point of Starvation ... My Spirits Are Excellent'

'Are you lost?' I asked.

'No,' she said in a tone that suggested otherwise.

'I think we should have turned off at that track, just past the Kin Kin Creek.'

'Then we'd really be lost,' she said.

I didn't believe her but at this stage of the journey I hadn't yet discovered she was, in fact, almost as bad as I was with directions. Okay, not *as* bad, just nearly as bad.

When he heard we were going to Neebs together, Casey did what guys do when they're into directions. His eyes popped as if someone had asked him to solve a deep-seated mystery to the universe that only he could answer, then raced around in circles until he came to a stop at the dining room table where he had laid out a large map of the Great Sandy National Park with emphasis on the Wide Bay Military Reserve which, he assured us darkly, was run by the CIA, mention of which reminded me that I had to tell Maria that Isosceles was missing her and perhaps she could Skype him in a tight-fitting bosom-revealing singlet. She hit me and Casey said:

'You tell the geek to keep his fuckin' eyes off my girl's tits or else I am gunna fly down to Melbourne and take his Raquel Welch sheet and tear it into shreds and ask him at the same time who it was that gave him the fucking sheet in the first place. Ain't easy to find. How many kids these days even heard of Raquel Welch, let alone know where to find her semi-nude image on a sheet.'

Maria hit Casey too.

'Shut up and show us how to get to Neebs so we don't get lost.'

'Okay babe, okay. Jesus. Just trying to look after you from being perved at. Here,' he stabbed his finger at a point on the map. 'This is where everyone gets lost 'cause the road is shit. Actually it ain't even a road, it's just a fucking nothing. There.'

His finger was stabbed into an intersection, if that was the appropriate word, between Tin Can Bay Road and Courier Road.

'That's where you're gunna get lost.' He looked at us. 'Who's driving?' he asked.

'I am,' we both said at the same time.

'I am,' she said.

'I am,' I said.

'You have the worst sense of direction in the history of mankind,' she said.

'That's an absolutely appalling thing to say,' I said, thinking it was actually pretty close to the truth.

'You have, mate,' said Casey. 'Worse than fucking Burke 'n Wills.'

'I am not,' I said. 'I may not be … the best, but I'm not–'

'I'm driving,' she said forcefully.

We had been on the road for two hours and now, having missed the intersection between Tin Can Bay Road and Courier Road because it was neither a road nor a track nor was there any sign or path or anything aside from an endless forest of gum and melaleuca trees, we were on the road to God knew where.

'At this rate we're just going to end up in Tin Can Bay,' I said.

'Shut up,' she responded.

I had the map spread out across my lap. It was as helpful as having the Koran.

'Or we might blunder our way into the Wide Bay Military Reserve and get shot for trespassing. Soldiers these days have itchy fingers.'

'Shut up.'

The road, if you could call it that – I wouldn't – was built of dirt and sand, and was narrow. Every now and then a branch would swipe across the roof or the window.

'Not that I want to add any pressure to the situation or anything but it *is* mid-afternoon and I have noticed there aren't too many street lights out in this part of the world.'

'Shut up. I know where I'm going. The turn-off is just ahead.'

'What? According to your innate navigational skill?'

This time she opted for silence.

'I could ring ahead and book a couple of rooms at the Tin Can Bay Motel. At least then we wouldn't have to sleep in the Toyota in the middle of nowhere.'

Silence.

'Did you know that, above all others in the category of terrible navigators, a man by the name of Robert Burke is considered to be the worst?'

Silence. This was the kind of silence that girls do when furious.

'With absolutely no sense of direction, known for even getting lost in his own town, he set off to cross Australia with over twenty-five camels and horses, twenty tons of supplies including a dining table, dandruff brushes and enema kits. He led nineteen men into the desert with no clue where he was going and promptly got them all lost and most, if not all – I'm a bit hazy on that fact – dead.'

Silence.

'Any resonance with that story?' I asked.

Silence.

I looked down at my phone.

'Even if you agreed with me and thought that spending the night in a motel room was preferable to being cooped up in the Toyota on the side of a track in the middle of this godforsaken Great Sandy National Park, there's no reception. So I can't call and say, "Hey, I'm travelling with the female Robert Burke of Noosa and could you put aside a couple of rooms? Might be there by Friday."'

Discernible seething. I decided that if Casey wasn't my best friend I'd try to crack on to Maria and see if we could make a go of it. I like the idea of dangerous women.

'But at least the view's great,' I said, staring out at the endless blank forest of ugly gum and melaleuca. 'Not to mention the conversation.'

Up ahead was a blind corner, turning to the right.

'Interestingly, although Burke knew he was going to die, having navigated his way into the heart of one of the world's largest deserts, he wrote to his father, "We are on the point of starvation ... my spirits are excellent," which makes you wonder if he was stark raving mad or just a complete fucking idiot. What do you think?'

No response. I looked at the map. I had zero clue where we were. I looked at the corner we were approaching.

'This is where the turn-off is, right? Up here, around the corner?'

'Yes,' she said.

'Awesome. I take back everything I said about you being the modern-day Robert Burke. Complete retraction.'

She slowed as we began to turn the corner. The road was really narrow and the blind turns would be dangerous if there were another car on the road – about as likely as seeing a spaceship.

The turn gave way to a short stretch of white sandy dirt track that ran for about two hundred metres until it stopped at a massive wall of forest, completely impenetrable. A dead end.

Maria brought the car to a stop. She stared ahead at the end of the road.

'We're lost,' she said.

'On the tip of my tongue,' I replied.

She put the car into reverse and said, in all seriousness: 'This is your fault.'

Instinctively I knew it was best to stay silent and let that pass. She turned the car around, pointed it in the direction from where we had come and pressed down on the accelerator.

42

Step 8: The Photo

It's important that you think of yourself as a professional. What we're doing is a craft, a trade. If you look at this as a hobby you're fucked up. It's not. This is your life's work, brothers and sisters. I take care of other business too, like getting a job. Not only to appear normal but also so I can get some money coming in when my mum gets angry with me and says she's not putting any money into my account for another week or two. I really want to kill her and inherit her money but I can't.

I also studied up real hard on the law. Brothers and sisters, it's important to know all about the law. For instance I started young but I knew that, being a kid, the courts had to protect my identity. They couldn't tell anyone of all the stuff I'd gotten up to. But that doesn't last forever. When you grow up they don't do that sort of thing. It's only for kids.

After I left Brisbane and moved to the Sunshine Coast I spent a lot of time preparing before I took the first girl. I laid out all the steps, one by one, in a long list that starts with targeting and ends with disposal and, finally, the chain.

Ssshhh, my friends. I'll tell you what the chain is. But not now. Not yet.

By the way my friends, it's important to do your work in a place that's user-friendly. Up here on the Sunshine Coast there are so many backpackers and people who come in and out to work in pubs or whatever and so many places in the bush and the forest that people don't ever go, that it makes the craft really easy. I went to

Bali on a holiday once and tried to do a bit of work over there but there were so many fucking people, you couldn't move. Fucked if I know where you'd dispose of a body over there. No fucking room. Still, I killed a couple of kids and dumped them in a forest and scadoodelled outta there quick smart before they were found.

Early on, up here, I knew I had to bury the bodies. You see, friends, cops love bodies. I'd read this book called *Dead Men Tell Tales* which is the first book, and the best I reckon, on the clues you can leave behind: fingerprints, hairs, fibres and DNA. Dumping bodies for the cops to discover is dumb dumb dumb. You may as well ask to be caught.

I searched and searched but eventually I discovered my dumping ground. It's perfect. And yours should be too. Don't rush this stage. In fact, don't rush any of the stages I'm talking about.

Like the plan. The steps. With each of the steps I knew that to keep the cops out of whack, I needed to have different working places: one place to keep the girls and play with them; another place – it has to be remote, friends – to take the photos; another place to kill them; another for the cooking; another place for the burials. And another place, the final place, for the chain. Sometimes I get a bit slack and do the kill and cooking at home.

What's the cooking, Winston? What are you talking about? I can hear you asking. Ha ha friends. Maybe I'm being boomy on you.

Cops look for a serial killer's 'trophies'. Most trophies are locks of hair or jewellery or other random pieces from victims. I'm not into that; it's childish, I reckon, but don't let me put you off. To each his own, I reckon.

The chain is super cool. It's historical too. It's an Inca thing. The girls never appreciate the importance of the chain. But fuck them. And fuck the cops too; the chain isn't for them, it's for humanity. Winston's Legacy.

Luck is also important. I was just lucky that I came across this deserted resort on the Noosa North Shore. It's real remote over there, hard to get to. Works real well. That's where I do my photos.

I told you about fear, remember? So I decided, early on, to take a snap of the package, all tied up and nude and scared, on a chair and then send it back to the package's family. Freak 'em right out. Freak out the cops too. You gotta be careful with this sort of stuff though because if you don't know how phones work and how they can be traced while the battery's still in them, then you can get caught. But it's really cool. I love taking snaps of the packages. After I die I'm putting out my movie and a big glossy photo book.

First thing I do, once the package is secure and tied, is find her phone and remove the battery. Dead. She is off the radar, friends. All mine.

It can be real hard to keep freaking out the girls, after you've got them and read them the rules and after they've spent a few days and nights in the room with all the photos on the wall, they get all numb and hard to scare. Taking more photos scares them; that gives them a *bolt*. Making them look at the millions of photos on the wall of their room also gives them a *bolt*. But nothing gives them the *bolt* more than when I tell them about the chain. I save that for last. After that it's over. Kill, dispose, add to the chain.

—

I LOAD UP my backpack with the hard drives, the power boards, the cameras, the laptop, the girls' phones, my knives, the duct tape and the cling wrap, and store it in the back of the van. I go down to the girls' room and lift Jenny-little-tits off Helen-big-tits.

'Jeez, she's gone all stiff now,' I say to Helen and then carry her out, down the corridor and out into the garage, where I lay her on one side in the back of the van. Even though she is as stiff as a plank I secure her tightly to the side of the van so she won't roll about as I drive.

Then I go back down to Helen-big-tits and say: 'Back we go, in the canoe,' and untie her from the bed. Her wrists and ankles are still tied up so she can't move. I toss her over my shoulder and carry her down the corridor and put her in the back of the van, securing her to the other wall so she won't roll about. I throw a blanket over them, not because I care if they are cold or that they are nude, but just in case I ever get stopped and made to open up the back of the van. Better to see two rolled-up things under a blanket than two nude girls. 'Statues, mate,' is what I'd say if that ever happened. 'Fragile, gotta keep 'em rolled up in blankets.'

I check my watch. Six o'clock. Perfect. No suspicion when your neighbour drives out in the late afternoon. In a van. I'm off to do shift work or get a pizza.

Drive carefully along the streets. Obey the rules, no running the orange lights, brothers.

I get to the river mooring. Gotta be careful here, have to make sure the nude girls don't drop out of the blanket as I carry them to my boat while a dumb fisherman is cruising past. One of the good things about the river is that it carries noise from far away. So I stare at the river in both directions and listen for any boat movement or the swish of a fishing line being cast into the water. In an hour it's going to be dusk. The river gets busy at dusk. That's when the fishermen reckon they can catch the most fish. Now, though, it's quiet. The fishermen were getting ready for the evening, just like me.

All clear.

My little boat is moored at a little beach on the edge of Tewantin. The North Shore is on the other side of the river, less than a hundred metres away. The little beach is a semi-public mooring. Lots of the locals use it. There are always a couple of boats, little tinnies like mine, although I call mine a canoe because that's what Pocahontas travels in, on the beach, held tight by rope or an anchor.

Open the back of the van. Same routine as before: the backpack first, then the girl. Tonight, two girls. Dead-stiff girl first then Helen-big-tits. Put them on the floor of the boat. Out of sight now.

I always dress the same: in complete black. Like a ninja or a ghost. I move real quiet too. Look upriver: empty. Downriver: empty. Big strong flow tonight. The moon is going to be hidden by dark cloud cover, which is good. Lock up the van, which I park under a big old tree. Looks anonymous. Push the boat away from the sand and as it slips into the water, jump into it, grabbing an oar to guide it across the water.

It only takes me a few minutes to cross the river. Row upstream about fifty metres until we reach a narrow estuary. In we go. This is much easier. No tidal flow. Sometimes the river current can be real angry. Once I saw this kid fall out of a hire boat and watched as he was swept away as quickly as the speedboat chasing him. The kid sank. I watched the speedboat and all these other boats as they joined in the search. People screamed as the boats went around in circles where the kid had gone under and every now and then somebody jumped in but they too were almost swept away with the force of the current so, after a while, they all left and the kid was probably stuck in the mud down at the bottom of river, dead dead dead.

The estuary is real thin. I could stretch out both arms and touch the mangroves on either side as we paddle down towards the empty Noosa North Shore Dreaming Resort.

I grab the branches of the overhanging trees and steer the boat into a mooring. Like clockwork. Same every time. Nothing changes. The apartment is nearby. On the second floor. The resort is always dark and real silent. There are a few people who live in some of the other buildings but they're too far away to notice me creeping through the scrub, from the estuary to my apartment. I've chosen it carefully. Easy access, in and out.

Backpack first usually. It's heavy, but I am strong. I could carry it and a package slung across my other shoulder at the same time.

Let's leave dead-stiff-Jenny in the boat and carry Helen-big-tits in first. I'll drop her on the floor, up against the wall where we take the photos, leave the backpack then go back out to get dead-stiff-Jenny. I reckon there are going to be lots of cool ways of laying them out together.

I was pretty angry with Jenny-little-tits at first because the way I was going to pose them together was really cool but, you know, after I got used to the fact she was dead-stiff, I came up with other ideas for photos that'll be even more cool. And boy oh boy, is the-number-one-best-homicide-investigator going to be impressed with me.

Ready, captain?

I love this apartment. Real good memories of the girls and the looks on their faces as I set them up for the sayonara photos, all nude and being told of Steps 9, 10 and 11.

Snap on being told of Step 11. I really laugh at the looks on their faces when I tell them about that. Best photos ever.

Open the sliding doors to my empty apartment and step inside, Helen-big-tits slung over one shoulder, backpack over the other.

What the fuck?

43

Edinburgh of the Seven Seas

ISOSCELES RARELY LEFT HIS APARTMENT. FOOD WAS ORDERED in. He did all his shopping online. When he ventured into the city below, it was at night. Sitting atop the city, on the top floor of one of the tallest buildings in the centre of Melbourne, he enjoyed the view of the flat, vast stretch of lights in all directions. For that reason he preferred the night. He had always been nocturnal, ever since he was given his first computer. Soon he became hooked on the darkness and considered people who went out in the day to be boring. He saw himself as a bat. Work, however, required him to spend daytime hours at 'the Pulse', his work station, a massive glass-topped desk holding laptops, keyboards, three large screens and five hard drives that hummed quietly by his feet. The outload was huge and as he had to keep it running twenty-four seven it required a temperature of two degrees Celsius. It was important that the machinery didn't overheat. If it did: crisis.

As such Isosceles dressed in over-large puffer jackets and thick wool-lined boots. He wore a wool-lined cap that covered his ears. His headset fitted neatly under it. Whenever he caught sight of his reflection in the glass windows he thought he looked like a yak hunter, armed and at the ready in the frozen wilds of the Yukon. Thus he dreamed of holidays in remote deserts, like his trip to Burkina Faso, which he was looking forward to, as soon as the nasty little serial killer on the Sunshine Coast was captured.

Isosceles adored working for Darian but made his money as a freelance operative in espionage cyberspace. He was often hired for one-off jobs by the CIA or ASIS. He was well known in the small but revered world of cyber geeks.

He rarely moved from his desk. He scanned newspapers from across the world and kept a watch on the various surveillance cameras he had in place around the country – six in all: two for Darian, the others for the FBI, tracking a potential Sudanese terrorist who Isosceles believed was no more dangerous than a stamp collector.

While reading the morning's edition of *The London Independent* he heard the rare sound of intrusion.

Each surveillance camera was programmed to set off a distinct alarm. He learned this from Darian and his clever designation of songs for people. Isosceles didn't use songs. He preferred tonal sounds, and the one that was going off, a high-pitched noise, immediately told him that Danny Jim Promise had just entered the apartment in the Noosa North Shore Dreaming Resort.

Reaching for his keypad to speed-dial Darian, he glanced at the monitor. All he could see was a shadowy figure, frozen in the doorway. The guy knew. Somehow, he knew.

'Leave a message,' said Darian's voice.

'Call me. There's a breach. He's at the resort, in the apartment.'

He dialled Maria.

'Hi, this is Maria. Leave a message and I'll call you straight back. Thanks.'

'Isosceles. Call me.'

He dialled Casey.

'She ain't here and you get your eyes off her tits, all right?' was the response as soon as the call was answered.

'Where are they? I need them. Urgent.'

'Then fuckin' call them.'

'I have. I can't get through.'

'They'll be out of range. In the middle of that fucking swampland. They may as well be in Edinburgh of the Seven Seas.'

'Noted. Is there any way you can make contact?'

'Nup. But I'll try, every few minutes, tell them you're on fire.'

Isosceles hung up without saying goodbye. He kept staring at the monitor. The killer hadn't moved. In the grainy image he could barely make him out but he was there. The alarm kept ringing, alerting him to the intrusion. He killed its sound and thought about his colleagues in the middle of nowhere. He liked Casey; they would probably be among the very few who could talk in a language that few others would follow. Tristan da Cunha was the most remote island on earth and its capital, Edinburgh of the Seven Seas, the most remote town. But while they didn't have television until 2001 they had phone lines and he'd be able to make a call and find a person at the other end.

44

Goodbye to All That

CAPTAIN, THERE'S BEEN A—

I know!

Friends, my brothers and sisters: as we've travelled along this journey I've told you of many things. I've been your guide and mentor and you've been good to me in return. Above all, my friends, I've been honest. Great men are always honest. They reveal their strengths and weaknesses. I'm like that.

Don't be alarmed, friends. I want you to pay close attention because this could happen to you.

You remember how Superman gets all wrecked if he is near Kryptonite? The same sort of thing can happen to us. It's called *catastrophising*. That's what the cops and the shrinks call it, anyway. It's really, really horrible. It's not fair. Us serial killers have it hard enough as it is. I mean, you know, you understand how hard it can be. People think it's easy. It's not. The amount of planning and thought that goes into the craft is huge.

—

I AM STANDING real stiff at the entrance to the apartment, Helen-big-tits over one shoulder and my backpack over the other. I'd slid the door open and was about to walk in when I sensed that there had been an intrusion. (Remember: be alert.)

Somebody has come in since I was last here. I can feel the intrusion but there is *something else*. Since the apartment doesn't have any furniture the only way I'm able to tell is to look at the floor and see if there are any signs of footprints. (Don't freak out if you can avoid it. Stay calm and check out the situation.)

Very slowly I walk backwards, to the other side of the sliding door, half-in, half-out, on the balcony. This is a dangerous situation. What if they are close by? I have to do something quickly. I am not in control and someone has entered my place. (You must be in control at all times.)

Part of my weaponry is expertise in surveillance. Like snipers. I've watched and followed the movements of my targets for years. I know that if I am ever getting too close when to step back, retreat, when to draw closer again and pretend to be a dumb lost tourist. It's an art form, learned through years of practice. As much as I know how to watch without being seen, I also know when I'm being watched. (That comes with experience, friends.)

Which isn't very often. But that's what is happening now. Not only has the feeling of the empty apartment changed but there is something else.

It takes me a few minutes to let the darkness go all through me so I can see properly. That's when I see the wire. A thin black wire, running along the skirting board of the room. I try to figure out where it starts from and where it goes to, but can't.

I lose sight of it in the kitchen area. I know it connects to a camera. Has to. If I was the-number-one-best-homicide-investigator-in-the-country that's what I'd do. (Try and put yourself in the shoes of the cops who are hunting you. Think like them. It's really helpful.)

How did this happen? My mind is all mumbo jumbo but I figure it out quickly. It was their mobile phones. I always knew it was a risk putting the battery back into them so I could load the photos. Even though it only lasted a minute or so the phone would send out those signals. I know, my friends: it was a professional gamble and it paid off. Until now. Won't be doing that again, that's for sure.

I know the camera isn't staring at me. I scope out the whole apartment and can see that there are no cameras, nothing, pointed at where I stand. (Know, as best you can, what sorts of technology the cops use so you can be alert to this.)

It is probably above me. Most likely it will've been triggered on my entry through the front door. That way they'd have a good clean front-on shot of me. At the moment, all they've got is my shadow, that's it. Lucky that. Lucky I come in via the balcony. (Remember, friends: luck plays a part.)

I take another step back and lay Helen on the floor of the balcony. Pause, think clearly about the problem. I'd really like to go in and find the camera and the recording machine and break the thing but I can't because I'd be seen.

I stomp on Helen's face because I am angry and if it wasn't for her none of this would've happened.

I don't go back in. I don't leave. Like I should. Friends, I am frozen. I don't know what to do. I am lost. No longer in control. He is.

45

Range

Light was fading, but Maria was determined to keep driving until we found the right turn-off and made our way to Neebs. I'd long come to the conclusion that we didn't have a ghost's hope of getting there tonight, that we were destined to spend the night on the side of the road or slink back to Casey's and, like Burke and his caravan, proceed with the journey again at first light. I knew that it was best to keep these thoughts to myself. After all, it was all my fault.

As we turned another blind corner on our silent journey back to the hidden intersection, shrouded by forest, our phones began to buzz at the same time.

'Pull over,' I said, 'while we've got range–'

She ground the Toyota to an uncomfortable stop. My seatbelt held me back from flying through the window.

'Eight messages,' I said as I dialled to listen.

'Me too.'

My messages started with the oldest, that being from Casey reminding us that the turn-off to Courier Road was really hard and to look out for a gum tree that looked like a chair.

Maria's messages started with the most recent.

As I was wiping his and moving on to the second, the car jolted and this time I was flung backwards, held from being hurtled against the back window by my seatbelt again.

'What–'

'It's him. He's at the apartment. Now.'

I dialled as she sped along the road in an extremely hazardous manner.

'Where are you?' asked Isosceles.

'Lost.'

'I'm driving back down Tin Can Bay Road. It links to the Resort road,' shouted Maria so he could hear her.

'I'll guide you,' he said. 'Make sure Maria keeps her phone off so as not to disrupt the frequencies with another call. I'll track her and GPS you at the same time. Doesn't matter if you drop out of range. You'll come back in. There. Got you. You are going in the wrong direction.'

'What?' I said.

'What?' she asked.

'Turn around. You are travelling in a south-west direction along Tin Can Bay Road–'

'Turn around,' I told Maria.

'But–'

'If you continue in that direction you will have to find a track called Courier Road, which appears to be a name and nothing else, then you have to traverse that for six kilometres, get to Harry's Hut Road, which looks equally invisible, drive along a walking track to a place called Fig Tree Point then head due east, through the forest for about three kilometres then turn south and drive through the forest for another eight or nine kilometres.'

I'd pressed speaker so she could hear him, which at least made her stop arguing and turn the vehicle around. *Whack* as the rear of the vehicle hit a tree, *whack* as the bullbar hit another tree, *whack* as the rear hit a second tree and *whack* as the bullbar swiped yet one more as she executed the three-point turn on a narrow dirt track. Now we were heading in the direction we had come from.

'This leads us to a dead end,' I said to Isosceles.

'No it doesn't. Shortly you will come to a v in the road. Steer to the right.'

'We're about to come to a v–'

'I heard him, okay?'

'And,' continued Isosceles, 'you will then, after two point three kilometres, arrive at Rainbow Beach Road. Take that to the Cooloola Creek. It may not be marked, in fact it most likely won't, but the road does an abrupt turn north. That's left, Darian. Do *not* turn left. At the creek is a four-wheel drive track. It leads directly to the beach where you will emerge at Little Freshwater Creek. No more than four kilometres. Then you are on the beach highway. You will be about thirty kilometres away from the resort but you'll be able to drive in a straight line and very fast.'

The Mad Max highway: here we come.

'Got that?' I asked.

She nodded then indicated something up ahead: the v in the road that we had not even noticed.

'Steer to the right,' I said.

'Shut up,' she replied.

'What can you see on the screen?' I asked Isosceles.

'At the moment? Nothing. He came in through the sliding door on the balcony. Then stopped. Froze.'

'And then what?'

'He stood like that for about forty seconds. I could barely see him, only a shadow at the bottom edge of the screen. Then he retreated.'

'So he's gone?'

'Perhaps. Perhaps not. I thought I saw a shadow, the merest glimpse, a few moments ago. It could be that he is still on the balcony. Maria is driving awfully fast.'

An understatement. Along a narrow track that barely deserved to be called a track she was – I leaned across to look – clocking a hundred and ten. Good speed for a four-lane highway. As there was less than a metre separating either side of the vehicle from thick bush and heavy trees, it was, to say the least, exhilarating.

She was getting sexier by the minute.

'Drive faster,' I said.

'Shut up,' she replied.

Back to that again. But at least we knew where we were going, and we were being guided.

'How long before we get there? We're doing a hundred and ten.'

'At that speed? Twenty-two minutes.'

Maria's phone buzzed.

'Don't answer it,' I said.

'I'm not,' she shouted back as she looked down to see who was calling.

'Keep your eyes on the road!' I shouted and took the phone from her lap.

'It's "Boss".'

'Adam. What's he want?'

'Probably another group-therapy meeting,' I said as the call went to voicemail.

'Give me back my phone.'

'You drive, I'll hang on to it.'

'Give it back.'

'Okay,' I said and placed it in the console between the two front seats. A sort of compromise, I thought. She scooped it up and placed it back in her lap without speaking.

46

Zigzag

It feels like you're being sucked into a vortex. It's very scary. Nothing makes sense.

The shock of the breach, the shock that they'd found one of my hideaways is overwhelming. How can that have happened? What did I do wrong? My mind is racing over all the times I'd been here, trying to figure it out. I can't move.

Rage tears through your body. I want to burst in there – into *my* place – and grab that camera and smash it to pieces. That's what I really want to do. Even better I want to grab the camera and hold on to Helen as I cut off her head and swing it in front of the lens then smash the glass with her forehead.

But you can't do any of those things, captain! Run! Quick! There might be soldiers in the other apartments! Run away now.

I don't. I can't. I can only stand on the balcony and keep staring inside at the black wire as it runs along the skirting board, vanishing somewhere in the kitchen.

You can't keep standing like this.

I know.

You have to run.

I know.

An alarm will have been triggered.

I know.

*People will be coming **now**.*

I know.

That cop. The-best-in-the-country. Him.

I know.

If you stay there like this he will catch you.

I know.

You will be safe. He will come by road. He won't even discover the creek until long after you've gone and even then he may not realise that's how you gain entry.

Good point. A plan. Escape. Retreat. Go back to the boat and navigate quietly through the swamps back into the river. I'll be safe.

Do it now.

But what about the girls? The photos? Telling them about the chain? What about the phones with their photos on them? I can't do that at home. I have to do it here, where it's safe. That's why I come here. Steps 9, 10 and 11. What about them? How do I deal with that? They won't work at home. They have to be done here. Can't be done in the apartment either. That's for Steps 12 and 13 only. What do I do with the girls?

Kill them. Leave them.

No!

I hit myself across the head as hard as I can. Bang, whack. Where did that idiotic idea come from? Leave them? That's breaking the first basic rule of my work: never leave behind a body. Jesus! Stay focused! Sometimes the voice says dumb dumb stuff.

Then you have to take them back home again.

I don't want to. I hate Helen-big-tits and Jenny's all stiff and soon she's gunna start to smell. Killers have got caught because of the smell of their dead.

Then go upriver. Go to Neebs.

I can't, you idiot! That's where he is! That's where I just sent him!

No. He's coming towards you. It had to be him who planted the surveillance. He will be driving to you now. Run. Take the girls. Figure it out later.

Figure it out later, figure it out later, figure it out later. Fuck!

I don't move.

47

Clear Shot

ONCE WE BASHED OUR WAY THROUGH THE FOREST, ALONG narrow tracks with heavily overgrown bush on both sides, gigantic potholes and areas where the road simply vanished, we emerged between two massive sand dunes onto the vast sweep of the South Pacific Ocean, bathed in the brilliant afterglow of sunset.

Maria ground the gear shift into first and slowly navigated our way across the thick, soft sand that can dangerously trap the unwary in a bog. You're supposed to let down the pressure of your tyres but we decided not to bother. Any delay seemed deadly.

The beach highway was busy. Most of the traffic was coming in our direction, heading up towards Fraser Island. As it was dark we could only really make out the cars by their headlights. Once we reached firm, solid sand Maria quickly aimed the Toyota down towards the direction of Noosa and floored it.

She hit a hundred and sixty within seconds. It was a blast. We stayed close to the water's edge, me keeping an anxious eye on the waves, knowing that we'd be in real trouble if we got caught by an undertow. Being so close to the ocean also meant we were a good distance away from most of the oncoming traffic, which moved at speeds between eighty and a hundred and twenty. It was the drunks who sat on the high speeds: they'd see us coming and swerve towards us, as if generating some form of primal greeting, then veer away at the last minute. Maria drove hard and with a clear determination, never once making way for the traffic coming towards us. It felt a little like that old movie *Rollerball* but I knew we were making good time and this was the fastest way of getting down there.

Isosceles kept us updated on what he saw on the monitor. Nothing. Just an 'inkling' he called it, that our boy might still be out on the balcony.

I was starting to get excited.

Being on a highway of sand, there were no lights. The moon was hidden behind a thick black cover of cloud. The oncoming cars began to thin out, and Maria hit the high beam. We had to be careful not to miss the turn-off. It's not like it was signposted – a gap between two sand dunes, that was the turn-off.

'There,' I said and pointed.

She nodded and swung the car inland. The resort was only a few minutes' drive away now.

Again she had to slow down and grind through the soft, thick sand in first gear. We drove at a snail's pace between the sand dunes and then, making sure she didn't hit any of the people wandering around the car park, she ramped up to a hundred and sixty again. We were through the gates of the North Shore Dreaming Resort within seconds.

It had been almost forty minutes. Would he still be there?

Maria killed the lights, and for a moment we were blinded by the dark. Thankfully the road was wide, flat and straight – and it had a hard surface. She eased off the speed and pulled up out the front of Sunrise Breeze. We got out of the car quickly and quietly, leaving the doors open so as not to make any slamming noises that might alert him.

'You take the front, I'll go round to the balcony,' I said.

She nodded and ran off. Clever CIB girl that she was, she had taken a set of master keys from Eddie the Toad when she released him the other morning. She carried them now.

I carried my gun, which I'd kept hidden from her, tucked uncomfortably into the back of my jeans, since we embarked on the journey in what seemed like hours ago. We kept an open line, whispering to each other as she made her advance and I mine.

'I'm just coming to the door now,' she said as I rounded the building and saw the balcony.

'He's gone,' I said. The balcony was empty. As I ran towards it I could see that the sliding glass doors were still open.

'Or else he's inside,' she answered.

'No. Isosceles would have seen him.'

'Most likely,' she answered. 'Still ...'

'I'm about ten metres away,' I added, my eyes focused on the balcony and the open door. If he were inside – and it was possible, the camera did not have 360-degree range – then she was in grave danger. Guys like Promise don't respond well to being arrested; they prefer to go out in a hail of bullets.

'Going in now,' I heard her say as I drew up to the balcony and began to climb when, off to my left in the distance, maybe two hundred metres away, I thought I saw a blink of light. The merest flash, like a torch, lasting just a second. It came from deep in the forest and, now, was gone. I couldn't afford the distraction and kept my eyes on the apartment as I crept onto the balcony and stepped inside as Maria came through the door. We both stared at each other, silent. Was he here? No noise. Nothing. She indicated the bedroom and crept towards it. I shadowed her.

'Empty,' she said. 'He's gone.' It was what we expected, but the sense of deflation was severe. It was close.

'Darian?' she asked, 'What are you doing?'

'I thought I saw something.'

I stepped back onto the balcony and peered into the dense forest of black shadows.

'What?' she asked, joining me.

'I dunno. A light maybe. A reflection. Lasted less than a second.'

'What's out there?' she asked.

'Scrub, more scrub and then a bit more. There's a creek–'

And then it hit me. 'The creek,' I said. 'That's his way in and out.'

I leaped over the balcony and ran towards the creek, where I'd stumbled and fallen the other night. Maria was close behind.

'Where does it lead?' she asked as we ran to its edge.

'Back to the river.'

'How far away was the light?' she asked as she dialled Isosceles.

'Maybe two hundred metres,' I answered.

'There's a creek that runs behind the resort. What's the distance to the Noosa River?' she asked him.

She snapped the phone shut and said, 'One point two k's. Are you sure it was a light?'

'No!' I said as I began to run in the direction of the blink – whatever it was – keeping as close to the edge of the creek as possible. 'I'll get a boat on the river,' she shouted back to me as she dialled her phone again.

Did it matter what it was I saw? It was *something*. And that something might be our guy. It had been nearly an hour since he triggered the alarm by stepping into the apartment. Any normal, clear-thinking person would have turned and fled, and if he did we had no chance. Sixty minutes of clean time would have him now sitting back at home in front of the TV. But if he'd frozen and if Isosceles's inkling was right and he had hung around the balcony trying to figure out what to do, then there was a real possibility that he was close.

Running along the edge of a crumbling creek bed through tall grass, dodging scrubby roots, tree stumps and a forest of tea-trees in the sheer dark was a new experience for me. All the perps I'd chased were headed down streets and alleys. I felt like a sheriff in the Mississippi Delta a hundred years ago. I tried to run in the creek itself, jumping in from the edge, but that was both stupid and wet. Although the creek was shallow it offered even less surety: I stumbled over potholes and fell face down into the disgusting water. The creek was so far inland that the tides from the river washed it clean about once every decade when the whole place flooded. It stank. So did I.

I hadn't seen anything that resembled a boat or a person – just that momentary blink of light as I was climbing onto the balcony. My eyesight had become well accustomed to the darkness now and I could see the shapes and form of the landscape around me – although the trees were doing a magnificent job of obscuring my line of sight – but only for about a hundred metres. After that, no more visibility. And the creek itself was a still black line that snaked unpredictably, merging into the blackness ahead without giving anything away. Still I stumbled on, knowing it was our only hope.

Hopefully not our last. I knew there was a very real danger that this experience would spook him so much he'd up-stumps and leave the area. We had forced him to re-evaluate his plan. He'd be freaking out because the comfort level of an intricate and much-loved part of his plan was now destroyed. He'd have to re-think everything.

—

'Arch, it's Maria. Can you get a boat in the water and meet me at the ferry landing? Now. I'll be there in about five. Torches.'

'No dramas,' she heard from the other end and snapped shut the phone as she ran down the corridor of the apartment block.

Arch lived downriver, not far from Darian. He was an old friend and the sort of guy you could impose on at three in the morning and he'd do whatever you wanted, no questions asked.

She'd seen that Adam and the office had rung her eight times throughout the afternoon. She hadn't listened to any of the messages, but she knew it was either because they'd discovered something new about the killer or he'd discovered she'd been snooping.

She didn't really have any friends at the station, nobody close in whom she could confide. A penalty of beauty. She chose Billy. He was dumb and more in love with her than any of the others.

'Hey Maria, what's up? Heard you been sick?' he said.

'Yeah. I reckon we gotta bust Sil the Onion, Billy. That bloody fish he sold me, I tell ya, I've been chuckin' nonstop for about ten hours.'

'He sells shark and pretends it's mangrove jack. We'll put the squeezers on him and get some freebies. French fries only, though.'

They laughed.

'I was just calling in to see how the rest of the day went.'

He became serious. 'Jesus. You know we found eight bottles of vodka in that car? Mickey reckoned it was the worst he'd ever seen.

Been on the news all night. Even the boss got all teared up. Don't blame him. No way I'm going to bed tonight. Too many nightmares on that one. Watching all my Clint Eastwood films. You ever seen *The Good, the Bad and the Ugly*? Awesome.'

'So that was it? Just that terrible roadie?'

'Yep. What else you want? Eleven bodies. Gotta be a record. That's what Mickey reckoned anyway.'

'Okay. Thanks Billy. Just wanted to make sure nothing else happened, like our serial killer popping up again.'

'Shit no. How to make a fucked day even more fucked? Nah. You on tomorrow?'

'Day off, but I got a couple of messages from Adam so ...' she lingered out a silence to see if he would fill it.

'He's a real pain, that bloke. Dunno how he ever got the job in the first place. Shoulda gone to Mickey.'

'Yeah, well, Mickey has the experience.' Time to get off the line now.

'He knows more about the area than anyone and he has the seniority—'

'Billy, I gotta go! It's that bloody fish again. Sorry!'

'No worries, Maria. See ya,' he said, laughing as she hung up on him.

As she drove through the gates to the resort and turned onto the ferry road, she thought to herself: I am in trouble.

Moments later she arrived at the ferry landing. The river, reflecting the street lights from Tewantin on the other side, was still. She recognised a large tinnie approaching. The speed limit on the river was forty knots. Arch looked like he was doing at least a hundred.

—

I MOVED THROUGH a world defined by a dark and narrow estuary, scrub and thickets of bush. The killer's creek. It had to be his way of access. He would know it backwards. For me, it was unknown terrain.

As the creek did yet another unexpected U-turn, causing me to tumble in, cutting myself for about the tenth time as I scraped a tree root, I told myself to keep going. Ignore the unknown – the fears within – and just keep running. Don't give up.

I still hadn't seen anything but a tangle of black shadows in a pungent forest.

Maria had texted me and said she and Arch were leaving the ferry landing and heading upriver. I guessed that meant they were sort of close, although I really had no idea. I just knew that the horrible little serpentine creek would eventually open onto the river.

And then it did.

About eighty metres away, at the journey's end of the little creek, was the wide expanse of the Noosa River. There was light on the river, reflections from the pockets of civilisation nearby – houses, the bright lights of the Tewantin park a kilometre away, houseboats – and in the middle of it I was sure I could see the gliding progress of a little narrow tinnie heading directly towards shore, as if it had exited the path of the creek that I was now bolting along at top speed. It looked like an eel and it made no sound. It moved with a swift efficiency as if it were fleeing something or someone. It was close to fifty metres away.

A wash of bright white light hit the tinnie; it had to come from Maria and Arch. I reached the end of the creek and stood at the river's edge, its water lapping across my ankles. I tried to get a clear line on the person in the boat but it was hard to see. He seemed to be crouching down, out of sight. But there *was* someone, hunched over the rear of the boat, by the motor. It was moving faster now and the other side of the river was fast approaching him. There was a landing with a few cars and four-wheel drives. It was hard to tell because there weren't any lights but one of the vehicles looked like a white van.

It was him. I was sure of it.

I kneeled down with the Beretta, my left hand held firmly gripped onto the wrist of my right. I was a good shot but it was a pistol and range would be an issue.

Maria and Arch kept him illuminated. If they knew what I was about to do, they might not have been so generous.

'Promise!' I shouted. My voice echoed along the river.

The figure at the back of the boat spun around towards me. He was too far away for me to see the look on his face but I didn't care. It was a clear shot. I pulled the trigger.

48

Payback

Arch laughed. 'Your boy's on the hunt,' he said to Maria. Shocked, she barked back:

'Turn off the light!'

Promise was moving faster now, panicked; my bullet had missed. He was close to the shore. He'd ducked down out of range. I kept my sights on where he would appear, just above the motor, waiting for the next shot. The range was good; the 92 would reach across the river. I just had to make sure the next shot connected and took him down.

And then the spotlight went out. My moving target, bathed in Arch's glow, was suddenly cut back into blackness. It would take a few moments for my eyes to adjust. By then he might be away from me, up on the sand, packing towards his van.

'Turn the light back on!' I shouted downriver. I could see their vessel approaching. There was no way they'd get to Promise in time. He was getting away.

'Darian! Do not fire!' I heard Maria's voice boom upriver towards me.

—

I hear my name booming out from across the river. At first I'm confused but as I turn around to see who it is, I realise it is the cop and then I feel this whish sound thing next to my ear, passing like a comet and a second later the sound of a crack, like mini-thunder, which I realise is a gunshot. Holy fucking jumping tornadoes. The cop is shooting at me.

'Turn the light back on!' I hear, realising now that the shooter – the-number-one-best-homicide-cop-in-the-country – has lost sight of me as a target. I look downriver and see the big speedboat heading towards me.

I look at the shoreline and realise I am going to make it. Their boat is too far away.

And it hasn't beamed its big spottie on me again. I am in the dark. Move quick.

This was catastrophising. Up until a few moments ago, I'd been running crazy, without plan or focus. Brothers, talk about breaking the rules. Back on the balcony after that crazy cacophony of mad thoughts went all through my mind like a zigzag I just did what a good soldier should do under enemy fire: pack up and retreat to fight the good fight another day.

There are many things to think about now. My entire life has just been turned upside down and inside out and I feel like Willy Wonka in a washing machine. Even as I was navigating down the creek with the girls on the floor of my canoe, even before I heard the whish, the sound of the gunshot, even though I was running away and thought I was safe safe safe, I felt all a jumble, barely able to focus on the need to get back across the river, into the van and get home.

Get-home-get-home-get-home. That makes sense and in the spin of catastrophising, it's about the only thing that makes sense. It's giving me something to do. Just stick with the idea of getting home and forget about the dead-girl smell and Helen-big-tits and the phones and do what the zeppelin said: concentrate.

If you have a problem place it on a leaf and watch it flow away down a stream. See. There it goes. Gone now. Do not fret over a problem if you cannot solve it then and there. Put it on the leaf, watch it float away and come back to it when you need to. That's called cognitive thinking. Thanks zeppelin.

But the swishing noise and the sound of the crack that followed straight after, that's changed everything. The-best-homicide-investigator-in-the-country is trying to kill me. And nearly did!

Wow. Talk about a focus moment.

I hope it never happens to you, brothers and sisters, but, if it does, think of it as a focus moment. I'm not recommending it but it sure is an excellent way to stop the catastrophising. All the zigzag went away.

Now I am calm.

—

MARIA HAD A moment of clarity. The killer was beaching his tinnie. She and Arch were closing in on him. Darian was stuck on the other side of the river with no chance of getting across. His shot had missed and he wouldn't bother again because the range was too far. Darian was, in effect, out of the game.

The capture was now all hers.

'Gun it,' she said to Arch.

The end of his boat dug into the water and they ploughed ahead with greater urgency.

She watched as, in the narrowing distance, the killer ran his tinnie onto the sand, leaped out and grabbed his backpack, then a young woman, who he threw over his shoulder like a sack, and ran to the van. Holy shit, thought Maria: he's taken another girl. He threw them into the van then ran back down to his boat. He glanced downriver at them. Too far away to get any indication of what he looked like. Dressed all in black. He was tall and thin, that was about all she could get from her distance. They were getting close, really close.

She watched as he reached into his tinnie and lifted up another girl.

Holy shit, thought Maria: he's taken a second girl they don't know about. Then she saw the way he carried her, like she was a statue. A dry fact, copied neatly into a notebook, taken down at one of her night classes, since forgotten, echoed through her. Rigor mortis occurs twelve hours after death and lasts for three days.

She felt Arch push the motor harder but the speed of their boat didn't increase. They were already gunning at its max. She watched as the killer ran up to his van, threw in the second girl and slammed its doors shut. Without another glance in their direction he ran to the driver's side and got in.

They were too far away. He was going to escape.

She watched as the van took off. No headlights. She couldn't make out a number plate. She watched as the van turned a corner into the street above the mooring and disappeared from view.

It was no use calling it in. All the police stations in the area were closed at night.

—

GET-HOME-FAST-get-home-fast-get-home-fast.

I took backstreets. I know all the streets. This was close, way too close. I don't like anxiety, friends, and this was really stressful. But after ten minutes of very careful driving, checking in my rear-view mirror that I wasn't being followed, I was back in the comfort of my garage.

Helen-big-tits and dead-stiff-Jenny had rolled around like lollies. Helen looked as if she might actually be dead. I did stomp on her head pretty heavily, but she deserved it. They were a mess. It was really funny. 'Specially dead-stiff-Jenny because she looked like a mannequin. She was all pale and pasty white. And her eyes were sort of weird. I wanted to fuck her. I'd always wanted to fuck a mannequin but then I remembered she was gunna start to smell, but then ...

—

I GOT AWAY but things are really tospy turvy now. Real improvisation is needed here, friends. But not too much. I can hear you say, *Don't get carried away, Winston, don't do anything that might go too far off-track or else you'll get caught*, because the plan is a well-worn track, a very safe track.

So what I'm gunna do is sit down and write a long list. A new list. A list of payback. A list of what I could think of that would really hurt and damage the-best-homicide-detective-in-the-country.

49

Neebs

'Jesus, will you two just shut up?' said Arch as he navigated the boat downriver. After I realised my second shot was not going to happen, I had no choice but to watch the killer's vehicle drive away, a shadow in the night. Arch's boat turned back towards me on the other side of the river, shone the light directly into my eyes and I heard: 'You bloody idiot!' from Maria.

That was five minutes ago. They'd come across the river, helped me up and over the side into the boat and now we were headed back to Arch's landing where Casey was waiting for us.

'I'm goin' back to bed. Wake me if you need me,' was Arch's first comment, followed by the admonishment as we kept arguing about my having a shot at the killer.

'I can't believe how dumb you are,' she said.

'Shut up,' I said in response.

'Give me the gun,' she answered.

'No way,' I replied.

'I'm already in the shit. Adam knows I'm onto him and if he hears about gunshots on the river–'

'Nah, I'll just tell everyone we were shooting off a few old fireworks,' said Arch confidently. This was the guy who set off the hand grenade in the mayor's office. He had a strong sense of command about him.

'You sulking over there, sister?' he said.

'No,' Maria mumbled.

'So what's the plan now, team?' he asked.

We looked at each other. Good question. Promise was gone, maybe for good, with two new victims, one of them dead. Maria's frustration with not having caught him was acute. I knew what she was thinking. Every second we were unable to catch him was another second of agony for the girl. Every second felt like a month of complete uselessness. This is where you beat yourself up. This is when it becomes your fault.

We were still to arrive at our original destination. We needed to be moving, be active. It wouldn't help release the girl immediately but then, nothing short of carpet bombing the entire area with home searches was going to do that.

'Neebs Waterhole,' I said even though it was just after midnight.

'Glad it's you and not me. Shithole,' he said. 'Why do you wanna go up there?'

'The killer left something for us,' answered Maria, though I could tell her heart wasn't in it. She wanted to go searching, driving up and down roads hoping she might find something. Like driving through your neighbourhood at night searching for a lost puppy.

'Like a trap? Good thing Casey's taking you up. Even so, you better watch out. This bloke's onto you now. No-one hears the whistle-sing of a bullet without sending something back in return. Trust me. I know.'

Casey was standing at the end of the jetty. 'Hey brother,' shouted Arch as he steered the boat to its edge and stepped out. 'You want to take these maniacs upriver? I've had all the fun I need for a night. Goin' to bed. Hooray,' he said and ambled off towards the open doors of his home, which like mine faced onto the river.

—

'You guys are losers. I told you to look out for the curve where the tree looks like a chair which is where Courier Road turns off Tin Can Bay Road.'

'If you say another word, I am going to hit you,' she said.

'Alright, alright! Jesus, just trying to make a bloody point. Thanks for all your help, Case. So what are we doing? Going up to Neebs now?'

'How long will it take to get to Neebs by water?' I asked Casey.

'Now? Six to eight hours.'

I looked at my watch. It was 12.15 a.m.

'What about Adam and you?' Casey asked Maria.

She was lost, staring into a dark place that her imagination enticed.

'I want to find the girl,' she said.

I didn't answer, just held her gaze. She knew it would be futile, a waste of our time. I knew what she was thinking. I'd been there too often.

'It's not an abrogation,' I said.

'Let's go to Neebs,' she said.

—

ANOTHER ISSUE I have with water is that when you're on a boat you can't get off – which is what I wanted to do from about the moment we set off. Casey did not draw breath for the entire journey. It seemed he had become encyclopaedic and obsessed with both the geography and the flora of his new land.

'There. Look, it's a bloodwood tree. We'll be seeing more of those,' or 'Here: this is Lake Cootharaba. It's the largest saltwater lake in Australia. And the shallowest! You could walk right across it,' he said and even jumped out and walked alongside the boat in the waist-high water. 'Look. Look, Darian, look. Come on in. Amazing. The whole place is this shallow. And did you know, this is where Eliza Fraser, who was shipwrecked, walked to safety …'

Maria – who was used to dealing with this onslaught of information, all of which might have been intriguing to a bunch of paying tourists – had fallen asleep and left me to nod and smile until finally I said: 'Casey, just shut up.'

'Just wait till you see what happens after we go past Harry's Hut. Awesome. Hey Darian?'

'Yeah?'

'What do you reckon about them photos of Lady Gaga wearing a meat dress?'

On and on. Dawn came and went.

Then we passed through the next lake, Como, the third in a string of massive shallow lakes. That's when everything changed. I felt as though we'd just crossed a boundary into another country. The Noosa River becomes narrow, both sides of the river pressing in with mangroves, melaleuca, bloodwood and scribbly gums, where the tea-tree and paperbark trees stain the water with rotting vegetation, the sky is blotted out by a canopy that hangs over you and a stillness takes over. The tourist boats come up here, as far as a landing called Harry's Hut. No further. We were going about another twenty kilometres on.

Thankfully the spookiness of the river now had the effect of silencing Casey. Even the passing by Harry's Hut was communicated by a nod only, in the direction of the water below us. What had been greenish brown suddenly became black. A clear line of delineation, where the river was no longer salt but fresh water, where its natural colours turned deeply unnatural and eerie. 'Fresh,' is all he said as he leaned down and scooped up a handful and drank it. From then on, as far as we could see upriver it was black.

As we plunged slowly forward, the edges of the river also changed, disappeared as we entered the everglades. On either side behind the walls of thick green bush I could occasionally spot the black water spreading into marshlands of grass and reeds.

'How much further?' I asked, dreading the answer.

'Another couple of hours. We get to Teewah Creek, then cut across west towards Cooloola Way.'

I sank deeper into the bottom of the boat and tried to sleep. Impossible.

'Easier than going by road, eh?' he offered. 'Can't get lost this way.'

I checked my phone; we were out of range again. Maria's phone had buzzed five times. Adam was on the hunt. Although she seemed pretty relaxed about the fat guy. After all, she *did* hold the cards.

He could intimidate her all he wanted but she'd bring him down like a sack of potatoes in a second.

The normal sounds of the river had long gone. There were no echoes of other boats or voices, no distant sounds of cars or the chattering of fish under the surface. Not even the sounds of birds. Everything seemed to have been swallowed up into the black water beneath us. Casey continued his silence and I began to consider the options.

Promise had abducted another two girls but their disappearances hadn't been rung in. Yet; that would most likely change, depending on whether they had parents or someone who'd notice they hadn't come home. If they were tourists, like Ida, one of the tens of thousands who flit in and out for a holiday, then they might never be called in.

What was important now was his state of mind. He'd obviously catastrophised at the apartment but managed to pull himself out of it. And that was him, not us. He'd fled before we arrived. We didn't prompt him. *He* did. That showed me he had strong will. No doubt it was the numerous cognitive-therapy courses he'd been made to take when he was a juvenile offender, his identity protected by the courts. It was impressive, though, and made me think he would stay in the area and not cut his losses and flee. He liked it up here, and this trip to Neebs he had sent us on had been based on a new form of boasting.

It was the newspaper article that did it. My 'fame' appealed to him, made him change direction with Ida and the message to go upriver. He was showing off. That was good. These guys are all narcissistic but Promise, up until now, had done an impressive job of keeping it in check.

His own fantasy world had been enough for him. The real world didn't seem to matter. He didn't need to make an impression on it, except for the mobile phones, but I figured that was more for his own sadistic pleasure. By the way Maria had described it, he was generating terror on the girls' faces for the photographs. I guess if he told them that the phones were being sent home they'd freak. It also allowed him to spread his pain across more people, in a very specific way. Their grief at the sudden loss of their daughter would mean less to him than a change in weather, but he could imagine and feel the horror at seeing their loved ones in their helpless, final stages of life. Control at its most horrible.

Despite what we'd find at Neebs I would have to try and entice more boasting from him. Whatever it was we were about to find, he was proud of it. If I dismissed it as the work of an amateur or ignored it altogether he'd probably respond by doing something to prove it really *was* impressive. *Here let me show you again but this time it's even better.*

Now one of two things would most likely happen: he'd lie low and maybe dispose of the girls without the phone photos, or he'd ramp up and become more audacious. There was a third possibility, but it was pretty unlikely: he'd stay on track, operating as before. But he was too smart for that. Survival had kicked in. The apartment at the North Shore resort was redundant now; so too the apartment at Mudjimba with its collection of sand and stones. I had to assume he'd never use it again, but I told Isosceles to keep the surveillance on. Narcissism leads to blindness. He might still think he had outwitted us on that one.

I had a bad feeling that we were back to square one, that he'd lie low, erase the beloved and established procedure and rebuild anew, alert to the enemy that was waiting: me.

'There's Teewah,' said Casey. I looked up and saw the narrow black river curve off to the right. Casey steered the boat to the left. This was still the Noosa River but, if possible, it was even narrower and creepier-looking than before. I had to duck to avoid being hit by the overhang of a mangrove.

'Only about another ten k's now,' he said. We were travelling at the speed of a one-legged dog. A person could walk faster. The river was shallow and Casey had to be careful that the propeller of the motor didn't get stuck in the black mud. He'd repositioned the motor upwards so the blades cut through the water just inches below the surface. The banks of the river were even closer. The feeling of claustrophobia was hard to ignore. I stared upwards, waiting for the occasional glimpse of the blue sky beyond the gnarled green canopy that stretched over us.

Maria was awake but sat on the floor of the boat, staring ahead.

'What do you reckon we're gunna find up there?' asked Casey.

I looked at him. 'No idea,' I said. 'But you know why he's sending us.'

Casey nodded. 'Yep.' We all knew it was designed to bring demons to our minds.

I'd lost track of time when I heard: 'We're here. Neebs Waterhole.'

The river – which now was so narrow it had become a stream – suddenly opened out onto a large circular pool of water, like a very small lake. It was surrounded by tall grass. Paperbark trees with their ghostly white limbs were dotted in all directions, growing right to the edge. They leaned over the water, looking like they wanted to fall in. Casey killed the motor, lifted it up out of the water and let the boat glide to an open patch of grass. I looked around me. The river found an exit, yet again a narrow tributary, at the other side. There were no signs of anything like a walking track or a stand-out tree or stump, a hint or a pointer to where we should go or what we should look at.

'There's a clearing over there,' said Casey, pointing. 'You can't see it 'cause it's hidden behind all the trees but it's where you're meant to camp.'

'People camp here?' I asked.

'Nah, don't think so. Not unless you're a desperado.' He looked around, as did Maria, as did I, all of us thinking: *Where do we go now?*

'This is one creepy place,' he said.

We stepped out of the boat and started to make our way towards the camping ground. 'Watch out for red-bellied blacks and browns. They're all over the ground up here.' Snakes, both of which are among the deadliest in the world – the ten-seconds-after-you're-bitten-you're-dead sort of deadly.

Like explorers on the search for the great inland sea, we trekked through the bush, making our own path, until we arrived at Neebs Waterhole Camping Ground, a flat, open patch of ground that had all the charm and allure of a gravel pit. Like most of the ground up here in the Great Sandy National Park, it was hard, white sand. It was a small area. We could see the sky. Visibility past the thickets of tall grass and scrubby thin melaleuca and bloodwood was about eighty metres. After that: dense forest.

We stood in the middle of the camping ground and looked around us.

'I'm seein' trees,' said Casey.

Neither Maria nor I had anything to say. We were all seeing trees.

'And grass,' he added.

I'm not an expert on camping grounds. My crime scenes were streets and houses, apartment blocks and inner-city parks. I was in the middle of nowhere, remote, out of range. Still, I needed to treat it like a crime scene. He'd been here. In person or imagination. I closed my eyes and tried to become him. I pictured the map on my wall at home: the lines and traces of his victims, of him, a shadow, an expert in deception, thorough, a man who knew the river and its estuaries. The entire landscape had become his, from the car park at the end of Hastings Street to the shopping centres to a narrow little creek with no name on the North Shore. He moved with ease. He chose this place because he liked it. It was another home to him.

After a moment I opened my eyes and scanned the camping ground again. Pretty white bark on the trees. A patch of deep green grass, soft, different from the rest, almost like lawn. Like a cemetery. I walked towards it, over to the edge of the camping ground, where the scrub began to take over. Like a final resting place.

About three metres wide. A green soft patch in the scrubby, sandy area. What grows in sand?

I stood in the middle of the green patch and wondered how long it would take us to find whatever it was we were looking for.

Casey and Maria had been walking the area to its far edges and came back to meet in the middle. Maria turned and was about to speak when I saw a look of horror cross her face. She was staring above me.

I looked up.

Hanging from the tree under which I stood was a skull.

Two holes had been neatly drilled into the cranium; through them a piece of twine had been threaded and then tied to a branch;

about four feet below the branch the skull hung, swinging in the soft breeze.

Casey responded immediately by walking across to the tree, climbing it like an insect and then, positioning himself on a branch that looked as if it would snap under his weight, carefully undid the knot and slowly climbed back down, careful not to knock or drop the skull.

He laid it down on a patch of white sand.

'Jesus wept,' he said.

All three of us have lived on the fringes of dark humanity, but what lay below us was simply appalling. Skulls as we see them on TV or in clinics or hospitals have been cleansed. They have gone through a process that takes some time, a process that removes human fat, tissue, hair. None of this had happened with the skull that we had retrieved. What was left of the girl's face was still rotting off the bone. Promise had incised a line around the throat, chopped through the various muscles that connected the head to the rest of the body and then peeled her face off, leaving behind the thing that he wanted us to find.

I know a little bit about the body and its decomposition. I've seen hundreds of dead bodies and followed a lot of them back to the morgue, have seen them in the clinical way that nobody should ever see, through the process of autopsy. I'd never seen anything like this. But I knew enough to say: 'This is Brianna.'

I looked at Maria. She was frozen. This had taken her to a new place.

'We'll call it in,' I said quietly. 'Casey, you can say you were four-wheel driving, looking around for any remnants from the old mines–'

'Aren't any old mines, not round here.'

'They won't know that. You're a collector. You go anywhere. Make it up. They'll believe you.'

I turned to Maria. 'You're home, still suffering from food poisoning. Okay?'

She nodded, but she was like a boxer in the final round: exhausted. In the normal course of events she would be in a safe place: the perp had a name, he'd had a job, he could be photo-fitted, his image and profile could be spread across the coast in the newspapers and evening news. CIB could sit well. That was the way she knew it went down. There was comfort in that way. Instead she'd gone rogue. A game of improvisation, based on his moves and our instincts, guided by some of the most sophisticated spywear on the planet.

In the States the cops use a phrase to describe when someone goes rogue, shakes off surveillance, vanishes and can't be found: 'in the wind'.

That was her now. In the wind. Lost.

'Okay?' I asked again.

She just nodded.

'They'll test DNA, confirm it's Brianna,' I said.

'Do you think this is like …' Casey paused. 'His dumping ground?'

'No. This is a one-off. This is meant to taunt me. Disgust me. Show me he's completely in charge. But there won't be any bodies here, not by a long shot. They're kept secret. He knows that the bodies can bring us closer to him. He's taken a risk with this, but it'll be clean. There'll be nothing but confirmation of identity.'

'And a few fuckin' nightmares.'

'Yeah. That was part of the point.'

'Jesus, the sooner you get rid of this guy, the better,' he said and crossed himself. It was the first time I realised he believed in God.

50

Improvisation

'Hello, I want to buy a freezer.

'No, that won't be necessary, I have the webpage open in front of me and I know exactly what I want. If you could tell me it's in stock, then I can pay for it on my credit card, but you have to deliver it to me. I notice that delivery is an extra fifty dollars, is that correct?

'Yes, I live on the Sunshine Coast.

'Tuesday? Gee. Wow. The thing is I've just gone fishing and I've caught a ton of fish and I need to freeze them asap. Know what I mean? It's like super urgent.

'Well ... There was some bream and whiting. Yeah, the whiting are really biting. Ha-ha, that's really funny. What's your name?

'So, Jack, what do you reckon? Do you think I could get it delivered sooner?

'Tewantin. Not far from your shop at Noosa Civic at all.

'Yeah, it's the Kelvinator. The big one, yeah. Sure, I'll hang on.

'Awesome! That's great news, Jack. You are a champ. Okay then, here's my credit card. And they'll deliver first thing tomorrow morning?

'Wow. You should be promoted to manager, Jack. Ha-ha. Okay. Ready for the numbers on the card?'

—

BTK GOT CAUGHT because he sent a computer disk to the local newspaper and they tracked it back to a computer he used at his local church. Pretty much everything can be traced. They'll examine the paper and the best they'll get is that it's the cheap office brand that's sold at Woolworths. So what? That won't lead them to me. They'll examine the ink and the best they'll get is that it's for an HP LaserJet printer. Big W sells heaps of them. So what? That won't lead them to me. Really-really-really important is the backdrop. I've got to do what those Arab terrorists do when they slash a person's throat in front of a camera, and put up a white sheet in the background so that there is nothing they can see that might tell them what the colour of the wall is or anything. No furniture. Just lay a white sheet on the floor and hang a white sheet on the wall. Lay the two girls out on the white sheets, take the photos, download them onto my laptop, print them onto the plain Woolworths paper on the HP LaserJet, pop them into the brown envelopes with the phones. It's important they have the phones because they gotta hear their own voices calling for Helen-big-tits and dead-stiff Jenny, getting more and more desperate. It's a real shame the photos can't be on the phones anymore but that's life. Gotta go with the flow, Mr-Darian-who-tried-to-shoot-me-with-a-bullet-whoosh-past-my-ear. God protects me. And in improvisation comes improvement. I've just discovered this. Because now I can take more than one photo. Before I could only do Step 8, which was the photo of them being told about Steps 9, 10 and 11. I couldn't photograph those steps but now I can. And I will. Actually I could have, I just didn't think I could have. I was trapped by my thinking and planning but now because I am improvising I am actually making it better.

Step 8 was the horror-show look on their face as I told them what Steps 9 to 11 would entail. Snap. Send.

Now – thanks Mr-best-homicide-detective-investigator-in-the-country for making me have to improvise and get the process even better.

Now – Helen is not dead, which is good. You can't get the look of horror from a dead person. She's all clean and showered and even though she's got a big bruise on the side of her face, that's from when I stomped her, and she's got big bruises on her ankles, that's when I stabbed her, she looks real pretty. I've tied her hands behind her back and her ankles together so she can't go anywhere.

'Hi Helen.'

She's just staring at me.

'You're alive, right? You wanna blink for that?'

Nup. Okay. Have it your way.

'This is called step eight. Normally we would've done this on the night we got together or maybe the night after but things have been so crazy lately it's all been zigzaggy. How about last night? Can you believe that guy shooting at me? Step eight is me taking a photo of you. Normally I do it another way but I'm improvising so I'm using my digital camera. It's much better this way. Smile.'

My first photo is of Helen leaning against the wall of white sheeting, naked and bound.

'Now I'm gunna do a real close-up of you. Smile.'

In the next photo, it's her head only. That's funny, her eyes are open but she looks dead already.

More photos of her: wide, tight, her breasts, the pubic area between her legs.

'Cool. You don't look very happy in these photos. You do know they are the last photos your loverboy is going to see of you so it would have been nice if you tried a little harder but that's your call. Done now.'

I take out the duct tape and cover her mouth. Taken a bit of a risk snapping the photos without it because she might have screamed but I'm pretty much an expert on how the packages react and I could tell she was too far gone. But now things are about to change. Ramp up, captain! Now she is silenced.

I leave her and go down into the bathroom where dead-stiff-Jenny is in the shower, leaning against the wall beside the taps.

Lift her up and carry her back to the room and say: 'Look who's here,' Ha ha. Then I lay little Jenny's body across big Helen's in the form of a cross.

There is nothing to say to Jenny so I just take photos of them laid out together. Then I place Jenny up against the wall, ramrod stiff, and take a couple of wide shots. Awesome. Good thing I'm getting the freezer tomorrow.

'Now I bet you've been wondering how all this ends?' I say to Helen. This is the best bit. 'Because you know you made a mistake on the counting, don't you? You completely forgot to tell me when you'd got to thirty-two. Doesn't matter. It all ends the same anyway.'

—

I AM DEAD. I cannot hear this man. He is not here. I am dead. I am in a coffin. Buried. Where are you, God?

He was talking at her again. He sounded faraway but she heard enough of his words to understand his meaning.

Snap. Another photo.

I am dead. I am dead. I am dead.

Snap. Snap. Snap. 'The look on their faces when I tell them of the decapitation; it's so cool.'

'But I'm gunna do Jenny first. You can watch so you can see how it's done. I'm also going to take lots of photos of you as I do it and then I'm going to put her head right there.' He pointed between her legs. 'That is going to be the photo that everyone is going to remember.'

Helen stared as he removed a saw.

She closed her eyes. *I am dead. I am dead. I am dead.*

'Open your eyes!' she heard him shout.

She didn't. *I am dead. I am dead.*

She felt the sting of his open hand slapping her across the face.

'Open your eyes!' he shouted.

And suddenly a calm came over her. She realised she had, in her final moments, power over him. He couldn't force her to open her eyes. She would endure the rest of her life knowing that she beat him at the very end.

'Open your eyes.'

He bent over her and prised them open but she shut them again, straightaway. He hit her and hit her and hit her, screaming, 'Open your eyes!'

'Fuckin' bitch,' was the last thing she heard and then suddenly, without warning and not at all as he'd described, everything went black.

51

Juanita And Jim

You can do it a thousand times but you'll never be ready. I stood and stared at the front door and hesitated before I knocked. I stepped back and took a deep breath. I could hear footsteps approaching, and the door opened. Juanita, Brianna's mother, stared at me. She was the smart one, the one who knew I was lying to them the morning when they confronted me.

The look on my face said it all. She sagged and fought back tears.

'I wanted to come and see you,' I said.

She stepped back to allow me in. I remembered to take off my shoes; left them at the front door and walked into the house in my socks.

'I'll get Jim,' she whispered. She pointed to a couch. 'Do you want to–'

'Yeah. I'll just wait. Get Jim.'

She moved off, calling, 'Jim!'

I hadn't done this in a long time. When you run the crews you task out the job of informing the parents. You do it fairly, spread the load equally. If it was really bad I'd do it myself. After all, I was the boss. I believed in responsibility. Don't ask them to do what you won't do yourself.

'Jim!' I heard from further away.

In the emergency services they teach you how to communicate the news of death. Don't say they've 'passed on' because you might get asked, 'To where?' or 'They're no longer with us' because you might get asked, 'What hospital did they get sent to?' or even 'I'm sorry' because that's often met with, 'What for?'

Juanita and Jim walked in, hand in hand. Her sombre reaction hadn't filtered to him.

'Hi Mr Richards,' he said.

'Hi Jim.' I looked at both of them. 'I'm not here officially. But earlier today I found a body. It's Brianna. She's dead. I'm very sorry.'

Jim collapsed onto the couch and began to sob. Juanita remained standing, fighting back the tears. She'd known all along.

'How do you know it's her?' she asked.

Everybody reacts to tragic news in their own unique way. She was being clinical. Her breakdown would come later, after I'd gone.

'When she was eight, she was hit by a shard of glass. It cut across the side of her head, above the left ear. A really deep cut. Sixty-three stitches?' It had left a scar that embarrassed her. She only told her closest friends about it, one of whom was Henna, who told me.

Juanita nodded.

'I made my identification based on that cut and the scarring it left behind.'

'Why aren't the police telling us this? Why you?' she asked.

'They will. Eventually. But first they'll do a lot of tests. There will be a lot of press coverage. The police don't think about the limbo that puts you in. The waiting. The not knowing. I wanted you to know now.'

She nodded, as if to say thank you. She sat next to Jim and hugged him. He didn't seem to know I was in the room.

I hesitated, unsure if I should just leave them alone or tell them the rest, which they were going to hear about, if not formally, through the tabloid rumour mill. Fat Adam's army couldn't be relied upon to hold in the gruesome details.

She knew I was holding something back.

'What?' she asked.

'Nothing,' I said.

She knew I was lying.

'Once again, I'm very sorry for your loss. I'll go now.'

I turned and began to walk to the front door. She got up from the couch and walked out with me, closing the door when we were on the front balcony.

'Should I call the police?'

'No. Like I said before, I'm not on this officially. They won't confirm or deny. You'll only get angry with them.'

'What didn't you tell us? Back inside, just then. What is it?'

'She would have died very quickly and she would not have suffered,' I lied.

'That's it? That's what you wouldn't tell us inside?'

'No, but that's what I want you to remember.'

She held my gaze.

'Do you believe in God?' I asked.

She nodded. 'He took her the moment she died. Remember that.'

52

Cop Land

MOST PEOPLE ARE INTIMIDATED BY COPS. WHEN SOMEONE IS asked a question by a cop they become deferential. I'm a good citizen with nothing to hide. It's part fear and part subservience. Ninety per cent of people believe and respect and trust people in uniforms. Even chemists get a lucky break on this one. Cops trade on it. One of the first realisations after putting on the uniform is that people treat you differently. Look up to you. Seek your help and guidance. You get used to being respected pretty quickly. Of course that's also the moment where cops can turn, and down that road lies the abuse of power. It's the road that led Fat Adam to his sixty-eight minutes with Izzie. But even if you don't travel that path, even if you're a constable with a duty of care and quietly go about the job, you don't take kindly to civilians acting like they don't understand the line of respect.

'Sir, you can't walk through there,' said the uniformed constable on the front bench at the Noosa Police Station as Casey walked across the foyer and straight past him, into the corridor that led down to the main room.

'No need to fret, brother,' Casey said and kept walking. The Constable was about to chase after him then noticed the man was swinging what appeared to be a human skull on the end of a piece of rope. He called down the back to warn them, and to cover his arse as Casey stepped into the war room where all the detectives were huddled and said: 'Where's Fat Adam?'

As much as they loathe disrespect, cops are also wary of those who breathe it. They all knew Casey, not so much as Maria's lover but as an ex-gangster from Melbourne. He knew more about the law than most of them and he was a cowboy. He was also just as likely to set off a grenade in the mayor's office. The lines of respect and contempt blurred considerably with a guy like Casey.

And what the hell is that he's holding? they were all thinking.

'I'm here, you prick, what do you want?' said a voice. Adam emerged from the doorway beside the Fisheries desks – which led to the toilet.

'To give you this.' He held up the skull.

'It's a skull,' said Adam.

'Yeah, I noticed that,' said Casey.

Adam stared at it as he took it – by the string, and held it at arm's length – from Casey.

'Jesus.'

'I found it up by Neebs Waterhole. It was hanging in a tree. I came directly here to the station to give it to you.'

'Jesus,' said Adam again as he stared at it. His experience with dead bodies was limited to road accidents and overdoses.

'I thought it might have something to do with your serial killer,' said Casey.

'Here, Boss,' said Billy as he walked up to Adam. 'I'll call the lab in Brisbane. You want me to drive it down?'

Adam was still staring at it as if trying to equate it with an actual person.

'Boss?'

'Yeah,' he said, snapping out of it. He handed it to Billy. 'Get it down there straightaway. If it *is* one of the victims ...' He was going to say that they would have been given a huge break in the case, but then his gaze returned to Casey.

'You found it?' he asked suspiciously. 'At Neebs? What the fuck were you doing up at Neebs?' The implausibility of it began to hit like waves on a beach. 'Nobody goes up there. What the fuck is going on?'

'*I* go up there. I go all round there. Go searching the old mines for any equipment I can scavenge.' He quickly added: 'Always checking in with Parks and Wildlife before I remove anything. That place is littered with old gold mines. You should come out to the Emporium, Adam, next time you're looking for an anniversary present for your wife.'

'And what, you just saw it?'

'Yep. You know that camping ground area? I found it hanging from one of the trees there.'

'And what? You climbed the tree and cut it down?'

'Yep.'

'That's called tampering with evidence.'

'Fuck off, Adam. I'm doing you a favour, you fat dick. There's no mobile service out there. I couldn't call it in. I coulda got back in me boat and driven eight fuckin' hours back to Noosaville and called it in and then we coulda all driven another eight fuckin' hours back, by which time it coulda been gone. So I didn't. "Tampering with the evidence." Jesus, mate, get a life. All right. I'm outta here.'

He turned to leave.

'Where's your missus?' asked Adam.

'Sick, mate. Food poisoning. Ate some dodgy fish.'

'Tell her I want to see her.'

'Yeah, she got that message already. But when you're dividing all your time between the toilet and sleeping, it ain't too easy to comply.' Casey knew the bureaucracy. 'She called in sick, left a message. It's her day off today too. She'll have a doctor's certificate when she comes back to work. Probably tomorrow.'

'I don't need a doctor's certificate, I just wanna see her.'

'Not at the moment you don't, trust me.' He heard some of the other cops laugh at that.

He was about to keep going then stopped. 'Hey? Isn't there a reward going for a break in this investigation? Yeah, there is. Answered my own question. Fifty k's, right?'

Adam stared at him incredulously.

'That's okay, I won't claim it now because it has to lead to the arrest of the killer. But make sure you've got my name down. Top of the list. Casey Lack: skull. This could be the break you're after, big fella. See youse,' he shouted to the assembled cops as he ambled out.

Adam stared after him with anger equal to what he felt towards his missus and that hot shot from Melbourne. He was sure they were all in on it together. All conducting some sort of rogue investigation. But, at the moment, he had more important issues to deal with.

'Toyne,' he called out. 'Get up to Neebs. Take a crew. Fine-tooth comb the whole place.'

'Where the hell is Neebs?' she asked.

'It's easy, don't worry,' said one of her colleagues. 'You go up to Tin Can Bay and just take the turn-off marked Courier Road.'

Adam went back into his office. He never closed the door because he liked to listen in on his team's conversations even when they were inane, like the one going on now – how to get to Neebs without getting lost – because he could tune out. He was good at that. Keep the mind focused. There was nothing he could do about Maria yet. He wasn't sure whether to believe she was sick. Why would she be playing for time? Looking at it from the very worst possible angle, she would rat on him to the Crime Commission, but that wouldn't necessitate an absence from work. She could easily spend days in the office knowing she'd set him up. In fact it made more sense to do it that way: keep up a normal profile while ratting below the surface. Maybe she was sick. Either that or she was moonlighting with Richards and Casey.

He'd bought the line about scrapping around the old mines. That's what guys like Casey Lack do. But now, settling back into his chair and opening up a box of doughnuts, he realised he'd been fooled. First law of an investigation: there's no such thing as a coincidence. Casey just happened to stumble on a skull that probably belongs to one of the missing girls? Bullshit.

Suddenly he had lost his appetite, which was what always happened when he felt threatened. Time to become more proactive, he thought. Too much sitting back and letting things happen around him.

No more.

53

The Invisible Man

I'd been evading the press since I gave them the slip and narrowly avoided running them over. Some still lingered, stretching out their all-expenses-paid job up at Noosa for as long as possible, but most had been summoned back. In the old days their editors could have spent the money to have them stalk me until there was a break. Not anymore.

As I pulled into the house I noticed a couple of diehards who were still hanging on. They ran every time they saw me in the hope of something meaningful to fill a news slot. The tabloid nature of the story hadn't gone away. It had fallen slack due to a lack of fuel. I was about to pour a bucket of kerosene on it.

'What we've got here is a guy desperately craving attention but no-one's listening because he's a rat-faced loser with nothing to say. He probably thinks he's clever, but he's not. These sorts of creeps live in the shadows because they're too scared to come outside. I'd be surprised if this guy has the guts to leave his house except when he creeps out at night to abduct these girls. He's an ordinary, pathetic, little guy who's running scared. No-one cares or notices him; it's all about the girls: Jenny, Marianne, Izzie, Jessica, Carol, Brianna.' There were two others of course but I didn't know who they were. Not yet.

'It's all about them. That's who we're going to remember, not the frightened creep who took them. This guy is such a loser he won't even have been on a school date. Forgettable. That's the guy we're searching for: Mr Mundane; Mr Forgettable. Compared to what

I'm used to, this guy is nothing. Mr Bland, that's who we're looking for. The most unimaginative, boring waste of space.'

This was a shock for the press. They were used to the curt 'No comment' and 'Fuck off or I'll kill you'. Once I'd finished my piece, they were silent for a moment. Before that could change I said, 'Thanks,' and turned to walk inside.

And then they came to their senses. They all barked questions at me at the same time.

I took one.

'Yeah, the reason why I'm going on the record to say what a pathetic creature this guy is, is because he's tried to impress us today.'

I looked into the camera.

'Wow,' I said, acting as unimpressed as I could. 'Loser. Amateur. Down where I come from, school kids could have done better.'

'Tried to impress? How? What does that mean?'

'Sorry, fellas, that's all I've got,' and walked inside, shoes on.

—

BEING NOOSA, THE Officer in Charge doesn't have a TV in his office. He has a 1980s airconditioning unit that doesn't work very well. That's about the sum total of his electronic items. It took a little while for Fat Adam to hear that I had gone Oprah on him.

So when the press charged through the open-to-the-public police station and demanded that he answer the curious reference to the killer 'trying to impress', Fat Adam had no idea what they were talking about. By the time he saw the TV commentary he still had no real clue, only the thought that it might have something to do with the grisly skull.

He rang Casey.

'Lack, did you tell Richards about that skull?'

'Yep, thought he'd be interested.'

'Well next time, fucking don't, all right!'

'Sure thing, Boss,' Casey said.

Adam was losing control. Normally he would have told Billy to go out and answer the questions from the press but he was down in

Brisbane delivering the skull to the forensics lab for testing. Second choice would have been Toyne but she and a crew had gone to Neebs and they were all out of range. So he waddled out and faced them with a curt 'No comment at this time' and went straight back into the safety of his office.

54

Tsantsa

FROM NOWHERE, MY FRIENDS, AND WITHOUT WARNING, THEY came with the hammer sound of the devil's drumbeat. That's how they felt and sounded. Nightmares. I was nineteen when they came. By then I'd raped eleven girls and women. I started young. The killings came later. After the girl in the park. I have to confess I needed to get up my nerve for killing. There was a lot of planning but after it was done it felt like the easiest thing in the world. The planning helped. Everything was really carefully worked out and executed accordingly – from the stalking to the disposal. Just like a soldier on an enemy mission. I knew that killing girls was going to be a part of my life from then on. It gives me such a thrill, can't imagine living without it. But the nightmares weren't part of the plan. After disposal, you see, there was just a blank space. That was the end. I'd thought so carefully and planned everything according to any possible random act of God that you can imagine how shocked I was when, at about three one morning, I woke with a horror, a truly awful horror. The horror of those dead girls haunting me. Why? How could this happen? They wouldn't go away. They kept staring at me as I slept, like spirits, swirling around my bed, whispering things to me. I didn't know what they were saying but I knew it was bad. Real bad, my friends. I knew they couldn't do anything to me – they were dead and well buried – but they wouldn't go away.

Nightmares.

What if they got so bad that I couldn't continue killing the girls? What if I really got haunted? Friends, this was unimaginable.

It seemed like it was beyond your Awesome One's control. Imagine that: having to stop the craft because of your weak, stupid, dumb brain.

I tried sleeping pills, hot chocolate, alcohol. Nothing worked. I tried meditation, weed. Nothing worked. I prayed. Nothing worked. The haunting spirits of the dead girls would not go away. Only time helped. Slowly, after months of having to put up with the horrors of their horrible spirits, I had a night where they left me alone. But then they came back a couple of nights later. And if I was to continue killing girls – which I had to – then I needed to sort out the problem. This was as bad as a girl escaping and running to the cops. This was a triple-A threat. It was a survival issue. There was no way I could put up with the wracking sobs and howls of these demons every night. And I needed to kill again – desperately. I'd found the next girl and I was so excited about stealing her and taunting her and killing her but couldn't because I knew she'd come back, joining the others. Imagine what it would be like when I was thirty and had killed over a hundred girls, maybe more? I was loving it and it was so easy – how could I handle having that many demons in my head every night? I'd read about people shooting themselves to get rid of nightmares. Now I understood why.

And that's exactly what could have happened were it not for divine intervention. I never believed in God. But there *was* something. Things didn't just happen for no reason. There was a spiritual guide. Maybe it wasn't God as in the old guy with the white beard who had Jesus as his son. Didn't matter. There was a force greater than him and it was on my side. There I was, my brothers and sisters, sitting on a seat in the underground railway station at Fortitude Valley, when this old man turned and said: 'Do you want this?'

He was holding out a newspaper that he'd finished reading. Normally I would have told him to fuck off. I hate newspapers unless they've got things in them about me but, for some reason that only God knew, I took it and, because the train was late, decided to read it to see if there were any pictures of pretty girls and, just before I was about to dump it, there was a little article, snuck into the bottom corner of page eight, that caught my attention. It was about a tribe in the Amazon forest called the Shuar. That's what's saved me.

—

I'D REALLY LOST my temper with Helen-big-tits and killed her just to stop her from keeping her eyes closed. Now they were open and she was watching me. But I won! You lost! Because I was angry I made a bit of mess. There was some blood spray on the wall. But that was okay. Worry about that later.

Now I was focused on the tsantsa process. Normally I do this at my little apartment in Mudjimba but I can't afford to take that risk. I'm not going back there again. They'll have cameras there, waiting for me.

Listen up, my good brothers and sisters. One day, when the Awesome World will be revealed people will marvel at this. You, my friends, my followers, my champions, are getting a sneak preview.

—

FIRST UP YOU remove the head. I like to use a saw. Just a simple one from any hardware store will do but I like Bunnings because you can often get things on special there. (Oh, I should have said that before you do this you need to lay out some sheets of plastic on the floor.)

Put it aside. Next I roll the bodies in lots of cling wrap, tight as a drum and all shiny like caterpillars. I've had to use an extra roll on Helen. She is such a bitch. She's ruined a lot of my plans but yes, friends, I am to blame also. I admit that. After all, she was older. Mature. Not my usual type. Never going to take one of them again. Well, I am but that's for a specific purpose, isn't it Darian?

Next is a little tricky so try not to rush. You have to remove the face from the skull. Because of the chain I take lots of time with this stage. The last thing I want is a slip of the knife. If that happens I could scar the face and then the chain wouldn't look as good. Work the knife from the bottom of the back of the head. Cut upwards, just like if you were cutting away the peel of an orange.

Now my brothers, listen up. You have to sew. Luckily mum taught me when I was little. She said every good boy needs to sew. Don't use cotton. Thin plastic twine. Cotton dissolves. Then it's down to the kitchen.

All you need is a big pot. Fill it up with water. I like to use some dried herbs, like thyme and garlic so the smell doesn't make your next door neighbours think something weird is going on. Boil for ninety minutes. Friends, don't do this at home. I would always do this at my little apartment in Mudjimba. The plumbing down there is totally riddled with the DNA of my packages. Now the pipes at my home are going to have Jenny G's and Helen's DNA. But that's okay because pretty soon I'm moving. I'm going to get myself a ranch. Like a cowboy.

Don't stare at the pot for ninety minutes, friends. Get a life. Play some games, watch some TV, go online. You might need to top up the water level a few times though, so keep an eye on that.

After the ninety minutes is up, drain the water, take out the head. Use rubber gloves, not tongs. Tongs can tear it. It's little now. All that boiling has really reduced its size.

You need to have a supply of little round stones and some sand. Smooth stones, fine sand. What you do for the next stage is pop the little round stones, one by one, into the head. Like filling a pouch with lollies. Then, next, you pour in some sand. Fill it up. Not too much, not too little. Give it a shake, let the sand settle. This, friends, gives it form and shape.

Should fit into the palm of your hand.

—

THE SHUAR WERE a tribe of Indians who lived in the Amazon forest. They believed that spirits were a real part of the world, like the nightmares in my bedroom. And they had ways of dealing with them. Especially the 'muisak' spirit, which was the vengeance of a person they'd killed. It was a powerful spirit but it could be stopped.

They and some of the other tribes in the Amazon figured out clever ways to keep the muisak spirits away. Like garlic and vampires. But that was Hollywood silly. This was real. The spirits of vengeance were real and so too was this way of stopping them. I know.

The Shuar believed in three spirit forces. The muisak, which was the vengeful spirit after you killed someone; the 'wakani', which was a basic one that survived after a person died; and the 'arutam', which was the problem spirit that caused the nightmares. This spirit protected, or was meant to, a person from being murdered. So if they *were* murdered it turned into the muisak, which created the demons that haunted my nights.

They'd found a way to stop the demons. And from them I found my answer. I started making a tsantsa, which means a shrunken head in English to ward off the muisak spirit. As soon as I read about them and what they did, I did it as well. It stopped them.

Haven't had a nightmare since.

55

The Powers of Arrest

TRY TO CATCH A SHADOW. YOU CAN'T. IT'S IMPOSSIBLE. It doesn't exist, even though you can see it, even though it follows you everywhere you go. Try to catch a serial killer. You can't. It's impossible. What's worse than the shadow is that you can't even see him. All you have are his traces, pathways and journeys travelled long ago. I'm an expert on catching serial killers, but what that really means is I'm an expert on how serial killers think and act. If I'm lucky I can think like them and place myself ahead of them. Anticipate and prepare like they would. Be ready for them. Act like their twin, their shadow.

You don't catch them. They catch you. The trick is to be sure you're ready when they aren't; when they stumble. Before they realise what it is they've stumbled into – that's when you need to be alert. Otherwise they will vanish again and won't return.

—

FROM NEARBY I heard the sound of a car pulling up. I heard the gravel crunch of two men walking across my backyard. Cops. Fat Adam had sent them to arrest me. You get to discern the sounds of cops from the press or civilians or gangsters; each one sounds different. And then you get to discern the sounds of why they are coming. To pass on sad news; to ask questions; to set you up; to beat the shit out of you; or to make an arrest. Even before they reached the door and could knock on it with the righteous anger of an officer of the law empowered to make an arrest in the good name of justice, I'd figured it out. I took two phones and dialled a different number on each, at the same time.

'They've come to arrest me,' I told Isosceles on one. He knew what to do, who to ring, how to carry out the plan.

'Me too,' said Maria on the other.

'Don't cooperate,' I said. 'Make it as hard as possible for them.'

'Okay,' she replied in a voice that didn't convince me.

'Cooperate with them, you're fucked.'

There was a pause. 'Gotcha,' she said in a much stronger voice. I hung up on her.

I got to the front door before they could knock.

'You gentlemen are trespassing on my property,' I said. It wasn't what they expected. Cops rely on people to act a certain way because of the uniform. Ninety-nine per cent of the time it works. Not this time.

All of the men on the hill had started to look the same to me: tall, beefy, blond, tanned, dumb-looking.

'Fuck off,' said one of them.

'Excuse me?' I said in my interpretation of civilian shock. 'What did you just say to me?'

Cops tell people to fuck off all the time, but it's against the law and they know it. They get so used to throwing it around without question they forget to observe it.

'Forget it,' said the other and was about to continue when I interrupted him.

'I certainly will not. As I first mentioned, you are trespassing. Then I was verbally assaulted. If you do not remove yourselves from my property immediately I will make a Citizen's Arrest under section five-forty-six of schedule one to the Criminal Code Act. Section two-sixty of the same Act refers to a breach of unorthodox peace, in which your "Get fucked" comment to me squarely sits.'

With that I closed the door and figured I'd bought half an hour. In Melbourne it would be ten minutes. After a few moments of uncertainty I heard the crunch of their retreat.

I called Maria.

'She's gone,' said Casey.

'What was the arrest?' I asked.

'There wasn't one. Just a "You better come with us". Adam ain't as dumb as we sometimes think he is.' He was keeping her under the radar. That was wise, given he had a long way to fall and she held the knowledge to precipitate his journey down.

'What about you?' he asked.

'I've got them looking up the balance between their warrant, trespass, verbal assault and a threat of citizen's arrest,' I said as I made my way through the house, out the front and down the jetty. Arch's tinnie was pulling up as I reached the end. I stepped aboard and lay on the floor, out of sight. He gunned it upriver. 'I've got a play on. Getting arrested isn't part of the script.'

'You on the river?' he asked.

'Yeah.'

'Say g'day to Arch for us. Remind him he owes me two bottles of rum.' He signed off.

'Where to, brother?' asked Arch.

'Can I borrow your four-wheel drive?' I asked.

'No dramas.'

'Then, to your place.'

He did a lazy U-turn and the wake of his wave washed across the nearby shore as he headed back downriver.

Since they hadn't served me with an arrest warrant I hadn't been put in custody and I wasn't officially on the run. I was, as the cops said in America, in the wind.

56

The 'Play'

INCARCERATION WAS NOT AN OPTION. WHATEVER CHARGES Fat Adam had designed to bring me in on, I'd be held in custody for at least half a day. That's just to get through the paperwork. If he was smart he could smack me with an impossible-to-disprove charge such as impeding a police investigation or worse – which would achieve what he wanted: me out of the frame. He could have me tangled up in court and bail applications for days. Obviously I had stretched his patience and he wanted to remind me who was running the show. I would have done the same, but I wouldn't have let me escape. By now the clodhoppers would have figured out a way to drag me in, realising that my threats laced with legal jargon were empty. By now they'd be returning to the front door.

I needed to stay free. As soon as I got into Arch's pick-up, I dialled Isosceles and told him I was good to go.

'What about Maria?' he asked.

'Dunno,' I said but I figured she'd hold her own against the fat guy on the hill.

—

NOBODY KNEW WHAT the problem was. They just knew there was one. Why else would the boss send two of the boys up to get Maria and drag her in on her day off when she's got food poisoning? It was a close-knit community, a brotherhood, a clan. Their work put them in the line of fire, and that created a bond. The uniform united them, but being on the 'team' kept them together.

Maria had grown up on the Coast. Some of the boys had gone to school with her. They thought her choice of boyfriend weird, but she was one of them. The boss was new. He came from down south, and rumour had it he bribed his way into the job. Running the station on Noosa Hill was about the best job a cop in Queensland could ever get. Mickey had been a slogger at the hill for over twenty years. Everyone knew the job should have gone to him.

But as they watched Maria being escorted to the boss's office they were all thinking the same thing: *If he's going after her, then why wouldn't he go after me?*

'I'm sick,' she said as she walked into his office.

'Close the door,' said Adam.

She turned away from him and, as she did as requested, caught the look of her fellow officers through the glass wall. She rolled her eyes as if to say: *What a jerk*. They all saw it. They all felt it. They all heard the burst: what a jerk. Camaraderie.

Adam's original plan was to transfer her to a remote outpost on the edge of his jurisdiction, a one-hippy town with a nine-to-five station. But the more he thought about it the more he realised that was just putting the problem out of sight. On this occasion 'out of sight' would not lead to 'out of mind' – indeed it would probably exacerbate it.

'If I puke all over your desk, don't say you weren't warned.'

Smart-arse little bitch. He was convinced the food-poisoning thing was an act to keep her out of the station and on the road with her buddy Darian Richards.

'I'll try and keep it brief. I've had a complaint,' he said.

'Really?'

'Really.'

It was either that or a transfer, but the complaint was what she expected. She wondered just how imaginative he was. She knew he could stitch her up but she also knew she could do the same to him – and worse.

'One of your colleagues has made an allegation of sexual harassment against you.'

This was unexpected. Who on earth would have colluded with Fat Adam to set this one up? Which one of the guys could possibly allege that sort of conduct? She was about to find out, she figured.

'I've got a report,' he said, holding a piece of paper, 'but I've asked the officer in question to let me talk to you first before it goes any further. I do have a duty, you understand, to ensure that this matter is handled appropriately, but before I submit this report and make it official, which would have a dreadful impact on your career, I thought I better talk to you about it first.'

She felt a chill as she remembered Darian's angry words about her male colleagues: *They'll fuck your head space because at least they get to fuck you – one way or the other.*

'I deny any sexual harassment,' she said.

'Of course you do. That's why we're having this conversation: so I can determine the truth of the matter and make an informed decision as to whether or not it becomes an official complaint, in which case I'd have to relieve you of your duties. With or without pay: that's a union issue and something the boys at Internal would have to determine. And the Crime Commission boys of course, too. Can't forget them fellas.'

He held her with a steady gaze. His phone rang. He looked annoyed, picked it up and barked: 'I said no interruptions,' and hung up.

'I just want you to understand the gravity of the situation. You're a good cop, Maria. Think real carefully about how you respond and proceed with this situation.'

'Thanks, Boss. Why don't you begin by telling me exactly what these false allegations contain?'

His phone rang again. 'Jesus, what is it?' He listened, his gaze not leaving Maria. After a moment he said: 'Tell them to perform their duties as officers of the law and stop being ordered around by a fucking civilian!' He hung up.

He looked at the piece of paper. The allegations.

'According to the officer involved, you came up behind them, put your arms around their shoulders, reached down to the area between their legs and then "squeezed" said area.'

'When was this meant to have occurred?' She couldn't help feelings of rising anger.

'Gettin' there. Hang on. It was on Tuesday the eighteenth of July. Approximately two-fifteen in the morning. The officer rebuffed you but on the following night, at approximately eleven-thirty, you followed her into the toilet and rubbed her breasts.'

Her?

'Senior Constable Toyne lists another four occasions on which you made similar advances to her. She told you that she was not "lesbian-orientated" but that you replied, "All girls have a bit of lesbian in them."'

—

I'D BORROWED A pair of Arch's sunglasses and a cowboy hat. That was the extent of my disguise but it worked as I drove past the two cops making their way back across the road and into my place. I even waved. I guess that was the clincher.

I fuelled the pick-up and checked my gun was loaded. I plugged my mobile charger into the cigarette lighter to keep my phone fully charged and drove down towards Buderim, to a town called Tanawha.

—

THERE I WAITED. The first of what would be many texts arrived:

Was there a man dismayed?
Not though the soldiers knew
Someone had blundered:
Theirs not to make reply,
Theirs not to reason why,
Theirs but to do and die:
Into the Valley of Death
Rode the six hundred.
Tennyson on the Charge of the Light Brigade.

ADAM HAD HER by the ovaries. Two female detectives, one female toilet. It was a perfect play. Her word against Jack's. No witnesses. Jack puts out. Maria? Well, she's different. Quiet. Not one of the guys. Jack's hetro: no question on that one. Maria? Thought she was but given that none of us had fucked her, given that she was pretty uptight when it came to jokes about sex, we all left her alone. Makes sense, when you think about it. Who woulda thought she was a lezzo? Poor Jack, getting the come-on in the toilets.

Even if Darian and Casey did what they had promised and made Adam wish he was never born, she would always carry the stigma, and worse, she'd never be able to prove her innocence. She was screwed.

She let Adam continue, get to the deal.

'I've spoken to Senior Constable Toyne about the gravity of making a complaint like this official. She understands. I told her I like to resolve matters without bureaucracy. That's the way I like to run my ship. I explained that we're all under extreme and unusual pressure with the serial-killer case upon us. It's like a weight you can't shake off.'

His phone rang again. He lifted the receiver and placed it straight back down again, then took it off the hook.

'Everybody makes mistakes. Human foibles. Where would we be without 'em? Eh? I said to Toyne: "Maybe Maria was under stress. Maybe it was an aberration. Maybe if she agrees not to do it again, if she understands the score, we can put it behind us. Move on. Give and take." I give. You give. Toyne said she thought that was fair. What about you, Maria? What are your thoughts on all this?'

'That sounds fair,' said Maria slowly, knowing she had no choice.

'That's what I think. Good. I'm glad you're of that opinion.' He leaned forward to emphasise his next point. He saw one of the duty officers trying to get his attention through the window and ignored him.

'What we don't want,' he said, leaning as far across the desk as his fat gut would allow, 'is to ruin an officer's reputation over a foible. It's not a *crime*, Maria. It was desire. No crime intended. None done. If you're prepared to move on, then so am I.'

She nodded. Silence: that was the deal. She reveals he fucked thirteen-year-old Izzie, he goes down and she goes with him. The odds were against her. Jack would play witness. Sexual harassment and being lesbian: dead career. Chances were he'd get off too. He'd manipulate those sixty-eight minutes, and some poor fuck like Mickey would take the blame. After all, there were twelve of them who watched Izzie as she fucked and sucked like a Bollywood slut.

'Deal,' she said.

He smiled and leaned back, giving the desk a chance to breathe. 'Good on ya.'

He then looked up, through the windows. 'Billy! Mickey!' he shouted through the closed office. They came running.

'Yeah, Boss?'

'Take this poor bloody girl home. She's got food poisoning. If we're not bloody careful, she'll spew her guts all over the fuckin' office. Go on, get outta here.'

As she rose to leave she noticed that Jack was nowhere in sight. Billy and Mickey seemed relieved that whatever was going down had gone down and gone away. Stability and order had returned. They'd ask her what it was all about but not yet. Never ask straight off. Always leave it a week.

'Oh, by the way,' said Adam, as if suddenly remembering something. 'Since you're part of the team – even though you'll be at home while you get over the food poisoning – you should know the latest on the serial killer.'

She assumed he was going to tell her about the skull – now that she was part of the team.

'I've had to issue an arrest warrant for Darian Richards. I've got reason to believe he's colluding with the killer. I think they're in on it together.'

'*What?*' asked Mickey. 'That's about as likely as–'

'Strange things happen, Mickey,' said Adam, cutting him off.

'People are strange. You should know that by now. You can never tell a person by what they look like, what they pretend to be. Underneath, who knows what goes on?'

Maria stared at him.

'Yeah, I know. I couldn't believe it either. But we found his prints on a skull that the killer presumably left at Neebs – you'd know about that. It was your boyfriend who found it and brought it in to us.'

—

I LIKE A clean kitchen. Nothing worse than mess. Now that Jenny and Helen had been shrunk, their little heads sitting in a ceramic bowl, I scoured the pot, cleaned out the sink, loaded up the dishwasher and turned it on – full cycle – and then left to go and play on my PlayStation. The tsantsa process wasn't complete, it would take another two days but you couldn't rush things if you wanted it done properly.

I flopped on the couch to play the PlayStation but then changed my mind. I went online and played Warhammer instead.

I lasted ten minutes before I realised I needed a snooze. I told the other players I was going offline and lay down and within seconds was sound asleep. There were no nightmares.

—

STILL I WAITED.
Stormed at with shot and shell,
While horse and hero fell,
They that had fought so well
Came through the jaws of Death,
Back from the mouth of Hell.

—

AS HE TURNED the corner and rode into Park Street, Harold thought to himself: houses have personalities. There were eighty-four houses in Park Street and they all looked alike. They were all brick and built to look the same. He delivered the morning newspaper to each one of the houses which allowed his mind to wander as he rode down the middle of the road, hurling the rolled-up copies onto the front lawns, occasionally onto the front walls. Lately he'd been doing that more often because it was fun and his boss, Cliff, seemed like he was on another planet since his daughter, the really hot Henna, got mixed up in the weird shooting where the guy got whacked on the side of the road and she was witness to it. So either people had stopped complaining or, more likely, Cliff didn't care. Looked to Harold like his boss had pretty much gone and died. Walking corpse.

Without exception, the weirdest house in Park Street was number 36. He knew someone lived there because each morning the lawn was empty of yesterday's paper. Whoever lived inside had come out to pick it up. But that was the point, why it was so weird: it was empty of anything. All the houses – except number 36 – had a car out the front, or a bike, or a pet or a kooky sign that named the house or a barbeque on the front or down the side. Something. Not 36. Nothing. It was always closed up. Curtains fully drawn. No sign of any life.

It intrigued Harold more and more. Now that his boss had gone off onto planet nine, he decided to hurl the rolled-up paper against the front wall of 36 as hard as he could, every morning, in the hope that maybe the person living inside would burst out and shout at him. Anything.

But nothing. The harder the whack, the same result. What was going on in there? For a brief moment, as he drew closer to 36, Harold thought about aiming at the front window and seeing if he could shatter it. That, surely, would bring a response. That also would surely lead to him being fired.

He slowed down as he reached 36. Yep: look at it. Nothing. He looked at 34, 38, the houses on the other side, the odd-numbered houses. Each one had something going on. He sighed. It was going to be a mystery he'd never uncover. With that he raised his arm and threw the rolled-up paper at the front door with as much force as he could summon.

WHACK!

That little fuckwit! I was in the middle of a deep sleep. In my dream I'd been floating in a golden palace with lots of girls who had long flowing blonde hair. It was like they were all underwater.

Four a.m. Same time. That little kid is really starting to get on my nerves. I'm sure the little prick is throwing the newspapers onto the front wall or door of my house on purpose. Every morning it seems to get louder and louder.

I swear if that little shit does it one more time I am going to break the rules and take him. I'll just kill him – no, I'll shove a broom handle up his arse then I'll kill him – and bury the little prick in a pit near the girls. I've never killed a boy before, but this is different. This is like paying the bills or going to see the doctor; something that has to be done to keep the natural order of life in place.

There are no girls to play with this morning so friends, this is my normal routine, the one I have when I'm alone. Shower. Shave. Dress. Get the paper. Little fuckwit long gone. Make breakfast. Baked beans on toast. Eat and read.

—

MR BLAND? PATHETIC? Rat-faced loser? Amateur?

'Regarded as the most experienced expert in homicide investigations, specifically in relation to serial killings, Mr Richards broke his silence this afternoon and told us that the killer had "tried to impress" the police. There was no official comment from the police but sources close to the investigation said the killer had attempted to boast about his killings. Mr Richards was dismissive of the boast, which the newspaper cannot verify at this time and referred to the killer as a "loser" and coined the phrase, intentionally or not, "Mr Bland".'

My brothers and sisters, can you imagine how I felt? He wants to see a bland loser, he's about to see one. I'd already planned my revenge on Darian but, friends, I've been careful to stick to the list and the routine. I hadn't intended to advance for another week.

No longer.

Like a warrior with new orders, I stood and marched into the garage, took out my kit, blankets, my rope and put them in the back of my van. I sat in the front seat, closed the door, pressed the zapper and heard the sound of the garage doors open. Saw the light of the early morning. Reversed the van out, paused as I zapped the garage shut again, watched it close, locking up the house, then drove on down onto the street – empty at this time of morning – driving in the direction of Tanawha.

PART III

'Nor would the depths of Hell receive them in,
lest truly wicked souls boast over them.'

DANTE ALIGHIERI – 'INFERNO'

57

Red Sky at Morning

... SHEPHERD'S WARNING, I THOUGHT AS I WATCHED THE dawn break.

My phone buzzed. Maria.

'I'll call you back from another phone. I need this one open,' I said and hung up. I took a second phone and called her back.

'What happened?' I asked.

'He had me on a sexual-harassment charge – a lesbian sexual-harassment charge. I bought the deal. My silence. His silence.'

'That's it?'

'That's it. For me, Darian, but he's got a warrant out for you.'

'I know.'

'He's going to tie you in to the killings. He's claiming there's a print on the skull that's yours. Every cop in the area is crawling for you. And it's payback. They haven't forgotten what you did to Dennis.'

'Who's Dennis?'

'The cop whose arm you broke like a twig.'

'Oh, that guy. I'm fine. They won't catch me.'

'Don't be so sure.'

'Okay, I'll be cautious.'

'Where are you?'

I paused. Mistake. 'I'm just cruising.'

'No you're not. You just lied to me. Where are you?'

I didn't want her involved anymore. If everything worked the way I intended she was going to be a problem. She would try to prevent me from finishing the job. If – of course a big if – I found him.

'So where are you?'

'I'm lying low at Boreen Point.' It was about eighty kilometres away.

'You know that spywear Isosceles uses to locate the position of people through their mobiles?'

'Yeah. Without it we'd be stuffed.'

'Yeah. Totally stuffed. Anyway, I thought I better call him up since he'd been so keen to talk to me.'

'Hope you wore a tight singlet,' I said, laughing.

'Really tight.' She laughed along as well. 'That's how I managed to convince him to let me have it.'

The passenger-side door to the pick-up opened. There she stood, phone pressed to her ear, staring at me. 'And it works really well.'

She hung up, climbed in and closed the door behind her.

'Hello partner,' she said.

—

ANGIE CHECKED HER reflection in the mirror. It was only a lecture – she'd be sitting in the semi-dark of the theatre listening to a speech about Yeats – but she liked to look good. Some of the students looked (and acted) as if they didn't care. Not her. Whenever she went to uni she chose her clothes carefully and put on make-up. Not to impress anyone, just because she thought it was important to look professional. She dreamed of being a writer like Flannery O'Connor, even though she was poor. Better, of course, to be like JK Rowling or Stephen King – writers who started out poor but whose talent and perseverance made them rich. She couldn't believe how much it cost to go to uni. Her mum and dad went in the seventies, when it was free; she had to pay $4000 per semester. Then there were the extras – the books and rent, food, transport. And the Sunshine Coast had a scarcity of part-time work. Everything was scattered up here. Little towns and villages, mostly. There was some bar work in Noosa but she missed out on that. There were a couple of jobs going at the shopping centre in Maroochydore but she missed out on those too. Then she overheard two girls in the toilet talking about how they'd taken a week off and gone down to the Gold Coast during the Indy, hired an apartment and made over two thousand dollars a night as escorts.

Escort? That's a polite word for 'prostitute', right?

Right. She did some research and realised it was highly paid and seemed well organised and safe. She figured that if she charged top money it would separate the creeps from the nicer clients, but after a little while she realised it wasn't quite that simple. She knew she was pretty. She knew she could make money from it after she went into a brothel to ask some questions and they begged her to join. She had no qualms about the work. She was always a bit nervous with a first-time client but now, after doing it for two years, she had a regular client list and made more than enough money to pay the uni fees, rent and food with the prospect of having a deposit to put on an apartment next year.

She didn't tell anyone. It was like having a secret life – a shadow personality. At the end of uni she'd give it up even though she sort of enjoyed it. Some of her clients were more than clients. They were lovers. To them she meant a lot. To some, like Darian, she was a means of survival. She loved him more than anyone. As much as she knew what love was.

On Tuesday he'd given her a ring. A narrow band of gold with tiny speckles of diamonds. 'Wear it at all times,' he said. 'It's based on a Celtic design that brings protection to the one who wears it.'

'I'll never take it off,' she said as she held it out and watched the sparkle of the diamonds.

'Promise?' he asked.

'I promise,' she replied.

Angie closed the door to her apartment, locked it and walked down the corridor to the lift. Her car was parked in the side street around the corner. She looked at her watch. She was running a little bit late but she'd get there just in time for the beginning of the lecture.

—

'Boreen Point?' said Maria.

'It's best that I handle this stage on my own,' I said.

'So you can kill him. Forget it. It's not going to happen. He's going into custody. Now tell me what's going down.'

I stared at her. Assuming my plan worked, we were going to have a profound disagreement, now or in the middle of a high-octane situation. I had to kill Promise but she'd try to prevent me. After all, murder *is* illegal. It was going to be ugly. But did I need to have the fight now? It wasn't a fight either of us could win. I decided lying was the best option.

'I'm not going to kill him.'

She looked surprised.

'Are you superstitious?' I knew she was. She didn't answer. 'Because I am, at times like this. I've set a trap, but whether or not it works depends entirely on chance. This is the stage where I *hope* things go according to plan. But they rarely do and I have no control. That's why I don't talk about it. The minute I articulate the plan it's destined to turn in on itself.'

'You don't want to articulate it because you know I'm going to stand in your way.'

'Ever heard of the train-rider?'

'The killer in Melbourne? The guy who abducts girls from trains. You never caught him.'

'I almost did. Once. I'd set a trap. It was after the seventh girl had gone missing and I thought I knew his patterns. I thought I could anticipate him. I told the crews what the plan was. I was confident. I was more than confident; I was sure I'd catch him. But I didn't. Maybe he woke up with a headache. Maybe it was his mother's birthday. But he didn't behave the way I expected. Maybe it was hubris on my part. But it taught me never to rely on hope and left me with the only thing I am superstitious about. So,' I concluded, 'wait and watch.'

NOT MY TYPE at all. Twenty-something, golden blonde hair, big breasts. Too old, too confident, fully developed. Still, that's not the point, is it? This isn't about me. This is about him and me.

'Hi.'

Angie heard somebody come up from behind her as she turned around. What strange-coloured eyes, she thought–

IT WAS UP to him. Everything depended on Isosceles. Even though he was two thousand kilometres away, he watched and waited, as he had been since Darian outlined the 'play'. He was buzzed but this part of the job also scared him. A person's life was in his hands. If he lost them they'd be dead. He didn't eat, sipped tiny mouthfuls of Coke and had his music up really loud so he could totally concentrate.

It reminded him of staring at the stars in the night sky, waiting for one to turn off. He used to do that as a kid, when he learnt they were so far away they were already dead. They had all blinked off. It just took millions of years for them to reach across the universe and tell us.

There it was: just like a star that turned off. Angie's mobile phone transmittance. Gone. He speed-dialled Darian.

MY PHONE RANG. 'He's got her. Her phone transmittance just vanished.'

'Where?' I asked.

'Her apartment block.'

I put the pick-up into gear and drove, speaking to him at the same time.

'Good. I'm two blocks away.'

'He's moving.'

'But you've got the signal?'

'Yep. They're travelling – hang on – along Morris Street. North. That's in the "up" direction, Darian.'

'What's happening?' asked Maria.

I indicated a GPS car system I'd recently bought. It was plugged into the cigarette lighter in the back seat. 'Plug in Morris Street. We need to find it.'

She did as she was told. 'Is it him?'

'Yes, I think so,' I replied.

'He's taken somebody you know?'

I didn't reply.

'You've got a girlfriend?' She sounded surprised.

'Have you found Morris Street?'

'Next turn on the right.' She was staring at me. I kept driving, ignoring the questions.

'Does this girl know she's part of your plan?'

I turned into Morris Street. I spoke to Isosceles. 'We're in Morris Street.'

'Yeah, I can see you. He's about four k's up ahead of you. He's not speeding, doing no more than fifty k's. You're both headed in the direction of the motorway that leads up to Noosa and Tewantin.'

'Okay. Thanks,' I said. She was still staring at me.

'Jesus Christ. You've tagged her with a radio frequency chip, right?'

I nodded.

'But she doesn't know, because the plan only works if she's ignorant. And the chips are so small and sophisticated these days it could be in a bracelet. Or a ring. A gift. Something she'll keep on and he won't bother taking off until after he's got her secure in his house, or wherever it is he's leading us. Jesus Christ,' she said again. She looked away. 'I hope she's the forgiving type.'

With the gunshot I'd placed myself in his firing line. But he wouldn't come after me, only what could hurt me. He knew where I lived, and it wouldn't take longer than a week for him to see Angie was the sum total of my private life. He could have made a point with Henna, since I'd gone out of my way to protect her, but she was down in Brisbane, in a private hospital, being counselled for the trauma of witnessing the 'mysterious and unsolved shooting' that had brought her a bout of amnesia. And Angie was the better target. In fact the only target, the only person I cared for. With Angie he could really hurt me.

I had set her up. The only person I really cared about: I had put her into the arms of the killer. It was my only choice. I hated myself for doing it and I knew that in doing so I would kill the only love that I had. She wouldn't forgive me. I wouldn't forgive myself.

I turned onto the Sunshine Motorway and took the pick-up to a hundred k's, the limit. I also needed to be careful not to draw attention to myself. The cops were looking for me. Up ahead, about two k's in the distance, I could make out a white van. Maria saw it too. She sat up and stared with intensity. The killer: Danny Jim Promise.

We didn't speak. There was nothing to say.

—

ANGIE KNEW IMMEDIATELY that this was the killer and that he'd taken her in revenge for what Darian had been doing. She knew she wasn't his type; no, this was all about boasting. Darian had put pressure on him, got too close, touched a nerve, and now he was going to get revenge by using her. She knew she was going to die and that the time between now and when he finally did kill her was going to be unimaginably horrific. She tried very hard not to let her imagination take her to the depths of human depravity, to the faces of the dead girls on Darian's wall board, to the stories she'd heard of what these guys do – the prolonging of pain, the removal of trophies. He would hurt her. He would agonise her and terrorise her. Record it, film it, taunt Darian with it.

It was Thursday. That meant Darian wouldn't know until next Tuesday. Until then everything would be normal. On Tuesday night, after she failed to turn up or call him, he'd know something was wrong. Then he'd go looking for her. Next Tuesday night. Five days away. She hoped he'd kill her before then. She hoped he'd get it over and done with as quickly as possible.

But she knew, deep in her heart, that was not going to happen. He was going to prolong it. The longer she was in agony, the greater pleasure he'd have knowing that Darian was worried and looking for her. He'd keep her alive for longer than five days. That would be part of the plan.

For a moment she felt fury at Darian for allowing this to happen. He should have anticipated this! It subsided as quickly as it had overwhelmed her. Because really, who was she? A prostitute he conveniently fucked every Tuesday night. Angie: it wasn't even her real name. She hadn't even told him her real name. She only had herself to blame.

—

WE HAD TRAVELLED another ten k's of straight motorway when I heard the sound of a police siren, looked in my rear-vision mirror and saw I was being tailed by a local cruiser.

'Shit!' said Maria.

'I'm being pulled over,' I told Isosceles. 'You've still got her?'

'Yep.'

'Okay. This shouldn't take too long.'

'Too long!' shouted Maria. 'This shouldn't take too long? What alternative universe are you living in? These guys are going to arrest you, you idiot! You're just lucky I'm here so I can take over and follow him!'

I stopped the car but left it idling. I opened my door and stepped out.

'Morning boys,' I said to the two grunts as they approached.

'Darian Richards?' asked the one on the left.

'The very same,' I said.

'We have a warrant for your arrest. You're going to have to come with us.'

Police officers in Queensland are well armed. They carry a Glock and a taser gun. Most of them, like these two, are fit and strong. Except for the fact I'd studied karate and judo, and some of the other martial arts, I was heavily outgunned. I waited until they were in striking range. Two Glocks, two tasers, two of them and just one of me. They were pretty relaxed. In the normal course of events one ex-cop doesn't take out two armed cops on the side of a busy motorway. But that's what I did. I lifted myself off the ground, spun with my right leg and kicked the cop on the left in the neck – he went down – and kept circling in the same spin, using my other leg to take out the second cop – who also went down. No more than five seconds.

'What the fuck have you done?' Maria screamed from the car behind me. I paused to make sure they were staying down. They were. I'd connected where I'd intended and they'd be paralysed for the next ten minutes.

'Sorry boys,' I said and ran back to the car, slammed the door shut, put it back into gear and, ignoring Maria who was on the nuclear side of ballistic, drove off at great speed.

'Oh my God, oh my God, oh my God, have you got any idea of the trouble we're in? Oh my God.'

'Isosceles?'

'Yep?'

'Is there a turn-off up ahead? I think I'll need to get off the motorway shortly and take some back roads. I need you to get Casey to meet us, as well; we're going to need to change cars. Although I don't know if there'll be enough time. How far to civilisation?'

'There's a turn-off three k's away. It's an old road that will take you into Tewantin and Noosa. Looks like it used to be part of the old highway. He's still on the motorway and will be in the suburbs in eight minutes. You'll be between five and ten minutes behind him.'

'You idiot!' was all Maria could offer.

'I'm listening to the police frequency radio now. I don't think they called it in before they pulled you over. Probably wanted to confirm it was you in Arch's pick-up. No mention yet of officers down either.'

'Well there bloody will be!' shouted Maria.

I didn't pay close attention to the traffic, but there were enough cars passing us during the altercation for people to have seen me take down the boys. Chances are it'd be on the airwaves soon.

'Do they have a helicopter up here?' I asked Maria.

'No. Yes. Sometimes.' She was pretty agitated. 'They use the emergency medivac chopper down at Coolum when it's available. It's the only one on the Coast.'

'One kilometre before your turn-off,' said Isosceles.

'It's not a great road. It's narrow. Trucks use it. Hard to overtake on,' said Maria.

'You've still got her?' I asked Isosceles.

'Loud and clear. She'll take us to him,' he said.

'Okay,' I said and began to swerve into the left lane, to take the back road.

'That gives him between five and ten minutes with her before we arrive,' she said.

I didn't reply. I was fully aware of that already and didn't need to hear it from her. But staying on the motorway wasn't an option. I turned off and immediately found myself grinding to a slower pace: a tractor was up ahead, about a kilometre, driving in the same direction and taking up the entire width of the road.

—

ANGIE FELT THE van slow down. They'd left the motorway about fifteen or twenty minutes ago. Sometimes she was clear in her thinking, other times it was a fog of terror and she had no clue. But for the past little while it felt like they were driving through suburban streets, turns left and right, a slow pace. Now the van slowed right down and seemed to crawl up a little hill. Then it paused. His home, she thought. She heard the electronic whir of a garage door being opened. The van accelerated. A darkness enveloped it. She was inside the garage. She heard the whirring sound of the garage door close and with it came even greater darkness. She tried to stretch around and look in his direction, where the driver's seat was. It was empty. The door seemed to be open but it was hard for her to tell. He must have climbed out without her having heard him.

She tried to struggle free but that was, she knew, both futile and painful. She lay. And waited.

THERE WAS NOTHING Isosceles could do but wait. He stared at the repetitive blink of the radio frequency antenna – now stationary – and at the distance between 36 Park Street and where Darian's pick-up was on the one-lane highway. He tried not to think about what might be going on inside number 36 Park Street and now that he'd done the job, thought about leaving the desk to stretch his legs. He'd been crouched over the monitors for many long hours. But he didn't move. He kept his eyes on the snail pace of Darian and Maria wishing there was a way in which he could send bolts of thunder down on the trucks and tractors that seemed to be constantly in their way.

—

I'M NOT GOING to waste time with this one. Hey, I don't even know her name. She's just the girl who goes to the-number-one-best-homicide-detective's house on Tuesday nights. Girlfriend. I've been so much out of sorts with my recent problems that I am really missing the comfort and pleasure of having a baby girl staying in the girls' room with me. I've found the next one. I always keep track of the possible targets. There is a list that I add to every day. At the moment there are eight names on it. Belinda will be next. She's fourteen and works weekend shifts at KFC. She's going to be easy to get. She walks home after work and this weekend she's on night shift. I'll grab her at the entrance to the third street down from KFC. Park the van just around the corner and scoop her up as she walks past me. I am really missing having a baby girl all to myself. There's been so much topsy-turvy lately.

I know, friends, I know. *Winston*, you're saying, *why deviate from the plan? Why are you so determined to get revenge? Isn't it an indulgence?*

I have to make my point to the smart-arse cop. I have to hurt him and I want to do it quickly. It's not indulgence. It just needs to be done. Don't worry, friends, I'm not going to stuff around with this girl – *nameless, that's what we'll call her* – I'm not even sure if I'm going to fuck her. What's the point? It's not as if she's a sexy turn-on like Belinda. Better I just get her into the room, take some photos of her all nude with her eyes popping out in horror as I tell her what I'm going to do. Then I'll just bag her and dump her body with the other two first thing in the morning.

Deliver the photos to the-best-cop-there-ever-was and take Belinda in the afternoon – forget the weekend, do it tomorrow – and have lots of baby-girl sex in the evening. Perfect.

I made sure the shrunken heads process was going okay. Final stage now as I've put the sand and the round stones in them, like marbles in a pouch. Don't forget to sew up the mouth and eyes so the sand doesn't fall out. Gotta be tight. It is. No sunken cheeks or moulding collapses anywhere. They are perfect tiny likenesses of Helen's and Jenny G's heads.

—

ANGIE HEARD THE back of the van door open quickly.

'Hello nameless,' said the man. He climbed in and stared at her. 'Normally we do lots of things, starting in here, in the back of the van, but we're not going to do them, not even going to look at the list on the fridge because I'm in a hurry. We're going down to the girls' room and we'll spend a bit of fun time in there and that'll be it. Okay?'

He untied the clasps that held her bound wrists to the wire mesh at one end and then released her bound ankles from the other. He stepped out and dragged her along the floor of the van, then grabbed her, chucked her over his shoulder and carried her inside.

She didn't fight, or even try to. She was inert. She knew she was going to die.

She saw the garage disappear from view as they entered a clean-looking kitchen.

Jesus, did I just see two shrunken heads?

They moved into a corridor and through the normal-looking house. She had a glimpse of a living room, a bedroom, a bathroom before they stopped and he opened a door. Suddenly she was in a white room, a bedroom. On the floor, she wriggled to get a clear view of what was in the room.

Were they heads?

She saw a wall covered with hundreds of photos. Dozens of girls. She saw their faces, the looks of agony and horror; she saw fresh blood streams on the wall. Suddenly she was being pulled by her feet, pulled across the room. He was moving quickly and clinically. He wasn't even looking at her. He'd put her in some sort of position in the middle of the room.

Jesus, he's got a knife. He's sitting on me. Staring at me. I wish I could scream. Do anything. He's so heavy I can't move.

'Time to make you nude,' he said and she watched as he lowered the knife.

Jesus, where is the knife? What's he doing with it?

She could feel him ripping off her shirt and cutting through her bra.

Oh my God!

He pulled down her jeans and cut off her underwear, nicking her thigh.

Ow! Jesus. What's he going to do next? Just kill me. Please, just kill me.

He leaned back and grabbed the camera. Snap. A photo of her head. Snap. Her body up close. Snap. A whole-body shot. Snap. Snap. Snap.

'Do you believe in improvisation? I do. You're pretty fuckable but I want to get Belinda, so I'll do you quick. Darian Richards is going to love seeing these photos.'

—

WE PULLED UP. It had been seventeen minutes since Angie and Promise arrived.

A plain white Mitsubishi Pajero was parked out the front of Promise's house. Casey. Park Street was part of a recent building estate. Each house had a backyard that connected to another three backyards, one at the back, one on either side. Each had an eight-foot brick wall done out in the popular Tuscan style for privacy. That was helpful; scaling an eight-foot brick wall would not be an easy escape.

I looked around. The street was empty. It was a mortgage-belt street. Nine-to-fivers lived here. Except in number 36.

Maria and I ran to the front door, Casey went down the side, to take the back entrance.

—

WHAT THE HELL is that noise? Is that someone knocking on my door? Piss off! I'm busy! Forget about them, back to nameless–

What is it with some people? Go away! Forget about them, nameless, they'll go away–

Jesus H! This is worse than little-creep-newspaper-kid! It must be those fucking Mormons or whoever they are that go round handing out their God letters. Fuck off! I'll have to go tell them to fuck off–

Hang on, captain. Any blood on you?

No. Okay. Shut up with the door-knocking! I swear as soon as I'm out of this house I'm going to think about a ranch in the woods. That's just as anonymous and I won't have to put up with people.

—

IT HAD BEEN over sixty seconds. That was eighteen minutes he'd had with her now. I looked at Maria. We didn't need to say anything. She knew what I was thinking and nodded. I stepped back, then kicked. The doorjamb shattered right out of its place at the handle. I kept moving as it splintered free and open, pushing inside, Maria right behind me.

58

Red Sky at Night

'Hey Darian, did you count how many girls were on the wall? Did you? More than eight, weren't there? Lot more. Did you count? I can tell you but I'm really interested to know if you counted. Being all clever, the-number-one-best-homicide-detective, I want to know if you read the scorecard.'

We were driving along an unnamed dirt road. I was in the driver's seat, Maria in the passenger seat and Promise cuffed at hands and ankles, in the back seat. He was a tall and thin guy with wavy blond hair. Clean shaven, he looked like a surfer except he was pale. He wasn't the type who spent much time in the sun. He was completely ordinary on the outside, but for his orange-hued eyes which were creepy. In his mid twenties, Promise was a blend of man and child. He whined and boasted and asked me questions respectfully, as if he was considering a job with the police. He was polite to Maria and excellent on directions. He told us how he learnt the ways of the rivers and estuaries as a means of travel, he told us about his canoe, he told us how he moved to the Sunshine Coast because of the lifestyle. Laid back, cruisey. He told us he did well in History at school and asked if we knew anything about Cecil Rhodes.

'Forty? More than forty? Or less than forty? What do you think?'

We were in Casey's white Pajero. It was a recent model; had an automatic door-locking device that I controlled. I'd also tied a chain to his belt, which was then tied to a bolt in the very back of the vehicle.

'Do you want me to give you a clue?'

Even though it was not a road we'd been along before, the terrain was familiar. We were back in the Great Sandy National Park, in the Cooloola Forest.

'If I say nine, does that help?'

Following Promise's directions, we had arrived at a river landing called Fig Tree Point, situated between the second and third of the three lakes, then driven through bush, along a walking track and over a wooden bridge before we turned left and headed north.

'Thirty-nine? Forty-nine? Fifty-nine? Sixty-nine? Hot or cold, what do you think?'

We were headed towards the Coloured Sands, or just inland from them. It was one of the tourist attractions on the coast: a long, tall section of sand dune facing the ocean, made up of the colours of the rainbow.

'On the wall, I'm talking about, just the girls from Sunshine. Otherwise, if we were talking about the total as in *total*, we'd be well into the triple figures. I lost count actually, after a hundred and forty-seven. Like counting stars. What's the point? Don't you agree? Darian? Don't you agree?'

I could see Maria was about to lose it. I put my hand on her knee, mock-punched it. *Chill. Don't let him get to you.* She got the message, nodded imperceptibly.

———

THE FORCE OF my kicking open the door connected with Promise, who was standing on the other side, about to open it. He fell backwards, momentarily shocked and in pain.

'What the fuck?' he screamed.

I grabbed him, threw him face-first into the wall, spread his legs with my feet, cuffed him and patted him down for any weapons. Nothing.

'Where is she?' I spat in his face. Maria had already run through the living room and down the corridor. I could hear doors being opened. I could hear Casey at the rear of the house.

'Casey coming in through the kitchen,' he announced.

'Darian!' I heard from deep within the house. It was Maria.

'Darian,' Promise echoed in a mock high-pitched, nasal voice. Far from being freaked that we'd caught him, he seemed delighted. He acted like a kid at their twenty-first birthday party. 'Better go see if she's still alive or headless, *Darian.*'

I resisted the urge to shoot him then and there. We had business to do. Stay patient, I told myself. Stay focused. Don't lose it. Casey took over. 'I've got him,' he said as I turned and walked out of the living room and into the corridor that looked grimly like the tunnel of my nightmares.

'Where are you?' I asked.

'Here. Third room on the left. She's alive,' she answered.

'Another two minutes and she would have … ' I heard from behind me. I also heard a thud, which I presumed was Casey banging his head against the wall to shut him up. 'Ow!' he screamed.

I got to the door but hesitated. We'd saved her, but we – I – had put her in his trap. I walked in. Maria had her arms around her. Angie was partly naked, had managed to grab a hold of some of her torn clothes but not bothered to put them on. She was huddled, like Ida had been on the end of my couch, holding herself, rocking back and forwards, weeping. On the floor was a saw. I noticed a trickle of blood running down the side of her neck onto her chest. He'd begun to cut.

I kneeled down in front of her but was careful not to touch her, not to intrude.

'You're okay, you're safe,' I said. Hollow words.

'You did this to me. Didn't you?' She was talking into her arms and legs, her head still buried deep into her crouched body.

I didn't know what to say. I didn't want to lie or tell the truth. I had used her and was damned for it. She looked up at me. Her eyes were bulging with tears. The bloodline was clearer now. It would have hurt. And it would leave her with nightmares for the rest of her life.

'The ring,' she said, looking directly at me. I could see the comprehension creep into her face. 'When you gave me the ring, it was to set me up with a tracking device. I kept wanting you to come and rescue me. My hero. But when I heard you, just then, I suddenly realised. How could my hero know where I was? It's not a Hollywood movie, Rose. It's real life and in real life there are no heroes. Are there? It's just "them" and "us".' She turned away, burying her head into her knees again.

'I'll get her cleaned up. Casey can take her home,' said Maria.

I nodded. I wished I had something to say. I wished for redemption but I knew there was none. I had known it when I slid the ring onto her finger and made her promise never to take it off.

—

MARIA WAS GOING to break the case.

I noticed a white van stalking a teenage blonde girl and decided to follow it. A million-in-one chance, not worth calling in. It looked as though the van was indeed following the girl when it abruptly did a U-turn and drove away. Weird, I thought. I should follow it. Still a million-in-one chance. The van led me to 36 Park Road. Nothing unusual. I was about to leave when I thought I heard the sound of a girl crying for help from inside. The suspect had already entered the premises. As I approached the house, Darian Richards intercepted me and explained that he had set up a girl to be taken by the suspect and that she was inside. Together we broke in. It was immediately clear this was the home of the serial killer we have been searching for. I was in shock. Richards released the girl, who fled. I did not get to talk to her, barely even saw her. Richards then demanded that I refrain from calling in the crime scene as he wanted the suspect to take him to the place where he buried his victims. I refused but Richards both disarmed and secured me to the front seat of his vehicle where I was unable to use a phone or any other device to free myself or make contact with the station. Richards secured the suspect into the rear of the vehicle and then drove for some time until we reached the place of burial. All I can remember is that it was just inland from the Coloured Sands. We drove for some time. Once the suspect informed Richards we had arrived he parked the vehicle and took the suspect with him, leaving me in the vehicle. I was alone in the vehicle for *what seemed like two hours. Richards and the suspect then returned. The suspect was once again secured to the back seat and Richards drove us back to Noosaville. He parked the car outside the suspect's house, called my partner, Casey Lack, informed him that I and the suspect were at 36 Park Street and then left the crime scene. I have not seen Mr Richards since.*

She was happy with that story. 'But it puts you in a whole heap of trouble,' she said after I'd gone through it with her.

'More than punching out two cops on the side of the motorway who'd come to arrest me?'

I told her I'd navigate my way around the cops. I told her I was an expert at that sort of thing. I told her that even if she had reached a deal of silence with Fat Adam on the sixty-eight minutes of fuck-time with Izzie, I hadn't. I told her that I'd call in favours, that I had a lot of sway. All of which was true, none of which would matter. Her story was just that: a story. It would never be any more than that. She'd never get to tell it. I was going to intercept and intervene. I was going to secure and disarm her but in a way that was consistent with my story, not hers.

'Stop. You've gone too far,' said Promise from the back seat. 'Back up, soldier, you just missed the turn-off.'

I reversed then followed his directions down a narrow walking track not meant for vehicles. The Noosa River ran alongside us. Promise had ferried the bodies in his little tin boat. The river, its creeks and estuaries, were his. He'd known them like my train-rider knew the train timetables.

'Yep, this'll do,' he said. I stopped the car, turned off the engine.

'Did you bring a camera?' he asked. 'It's really special. My Aladdin's Cave.' I climbed out, opened the back door and began to unbolt him. Since we had released Angie – *Rose* – Promise had been cooperative. He was, in fact, childishly delighted by the revelation for us at journey's end. He'd been bragging nonstop since we set off, the three of us, over an hour ago.

'Follow me, Darian, and Miss I'm-All-Silent-Not-Going-To-Tell-You-My-Name. This way,' he said as if we were off on a picnic together. We walked along a track, barely able to see twenty metres ahead of us as the bush was so dense.

Most of this region had been fully logged by the end of the 1920s. Entire forests were cut down, stripped and then the logs were rolled into the river and ushered downstream to the old saw mill, at the site of what is now the Tewantin public jetty. At certain places pocketed throughout the region were the remains of the loggers' camps or, like the place that was looming up ahead of us, a cave dug into the earth and held in place by beams of hardwood. It looked like the entrance to an old mine. It would have been a place of storage – for their saws, axes, their tools – and a camp, a place where the loggers could rest, light a fire, eat, sleep. It looked like it had been uninhabited and forgotten since the 1920s.

'My special place,' said Promise as we walked through its open entrance. An estuary from the river, still and black, ran past us. I noticed the ground was solid, dark brown, a small patch of earth in the vast tract of sand. The ocean was nearby. I could hear the surf.

A hole had been dug into one of its sides. Maybe originally a second storage space, it was about ten metres deep and barely three metres high. It was pitch black, visibility lasting barely a metre in.

'In there,' he whispered. I shone my torch in.

'Holy Jesus,' said Maria.

Like a string of rosary beads a line of shrunken heads hung from the roof of the cave, forming a zigzag line above us. They swayed as if we had brought in a gentle breeze.

'The chain,' he said proudly.

We had already seen the two heads in his kitchen. We knew what to expect. What we didn't expect was the amount. As if reading my mind he whispered: 'Eighty-nine.'

'Where are they buried?' I asked.

'Underneath you,' he answered. 'Tsantsa,' he said. 'Keeps away the spirits of the dead.' He leaned towards me and smiled as if we were about to share a secret. 'It works,' he said.

'Okay,' I said. 'Let's go.' I reached into the back of my jeans and grabbed hold of the Beretta.

'Darian,' said Maria. When I turned I was staring down the barrel of her Glock. 'Give me your gun,' she said.

For a moment Promise looked confused but then he realised. 'Oh, was he going to kill me? Don't let him do that. Gee, that would be awful. Then nobody will know who I am. Nobody will know about the chain.'

Neither of us was listening.

'Your gun,' she repeated.

I handed it across to her.

'Thanks,' she said.

'Yeah, thanks,' said Promise. 'Horrible man,' he said.

I kept my eyes on Maria, waiting for her to take over and lead us back to the vehicle.

And on Promise, waiting for him to make his move. We were on his land. We were trespassers, physically and psychologically. He'd shown us his chain and made his impression. He'd got off on the look of surprise on our faces. Genuine surprise. Thirty thousand people go missing in Australia every year. Not many of them are voluntary. Most of them turn up again. Not many of them end up in a mass grave like the one we were leaving. Still, eighty-nine was beyond both our expectations. He enjoyed that. There was nothing left for him now but to escape. Jail wasn't an option. If we were going to deny him his reason for living, he'd quickly choose death if given the chance. He wasn't afraid of death. He dealt in it. It was his friend. All this I knew and anticipated, and I told Maria none of it.

She hadn't questioned me when I removed the cuffs from his ankles after I dragged him out of the back seat. I didn't even need to ask. It made sense: how could he walk through the bush with shackles around his legs?

It would be dark soon. A streak of red blistered across the sky. Red sky at morning: shepherd's warning. Red sky at night: shepherd's delight. A day of clear blue sky? I wondered.

Two guns and a perp in cuffs; Maria had every reason to think she was in control. I could see the quiet exuberance of success buoying her. Promise made his move as she opened the rear door for him to climb inside. She'd already opened the driver's-side front door and had inadvertently positioned herself perfectly for him. He suddenly lurched away from the door, pushing into her, sending her backwards into the car and then, with the swing of his back, slammed the door into her. It connected with her face and her knees. Blunt, basic, powerful. I was on the other side of the vehicle, as if to climb into the passenger seat. Out of the way. Unable to stop him.

He bolted. The still black waters were his. They had a trapeze life of their own: creeks, waterholes, rivers and estuaries. Once in the water he'd be lost to us.

'Stop!' she shouted.

'Don't let him get away!' I shouted. Both our instructions were entirely futile but heavily instinctual. She saw him running, slipping away into the dense forest. Gone for good. 'Stop!' she shouted again.

'Maria!' I shouted. 'He gets into the creek or past those trees and he's gone! Forever!'

'Stop!' One last time as she lowered her Glock and took aim.

'Don't let him escape!'

I watched her watching him flee. Everything about being a cop comes down to a moment like this. There was only one overwhelming instinct in her.

She pulled the trigger. Missed. Pulled it again. Hit him this time, in the back. An explosion of crimson popping where the bullet entered and blew apart his insides. He sagged and, as if running in quicksand, took another two steps then collapsed.

Even if it's the life of a serial killer, a beast who inflicted pain onto others, the taking of a life is a deeply haunting moment.

She ran to where he lay and I joined her a moment later.

I kneeled down and checked him. No pulse.

'You did what you had to do,' I said.

'Did I?' she asked. Maybe later she'd come to realise I set her up. For the moment, however, she was shaking, tremors of guilt and astonishment at having ended a person's life rattling through her.

'Come on,' I said, guiding her back towards the vehicle. 'Just sit,' I said. I opened the boot. Casey had left a shovel and a pick, in case the earth was hard. I wouldn't need the latter. I took the shovel and walked across the scrub to where he lay.

'What are you doing?' she asked in a voice soft and lost – a voice that needed no answer. She knew what I was doing. If there was any good reason for her to object she didn't offer one. There wasn't.

Never bury a killer next to his dead. It's an insult to their memories and their spirits. I carried him deep into the forest, then dug a hole and threw him in. I piled the dirt on top of him. Within half an hour he was gone.

I turned back towards the vehicle. Maria had fallen asleep, slumped over the wheel. I hoped the nightmares wouldn't harm her too deeply. The sky was brilliant red, the colour of blood, the colour of the shepherd's delight.

59

Darkness at Noon

Syd Barrett was afflicted by a mental disorder that was possibly induced by taking too much acid. It shows in some of his music. Personally my favourite album by Pink Floyd is *Dark Side of the Moon*. My dad gave it to me on my tenth birthday. By then he'd left home and fled to Thailand. I never saw him after his departure from me, the home and my mother. The record came by post. A piece of yellow paper was sticky-taped to the cover. 'Happy birthday kid' was all it said.

Harold Shipman was afflicted with a mental disorder too. He was the English doctor who silently killed over 250 of his elderly patients. No-one knows why. The shrink reports said he was a control freak, depressed, had grandiose thoughts and relied too heavily on painkillers. What separated Harold Shipman from Syd Barrett? Who knows.

Was Winston Promise mad? He held a job, when he wanted to, appeared normal to the people in the street where he lived and regularly visited a psychologist to discuss his issues. She never knew he was a monster, that her patient would capture and kill her young receptionist.

She's on leave now.

—

The discovery of a mass grave is big news. Helicopters buzzed while forensics and retrieval teams carefully unearthed his burial site. They've kept the search narrow, to his cave and its immediate vicinity. If they stray too wide, they'll find the recently buried body of a young male, age twenty-four. They won't find the bullet that killed him. It went straight through.

Our fingerprint search never revealed his identity. He did. If it wasn't for his determination to boast, by taking the photos of the girls with their phones, in order to spread fear and marvel, then we might never have found him.

One by one, the girls' families came to see me.

'Is it over?' they asked.

'Yes,' I replied.

They're still waiting for the official identification process to grind its way forward. They have to put up with the newspaper stories and the grim fascination with Promise's chain. The random snatch and kills by Promise left scars widely reverberating across the area.

—

I DROVE MARIA home and she left me without saying a word. I haven't seen or talked to her since. But the next day she alerted Fat Adam and the cops to a house in Park Street. Number 36. According to the news reports she'd driven past it, saw a pile of newspapers out the front and all the blinds closed. Acting on a cop's sixth sense, she got out of the car, checked with the neighbours who said the young man who lived there hadn't been seen for days. One also mentioned something about a strange odour emanating from inside. Now suspicious, Maria looked a little closer and noticed that the front door had been knocked off its hinges. She called inside but received no response. Believing that the situation required her to proceed, she entered the premises.

Later, after the forensics teams and specialist squads had fanned through Promise's house, the neighbours all said that the young man seemed so normal.

Maria was promoted for her excellent police work that led to the missing piece of the jigsaw. Danny Jim Promise's face adorns the

Most Wanted lists and a reward is out for his capture. He wanted fame and notoriety. He got it. I was happy to have given it to him.

Casey still asks me over for dinner. I decline.

—

THE CALM HASN'T returned to the community yet. In fact it's just the opposite but that'll pass. Over time, without any more girls being taken, Promise and his spread of terror will subside.

Fat Adam tried to rumble me.

I acquiesced to an arrest warrant. Two constables escorted me to the station whereupon I was charged with multiple counts of resisting arrest, assaulting policemen and a few hundred other charges.

I told him I knew about his sexual exploits with Izzie. How much did he want to punish me? I'm not usually into blackmail but if it works to ease the irritant, why not? He withdrew the charges. The survival instinct is always the primal and primary one. He wished me well, escorted me out of the station. We parted like buddies looking forward to catching up for a beer.

—

DAYS LATER I'M standing on the cliff face of Granite Bay, in the national park. Noosa Heads to my left, Sunshine Beach to my right. I'm alone. I'd returned to the gun and now it was time to hurl it back into the ocean. Casey won't forgive me but I'm going to lie, pretend I've treated the 92 with the due respect it deserves.

I look up at the sun. There's going to be an eclipse today. Bang on noon. The beaches are full of tourists and locals, all waiting for the moment when the moon crosses the sun. It will be a total eclipse. For a moment or two all sunlight will be blocked.

I'm thinking about my past life, the one I've left behind, the one that was defined by a never ending journey of murder, investigation and capture. Defined by death. Defined by killers. Defined by haunting nightmares, the wails of the victims' cries, calling out to me as I slept.

I'm not hearing the cries of Promise's victims anymore. I sleep well now. I don't have any more nightmares, the nightmares that haunted me, that I couldn't push back, that forced me to find him and kill him. Their cries have been silenced.

I think about Rose who used to call herself Angie. For a while I had imagined happiness through her and with her. I haven't tried to make contact with Rose. I'm not going to. I can't ask for her forgiveness. That would be too cruel. I can't ask for her understanding. That would be too selfish.

I look down at the ocean, at the gun in my hand. I look up at the sun. The eclipse is beginning. I can hear the distant sounds of the crowds of onlookers, gathered at the beaches. I imagine all the mums and dads and little kids, all stopping to look up at the sky, pointing to the eclipse. An event for the kids to always remember. I hear sounds of delight.

The sky turns a pale silver. A solar eclipse doesn't bring darkness but an eerie, unreal and other-worldly light.

The birds stop singing. A hush falls over the crowds. All is silent as the moon passes slowly across the sun. I imagine a complete and total darkness but there isn't one.

I remember *Dark Side of the Moon*. Syd Barrett was no longer with the band he formed when that record was made. He'd gone mad. It was their best record. In it are lyrics that describe the world in which we live and all that it contains, everything, thriving under the sun, but that the sun will always be eclipsed by the moon.

I hold the gun tightly. Down below me surf crashes up against the rocks.

I look back at the sun as the moon begins to edge away from it, casting a brilliant edge of light. I tuck the gun into my belt. It feels comfortable there.

Turn and walk away.

Acknowledgements

WRITING A FIRST NOVEL IS A FREAKY EXPERIENCE. I WOULD like to thank the people who helped make it possible. Claude Minisini, for his advice and guidance. Ross Macrea, for his help on the local terrains and life on the river. Thanks also to Claude and Ross for giving feedback and offering honest advice on early drafts. Any errors or mistakes are entirely mine. Jasin Boland, for his life-saving generosity and support. My editors and publishers at Hachette Australia: Bernadette Foley, for giving me the initial feedback and encouragement; Claire de Medici, Karen Ward and Kate Stevens for their perceptive and excellent editing; Vanessa Radnidge, for her unstinting advice, help, additional editing and constant support during the process. Thanks to Vanessa, also, for coming up with the title. To Rachael McGuirk, without whom this book and a whole lot of other things, wouldn't have happened. Thanks for the exceedingly honest feedback, help with the tenses and punctuation, love and support.

I'd also like to thank the many police officers I have worked with over the years, for sharing their experiences. My portrayal of the Melbourne and Noosa police is entirely fictional and the characters bear no resemblance to any real people. The officers in both these organisations are extremely competent and dedicated to their difficult work.

Thanks finally to you, the reader. If you got this far, I'm forever in your debt.